He leapt high and wide, trying to shake the thing that held his hand in a leathery grip, shrieking his denial in a black vault that echoed his cries like lunatic laughter. He leapt and cavorted, coming into momentary contact with the wall, tracing with his burning, supersensitive flesh the tentacled monstrosity that gloated there in bas-relief, feeling its dread embrace!

Something furry and slimy-damp arched against his naked thigh – and again he leapt frenziedly in the baying darkness, gibbering now as his mind teetered on the very brink of madness.

Bounding from the wall he tripped, sprawled and clawed at the casket which, in his mind's eye, he saw where he had last seen it at the foot of her couch. Except now . . . his fluttering fingers dared not accept that which his eyes couldn't see . . . *the fact that the lid lay open!*

About the author

Brian Lumley is the internationally bestselling author of the *Necroscope* and *Vampire World* series. A career British Army Military Policeman for over twenty years, he has been a full-time writer since leaving the army. He lives in Torquay, South Devon.

The Second Wish and Other Exhalations

Brian Lumley

NEW ENGLISH LIBRARY
Hodder and Stoughton

British Library Cataloguing in Publication Data

Lumley, Brian
Second Wish and Other Exhalations
I. Title
823.914 [FS]

ISBN 0 340 62300 4

Typeset by Phoenix Typesetting, Ilkley, West Yorkshire

Printed and bound in Great Britain by
Cox and Wyman Ltd, Reading, Berkshire

Hodder and Stoughton Ltd
A division of Hodder Headline PLC
338 Euston Road
London NW1 3BH

THE SECOND WISH

Contents

INTRODUCTION

A couple of years ago I cropped *Fruiting Bodies & Other Fungi*; then *Dagon's Bell & Other Discords* rang out; by all rights *The Second Wish & Other Exhalations* should be the last gasp, so to speak. A trilogy, with each book containing a witch's dozen of stories from across my twenty-five-year span as an author. So that by the time this one sees print, all or most of the short stories and novelettes that I would wish to preserve will have been collected in this, that, or the other volume.

That's not to say that there aren't more short stories and novelettes; there are, but they have already been collected, or they were 'theme' stories that wouldn't fit in. My tales of the *Primal Land*, and my *Dreamlands* stories, for example, would feel out of place here; many of them wouldn't be sufficiently, well, macabre. And if there's any theme at all to what I've tried to present in these books, that's it: the macabre, or what I continue to think of as 'horror stories', despite the fact that a good many authors nowadays tend to shy away from the horror tag.

But while the collections themselves haven't had specific themes – except horror, of course – the introductions have; they were platforms for my own ideas about the horror story. I prefaced *Fruiting Bodies* with a 'What's wrong with horror?' introduction; not an apology for the genre, just a brief examination of what, to my way of thinking, has gone wrong with it. And I came to the conclusion that while a good many recent tales of terror are still recognizably 'horror' stories (how else can we describe them? A month-old corpse by any other name, etc), far too often the modern variety fails to entertain but merely . . . horrifies!

And in my introduction to *Dagon's Bell* I tried to describe what a horror story should be all about; not its contents, but the feeling it evokes: the need to look back over your shoulder when the house is dark and still. So, entertainment by *frisson*: the continuing theme that blood and guts aren't enough in themselves but – like good food – the real measure of the art is in the presentation, the way it's served up.

And so in *The Second Wish*, for the third time, I'm attempting to serve up horror stories that won't *just* horrify but satisfy, too, and might occasionally make you want to take a peek over your shoulder, or maybe gasp out loud.

If, on the other hand, you're looking for something to make your stomach heave, forget it – you won't find it in this corner of the bookshop. The chemist's (or drugstore, to you American cousins) is next door. If you *should* find it here, however, then for sure I've strayed from the path and failed to achieve my real goal, which was always and only to entertain – albeit in a cold, shivery, gasping sort of way . . .

Brian Lumley
Torquay
February 1994

THE SECOND WISH

Among horror classics **The Monkey's Paw** *must rank with the very best. I don't think it inspired the present tale, though certainly both stories share similar macabre motifs.*

My first wish when I set about to write this story was to reiterate the theme of 'The Warning Ignored' and the resultant 'Payment Exacted'; that's what it's about. It's also a Cthulhu Mythos story, but despite the usual (unusual? obligatory?) references, it isn't typically Lovecraftian.

As for my second wish:

Sixteen or seventeen years ago when this story was written, I was still a soldier. I wasn't dependent upon earnings from my literary efforts; writing was only my hobby, while the Army was my real bread and butter. Which made me easy meat if an editor wanted changes made in a manuscript: I wouldn't kick and scream at the mere suggestion. At that time the important thing was to get my stuff into print.

In order to comply with editorial dictates, I re-wrote the original ending in a style that never entirely satisfied me: a case of 'who pays the piper calls the tune,' so to speak. This time around I've put the matter right. It's only a small thing – just a paragraph, that's all – but I can now consider **The Second Wish** *in its entirety published the way I want it.*

My third wish is that it should give you the creeps!

The scene was awesomely bleak: mountains gauntly grey and black towered away to the east, forming an uneven backdrop for a valley of hardy grasses, sparse bushes, and leaning trees. In one corner of the valley, beneath foothills, a scattering of shingle-roofed houses, with the very occasional tiled roof showing through, was enclosed and protected in the Old European fashion by a heavy stone wall.

A mile or so from the village – if the huddle of time-worn houses could properly be termed a village – leaning on a low rotting fence that guarded the rutted road from a steep and rocky decline, the tourists gazed at the oppressive bleakness all about and felt oddly uncomfortable inside their heavy coats. Behind them their hired car – a black Russian model as gloomy as the surrounding country-side, exuding all the friendliness of an expectant hearse – stood patiently waiting for them.

He was comparatively young, of medium build, dark-haired, unremarkably good-looking, reasonably intelligent, and decidedly idle. His early adult years had been spent avoiding any sort of real industry, a prospect which a timely and quite substantial inheritance had fortunately made redundant before it could force itself upon him. Even so, a decade of living at a rate far in excess of even his ample inheritance had rapidly reduced him to an almost penniless, unevenly cultured, high-ranking rake. He had never quite lowered himself to the level of a gigolo, however, and his womanizing had been quite deliberate, serving an end other than mere fleshly lust.

They had been ten very good years by his reckoning and not at all wasted, during which his expensive life-style had placed him in intimate contact with the cream of society; but while yet surrounded by affluence and glitter he had not been unaware of his own steadily dwindling resources. Thus, towards the end, he had set himself to the task of ensuring that his tenuous standing in society would not suffer with the disappearance of his so carelessly distributed funds; hence his philandering. In this he was not as subtle as he might have been, with the result that the field had narrowed down commensurately with his assets, until at last he had been left with Julia.

She was a widow in her middle forties but still fairly trim, rather prominently featured, too heavily made-up, not a little calculating, and very well-to-do. She did not love her consort – indeed she had never been in love – but he was often amusing and always thoughtful. Possibly his chief interest lay in her money, but that thought did not really bother her. Many of the younger, unattached men she had known had been after her money. At least Harry was not foppish, and she believed that in his way he did truly care for her.

Not once had he given her reason to believe otherwise. She had only twenty good years left and she knew it; money could only buy so much youth ... Harry would look after her in her final years and she would turn a blind eye on those little indiscretions which must surely come – provided he did not become too indiscreet. He had asked her to marry him and she would comply as soon as they returned to London. Whatever else he lacked he made up for in bed. He was an extremely virile man and she had rarely been so well satisfied . . .

Now here they were together, touring Hungary, getting 'far away from it all.'

'Well, is this remote enough for you?' he asked, his arm around her waist.

'Umm,' she answered. 'Deliciously barren, isn't it?'

'Oh, it's all of that. Peace and quiet for a few days – it was a good idea of yours, Julia, to drive out here. We'll feel all the more like living it up when we reach Budapest.'

'Are you so eager, then, to get back to the bright lights?' she asked. He detected a measure of peevishness in her voice.

'Not at all, darling. The setting might as well be Siberia for all I'm concerned about locale. As long as we're together. But a girl of your breeding and style can hardly—'

'Oh, come off it, Harry! You can't wait to get to Budapest, can you?'

He shrugged, smiled resignedly, thought: *You niggly old bitch!* and said, 'You read me like a book, darling – but Budapest is just a wee bit closer to London, and London is that much closer to us getting married, and—'

'But you have me anyway,' she again petulantly cut him off. 'What's so important about being married?'

'It's your friends, Julia,' he answered with a sigh. 'Surely you know that?' He took her arm and steered her towards the car. 'They see me as some sort of cuckoo in the nest, kicking them all out of your affections. Yes, and it's the money, too.'

'The money?' she looked at him sharply as he opened the car door for her. 'What money?'

'The money I haven't got!' he grinned ruefully, relaxing now that he could legitimately speak his mind, if not the truth. 'I mean, they're all certain it's your money I'm after, as if I was some damned gigolo. It's hardly flattering to either one of us. And I'd hate to think they might convince you that's all it is with me. But once we're married I won't give a damn what they say or think. They'll just have to accept me, that's all.'

Reassured by what she took to be pure naïveté, she smiled at him and pulled up the collar of her coat. Then the smile fell from her face, and though it was not really cold she shuddered violently as he started the engine.

'A chill, darling?' he forced concern into his voice.

'Umm, a bit of one,' she answered, snuggling up to him. 'And a headache too. I've had it ever since we stopped over at – oh, what's the name of the place? Where we went up over the scree to look at that strange monolith?'

'Stregoicavar,' he answered her. 'The "Witch-Town." And that pillar-thing was the Black Stone. A curious piece of rock that, eh? Sticking up out of the ground like a great black fang! But Hungary is full of such things: myths and legends and odd relics of forgotten times. Perhaps we shouldn't have gone to look at it. The villagers shun it . . .'

'Mumbo jumbo,' she answered. 'No, I think I shall simply put the blame on *this* place. It's bloody depressing, really, isn't it?'

He tut-tutted good humouredly and said: 'My God! – the whims of a woman, indeed!'

She snuggled closer and laughed in his ear. 'Oh, well, that's what makes us so mysterious, Harry. Our change-ability. But seriously, I think maybe you're right. It is a bit late in the year for wandering about the Hungarian countryside. We'll stay the night at the inn as planned, then cut short and go on tomorrow into Budapest. It's a drive of two hours at the most. A week at Zjhack's place, where we'll be looked after like royalty, and then on to London. How does that sound?'

'Wonderful!' He took one hand from the wheel to hug her. 'And we'll be married by the end of October.'

* * *

The inn at Szolyhaza had been recommended for its comforts and original Hungarian cuisine by an innkeeper in Kecskemét. Harry had suspected that both proprietors were related, particularly when he first laid eyes on Szolyhaza. That had been on the previous evening as they drove in over the hills.

Business in the tiny village could hardly be said to be booming. Even in the middle of the season, gone now along with the summer, Szolyhaza would be well off the map and out of reach of the ordinary tourist. It had been too late in the day to change their minds, however, and so they had booked into the solitary inn, the largest building in the village, an ancient stone edifice of at least five and a half centuries.

And then the surprise. For the proprietor, Herr Debrec, spoke near-perfect English; their room was light and airy with large windows and a balcony (Julia was delighted at the absence of a television set and the inevitable 'Kultur' programs); and later, when they came down for a late evening meal, the food was indeed wonderful!

There was something Harry had wanted to ask Herr Debrec that first evening, but sheer enjoyment of the atmosphere in the little dining-room – the candlelight, the friendly clinking of glasses coming through to them from the bar, the warm fire burning bright in an old brick hearth, not to mention the food itself and the warm red local wine – had driven it from his mind. Now, as he parked the car in the tiny courtyard, it came back to him. Julia had returned it to mind with her headache and the talk of ill-rumoured Stregoicavar and the Black Stone on the hillside.

It had to do with a church – at least Harry suspected it was or had been a church, though it might just as easily have been a castle or ancient watchtower – sighted on the other side of the hills beyond gaunt autumn woods. He had seen it limned almost as a silhouette against the hills as they had covered the last few miles to Szolyhaza from Kecskemét. There had been little enough time to study the distant building before the road veered and the car climbed up through a shallow pass, but nevertheless Harry had been left with a feeling of – well, almost of déjà vu – or perhaps presentiment. The picture of sombre ruins had brooded obscurely in his mind's eye until Herr Debrec's excellent meal and luxurious bed, welcome after many hours of driving on the poor country roads, had shut the vision out.

Over the midday meal, when Herr Debrec entered the dining room to replenish their glasses, Harry mentioned the old ruined church, saying he intended to drive out after lunch and have a closer look at it.

'That place, mein Herr? No, I should not advise it.'

'Oh?' Julia looked up from her meal. 'It's dangerous, is it?'

'Dangerous?'

'In poor repair – on the point of collapsing on someone?'

'No, no. Not that I am aware of, but—' he shrugged half-apologetically.

'Yes, go on,' Harry prompted him.

Debrec shrugged again, his short fat body seeming to wobble uncertainly. He slicked back his prematurely greying hair and tried to smile. 'It is . . . very old, that place. Much older than my inn. It has seen many bad times, and perhaps something of those times still – how do you say it? – yes, "adheres" to it.'

'It's haunted?' Julia suddenly clapped her hands, causing Harry to start.

'No, not that – but then again—' the Hungarian shook his head, fumbling with the lapels of his jacket. He was obviously finding the conversation very uncomfortable.

'But you must explain yourself, Herr Debrec,' Harry demanded. 'You've got us completely fascinated.'

'There is . . . a dweller,' the man finally answered. 'An old man – a holy man, some say, but I don't believe it – who looks after . . . things.'

'A caretaker, you mean?' Julia asked.

'A keeper, madam, yes. He terms himself a "monk", I think, the last of his sect. I have my doubts.'

'Doubts?' Harry repeated, becoming exasperated. 'But what about?'

'Herr, I cannot explain,' Debrec fluttered his hands. 'But still I advise you, do not go there. It is not a good place.'

'Now wait a min—' Harry began, but Debrec cut him off.

'If you insist on going, then at least be warned: do not touch . . . anything. Now I have many duties. Please to excuse me.' He hurried from the room.

Left alone they gazed silently at each other for a moment. Then Harry cocked an eyebrow and said: 'Well?'

'Well, we have nothing else to do this afternoon, have we?' she asked.

'No, but – oh, I don't know,' he faltered, frowning. 'I'm half inclined to heed his warning.'

'But why? Don't tell me you're superstitious, Harry?'

'No, not at all. It's just that – oh, I have this feeling, that's all.'

She looked astounded. 'Why, Harry, I really don't know which one of you is trying hardest to have me on: you or Debrec!' She tightened her mouth and nodded determinedly. 'That settles it then. We *will* go and have a look at the ruins, and damnation to all these old wives' tales!'

Suddenly he laughed. 'You know, Julia, there might just be some truth in what you say – about someone having us on, I mean. It's just struck me: you know this old monk Debrec was going on about? Well, I wouldn't be surprised if it turned out to be his uncle or something! All these hints of spooky goings-on could be just some sort of put-on, a con game, a tourist trap. And here we've fallen right into it! I'll give you odds it costs us five pounds a head just to get inside the place!' And at that they both burst out laughing.

The sky was overcast and it had started to rain when they drove away from the inn. By the time they reached the track that led off from the road and through the grey woods in the direction of the ruined church, a ground mist was curling up from the earth in white drifting tendrils.

'How's this for sinister?' Harry asked, and Julia shivered again and snuggled closer to him. 'Oh?' he said, glancing at her and smiling. 'Are you sorry we came after all, then?'

'No, but it is eerie driving through this mist. It's like floating on milk! ... Look, there's our ruined church directly ahead.'

The woods had thinned out and now high walls rose up before them, walls broken in places and tumbled into heaps of rough moss-grown masonry. Within these walls, in grounds of perhaps half an acre, the gaunt shell of a great Gothic structure reared up like the tombstone of some primordial giant. Harry drove the car through open iron gates long since rusted solid with their massive hinges. He pulled up before a huge wooden door in that part of the building which still supported its lead-covered roof.

They left the car to rest on huge slick centuried cobbles, where the mist cast languorous tentacles about their ankles. Low over distant peaks the sun struggled bravely, trying to break through drifting layers of cloud.

Harry climbed the high stone steps to the great door and stood uncertainly before it. Julia followed him and said, with a shiver in her voice: 'Still think it's a tourist trap?'

'Uh? Oh! No, I suppose not. But I'm interested anyway. There's something about this place. A feeling almost of—'

'As if you'd been here before?'

'Yes, exactly! You feel it too?'

'No,' she answered, in fine contrary fashion. 'I just find it very drab. And I think my headache is coming back.'

For a moment or two they were silent, staring at the huge door.

'Well,' Harry finally offered, 'nothing ventured, nothing gained.' He lifted the massive iron knocker, shaped like the top half of a dog's muzzle, and let it fall heavily against the grinning metal teeth of the lower jaw. The clang of the knocker was loud in the misty stillness.

'Door creaks open,' Julia intoned, 'revealing Bela Lugosi in a black high-collared cloak. In a sepulchral voice he says: "Good evening . . ."' For all her apparent levity, half of the words trembled from her mouth.

Wondering how, at her age, she could act so stupidly girlish, Harry came close then to telling her to shut up. Instead he forced a grin, reflecting that it had always been one of her failings to wax witty at the wrong time. Perhaps she sensed his momentary annoyance, however, for she frowned and drew back from him fractionally. He opened his mouth to explain himself but started violently instead as, quite silently, the great door swung smoothly inward.

The opening of the door seemed almost to pull them in, as if a vacuum had been created . . . the sucking rush of an express train through a station. And as they stumbled forward they saw in the gloom, the shrunken, flame-eyed

ancient framed against a dim, musty-smelling background
of shadows and lofty ceilings.

The first thing they really noticed of him when their eyes
grew accustomed to the dimness was his filthy appearance.
Dirt seemed ingrained in him! His coat, a black full-length
affair with threadbare sleeves, was buttoned up to his neck
where the ends of a grey tattered scarf protruded. Thin
grimy wrists stood out from the coat's sleeves, blue veins
showing through the dirt. A few sparse wisps of yellowish
hair, thick with dandruff and probably worse, lay limp on
the pale bulbous dome of his head. He could have been
no more than sixty-two inches in height, but the fire that
burned behind yellow eyes, and the vicious hook of a nose
that followed their movements like the beak of some bird
of prey, seemed to give the old man more than his share of
strength, easily compensating for his lack of stature.

'I . . . that is, we . . .' Harry began.

'Ah! – *English!* You are English, yes? Or perhaps
American?' His heavily accented voice, clotted and
guttural, sounded like the gurgling sound of a black
subterranean stream. Julia thought that his throat must
be full of phlegm, as she clutched at Harry's arm.

'Tourists, eh?' the ancient continued. 'Come to see old
Möhrsen's books? Or perhaps you don't know why you've
come?' He clasped his hands tightly together, threw back
his head, and gave a short coughing laugh.

'Why, we . . . that is . . .' Harry stumbled again, feeling
foolish, wondering just why they *had* come.

'Please enter,' said the old man, standing aside and
ushering them deeper, irresistibly in. 'It is the books,
of course it is. They all come to see Möhrsen's books
sooner or later. And of course there is the view from the
tower. And the catacombs . . .'

'It was the ruins,' Harry finally found his voice. 'We
saw the old building from the road, and—'

'Picturesque, eh. The ruins in the trees . . . Ah! – but there are other things here. You will see.'

'Actually,' Julia choked it out, fighting with a sudden attack of nausea engendered by the noisome aspect of their host, 'we don't have much time . . .'

The old man caught at their elbows, yellow eyes flashing in the gloomy interior. 'Time? No time?' his hideous voice grew intense in a moment. 'True, how true. Time is running out for all of us!'

It seemed then that a draught, coming from nowhere, caught at the great door and eased it shut. As the gloom deepened Julia held all the more tightly to Harry's arm, but the shrunken custodian of the place had turned his back to guide them on with an almost peremptory: 'Follow me.'

And follow him they did.

Drawn silently along in his wake, like seabirds following an ocean liner through the night, they climbed stone steps, entered a wide corridor with an arched ceiling, finally arrived at a room with a padlocked door. Möhrsen unlocked the door, turned, bowed, and ushered them through.

'My library,' he told them, 'my beautiful books.'

With the opening of the door light had flooded the corridor, a beam broad as the opening in which musty motes were caught, drifting, eddying about in the disturbed air. The large room – bare except for a solitary chair, a table, and tier upon tier of volume-weighted shelves arrayed against the walls – had a massive window composed of many tiny panes. Outside the sun had finally won its battle with the clouds; it shone wanly afar, above the distant mountains, its autumn beam somehow penetrating the layers of grime on the small panes.

'Dust!' cried the ancient. 'The dust of decades – of decay! I cannot keep it down.' He turned to them. 'But see, you must sign.'

'Sign?' Harry questioned. 'Oh, I see. A visitors' book.'

'Indeed, for how else might I remember those who visit me here? See, look at all the names . . .'

The old man had taken a leather-bound volume from the table. It was not a thick book, and as Möhrsen turned the parchment leaves they could see that each page bore a number of signatures, each signature being dated. Not one entry was less than ten years old. Harry turned back the pages to the first entry and stared at it. The ink had faded with the centuries so that he could not easily make out the ornately flourished signature. The date, on the other hand, was still quite clear: 'Frühling, 1611.'

'An old book indeed,' he commented, 'but recently, it seems, visitors have been scarce . . .' Though he made no mention of it, frankly he could see little point in his signing such a book.

'Sign nevertheless,' the old man gurgled, almost as if he could read Harry's mind. 'Yes, you must, and the madam too.' Harry reluctantly took out a pen, and Möhrsen watched intently as they scribbled their signatures.

'Ah, good, good!' he chortled, rubbing his hands together. 'There we have it – two more visitors, two more names. It makes an old man happy, sometimes, to remember his visitors . . . And sometimes it makes him sad.'

'Oh?' Julia said, interested despite herself. 'Why sad?'

'Because I know that many of them who visited me here are no more, of course!' He blinked great yellow eyes at them.

'But look here, look here,' he continued, pointing a grimy sharp-nailed finger at a signature. 'This one: "Justin Geoffrey, 12 June, 1926." A young American poet, he was. A man of great promise. Alas, he gazed too long upon the Black Stone!'

'The Black Stone?' Harry frowned. 'But—'

'And here, two years earlier: "Charles Dexter Ward" – another American, come to see my books. And here, an Englishman this time, one of your own countrymen, "John Kingsley Brown."' He let the pages flip through filthy fingers. 'And here another, but much more recently. See: "Hamilton Tharpe, November, 1959." Ah, I remember Mr Tharpe well! We shared many a rare discussion here in this very room. He aspired to the priesthood, but—' He sighed. 'Yes, seekers after knowledge all, but many of them ill-fated, I fear . . .'

'You mentioned the Black Stone,' Julia said. 'I wondered—?'

'Hmm? Oh, nothing. An old legend, nothing more. It is believed to be very bad luck to gaze upon the stone.'

'Yes,' Harry nodded. 'We were told much the same thing in Stregoicavar.'

'Ah!' Möhrsen immediately cried, snapping shut the book of names, causing his visitors to jump. 'So you, too, have seen the Black Stone?' He returned the volume to the table, then regarded them again, nodding curiously. Teeth yellow as his eyes showed as he betrayed a sly, suggestive smile.

'Now see here—' Harry began, irrational alarm and irritation building in him, welling inside.

Möhrsen's attitude, however, changed on the instant. 'A myth, a superstition, a fairy story!' he cried, holding out his hands in the manner of a conjurer who has nothing up his sleeve. 'After all, what is a stone but a stone?'

'We'll have to be going,' Julia said in a faint voice. Harry noticed how she leaned on him, how her hand trembled as she clutched his arm.

'Yes,' he told their wretched host, 'I'm afraid we really must go.'

'But you have not seen the beautiful books!' Möhrsen protested. 'Look, look—' Down from a shelf he pulled a pair of massive antique tomes and opened them on the table. They were full of incredible, dazzling, illuminated texts; and despite themselves, their feelings of strange revulsion, Harry and Julia handled the ancient works and admired their great beauty.

'And this book, and this.' Möhrsen piled literary treasures before them. 'See, are they not beautiful. And now you are glad you came, yes?'

'Why, yes, I suppose we are,' Harry grudgingly replied.

'Good, good! I will be one moment – some refreshment – please look at the books. Enjoy them . . .' And Möhrsen was gone, shuffling quickly out of the door and away into the gloom.

'These books,' Julia said as soon as they were alone. 'They must be worth a small fortune!'

'And there are thousands of them,' Harry answered, his voice awed and not a little envious. 'But what do you think of the old boy?'

'He – frightens me,' she shuddered. 'And the way he smells!'

'Ssh!' he held a finger to his lips. 'He'll hear you. Where's he gone, anyway?'

'He said something about refreshment. I certainly hope he doesn't think I'll eat anything he's prepared!'

'Look here!' Harry called. He had moved over to a bookshelf near the window and was fingering the spines of a particularly musty-looking row of books. 'Do you know, I believe I recognize some of these titles? My father was always interested in the occult, and I can remember—'

'The occult?' Julia echoed, cutting him off, her voice nervous again. He had not noticed it before, but she was starting to look her age. It always happened when her nerves became frazzled, and then all the makeup in the world could not remove the stress lines.

'The occult, yes,' he replied. 'You know, the "Mystic Arts", the "Supernatural", and what have you. But what a collection! There are books here in Old German, in Latin, Dutch – and listen to some of the titles:

'*De Lapide Philosophico . . . De Vermis Mysteriis . . . Othuum Omnicia . . . Liber Ivonis . . . Necronomicon.*' He gave a low whistle, then: 'I wonder what the British Museum would offer for this lot? They must be near priceless!'

'They *are* priceless!' came a guttural gloating cry from the open door. Möhrsen entered, bearing a tray with a crystal decanter and three large crystal glasses. 'But please, I ask you not to touch them. They are the pride of my whole library.'

The old man put the tray upon an uncluttered corner of the table, unstoppered the decanter, and poured liberal amounts of wine. Harry came to the table, lifted his glass, and touched it to his lips. The wine was deep, red, sweet. For a second he frowned, then his eyes opened in genuine appreciation. 'Excellent!' he declared.

'The best,' Möhrsen agreed, 'and almost one hundred years old. I have only six more bottles of this vintage. I keep them in the catacombs. When you are ready you shall see the catacombs, if you so desire. Ah, but there is something down there that you will find most interesting, compared to which my books are dull, uninteresting things.'

'I don't really think that I care to see your—' Julia began, but Möhrsen quickly interrupted.

'A few seconds only,' he pleaded, 'which you will remember for the rest of your lives. Let me fill your glasses.'

The wine had warmed her, calming her treacherous nerves. She could see that Harry, despite his initial reservations, was now eager to accompany Möhrsen to the catacombs.

'We have a little time,' Harry urged. 'Perhaps—?'

'Of course,' the old man gurgled, 'time is not *so* short, eh?' He threw back his own drink and noisily smacked his lips, then shepherded his guests out of the room, mumbling as he did so: 'Come, come – this way – only a moment – no more than that.'

And yet again they followed him, this time because there seemed little else to do; deeper into the gloom of the high-ceilinged corridor, to a place where Möhrsen took candles from a recess in the wall and lit them; then on down two, three flights of stone steps into a nitrous vault deep beneath the ruins; and from there a dozen or so paces to the subterranean room in which, reclining upon a couch of faded silk cushions, Möhrsen's revelation awaited them.

The room itself was dry as dust, but the air passing gently through held the merest promise of moisture, and perhaps this rare combination had helped preserve the object on the couch. There she lay – central in her curtain-veiled cave, behind a circle of worn, vaguely patterned stone tablets, reminiscent of a miniature Stonehenge – a centuried mummy-parchment figure, arms crossed over her abdomen, remote in repose. And yet somehow . . . unquiet.

At her feet lay a leaden casket, a box with a hinged lid, closed, curiously like a small coffin. A design on the lid, obscure in the poor light, seemed to depict some mythic creature, half-toad, half-dog. Short tentacles or feelers fringed the thing's mouth. Harry traced the dusty raised outline of this chimera with a forefinger.

'It is said she had a pet – a companion creature – which slept beside her in that casket,' said Möhrsen, again anticipating Harry's question.

Curiosity overcame Julia's natural aversion. 'Who is . . . who *was* she?'

'The last true Priestess of the Cult,' Möhrsen answered. 'She died over four hundred years ago.'

'The Turks?' Harry asked.

'The Turks, yes. But if it had not been them . . . who can say? The cult always had its opponents.'

'The cult? Don't you mean the order?' Harry looked puzzled. 'I've heard that you're – ah – a man of God. And if this place was once a church—'

'A man of God?' Möhrsen laughed low in his throat. 'No, not of your God, my friend. And this was not a church but a temple. And not an order, a cult. I am its priest, one of the last, but one day there may be more. It is a cult which can never die.' His voice, quiet now, nevertheless echoed like a warning, intensified by the acoustics of the cave.

'I think,' said Julia, her own voice weak once more, 'that we should leave now, Harry.'

'Yes, yes,' said Möhrsen, 'the air down here, it does not agree with you. By all means leave – but first there is the legend.'

'Legend?' Harry repeated him. 'Surely not another legend?'

'It is said,' Möhrsen quickly continued, 'that if one holds her hand and makes a wish . . .'

'*No!*' Julia cried, shrinking away from the mummy. 'I couldn't touch that!'

'Please, please,' said Möhrsen, holding out his arms to her, 'do not be afraid. It is only a myth, nothing more.'

Julia stumbled away from him into Harry's arms. He held her for a moment until she had regained control of herself, then turned to the old man. 'All right, how do I go about it? Let me hold her hand and make a wish – but then we *must* be on our way. I mean, you've been very hospitable, but—'

'I understand,' Möhrsen answered. 'This is not the place for a gentle, sensitive lady. But did you say that you wished to take the hand of the priestess?'

'Yes,' Harry answered, thinking to himself: 'if that's the only way to get to hell out of here!'

Julia stepped uncertainly, shudderingly back against the curtained wall as Harry approached the couch. Möhrsen directed him to kneel; he did so, taking a leathery claw in his hand. The elbow joint of the mummy moved with surprising ease as he lifted the hand from her withered abdomen. It felt not at all dry but quite cool and firm. In his mind's eye Harry tried to look back through the centuries. He wondered who the girl had really been, what she had been like. 'I wish,' he said to himself, 'that I could know you as you were . . .'

Simultaneous with the unspoken thought, as if engendered of it, Julia's bubbling shriek of terror shattered the silence of the vault, setting Harry's hair on end and causing him to leap back away from the mummy. Furthermore, it had seemed that at the instant of Julia's scream, a tingle as of an electrical charge had travelled along his arm into his body.

Now Harry could see what had happened. As he had taken the mummy's withered claw in his hand, so Julia had been driven to clutch at the curtains for support. Those curtains had not been properly hung but merely draped over the stone surface of the cave's walls; Julia had brought them rustling down. Her scream had originated in being suddenly confronted by the hideous bas-reliefs which completely covered the walls, figures and shapes that seemed to leap and cavort in the flickering light of Möhrsen's candles.

Now Julia sobbed and threw herself once more into Harry's arms, clinging to him as he gazed in astonishment and revulsion at the monstrous carvings. The central theme of these was an octopodal creature of vast proportions – winged, tentacled, and dragonlike, and yet with a vaguely anthropomorphic outline – and around it danced all the demons of hell. Worse than this main horror itself, however, was what its attendant minions were doing to the tiny but undeniably human figures which also littered the walls. And there, too, as if directing the nightmare activities of a group of these small, horned horrors, was a girl – with a leering dog-toad abortion that cavorted gleefully about her feet!

Hieronymus Bosch himself could scarcely have conceived such a scene of utterly depraved torture and degradation, and horror finally burst into livid rage in Harry as he turned on the exultant keeper of this nighted crypt. 'A temple, you said, you old devil! A temple to what? – to that obscenity?'

'To Him, yes!' Möhrsen exulted, thrusting his hook-nose closer to the rock-cut carvings and holding up the candles the better to illuminate them. 'To Cthulhu of the tentacled face, and to all his lesser brethren.'

Without another word, more angry than he could ever remember being, Harry reached out and bunched up the front of the old man's coat in his clenched fist. He shook Möhrsen like a bundle of moth-eaten rags, cursing and threatening him in a manner which later he could scarcely recall.

'God!' he finally shouted. 'It's a damn shame the Turks didn't raze this whole nest of evil right down to the ground! You ... you can lead the way out of here right now, at once, or I swear I'll break your neck where you stand!'

'If I drop the candles,' Möhrsen answered, his voice like black gas bubbles breaking the surface of a swamp, 'we will be in complete darkness!'

'No, please!' Julia cried. 'Just take us out of here ...'

'If you value your dirty skin,' Harry added, 'you'll keep a good grip on those candles!'

Möhrsen's eyes blazed sulphurous yellow in the candle-light and he leered hideously. Harry turned him about, gripped the back of his grimy neck, and thrust him ahead, out of the blasphemous temple. With Julia stumbling in the rear, they made their way to a flight of steps that led up into daylight, emerging some twenty-five yards from the main entrance.

They came out through tangled cobwebs into low decaying vines and shrubbery that almost hid their exit. Julia gave one long shudder, as if shaking off a nightmare, and then hastened to the car. Not once did she look back.

Harry released Möhrsen who stood glaring at him, shielding his yellow eyes against the weak light. They confronted each other in this fashion for a few moments, until Harry turned his back on the little man to follow Julia to the car. It was then that Möhrsen whispered:

'Do not forget: I did not force you to do anything. I did not make you touch anything. You came here of your own free will.'

When Harry turned to throw a few final harsh words at him, the old man was already disappearing down into the bowels of the ruins.

In the car as they drove along the track through the sparsely clad trees to the road, Julia was very quiet. At last she said: 'That was quite horrible. I didn't know such people existed.'

'Nor did I,' Harry answered.

'I feel filthy,' she continued. 'I need a bath. What on earth did that creature want with us?'

'I haven't the faintest idea. I think he must be insane.'

'Harry, let's not go straight back to the inn. Just drive around for a while.' She rolled down her window, breathing deeply of the fresh air that flooded in before lying back in the seat and closing her eyes. He looked at her, thinking: 'God! – but you're certainly showing your age now, my sweet' . . . but he couldn't really blame her.

There were two or three tiny villages within a few miles of Szolyhaza, centres of peasant life compared to which

Szolyhaza was a veritable capital. These were mainly farming communities, some of which were quite picturesque. Nightfall was still several hours away and the rain had moved on, leaving a freshness in the air and a beautiful warm glow over the hills, so that they felt inclined to park the car by the roadside and enjoy a drink at a tiny *Gasthaus*.

Sitting there by a wide window that overlooked the street, while Julia composed herself and recovered from her ordeal, Harry noticed several posters on the wall of the building opposite. He had seen similar posters in Szolyhaza, and his knowledge of the language was just sufficient for him to realize that the event in question – whatever that might be – was taking place tonight. He determined, out of sheer curiosity, to question Herr Debrec about it when they returned to the inn. After all, there could hardly be very much of importance happening in an area so out-of-the-way. It had already been decided that nothing should be said about their visit to the ruins, the exceedingly unpleasant hour spent in the doubtful company of Herr Möhrsen.

Twilight was settling over the village when they got back. Julia, complaining of a splitting headache, bathed and went straight to her bed. Harry, on the other hand, felt strangely restless, full of physical and mental energy. When Julia asked him to fetch her a glass of water and a sleeping pill, he dissolved two pills, thus ensuring that she would remain undisturbed for the night. When she was asleep he tidied himself up and went down to the bar.

After a few drinks he buttonholed Herr Debrec and questioned him about the posters; what was happening tonight? Debrec told him that this was to be the first of three nights of celebration. It was the local shooting carnival, the equivalent of the German *Schützenfest*, when prizes would be presented to the district's best rifle shots.

There would be sideshows and thrilling rides on machines specially brought in from the cities – members of the various shooting teams would be dressed all in hunter's green – beer and wine would flow like water and there would be good things to eat – oh, and all the usual trappings of a festival. This evening's main attraction was to be a masked ball, held in a great barn on the outskirts of a neighbouring village. It would be the beginning of many a fine romance. If the Herr wished to attend the festivities, Debrec could give him directions . . . ?

Harry declined the offer and ordered another drink. It was odd the effect the brandy was having on him tonight: he was not giddy – it took a fair amount to do that – but there seemed to be a peculiar *excitement* in him. He felt much the same as when, in the old days, he'd pursued gay young debutantes in the Swiss resorts or on the Riviera.

Half an hour and two drinks later he checked that Julia was fast asleep, obtained directions to the *Schützenfest*, told Herr Debrec that his wife was on no account to be disturbed, and drove away from the inn in fairly high spirits. The odds, he knew, were all against him, but it would be good fun and there could be no possible comeback; after all, they were leaving for Budapest in the morning, and what the eye didn't see, the heart wouldn't grieve over. He began to wish that his command of the language went a little further than 'good evening' and 'another brandy, please.' Still, there had been plenty of times in the past when language hadn't mattered at all, when talking would have been a positive hindrance.

In no time at all he reached his destination, and at first glance he was disappointed. Set in the fields beside a hamlet, the site of the festivities was noisy and garishly lit, in many ways reminiscent of the country fairgrounds of England. All very well for teenage couples, but rather gauche for a civilized, sophisticated adult. Nevertheless, that peculiar tingling with which Harry's every fibre seemed imbued had not lessened, seemed indeed heightened by the whirling machines and gaudy, gypsyish caravans and sideshows; and so he parked the car and threaded his way through the swiftly gathering crowd.

Hung with bunting and festooned with balloons like giant ethereal multihued grapes, the great barn stood open to the night. Inside, a costumed band tuned up while masked singles and couples in handsome attire gathered, preparing to dance and flirt the night away. Framed for a moment in the huge open door, frozen by the camera of his mind, Harry saw among the crowd the figure of a girl – a figure of truly animal magnetism – dressed almost incongruously in peasant's costume.

For a second masked eyes met his own and fixed upon them across a space of only a few yards, and then she was gone. But the angle of her neck as she had looked at him, the dark unblinking eyes behind her mask, the fleeting, knowing smile on her lips before she turned away – all of these things had spoken volumes.

That weird feeling, the tingling that Harry felt, suddenly suffused his whole being. His head reeled and his mouth went dry; he had consciously to fight the excitement rising from within; following which he headed dizzily for the nearest wine tent, gratefully to slake his thirst. Then, bolstered by the wine, heart beating fractionally faster than usual, he entered the cavernous barn and casually cast about for the girl whose image still adorned his mind's eye.

But his assumed air of casual interest quickly dissipated as his eyes swept the vast barn without sighting their target, until he was about to step forward and go among the tables in pursuit of his quarry. At that point a hand touched his arm, a heady perfume reached him, and a voice said: 'There is an empty table on the balcony. Would you like to sit?'

Her voice was not at all cultured, but her English was very good; and while certainly there was an element of peasant in her, well, there was much more than that. Deciding to savour her sensuous good looks later when they were seated, he barely glanced at her but took her hand and proceeded across the floor of the barn. They climbed wooden stairs to an open balcony set with tables and cane chairs. On the way he spoke to a waiter and ordered a bottle of wine, a plate of dainties.

They sat at their tiny table overlooking the dance floor, toying with their glasses and pretending to be interested in completely irrelevant matters. He spoke of London, of skiing in Switzerland, the beach at Cannes. She mentioned the mountains, the markets of Budapest, the bloody history of the country, particularly of this region. He was offhand about his jet-setting, not becoming ostentatious; she picked her words carefully, rarely erring in pronunciation. He took in little of what she said and guessed that she wasn't hearing him. But their eyes – at first rather fleetingly – soon became locked; their hands seemed to meet almost involuntarily atop the table.

Beneath the table Harry stretched out a leg towards hers, felt something cold and hairy arching against his calf as might a cat. A cat, yes, it must be one of the local cats, fresh in from mousing in the evening fields. He edged the thing to one side with his foot . . . but she was already on her feet, smiling, holding out a hand to him.

They danced, and he discovered gypsy in her, and strangeness, and magic. She bought him a red mask and positioned it over his face with fingers that were cool and sure. The wine began to go down that much faster . . .

It came almost as a surprise to Harry to find himself in the car, in the front passenger seat, with the girl driving beside him. They were just pulling away from the bright lights of the *Schützenfest*, but he did not remember leaving the great barn. He felt more than a little drunk – with pleasure as much as with wine.

'What's your name?' he asked, not finding it remarkable that he did not already know. Only the sound of the question seemed strange to him, as if a stranger had spoken the words.

'Cassilda,' she replied.

'A nice name,' he told her awkwardly. 'Unusual.'

'I was named after a distant . . . relative.'

After a pause he asked: 'Where are we going, Cassilda?'

'Is it important?'

'I'm afraid we can't go to Szolyhaza—' he began to explain.

She shrugged, 'My . . . home, then.'

'Is it far?'

'Not far, but—'

'But?'

She slowed the car, brought it to a halt. She was a shadowy silhouette beside him, her perfume washing him in warm waves. 'On second thoughts, perhaps I had better take you straight back to your hotel – and leave you there.'

'No, I wouldn't hear of it,' he spoke quickly, seeing his hopes for the night crumbling about him, sobered by the thought that she could so very easily slip out of his life. The early hours of the morning would be time enough for slipping away – and *he* would be doing it, not the girl. 'You'd have to walk home, for one thing, for I'm afraid I couldn't let you take the car . . .' To himself he added: And I know that taxis aren't to be found locally.

'Listen,' he continued when she made no reply, 'you just drive yourself home. I'll take the car from there back to my hotel.'

'But you do not seem steady enough to drive.'

'Then perhaps you'll make me a cup of coffee?' It was a terribly juvenile gambit, but he was gratified to see her smiling behind her mask.

Then, just as quickly as the smile had come, it fell away to be replaced by a frown he could sense rather than detect in the dim glow of the dashboard lights. 'But you must not see where I live.'

'Why on earth not.'

'It is not . . . a rich dwelling.'

'I don't care much for palaces.'

'I don't want you to be able to find your way back to me afterward. This can be for one night only . . .'

Now this, Harry thought to himself, is more like it! He felt his throat going dry again. 'Cassilda, it can't possibly be for more than one night,' he gruffly answered. 'Tomorrow I leave for Budapest.'

'Then surely it is better that—'

'Blindfold me!'

'What?'

'Then I won't be able to see where you live. If you blindfold me I'll see nothing except . . . your room.' He reached across and slipped his hand inside her silk blouse, caressing a breast.

She reached over and stroked his neck, then pulled gently away. She nodded knowingly in the darkness: 'Yes, perhaps we had better blindfold you, if you insist upon handling everything that takes your fancy!'

She tucked a black silk handkerchief gently down behind his mask, enveloping him in darkness. Exposed and compromised as she did this, she made no immediate effort to extricate herself as he fondled her breasts through the silk of her blouse. Finally, breathing the words into his face, she asked:

'Can you not wait?'

'It's not easy.'

'Then I shall make it easier.' She took his hands away from her body, sat back in her seat, slipped the car into gear and pulled away. Harry sat in total darkness, hot and flushed and full of lust.

'We are there,' she announced, rousing him from some peculiar torpor. He was aware only of silence and darkness. He felt just a trifle queasy and told himself that it must be the effect of being driven blindfolded over poor roads. Had he been asleep? What a fool he was making of himself!

'No,' she said as he groped for the door handle. 'Let's just sit here for a moment or two. Open a bottle, I'm thirsty.'

'Bottle? Oh, yes!' Harry suddenly remembered the two bottles of wine they had brought with them from the *Schützenfest*. He reached into the back seat and found one of them. 'But we have no glasses. And why should we drink here when it would be so much more comfortable inside?'

She laughed briefly. 'Harry, I'm a little nervous . . .'

Of course! French courage! – or was it Dutch? What odds? If a sip or two would help her get into the right frame of mind, why not? Silently he blessed the manufacturers of screw-top bottles and twisted the cap free. She took the wine from him, and he heard the swishing of liquid. Her perfume seemed so much stronger, heady as the scent of poppies. And yet beneath it he sensed . . . something tainted?

She returned the bottle to him and he lifted it to parched lips, taking a long deep draft. His head immediately swam, and he felt a joyous urge to break into wild laughter. Instead, discovering himself the victim of so strange a compulsion, he gave a little grunt of surprise.

When he passed the bottle back to her, he let his hand fall to her breast once more – and gasped at the touch of naked flesh, round and swelling! She had opened her blouse to him – or she had removed it altogether! With trembling fingers he reached for his mask and the handkerchief tucked behind it.

'No!' she said, and he heard the slither of silk. 'There, I'm covered again. Here, finish the bottle and then get out of the car. I'll lead you . . .'

'Cassilda,' he slurred her name. 'Let's stop this little game now and—'

'You may not take off the blindfold until we are in my room, when we both stand naked.' He was startled by the sudden coarseness of her voice – the lust he could now plainly detect – and he was also fired by it. He jerked violently when she took hold of him with a slender hand, working her fingers expertly, briefly, causing him to gabble some inarticulate inanity.

Momentarily paralysed with nerve-tingling pleasure and shock, when finally he thought to reach for her she was gone. He heard the whisper of her dress and the click of the car door as she closed it behind her.

Opening his own door he almost fell out, but her hand on his shoulder steadied him. 'The other bottle,' she reminded him.

Clumsily he found the wine, then stumbled as he turned from the car. She took his free hand, whispering: 'Ssh! Quiet!' and gave a low guttural giggle.

Blind, he stumbled after her across a hard, faintly familiar surface. Something brushed against his leg, cold, furry and damp. The fronds of a bushy plant, he suspected.

'Lower your head,' she commanded. 'Carefully down the steps. This way. Almost there . . .'

'Cassilda,' he said, holding tightly to her hand. 'I'm dizzy.'

'The wine!' she laughed.

'Wait, wait!' he cried, dragging her to a halt. 'My head's swimming.' He put out the hand that held the bottle, found a solid surface, pressed his knuckles against it and steadied himself. He leaned against a wall of sorts, dry and flaky to his touch, and gradually the dizziness passed.

This is no good, he told himself: I'll be of no damn use to her unless I can control myself! To her he said, 'Potent stuff, your local wine.'

'Only a few more steps,' she whispered.

She moved closer and again there came the sound of sliding silk, of garments falling. He put his arm around her, felt the flesh of her body against the back of his hand. The weight of the bottle slowly pulled down his arm. Smooth firm buttocks – totally unlike Julia's, which sagged a little – did not flinch at the passing of fingers made impotent by the bottle they held.

'God!' he whispered, throat choked with lust. 'I wish I could hold on to you for the rest of my life . . .'

She laughed, her voice hoarse as his own, and stepped away, pulling him after her. 'But that's your second wish,' she said.

Second wish . . . Second wish? He stumbled and almost fell, was caught and held upright, felt fingers busy at his jacket, the buttons of his shirt. Not at all cold, he shivered, and deep inside a tiny voice began to shout at him, growing louder by the moment, shrieking terrifying messages into his inner ear.

His second wish!

Naked he stood, suddenly alert, the alcohol turning to water in his system, the unbelievable looming real and immense and immediate as his four sound senses compensated for voluntary blindness.

'There,' she said. 'And now you may remove your blindfold!'

Ah, but her perfume no longer masked the charnel musk beneath; her girl's voice was gone, replaced by the dried-up whisper of centuries-shrivelled lips; the hand he held was—

Harry leapt high and wide, trying to shake off the thing that held his hand in a leathery grip, shrieking his denial in a black vault that echoed his cries like lunatic laughter. He leapt and cavorted, coming into momentary contact with the wall, tracing with his burning, supersensitive flesh the tentacled monstrosity that gloated there in bas-relief, feeling its dread embrace!

And bounding from the wall he tripped and sprawled, clawing at the casket which, in his mind's eye, he saw where he had last seen it at the foot of her couch. *Except that now the lid lay open!*

Something at once furry and slimy-damp arched against his naked leg – and again he leapt frenziedly in darkness, gibbering now as his mind teetered over vertiginous chasms.

Finally, dislodged by his threshing about, his blindfold – the red mask and black silk handkerchief he no longer dared remove of his own accord – slipped from his face . . . And then his strength became as that of ten men, became such that nothing natural or supernatural could ever have held him there in that nighted cave beneath black ruins.

Herr Ludovic Debrec heard the roaring of the car's engine long before the beam of its headlights swept down the black deserted road outside the inn. The vehicle rocked wildly and its tyres howled as it turned an impossibly tight corner to slam to a halt in the inn's tiny courtyard.

Debrec was tired, cleaning up after the day's work, preparing for the morning ahead. His handful of guests were all abed, all except the English Herr. This must be him now, but why the tearing rush? Peering through his kitchen window, Debrec recognized the car – then his weary eyes widened and he gasped out loud. But what in the name of all that . . . ? The Herr was naked!

The Hungarian landlord had the door open wide for Harry almost before he could begin hammering upon it – was bowled to one side as the frantic, gasping, bulge-eyed figure rushed in and up the stairs – but he had seen enough, and he crossed himself as Harry disappeared into the inn's upper darkness.

'Mein Gott!' he croaked, crossing himself again, and yet again. 'The Herr has been in *that* place!'

Despite her pills, Julia had not slept well. Now, emerging from unremembered, uneasy dreams, temples throbbing in the grip of a terrific headache, she pondered theproblem of her awakening. A glance at the luminous dial of her wristwatch told her that the time was ten after two in the morning.

Now what had startled her awake? The slamming of a door somewhere? Someone sobbing? Someone crying out to her for help? She seemed to remember all of these things.

She patted the bed beside her with a lethargic gesture. Harry was not there. She briefly considered this, also the fact that his side of the bed seemed undisturbed. Then something moved palely in the darkness at the foot of the bed.

Julia sucked in air, reached out and quickly snapped on the bedside lamp. Harry lay naked, silently writhing on the floor, face down, his hands beneath him.

'Harry!' she cried, getting out of bed and going to him. With a bit of a struggle she turned him on to his side, and he immediately rolled over on his back.

She gave a little shriek and jerked instinctively away from him, revulsion twisting her features. Harry's eyes were screwed shut now, his lips straining back from his teeth in unendurable agony. His hands held something to his heaving chest, something black and crumbly. Even as Julia watched, horrified, his eyes wrenched open and his face went slack. Then Harry's hands fell away from his chest; in one of them, the disintegrating black thing seemed burned into the flesh of his palm and fingers. It was unmistakably a small mummified hand!

Julia began to crawl backwards away from him across the floor; as she did so something came from behind, moving sinuously where it brushed against her. Seeing it, she scuttled faster, her mouth working silently as she came up against the wall of the room.

The – creature – went to Harry, snatched the shrivelled hand from him, turned away ... then, as if on an afterthought, turned back. It arched against him for a moment, and, with the short feelers around its mouth writhing greedily, quickly sank its sharp teeth into the flesh of his leg. In the next instant the thing was gone, but Julia didn't see where it went.

Unable to tear her eyes away from Harry, she saw the veins in his leg where he had been bitten turn a deep, dark blue and stand out, throbbing beneath his marble skin. Carried by the now sluggish pulsing of his blood, the creature's venom spread through him. But ... poison? No, it was much more, much worse, than poison. For as the writhing veins came bursting through his skin, Harry began to melt. It went on for some little time, until what was left was the merest travesty of a man: a sticky, tarry thing of molten flesh and smoking black bones.

Then, ignoring the insistent hammering now sounding at the door, Julia drew breath into her starving lungs – drew breath until she thought her chest must burst – and finally expelled it all in one vast eternal scream ...

THE SUN, THE SEA,
AND THE SILENT SCREAM

I think most writers know when they've written 'a good one.' And there's always a special pleasure in the memories that accompany or follow on from such an event. Charles L. Grant – a writer of many excellent parts and several entire persons, and an editor/anthologist to boot – rang me from the States after he read this one in The Magazine of Fantasy & Science Fiction *to say, 'Wow – what a story!' Coming from Charlie, that was something. And someone on the British Fantasy Society Committee told me if* Fruiting Bodies *hadn't won the BFS short story award for 1989, then SS&SS surely would have.*

So in many ways – what with those two short stories, plus The Picknickers, The Pit-Yakker, No Sharks in the Med *and others, and not forgetting first publication of* Wamphyri! *and* The Source *in England, and* Necroscope *in America – 1987-88 were very good writing and publishing years for me. Especially good when I remember that for two consecutive years I even managed to indulge my passion for the Greek Islands –*

– But not, I hasten to add, on the island in this story!

This time of year, just as you're recovering from Christmas, they're wont to appear, all unsolicited, *plop* on your welcome mat. I had forgotten that fact, but yesterday I was reminded.

Julie was up first, creating great smells of coffee and frying bacon. And me still in bed, drowsy, thinking how great it was to be nearly back to normal. Three months she'd been out of *that* place, and fit enough now to be first up, running about after me for a change.

Her sweet voice called upstairs: 'Post, darling!' And her slippers flip-flopping out into the porch. Then those long moments of silence – until it dawned on me what she was doing. I knew it instinctively, the way you do about someone you love. She was screaming – but silently. A scream that came drilling into all my bones to shiver into shards right there in the marrow. Me out of bed like a puppet on some madman's strings, jerked downstairs so as to break my neck, while the silent scream went on and on.

And Julie standing there with her head thrown back and her mouth agape, and the unending scream not coming out. Her eyes starting out with their pupils rolled down, staring at the thing in her white, shuddering hand—

A travel brochure, of course . . .

* * *

Julie had done Greece fairly extensively with her first husband. That had been five or six years ago, when they'd hoped and tried for kids a lot. No kids had come; she couldn't have them; he'd gone off and found someone who could. No hard feelings. Maybe a few soft feelings.

So when we first started going back to Greece, I'd suggested places they'd explored together. Maybe I was looking for far-away expressions on her face in the sunsets, or a stray tear when a familiar *bousouki* tune drifted out on aromatic taverna exhalations. Somebody had taken a piece of my heart, too, once upon a time; maybe I wanted to know how much of Julie was really mine. As it happened, all of her was.

After we were married, we left the old trails behind and broke fresh ground. That is, we started to find new places to holiday. Twice yearly we'd pack a few things, head for the sunshine, the sea, and sometimes the sand. Sand wasn't always a part of the package, not in Greece. Not the golden or pure white varieties, anyway. But pebbles, marble chips, great brown and black slabs of volcanic rock sloping into the sea – what odds? The sun was always the same, and the sea . . .

The sea. Anyone who knows the Aegean, the Ionian, the Mediterranean in general, in between and around Turkey and Greece, knows what I mean when I describe those seas as indescribable. Blue, green, mother-of-pearl, turquoise in that narrow band where the sea meets the land: fantastic! Myself, I've always liked the colours *under* the sea the best. That's the big bonus I get, or got, out of the islands: the swimming, the amazing submarine world just beyond the glass of my face mask, the spearfishing.

And this time – last time, the very last time – we settled for Makelos. But don't go looking for it on any maps. You won't find it; much too small, and I'm assured that the British don't go there any more. As a holiday venue, it's been written off. I'd like to think I had something, everything, to do with that, which is why I'm writing this. But a warning: if you're stuck on Greece anyway, and willing to take your chances come what may, read no further. I'd hate to spoil it all for you.

So ... what am I talking about? Political troubles, unfinished hotel apartments, polluted swimming pools? No, nothing like that. We didn't take that sort of holiday, anyway. We were strictly 'off-the-beaten-track' types. Hence Makelos.

We couldn't fly there direct; the island was mainly a flat-topped mountain climbing right out of the water, with a dirt landing strip on the plateau suitable only for Skyvans. So it was a packed jet to Athens, a night on the town, and in the mid-morning a flying Greek matchbox the rest of the way. Less than an hour out of Athens and into the Cyclades, descending through a handful of cotton-wool clouds, that was our first sight of our destination.

Less than three miles long, a mile wide – that was it. Makelos. There was a 'town', also called Makelos, at one end of the island where twin spurs formed something of a harbour; and the rest of the place around the central plateau was rock and scrub and tiny bays, olive groves galore, almonds and some walnuts, prickly pears and a few lonely lemons. Oh, and lots of wildflowers, so that the air seemed scented.

The year before, there'd been a few apartments available in Makelos town. But towns weren't our scene. This time, however, the island had something new to offer: a lone taverna catering for just three detached, cabin-style apartments, or 'villas', all nestling in a valley two miles down the coast from Makelos town itself. Only one or two taxis on the entire island (the coastal road was little more than a track), no fast-food stands, and no packed shingle beaches where the tideless sea would be one-third sun oil and two-thirds tourist pee!

We came down gentle as a feather, taxied up to a wind-blown shack that turned out to be the airport, deplaned and passed in front of the shack and out the back, and boarded our transport. There were other holiday makers; but we were too excited to pay them much attention; also a handful of dour-faced island Greeks – Makelosians, we guessed. Dour, yes. Maybe that should have told us something about their island.

Our passports had been stamped over the Athens stamp with a local variety as we passed through the airport shack, and the official doing the job turned out to be our driver. A busy man, he also introduced himself as the mayor of Makelos! The traction end of our 'transport' was a three-wheeler: literally a converted tractor, hauling a four-wheeled trolley with bucket seats bolted to its sides. On the way down from the plateau, I remember thinking we'd never make it; Julie kept her eyes closed for most of the trip; I gave everyone aboard As for nerve. And the driver-mayor sang a doleful Greek number all the way down.

The town was very old, with nowhere the whitewashed walls you become accustomed to in the islands. Instead, there was an air of desolation about the place. Throw in a few tumbleweeds, and you could shoot a Western there. But fishing boats bobbed in the harbour, leathery Greeks mended nets along the quayside; old men drank muddy coffee at wooden tables outside the tavernas, and bottles of Metaxa and ouzo were very much in evidence. Crumbling fortified walls of massive thickness proclaimed, however inarticulately, a one-time Crusader occupation.

Once we'd trundled to a halt in the town's square, the rest of the passengers were home and dry; Julie and I still had a mile and a half to go. Our taxi driver (transfer charges both ways, six pounds sterling: I'd wondered why it was so cheap!) collected our luggage from the tractor's trolley, stowed it away, waited for us while we dusted ourselves down and stretched our legs. Then we got into his 'taxi'.

I won't impugn anyone's reputation by remarking on the make of that old bus; come to think of it, I could possibly *make* someone's name, for anywhere else in the world this beauty would have been off the road in the late sixties! Inside – it was a shrine, of course. The Greek sort, with good-luck charms, pictures of the saints, photos of Mum and Dad, and icon-like miniatures in silver frames, hanging and jangling everywhere. And even enough room for the driver to see through his windscreen.

'Nichos,' he introduced himself, grave-faced, trying to loosen my arm in its socket with his handshake where he reached back from the driver's seat. And to Julie, seated beside him up front: 'Nick!' and he took her hand and bowed his head to kiss it. Fine, except we were already mobile and leaving the town, and holiday makers and villagers alike scattering like clucking hens in all directions in our heavy blue exhaust smoke.

Nichos was maybe fifty, hard to tell: bright brown eyes, hair greying, upward-turned moustache, skin brown as old leather. His nicotine-stained teeth and ouzo breath were pretty standard. 'A fine old car,' I opined, as he jarred us mercilessly on non-existent suspension down the patchy, pot-holed tarmacadam street.

'Eh?' He raised an eyebrow.

'The car,' I answered. 'She goes, er, well!'

'Very well, thank you. The car,' he apparently agreed.

'Maybe he doesn't speak it too well, darling.' Julie was straight-faced.

'Speaks it,' Nichos agreed with a nod. Then, registering understanding: 'Ah – *speak* it! I am speaking it, yes, and slowly. Very *slooowly*! Then is understanding. Good morning, good evening, welcome to my house – exactly! I am in Athens. Three years. Speaks it much, in Athens.'

'Great!' I enthused, without malice. After all, I couldn't speak any Greek.

'You stay at Villas Dimitrios, yes?' He was just passing the time; of course we were staying there; he'd been paid to take us there, hadn't he? And yet at the same time, I'd picked up a note of genuine enquiry, even something of concern in his voice, as if our choice surprised or dismayed him.

'Is it a nice place?' Julie asked.

'Nice?' he repeated her. 'Beautiful!' He blew a kiss. 'Beautiful sea – for swim, *beautiful*!' Then he shrugged, said: 'All Makelos same. But Dimitrios water – water for drink – him not so good. You drinking? OK – you drink Coke. You drink beer. Drinking water in bottle. Drinking wine – very cheap! Not drinking water. Is big hole in Dimitrios. Deep, er – well? Yes? Water in well bad. All around Dimitrios bad. Good for olives, lemons, no good for the people.'

We just about made sense of everything he said, which wasn't quite as easy as I've made it sound here. As for the water situation: that was standard, too. We never drank the local water anyway. 'So it's a beautiful place,' I said. 'Good.'

Again he glanced at me over his shoulder, offered another shrug. 'Er, beautiful, yes.' He didn't seem very sure about it now. The Greeks are notoriously vague.

We were out of Makelos, heading south round the central plateau, kicking up the dust of a narrow road where it had been cut through steep, seaward-sloping strata of yellow-banded, dazzling white rock to run parallel with the sea on our left. We were maybe thirty or forty feet above sea level, and down there through bights in the shallow sea cliffs, we were allowed tantalizing glimpses of white pebble beaches scalloping an ocean flat as a mill-pond.

The fishing would be good. Nothing like the south coast of England (no Dover sole basking on a muddy bottom here), but that made it more of a challenge. You had to be *good* to shoot fish here!

I took out a small paper parcel from my pocket and unwrapped it: a pair of gleaming trident spearheads purchased in Athens. With luck these heads should fit my spears. Nichos turned his head. 'You like to fish? I catch plenty! *Big* fisherman!' Then that look was back on his face. 'You fish in Dimitrios? No eat. You like the fishing – good! Chase him, the fish – shoot, maybe kill – but no eat. OK?'

I began to feel worried. Julie, too. She turned to stare at me. I leaned forward, said: 'Nichos, what do you mean? Why shouldn't we eat what I catch?'

'My house!' he answered as we turned a bend through a stand of stunted trees. He grinned, pointed.

Above us, the compacted scree slope was green with shrubs and Mediterranean pines. There was a garden set back in ancient, gnarled olives, behind which a row of white-framed windows reflected the late-morning sunlight. The house matched the slope rising around and beyond it, its ochre-tiled roof seeming to melt into the hillside. Higher up there were walled, terraced enclosures; higher still, where the mountain's spur met the sky, goats made gravity-defying silhouettes against the dazzle.

'I show you!' said Nichos, turning right onto a track that wound dizzily through a series of hairpins to the house. We hung on as he drove with practised ease almost to the front door, parking his taxi in the shade of an olive tree heavy with fruit. Then he was opening doors for us, calling out to his wife: 'Katrin – hey, Katrin!'

We stayed an hour. We drank cold beer, ate a delicious sandwich of salami, sliced tomatoes, and goat's milk cheese. We admired the kids, the goats and chickens, the little house. It had been an effective way of changing the subject. And we didn't give Nichos's reticence (was that what it had been, or just poor communications?) another thought until he dropped us off at Villas Dimitrios.

The place was only another mile down the road, as the crow flies. But that coastal road knew how to wind. Still, we could probably have walked it while Katrin made us our sandwiches. And yet the island's natural contours kept it hidden from sight until the last moment.

We'd climbed up from the sea by then, maybe a hundred feet, and the road had petered out to little more than a track as we crested the final rise and Nichos applied his brakes. And there we sat in that oven of a car, looking down through its dusty, fly-specked windows on Villas Dimitrios. It was . . . idyllic!

Across the spur where we were parked, the ground dipped fairly steeply to a bay maybe a third of a mile point to point. The bay arms were rocky, formed of the tips of spurs sloping into the sea, but the beach between them was sand. *White* sand, Julie's favourite sort. Give her a book, a white beach, and a little shade, and I could swim all day. The taverna stood almost at the water's edge: a long, low house with a red-tiled roof, fronted by a wooden framework supporting heavy grapevines and masses of bougainvillaea. Hazy blue woodsmoke curled up from its chimney, and there was a garden to its rear. Behind the house, separate from it and each other and made private by screening groves of olives, three blobs of shimmering white stone were almost painful to look at. The chalets or 'villas'.

Nichos merely glanced at it; nothing new to him. He pointed across the tiny valley to its far side. Over there, the scree base went up brown and yellow to the foot of sheer cliffs, where beneath a jutting overhang the shadows were so dark as to be black. It had to be a cave.

Something of a track had been worn into the scree, leading to the place under the cliff.

'In there,' said Nichos with one of his customary shrugs, 'the well. Water, him no good . . .' His face was very grave.

'The water was poisoned?' Julie prompted him.

'Eh?' he cocked his head, then gave a nod. 'Now is poison!'

'I don't understand,' I said. 'What is it—' I indicated the dark blot under the cliff '—over there?'

'The well,' he said again. 'Down inside the cave. But the water, he had, er – like the crabs, you know? You understand the crabs, in the sea?'

'Of course,' Julie told him. 'In England we eat them.'

He shook his head, looked frustrated. 'Here, too,' he said. 'But this thing not crab. Very small.' He measured an inch between thumb and forefinger. 'And no eat him. Very bad! People were . . . sick. They died. Men came from the government in Athens. They bring, er, chemicals? They put in well. Poison for the crabs.' Again his shrug. 'Now is OK – maybe. But I say, no drink the water.'

Before we could respond, he got out of the car, unloaded our luggage onto the dusty track. I followed him. 'You're not taking us down?'

'Going down OK,' he shrugged, this time apologetically. 'Come up again – difficult! Too – how you say?' He made an incline with his hand.

'Too steep?'

'Is right. My car very nice – also very old! I sorry.' I picked up the cases; Julie joined us and took the travel bags. Nichos made no attempt to help; instead he gave a small, awkward bow, said: 'You see my house? Got the problem, come speak. Good morning.' Then he was into his car. He backed off, turned around, stopped, and leaned out his window. 'Hey, mister, lady!'

We looked at him.

He pointed. 'Follow road is long way. Go straight down, very easy. Er, how you say – short-cut? So, I go. See you in two weeks.'

We watched his tyres kicking up dust and grit until he was out of sight. Then:

Taking a closer look at the terrain, I could see he was right. The track followed the ridge of the spur down to a sharp right turn, then down a hard-packed dirt ramp to the floor of the valley. It was steep, but a decent car should make it – even Nichos's taxi, I thought. But if we left the track here and climbed straight down the side of the spur, we'd cut two or three hundred yards off the distance. And actually, even the spur wasn't all that steep. We made it without any fuss, and I sat down only once when my feet shot out from under me.

As we got down onto the level, our host for the next fortnight came banging and clattering from the direction of the taverna, bumping over the rough scrub in a Greek three-wheeler with a cart at the back. Dimitrios wore a wide-brimmed hat against the sun, but still he was sweating just as badly as we were. He wiped his brow as he dumped our luggage into his open-ended cart. We hitched ourselves up at the rear and sat with our feet dangling. And he drove us to our chalet.

We were hot and sticky, all three of us, and maybe it wasn't so strange we didn't talk. Or perhaps he could see our discomfort and preferred that we get settled in before turning on the old Greek charm. Anyway, we said nothing as he opened the door for us, gave me the key, helped me carry our bags into the cool interior. I followed him back outside again while Julie got to the ritual unpacking.

'Hot,' he said then. 'Hot, the sun . . .' Greeks have this capacity for stating the obvious. Then, carrying it to extreme degrees, he waved an arm in the direction of the beach, the sea, and the taverna. 'Beach. Sea. Taverna. For swimming. Eating. I have the food, drinks. I also selling the food for you the cooking . . .' The chalet came with its own self-catering kit.

'Fine,' I smiled. 'See you later.'

He stared at me a moment, his eyes like dull lights in the dark shadow of his hat, then made a vague sort of motion halfway between a shrug and a nod. He got back aboard his vehicle and started her up, and as his clatter died away, I went back inside and had a look around.

Julie was filling a pair of drawers with spare clothing, at the same time building a teetering pyramid of reading material on a chair. Where books were concerned, she was voracious. She was like that about me, too. No complaints here.

Greek island accommodation varies from abominable to half decent. Or, if you're willing to shell out, you might be lucky enough to get good – but rarely better than that. The Villas Dimitrios chalets were . . . well, OK. But we'd paid for it, so it was what we expected.

I checked the plumbing first. Greek island plumbing is never better than basic. The bathroom was tastefully but totally tiled, even the ceiling! No bathtub, but a good shower and, at the other end of the small room, the toilet and washbasin. Enclosed in tiles, you could shower and let the water spray where-the-heck; if it didn't end up in the shower basin, it would end up on the floor, which sloped gently from all directions to one corner where there was a hole going – where? That's the other thing about Greek plumbing: I've never been able to figure out where everything goes.

But the bathroom did have its faults: like, there were no plugs for the washbasin and shower drainage, and no grilles in the plugholes. I suppose I'm quirky, but I like to see a grille in there, not just a black hole gurgling away to nowhere. It was the same in the little 'kitchen' (an alcove under an arch, really, with a sink and drainer unit, a two-ring gas stove, a cupboard containing the cylinder, and a wall-mounted rack for crockery and cutlery; all very nice and serviceable and equipped with a concealed overhead fan-extractor): no plug in the sink and no grille in the plughole.

I complained loudly to Julie about it.

'Don't put your toe down and you won't get stuck!' was her advice from the bedroom.

'Toe down?' I was already miles away, looking for the shaver socket.

'Down the shower plughole,' she answered. And she came out of the bedroom wearing sandals and the bottom half of her bikini. I made slavering noises, and she turned coyly, tossed back her bra straps for me to fasten. 'Do me up.'

'You were quick off the mark,' I told her.

'All packed away, too,' she said with some satisfaction. 'And the big white hunter's kit neatly laid out for him. And all performed free of charge – while he examines plugholes!' Then she picked up a towel and tube of lotion and headed for the door. 'Last one in the sea's a pervert!'

Five minutes later I followed her. She'd picked a spot halfway between the chalet and the most northerly bay arm. Her red towel was like a splash of blood on the white sand two hundred yards north of the taverna. I carried my mask, snorkel, flippers, some strong string, and a tatty old blanket with torn corners; that was all. No spear gun. First I'd take a look-see, and the serious stuff could come later. Julie obviously felt the same as I did about it: no book, just a slim, pale white body on the red towel, green eyes three-quarters shuttered behind huge sunglasses. She was still wet from the sea, but that wouldn't last long.

The sun was a furnace, steaming the water off her body.

On my way to her, I'd picked up some long, thin, thorny branches from the scrub; when I got there, I broke off the thorns and fixed up a sunshade. The old blanket's torn corners showed how often we'd done this before. Then I took my kit to the water's edge and dropped it, and ran gasping, pell-mell into the shallows until I toppled over! My way of getting into the sea quickly. Following which I outfitted myself and finned for the rocks where the spur dipped below the water.

As I've intimated, the Mediterranean around the Greek islands is short on fish. You'll find red mullet on the bottom, plenty of them, but you need half a dozen to make a decent meal. And grey mullet on top, which move like lightning and cause you to use up more energy than eating them provides; great sport, but you couldn't live on it. But there's at least one fish of note in the Med, and that's the grouper.

Groupers are territorial; a family will mark out its own patch, usually in deep water where there's plenty of cover, which is to say rock or weeds. And they love caves. Where there are plenty of rocks and caves, there'll also be groupers. Here, where the spur crumbled into the sea, this was ideal grouper ground. So I wasn't surprised to see this one – especially since I didn't have my gun! Isn't that always the way of it?

He was all of twenty-four inches long, maybe seven across his back, mottled red and brown to match his cave. When he saw me, he headed straight for home, and I made a mental note to mark the spot. Next time I came out here, I'd have my gun with me, armed with a single flap-nosed spear. The spear goes into the fish, the flap opens, and he's hooked, can't slip off. Tridents are fine for small fish, but not for this bloke. And don't talk to me about cruel; if I'm cruel, so is every fisherman in the world, and at least I eat what I catch. But it was then, while I was thinking these things, that I noticed something was wrong.

The fish had homed in on his cave all right, but as his initial reaction to my presence wore off, so his spurt of speed diminished. Now he seemed merely to drift toward the dark hole in the rock, lolling from side to side like some strange, crippled sub, actually missing his target to strike *against* the weedy stone! It was the first time I'd seen a fish collide with something underwater. This was one very sick grouper.

I went down to have a closer look. He was maybe ten feet down, just lolling against the rock face. His huge gill flaps pulsed open and closed, open and closed. I could have reached out and touched him. Then, as he rolled a little on one side, I saw—

I backed off, felt a little sick – felt sorry for him. And I wished I had my gun with me, if only to put him out of his misery. Under his great head, wedging his gill slits half open, a nest of fish lice or parasites of some sort were plainly visible. Not lampreys or remora or the like, for they were too small, only as big as my thumbs. Crustaceans, I thought – a good dozen of them – and they were hooked into him, leeching on the raw red flesh under his gills.

God, I have a *loathing* of this sort of thing! Once in Crete I'd come out of the sea with a suckerfish in my armpit. I hadn't noticed it until I was towelling myself dry and it fell off me. It was only three or four inches long but I'd reacted like I was covered with leeches! I had that same feeling now.

Skin crawling, I drifted up and away from the stricken fish, and for the first time got a good look at his eyes. They were dull, glazed, bubbly as the eyes of a fatally diseased goldfish. And they followed me. And then *he* followed me!

As I floated feet first for the surface, that damned grouper

finned lethargically from the rocks and began drifting up
after me. Several of his parasites had detached themselves
from him and floated alongside him, gravitating like small
satellites about his greater mass. I pictured one of them with
its hooked feet fastened in my groin, or over one of my eyes.
I mean, I knew they couldn't do that – their natural hosts are
fish – but the thoughts made me feel vulnerable as hell.

I took off like Tarzan for the beach twenty-five yards
away, climbed shivering out of the water in the shadow of
the declining spur. As soon as I was out, the shudders left
me. Along the beach my sunshade landmark was still there,
flapping a little in a light breeze come up suddenly off the
sea; but no red towel, no Julie. She could be swimming.
Or maybe she'd felt thirsty and gone for a drink under the
vines where the taverna fronted onto the sea.

Kit in hand, I padded along the sand at the dark rim of
the ocean, past the old blanket tied with string to its frame
of branches, all the way to the taverna. The area under
the vines was maybe fifty feet along the front by thirty
deep, a concrete base set out with a dozen small tables
and chairs. Dimitrios was being a bit optimistic here, I
thought. After all, it was the first season his place had
been in the brochures. But . . . maybe next year there'd
be more chalets, and the canny Greek owner was simply
thinking well ahead.

I gave the place the once-over. Julie wasn't there, but
at least I was able to get my first real look at our handful of fellow holiday makers.

A fat woman in a glaring yellow one-piece splashed in
eighteen inches of water a few yards out. She kept calling
to her husband, one George, to come on in. George sat
half in, half out of the shade; he was a thin, middle-aged,
balding man not much browner than myself, wearing specs
about an inch thick that made his eyes look like marbles.
'No, no, dear,' he called back. 'I'm fine watching you.'

He looked frail, timid, tired – and I thought: *Where the hell are marriages like this made?* They were like characters off a seaside postcard, except he didn't even seem to have the strength to ogle the girls – if there'd been any! His wife was twice his size.

George was drinking beer from a glass. A bottle, three-quarters empty and beaded with droplets of moisture, stood on his table. I fancied a drink but had no money on me. Then I saw that George was looking at me, and I felt that he'd caught me spying on him or something. 'I was wondering,' I said, covering up my rudeness, 'if you'd seen my wife? She was on the beach there, and—'

'Gone back to your chalet,' he said, sitting up a bit in his chair. 'The girl with the red towel?' And suddenly he looked just a bit embarrassed. So he was an ogler after all. 'Er, while you were in the sea . . .' He took off his specs and rubbed gingerly at a large red bump on the lid of his right eye. Then he put his glasses on again, blinked at me, held out the beer bottle. 'Fancy a mouthful? To wash the sea out of your throat? I've had all I want.'

I took the bottle, drained it, said: 'Thanks! Bite?'

'Eh?' He cocked his head on one side.

'Your eye,' I said. 'Mosquito, was it? Horsefly or something?'

'Dunno.' He shook his head. 'We got here Wednesday, and by Thursday night this was coming up. Yesterday morning it was like this. Doesn't hurt so much as irritates. There's another back of my knee, not fully in bloom yet.'

'Do you have stuff to dab on?'

He nodded in the direction of his wallowing wife and sighed, 'She has *gallons* of it! Useless stuff! It will just have to take its own time.'

'Look, I'll see you later,' I said. 'Right now I have to go and see what's up with Julie.' I excused myself.

Leaving the place, I nodded to a trio of spinsterish types

relaxing in summer frocks at one of the tables further back. They looked like sisters, and the one in the middle might just be a little retarded. She kept lolling first one way, then the other, while her companions propped her up. I caught a few snatches of disjointed, broad Yorkshire conversation:

'Doctor? . . . sunstroke, I reckon. Or maybe that melon? . . . taxi into town will fix her up . . . bit of shopping . . . pull her out of it . . . Kalamari? – *yechhh!* Don't know what decent grub is, these foreign folks . . .' They were so wrapped up in each other, or in complaint of the one in the middle, that they scarcely noticed me at all.

On the way back to our chalet, at the back of the house/taverna, I looked across low walls and a row of exotic potted plants to see an old Greek (male or female I couldn't determine, because of the almost obligatory floppy black hat tilted forward, and flowing black peasant clothes) sitting in a cane chair in one corner of the garden. He or she sat dozing in the shade of an olive tree, chin on chest, all oblivious of the world outside the tree's sun-dappled perimeter. A pure white goat, just a kid, was tethered to the tree; it nuzzled the oldster's dangling fingers like they were teats. Julie was daft for young animals, and I'd have to tell her about it. As for the figure in the cane chair: he/she had been there when Julie and I went down to the beach. Well, getting old in this climate had to be better than doing it in some climates I could mention . . .

I found Julie in bed, shivering for all she was worth! She was patchy red where the sun had caught her, cold to the touch but filmed with perspiration. I took one look, recognized the symptoms, said: 'Oh-oh! Last night's moussaka, eh? You should have had the chicken!' Her tummy *always* fell prey to moussaka, be it good or bad. But she usually recovered quickly, too.

'Came on when I was on the beach,' she said. 'I left the blanket . . .'

'I saw it,' I told her. 'I'll go get it.' I gave her a kiss.

'Just let me lie here and close my eyes for a minute or two, and I'll be OK,' she mumbled. 'An *hour* or two, anyway.' And as I was going out the door: 'Jim, this isn't Nichos's bad water, is it?'

I turned back. 'Did you drink any?'

She shook her head.

'Got crabs?'

She was too poorly to laugh, so merely snorted.

I pocketed some money. 'I'll get the blanket, buy some bottled drinks. You'll have something to sip. And then . . . will you be OK if I go fishing?'

She nodded. 'Of course. You'll see; I'll be on my feet again tonight.'

'Anyway, you should see the rest of them here,' I told here. 'Three old sisters, and one of 'em not all there – a little man and fat woman straight off a postcard! Oh, and I've a surprise for you.'

'Oh?'

'When you're up,' I smiled. I was talking about the white kid. Tonight or tomorrow morning I'd show it to her.

Feeling a bit let down – not by Julie but by circumstances in general, even by the atmosphere of this place, which was somehow odd – I collected the sunscreen blanket and poles, marched resolutely back to the taverna. Dimitrios was serving drinks to the spinsters. The 'sunstruck' one had recovered a little, sipped Coke through a straw. George and his burden were nowhere to be seen. I sat down at one of the tables, and in a little while Dimitrios came over. This time I studied him more closely.

He was youngish, maybe thirty, thirty-five, tall if a little stooped. He was more swarthy peasant Greek than classical or cosmopolitan; his natural darkness, coupled with the shadow of his hat (which he wore even here in the shade), hid his face from any really close inspection. The one very noticeable thing about that face, however, was this: it didn't smile. That's something you get to expect in the islands, the flash of teeth. Even badly stained ones. But not Dimitrios's teeth.

His hands were burned brown, lean, almost scrawny. Be that as it may, I felt sure they'd be strong hands. As for his eyes: they were the sort that make you look away. I tried to stare at his face a little while, then looked away. I wasn't afraid, just concerned. But I didn't know what about.

'Drink?' he said, making it sound like 'dring'. 'Melon? The melon he is free. I give. I grow plenty. You like him? And water? I bring half-melon and water.'

He turned to go, but I stopped him. 'Er, no!' I remembered the conversation of the spinsters, about the melon. 'No melon, no water, thank you.' I tried to smile at him, found it difficult. 'I'll have a cold beer. Do you have bottled water? You know, in the big plastic bottles? And Coke? Two of each, for the refrigerator. OK?'

He shrugged, went off. There was this lethargy about him, almost a malaise. No, I didn't much care for him at all . . .

'Swim!' the excited voice of one of the spinsters reached me. 'Right along there, at the end of the beach. Like yesterday. Where there's no one to peep.'

God! You'll be lucky, I thought.

'*Shh!*' one of her sisters hushed her, as if a crowd of rapacious men were listening to every word. 'Don't tell the whole world, Betty!'

A Greek girl, Dimitrios's sister or wife, came out of the house carrying a plastic bag. She came to my table, smiled at me – a little nervously, I thought. 'The water, the Coke,' she said, making each definite article sound like 'thee'. *But at least she can speak my language*, I had to keep reminding myself. 'Four hundred drachmas, please,' she said. I nodded and paid up. About two pounds sterling. Cheap, considering it all had to be brought from the mainland. The bag and the bottles inside it were tingling cold in my hand.

I stood up – and the girl was still there, barring my way. The three sisters made off down the beach, and there was no one else about. The girl glanced over her shoulder toward the house. The hand she put on my arm was trembling and now I could see that it wasn't just nervousness. She was afraid.

'Mister,' she said, the word very nearly sticking in her dry throat. She swallowed and tried again. 'Mister, please. I—'

'Elli!' a low voice called. In the doorway to the house, dappled by splashes of sunlight through the vines, Dimitrios.

'Yes?' I answered her. 'Is there—?'

'*Elli!*' he called again, an unspoken warning turning the word to a growl.

'Is all right,' she whispered, her pretty face suddenly thin and pale. 'Is – nothing!' And then she almost ran back to the house.

Weirder and weirder! But if they had some husband-and-wife thing going, it was no business of mine. I'm no Clint Eastwood – and they're a funny lot, the Greeks, in an argument.

On my way back to the chalet, I looked again into the garden. The figure in black, head slumped on chest, sat there as before; it hadn't moved an inch. The sun had, though, and was burning more fiercely down on the drowsing figure in black. The white kid had got loose from its tether and was on its hind legs, eating amazing scarlet flowers out of their tub. 'You'll get hell, mate,' I muttered, 'when he/she wakes up!'

There were a lot of flies about. I swatted at a cloud of

the ugly, buzzing little bastards as I hurried, dripping perspiration, back to the chalet.

Inside, I took a long drink myself, then poured ice-cold water into one glass, Coke into another. I put both glasses on a bedside table within easy reach of Julie, stored the rest of the stuff in the fridge. She was asleep: bad belly complicated by a mild attack of sunstroke. I should have insisted that Nichos bring us right to the door. He could have, I was sure. Maybe he and Dimitrios had a feud or something going. But ... Julie was sleeping peacefully enough, and the sweat was off her brow.

Someone tut-tutted, and I was surprised to find it was I. Hey! – this was supposed to be a holiday, wasn't it?

I sighed, took up my kit – including the gun – went back into the sun. On impulse I'd picked up the key. I turned it in the lock, withdrew it, stooped, and slid it under the door. She could come out, but no one could go in. If she wasn't awake when I got back, I'd simply hook the key out again with a twig.

But right now it was time for some serious fishing!

There was a lot of uneasiness building up inside me, but I put it all out of my head (what was it anyway but a set of unsettling events and queer coincidence?) and marched straight down to the sea. The beach was empty here, not a soul in sight. No, wrong: at the far end, near the foot of the second spur, two of the sisters splashed in the shallows in faded bathing costumes twenty years out of date, while the third one sat on the sand watching them. They were all of two or three hundred yards away, however, so I wouldn't be accused of ogling them.

In a little while I was outfitted, in the water, heading straight out to where the sandy bottom sloped off a little more steeply. At about eight or nine feet, I saw an octopus in his house of shells – a big one, too, all coiled pink tentacles and cat eyes wary – but in a little while I moved on. Normally I'd have taken him, gutted him and beaten the grease out of him, then handed him in to the local taverna for goodwill. But on this occasion that would be Dimitrios. Sod Dimitrios!

At about twelve feet the bottom levelled out. In all directions I saw an even expanse of golden, gently rippled sand stretching away: beautiful but boring. And not a fish in sight! Then . . . the silvery flash of a belly turned side-on – no, two of them, three! – caught my eye. Not on the bottom but on the surface. Grey mullet, and of course they'd seen me before I saw them. I followed their darting shapes anyway, straight out to sea as before.

In a little while a reef of dark, fretted rocks came in view. It seemed fairly extensive, ran parallel to the beach. There was some weed but not enough to interfere with visibility. And the water still only twelve to fifteen feet deep. Things were looking up.

If a man knows the habits of his prey, he can catch him, and I knew my business. The grey mullet will usually run, but if you can surprise him, startle him, he'll take cover. If no cover's available, then he just keeps on running, and he'll very quickly outpace any man. But here in this pock-marked reef, there *was* cover. To the fish, it would seem that the holes in the rocks were a refuge, but in fact they'd be a trap. I went after them with a will, putting everything I'd got into the chase.

Coming up fast behind the fish, and making all the noise I could, I saw a central school of maybe a dozen small ones, patrolled by three or four full-grown outriders. The latter had to be two-pounders if they were an ounce. They panicked, scattered; the smaller fish shot off in all directions, and their big brothers went to ground! Exactly as I'd hoped they would. Two into one outcrop of honey-combed rock, and two into another.

I trod water on the surface, getting my breath, making

sure the rubbers of my gun weren't tangled with the loose line from the spear, keeping my eyes glued to the silvery grey shapes finning nervously to and fro in the hollow rocks. I picked my target, turned on end, thrust my legs up, and let my own weight drive me to the bottom; and as my impetus slowed, so I lined up on one of the two holes. Right on cue, one of the fish appeared. He never knew what hit him.

I surfaced, freed my vibrating prize from the trident where two of the tines had taken him behind the gills, hung him from a gill ring on my belt. By now his partner had made off, but the other pair of fish was still there in the second hole. I quickly reloaded, made a repeat performance. My first hunt of the season, and already I had two fine fish! I couldn't wait to get back and show them to Julie.

I was fifty yards out. Easing the strain on muscles that were a whole year out of practice, I swam lazily back to the beach and came ashore close to the taverna. Way along the beach, two of the sisters were putting their dresses on over their ancient costumes, while the third sat on the sand with her head lolling. Other than these three, no one else was in sight.

I made for the chalet. As I went, the sun steamed the water off me and I began to itch; it was time I took a shower, and I might try a little protective after-sun lotion, too. Already my calves were turning red, and I supposed my back must be in the same condition. Ugly now, but in just a few days' time . . .

Passing the garden behind the house, this time I didn't look in. The elderly person under the tree would be gone by now, I was sure; but I did hear the lonely bleating of the kid.

Then I saw Dimitrios. He was up on the roof of the central chalet, and from where I padded silently between the olives, I could see him lifting a metal hatch on a

square water tank. The roofs were also equipped with
solar panels. So the sun heated the water, but ... where
did the water come from? Idiot question, even to oneself!
From a well, obviously. But which well?

I passed under the cover of a clump of trees, and the
Greek was lost to sight. When I came out again into
the open, I saw him descending a ladder propped against the
chalet's wall. He carried a large galvanized bucket –
empty, to judge from its swing and bounce. He hadn't
seen me, and for some hard-to-define reason, I didn't
want him to. I ran the rest of the way to our chalet.

The door was open; Julie was up and about in shorts and
a halter. She greeted me with a kiss, *oohed* and *aahed* at my
catch. 'Supper,' I told her with something of pride. 'No
moussaka tonight. Fresh fish done over charcoal, with a
little Greek salad and a filthy great bottle of retsina – or
maybe two filthy great bottles!'

I cleaned the fish into the toilet, flushed their guts away.
Then I washed them, tossed some ice into the sink unit, and
put the fish in the ice. I didn't want them to stiffen up in
the fridge, and they'd keep well enough in the sink for a
couple of hours.

'Now you stink of fish,' Julie told me without ceremony.
'Your forearms are covered in scales. Take a shower and
you'll feel great. I did.'

'Are you OK?' I held her with my eyes.

'Fine now, yes,' she said. 'System flushed while you were
out – you don't wish to know that – and now the old tum's
settled down nicely, thank you. It was just the travel, the
sun—'

'The moussaka?'

'That, too, probably.' She sighed. 'I just wish I didn't
love it so!'

I stripped and stepped into the shower basin, fiddled
with the knobs. 'What'll you do while I shower?'

'Turn 'em both on full,' she instructed. 'Hot and cold both. Then the temperature's just right. Me? I'll go and sit in the shade by the sea, start a book.'

'In the taverna?' Maybe there was something in the tone of my voice.

'Yes. Is that OK?'

'Fine,' I told her, steeling myself and spinning the taps on. I didn't want to pass my apprehension on to her. 'I'll see you there – *ahh!* – shortly.' And after that, for the next ten minutes, it was hissing, stinging jets of water and blinding streams of medicated shampoo . . .

Towelling myself dry, I heard the clattering on the roof. Maintenance? Dimitrios and his galvanized bucket? I dressed quickly in lightweight flannels and a shirt, flip-flops on my feet, went out, and locked the door. Other places like this, we'd left the door open. Here I locked it. At the back of the chalet, Dimitrios was coming down his ladder. I came round the corner as he stepped down. If anything, he'd pulled his hat even lower over his eyes, so that his face was just a blot of shadow with two faint smudges of light for eyes. He was lethargic as ever, possibly even more so. We stood looking at each other.

'Trouble?' I eventually ventured.

Almost imperceptibly, he shook his head. 'No troubles,' he said, his voice a gurgle. 'I just see all OK.' He put his bucket down, wiped his hands on his trousers.

'And is it?' I took a step closer. 'I mean, is it all OK?'

He nodded and at last grinned. Briefly a bar of whiteness opened in the shadow of his hat. 'Now is OK,' he said. And he picked up his bucket and moved off away from me.

Surly bastard! I thought. And: *What a dump! God, but we've slipped up this time, Julie, my love!*

I started toward the taverna, remembered I had no

cigarettes with me, and returned to the chalet. Inside, in the cool and shade, I wondered what Dimitrios had been putting in the water tanks. Some chemical solution, maybe? To purify or purge the system? Well, I didn't want my system purified, not by Dimitrios. I flushed the toilet again. And I left the shower running full blast for all of five minutes before spinning the taps back to the off position. I would have done the same to the sink unit, but my fish were in there, the ice almost completely melted away. And emptying another tray of ice into the sink, I snapped my fingers: *Hah!* A blow for British eccentricity!

By the time I got to the taverna, Dimitrios had disappeared, probably inside the house. He'd left his bucket standing on the garden wall. Maybe it was simple curiosity, maybe something else; I don't know – but I looked into the bucket. Empty. I began to turn away, looked again. No, not empty, but almost. Only a residue remained. At the bottom of the bucket, a thin film of . . . jelly? That's what it looked like: grey jelly.

I began to dip a finger. Hesitated, thought: *What the hell! It's nothing harmful.* It couldn't be, or he wouldn't be putting it in the water tanks. Would he? I snorted at my mind's morbid fancies. Surly was one thing, but homicidal—?

I dipped, held my finger up to the sun where that great blazing orb slipped down toward the plateau's rim. Squinting, I saw . . . just a blob of goo. Except – black dots were moving in it, like microscopic tadpoles.

Urgh! I wiped the slime off my finger onto the rough concrete of the wall. Wrong bucket, obviously, for something had gone decidedly wrong in this one. Backing uncertainly away, I heard the doleful bleating of the white kid.

Across the garden, he was chewing on the frayed end of a rope hanging from the corner of a tarpaulin where it had been thrown roughly over the chair under the olive tree. The canvas had peaked in the middle, so that it seemed

someone with a pointed head was still sitting there. I stared
hard, felt a tic starting up at the corner of my eye. And
suddenly I knew that I didn't want to be here. I didn't want
it one little bit. And I wanted Julie to be here even less.

Coming round the house to the seating area under the
vines, it became noisily apparent that I wasn't the only
disenchanted person around here. An angry, booming female voice, English, seemed matched against a chattering
wall of machine-gun-fire Greek. I stepped quickly in under
the vines and saw Julie sitting in the shade at the ocean's
edge, facing the sea. A book lay open on her table. She
looked back over her shoulder, saw me, and even though
she wasn't involved in the exchange, still relief flooded over
her face.

I went to her, said, 'What's up?' She looked past me,
directing her gaze toward the rear of the seating area.

In the open door of the house, Dimitrios made a hunched
silhouette, stiff as a petrified tree stump; his wife was a pale
shadow behind him, in what must be the kitchen. Facing
the Greek, George's wife stood with her fists on her hips,
jaw jutting. 'How *dare* you?' she cried, outraged at something or other. 'What do you mean, you can't help? No
phone? Are you actually telling me there's no telephone?
Then how are we to contact civilization? I have to speak to
someone in the town, find a doctor. My husband, George,
needs a doctor! Can't you understand that? His lumps are
moving. *Things are alive under his skin!*'

I heard all of this, but failed to take it in at once. George's
lumps moving? Did she mean they were spreading? And
still, Dimitrios stood there, while his wife squalled shrilly
at him (at *him*, yes, not at George's wife as I'd first thought)
and tried to squeeze by him. Whatever was going on here,
someone had to do something, and it looked like I was the
one.

'Sit tight,' I told Julie, and I walked up behind the

furious fat lady. 'Something's wrong with George?' I said.

All eyes turned in my direction. I still couldn't see Dimitrios's face too clearly, but I sensed a sudden wariness in him. George's wife pounced on me. 'Do you know George?' she said, grasping my arm. 'Oh, of course! I saw you talking to him when I was in the sea.'

I gently prized her sweaty, iron-band fingers from my arm. 'His lumps?' I pressed. 'Do you mean those swollen stings of his? Are they worse?'

'Stings?' I could see now that her hysteria had brought her close to the point of tears. 'Is that what they are? Well, God only knows what stung him! Some of them are opening, and there's movement in the wounds! And George just lies there, without the will to do anything. He must be in agony, but he says he can't feel a thing. There's something terribly wrong . . . '

'Can I see him?'

'Are you a doctor?' She grabbed me again.

'No, but if I could see how bad it is—'

'—A waste of *time*!' she cut me off. 'He needs a doctor now!'

'I take you to Makelos.' Dimitrios had apparently snapped out of his rigor mortis mode, taken a jerky step toward us. 'I take, find doctor, come back in taxi.'

She turned to him. 'Will you? Oh, *will* you, really? Thank you, oh, thank you! But . . . *how* will you take me?'

'Come,' he said. They walked round the building to the rear, followed the wall until it ended, crossed the scrub to a clump of olives, and disappeared into the trees. I went with them part of the way, then watched them out of sight: Dimitrios stiff as a robot, never looking back, and Mrs George rumbling along massively behind him. A moment later there came the clattering and banging of an

engine, and his three-wheeler bumped into view. It made
for the packed-dirt incline to the road where it wound up
the spur. Inside, Dimitrios at the wheel behind a flyspecked
windscreen, almost squeezed into the corner of the tiny cab
by the fat lady where she hunched beside him.

Julie had come up silently behind me. I gave a start when
she said: 'Do you think we should maybe go and see if this
George is OK?'

I took a grip of myself, shrugged, said: 'I was speaking
to him just – oh, an hour and a half ago. He can't have
got really bad in so short a time, can he? A few horsefly
bites, he had. Nasty enough, but you'd hardly consider
them as serious as all that. She's just got herself a bit
hot and bothered, that's all.'

Quite suddenly, shadows reached down to us from the
high brown and purple walls of the plateau. The sun had
commenced to sink behind the island's central hump. In
a moment it was degrees cooler, so that I found myself shivering. In that same moment the cicadas stopped
their frying-fat onslaught of sound, and a strange silence
fell over the whole place. On impulse, quietly, I said:
'We're out of here tomorrow.'

That was probably a mistake. I hadn't wanted to get
Julie going. She'd been in bed most of the time; she hadn't
experienced the things I had, hadn't felt so much of the
strangeness here. Or maybe she had, for now she said:
'Good,' and gave a little shudder of her own. 'I was
going to suggest just that. I'm sure we can find cheap
lodging in Makelos. And this place is such – I don't know
– such a dead and alive hole! I mean, it's beautiful – but it's
also very ugly. There's just something morbid about it.'

'Listen,' I said, deciding to lighten the atmosphere if
I could. 'I'll tell you what we'll do. You go back to the
taverna, and I'll go get the fish. We'll have the Greek girl
cook them for us and dish them up with a little salad – and

a bottle of retsina, as we'd planned. Maybe things will look better after a bite to eat, eh? Is your tummy up to it?'

She smiled faintly in the false dusk, leaned forward, and gave me a kiss. 'You know,' she said, 'whenever you start worrying about me – and using that tone of voice – I always know that there's something you're worrying about yourself. But actually, you know, I do feel quite hungry!'

The shadows had already reached the taverna. Just shadows – in no way night, for it wasn't properly evening yet, though certainly the contrast was a sort of darkness – and beyond them the vast expanse of the sea was blue as ever, sparkling silver at its rim in the brilliant sunlight still striking there. The strangeness of the place seemed emphasized, enlarged . . .

I watched Julie turn right and disappear into the shade of the vines, and then I went for our fish.

The real nightmare began when I let myself into the chalet and went to the sink unit. Doubly shaded, the interior really was quite dark. I put on the light in the arched-over alcove that was the kitchen, and picked up the two fish, one in each hand – and dropped them, or rather tossed them back into the sink! The ice was all melted; the live-looking glisten of the scales had disappeared with the ice, and the mullets themselves had been – infected!

Attached to the gill flap of one of them, I'd seen a parasite exactly like the ones on the big grouper; the second fish had had one of the filthy things clamped half over a filmed eye. My hair actually prickled on my head; my scalp tingled; my lips drew back from my teeth in a silent snarl. The things were something like sheep ticks, in design if not in dimension, but they were pale, blind, spiky, and looked infinitely more loathsome. They were only – crustaceans? Insects? I couldn't be sure – but there was that about them which made them more horrific to me than any creature has a right to be.

Anyone who believes you can't go cold, break out in gooseflesh, on a hot, late afternoon in the Mediterranean is mistaken. I went so cold I was shaking, and I kept on shaking for long moments, until it dawned on me that just a few seconds ago, I'd actually handled these fish!

Christ!

I turned on the hot tap, thrust my hands forward to receive the cleansing stream, snatched them back again. God, no! I couldn't wash them, for Dimitrios had been up there putting something in the tank! Some kind of spawn. But that didn't make sense: hot water would surely kill the things. If there was any hot water . . .

The plumbing rattled, but no hot water came. Not only had Dimitrios interfered with the water, introduced something into it, but he'd also made sure that from now on we could use only the *cold* water!

I wiped my trembling hands thoroughly on sheets from a roll of paper towel, filled the kettle with water from a refrigerated bottle, quickly brought the water toward boiling. Before it became unbearable, I gritted my teeth, poured a little hot water first over one hand, then the other. It stung like hell, and the flesh of my hands went red at once, but I just hugged them and let them sting. Then, when the water was really boiling, I poured the rest of the contents of the kettle over the fish in the sink.

By that time the parasites had really dug themselves in. The one attached to the gill flap had worked its way under the gill, making it bulge; the other had dislodged its host's eye and was half-way into the skull. Worse, another had clawed its way up the plughole and was just now emerging into the light! The newcomer was white, whereas the others were now turning pink from the ingestion of fish juices.

But up from the plughole! This set me shuddering again;

and again I wondered: *what's down there, down in the slop under the ground? Where does everything go?*

These fish had been clean when I caught them; I'd gutted them, and so I ought to know. But their scent had drawn these things up to the feast. Would the scent of human flesh attract them the same way?

As the boiling water hit them, the things popped like crabs tossed into a cooking pot. They seemed to hiss and scream, but it was just the rapid expansion and explosion of their tissues. And the stench that rose up from the sink was nauseating. God! – would I ever eat fish again?

And the thought kept repeating over and over in my head: what was down below?

I went to the shower recess, put on the light, looked in, and at once shrank back. The sunken bowl of the shower was crawling with them! Two, three dozen of them at least. And the toilet? And the cold-water system? And all the rest of the bloody plumbing? There'd be a cesspit down there, and these things were alive in it in their thousands! And the maniac Dimitrios had been putting their eggs in the water tanks!

But what about the spinsters? They had been here before us, probably for the past three or four days at least. And what about George? George and his lumps! And Julie: she wouldn't have ordered anything yet, would she! She wouldn't have *eaten* anything!

I left the door of the chalet slamming behind me, raced for the taverna.

The sun was well down now, with the bulk of the central mountain throwing all of the eastern coastline into shadow; halfway to the horizon, way out to sea, the sun's light was a line ruled across the ocean, beyond which silver-flecked blueness seemed to reach up to the sky. And moment by moment the ruled line of deeper blue flowed eastward as the unseen sun dipped even lower.

On the other side of the island, the west coast, it would still be sweltering hot, but here it was noticeably cooler. Or maybe it was just my blood.

As I drew level with the garden at the back of the house, something came flopping over the wall at me. I hadn't been looking in that direction or I'd have seen her: Julie, panic-stricken, her face a white mask of horror. She'd seemed to fly over the wall – jumped or simply bundled herself over I couldn't say – and came hurtling into my arms. Nor had she seen me, and she fought with me a moment when I held her. Then we both caught our breath, or at least I did. Julie had a harder time of it. Even though I'd never heard her scream before, there was one building up in her, and I knew it.

I shook her, which served to shake me a little, too, then hugged her close. 'What were you doing in the garden?' I asked, when she'd started to breathe again. I spoke in a whisper, and that was how she answered me, but drawing breath raggedly between each burst of words:

'The little goat . . . he was bleating . . . so pitifully . . . frightened! I heard him . . . went to see . . . got in through a gate on the other side.' She paused and took a deep breath. 'Oh *God*, Jim!'

I knew without asking. A picture of the slumped figure in the chair, under the olive tree, had flashed momentarily on my mind's eye. But I asked anyway: 'The tarpaulin?'

She nodded, gulped. 'Something had to be dead under there. I had no idea it would be a . . . a . . . a man!'

'English?' That was a stupid question, so I tried again: 'I mean, did he look like a tourist, a holiday maker?'

She shook her head. 'An old Greek, I think. But there are – *ugh!* – these things all over him. Like . . . like—'

'Like crabs?'

She drew back from me, her eyes wide, terror replaced by astonishment. 'How did you know that?'

Quickly, I related all I knew. As I was finishing, her

hand flew to her mouth. 'Dimitrios? Putting their eggs in the tanks? But Jim, we've taken showers – both of us!'

'Calm down,' I told her. 'We had our showers *before* I saw him up there. And we haven't eaten here, or drunk any of the water.'

'Eaten?' her eyes opened wider still. 'But if I hadn't heard the kid bleating, I might have eaten!'

'What?'

She nodded. 'I ordered wine and . . . some melon. I thought we'd have it before the fish. But the Greek girl dropped it, and—'

She was rapidly becoming incoherent. I grabbed her again, held her tightly. 'Dropped it? You mean she dropped the food?'

'She dropped the melon, yes.' She nodded jerkily. 'The bottle of wine, too. She came out of the kitchen and just let everything drop. It all smashed on the floor. And she stood there wringing her hands for a moment. Then she ran off. She was crying: "Oh Dimitrios, Dimitrios!"'

'I think he's crazy,' I told her. 'He has to be. And his wife – or sister, or whatever she is – she's scared to death of him. You say she ran off? Which way?'

'Toward the town, the way we came. I saw her climbing the spur.'

I hazarded a guess: 'He's pushed her to the edge, and she's slipped over. Come on, let's go and have a look at Dimitrios's kitchen.'

We went to the front of the building, to the kitchen door. There on the floor by one of the tables, I saw a broken wine bottle, its dark red contents spilled. Also a half-melon, lying in several softly jagged chunks. And in the melon, crawling in its scattered seeds and pulpy red juices—

'Where are the others?' I said, wanting to speak first before Julie could cry out, trying to forestall her.

'Others?' she whispered. She hadn't really heard me,

hadn't even been listening; she was concentrating on backing away from the half-dozen crawling things that moved blindly on the floor.

I stamped on them, crushed them in a frenzy of loathing, then scuffed the soles of my flip-flops on the dusty concrete floor as if I'd stepped in something nasty – which is one hell of an understatement. 'The other people,' I said. 'The three sisters and . . . and George.' I was talking more to myself than to Julie, and my voice was hoarse.

My fear transferred itself instantly. 'Oh Jim, Jim!' she cried. She threw herself into my arms, shivering as if in a fever. And I felt utterly useless – no, defenceless – a sensation I'd occasionally known in deep water, without my gun, when the shadow of a rock might suddenly take on the aspect of a great, menacing fish.

Then there came one of the most dreadful sounds I've ever heard in my life: the banging and clattering of Dimitrios's three-wheeler on the road cut into the spur, echoing down to us from the rocks of the mountainside. 'My spear gun,' I said. 'Come on, quickly!'

She followed at arm's length, half running, half dragged. 'We're too vulnerable,' I gasped as we reached the chalet. 'Put clothes on, anything. Cover up your skin.'

'What?' She was still dazed. 'What?'

'*Cover yourself!*' I snapped. Then I regained control. 'Look, he tried to give us these things. He gave them to George, and to the sisters for all I know. And he may try again. Do you want one of those things on your flesh, maybe laying its eggs in you?'

She emptied a drawer onto the floor, found slacks, and pulled them on; good shoes, too, to cover her feet. I did much the same: pulled on a long-sleeved pullover, rammed my feet into decent shoes. And all in a sort of frenzied blur, fingers all thumbs, heart thumping. And: '*Oh shit!*' she sobbed. Which wasn't really my Julie at all.

'Eh?' She was heading for the small room at the back.
'Toilet!' she said. 'I have to.'

'*No!*' I jumped across the space between, dragged her
away from the door to the toilet-*cum*-shower unit. 'It's
crawling with them in there. They come up the plugholes.'
In my arms, I could feel that she was also crawling. Her
flesh. Mine, too. 'If you must go, go outside. But first
let's get away from here.' I picked up my gun, loaded it
with a single flap-nosed spear.

Leaving the chalet, I looked across at the ramp coming
down from the rocky spur. The clatter of Dimitrios's three-
wheeler was louder, it was there, headlight beams bobbing
as the vehicle trundled lurchingly down the rough decline. 'Where are we going?' Julie gasped, following me
at a run across the scrub between clumps of olives. I
headed for the other chalets.

'Safety in numbers,' I answered. 'Anyway, I want to
know about George, and those three old spinsters.'

'What good will they be, if they're old?' She was too
logical by half.

'They're not that old.' Mainly, I wanted to see if
they were all right. Apart from the near-distant racket
Dimitrios's vehicle was making, the whole valley was quiet
as a tomb. Unnaturally quiet. It had to be a damned funny
place in Greece where the cicadas keep their mouths shut.

Julie had noticed that too. 'They're not singing,' she
said. And I knew what she meant.

'Rubbing,' I answered. 'They rub their legs together
or something.'

'Well,' she panted, 'whatever it is they do, they're not.'

It was true evening now, and a half-moon had come
up over the central mountain's southern extreme. Its light
silvered our way through thorny shrubs and tall, spiked
grasses, under the low grey branches of olives and across
their tangled, groping roots.

We came to the first chalet. Its lights were out, but the door stood ajar. 'I think this is where George is staying,' I said. And calling ahead: 'George, are you in?', I entered and switched on the light. He was in – in the big double bed, stretched out on his back. But he turned his head toward us as we entered. He blinked in the sudden, painful light. One of his eyes did, anyway. The other couldn't . . .

He stirred himself, tried to sit up. I think he was grinning. I can't be sure, because one of the things, a big one, was inside the corner of his mouth. They were hatching from fresh lumps down his neck and in the bend of his elbow. God knows what the rest of his body was like. He managed to prop himself up, hold out a hand to me – and I almost took it. And it was then that I began to understand something of the nature of these things. For there was one of them in his open palm, its barbed feet seeming poised, waiting.

I snatched back my hand, heard Julie's gasp. And there she was, backed up against the wall, screaming her silent scream. I grabbed her, hugged her, dragged her outside. For of course there was nothing we could do for George. And, afraid she would scream, and maybe start *me* going, I slapped her. And off we went again, reeling in the direction of the third and last chalet.

Down by the taverna, Dimitrios's three-wheeler had come to a halt, its engine stilled, its beams dim, reaching like pallid hands along the sand. But I didn't think it would be long before he was on the move again. And the nightmare was expanding, growing vaster with every beat of my thundering heart.

In the third chalet . . . it's hard to describe all I saw. Maybe there's no real need. The spinster I'd thought was maybe missing something was in much the same state as George; she, too, was in bed, with those god-awful things hatching in her. Her sisters . . . at first I thought they were both dead, and . . . But there, I've gone ahead of myself.

That's how it always happens when I think about it, try to reconstruct it again in my own mind: it speeds up until I've outstripped myself. You have to understand that the whole thing was kaleidoscopic.

I went inside ahead of Julie, got a quick glimpse, an indistinct picture of the state of things fixed in my brain – then turned and kept Julie from coming in. 'Watch for him.' I forced the words around my bobbing Adam's apple and returned to take another look. I didn't want to, but I thought the more we knew about this monster, the better we'd know how to deal with him. Except that in a little while, I guessed there would be only one possible way to deal with him.

The sister in the bed moved and lolled her head a little; I was wary, suspicious of her, and left her strictly alone. The other two had been attacked. With an axe or a machete or something. One of them lay behind the door, the other on the floor on the near side of the bed. The one behind the door had been sliced twice, deeply, across the neck and chest and lay in a pool of her own blood, which was already congealing. Tick-things, coming from the bathroom, had got themselves stuck in the darkening pool, their barbed legs twitching when they tried to extricate themselves. The other sister . . .

Senses swimming, throat bobbing, I stepped closer to the bed with its grimacing, hag-ridden occupant, and I bent over the one on the floor. She was still alive, barely. Her green dress was a sodden red under the rib cage, torn open in a jagged flap to reveal her gaping wound. And Dimitrios had dropped several of his damned pets onto her, which were burrowing in the raw, dark flesh.

She saw me through eyes already filming over, whispered something. I got down on one knee beside her, wanted to hold her hand, stroke her hair, do something. But I couldn't. I didn't want those bloody things on me. 'It's all right,' I said. 'It's all right.' But we both knew it wasn't.

'The . . . the Greek,' she said, her voice so small I could scarcely hear it.

'I know, I know,' I told her.

'We wanted to . . . to take Flo into town. She was . . . was so *ill*! He said to wait here. We waited, and . . . and . . . ' She gave a deep sigh. Her eyes rolled up, and her mouth fell open.

Something touched my shoulder where I knelt, and I leapt erect, flesh tingling. The one on the bed, Flo, had flopped an arm in my direction – deliberately! Her hand had touched me. Crawling slowly down her arm, a trio of the nightmare ticks or crabs had been making for me. They'd been homing in on me like a bee targeting a flower. But more slowly, thank God, far more slowly.

Horror froze me rigid; but in the next moment, Julie's sobbing cry – 'Jim, he's coming!' – unfroze me at once.

I staggered outside. A dim, slender, dark and reeling shape was making its way along the rough track between the chalets. Something glinted dully in his hand. Terror galvanized me. 'Head for the high ground,' I said. I took Julie's hand, began to run.

'High ground?' she panted. 'Why?' She was holding together pretty well. I thanked God I hadn't let her see inside the chalet.

'Because then we'll have the advantage. He'll have to come up at us. Maybe I can roll rocks down on him or something.'

'You have your gun,' she said.

'As a last resort,' I told her, 'yes. But this isn't a John Wayne Western, Julie. This is real! Shooting a man isn't the same as shooting a fish . . .' And we scrambled across the rough scrubland toward the goat track up the far spur. Maybe ten minutes later and halfway up that track, suddenly it dawned on both of us just where we were heading. Julie dug in her heels and dragged me to a halt.

'But the cave's up there!' she panted. 'The well!'

I looked all about. The light was difficult, made everything seem vague and unreal. Dusk is the same the world over: it confuses shapes, distances, colours and textures. On our right, scree rising steeply all the way to the plateau: too dangerous by far. And on our left a steep, in places sheer, decline to the valley's floor. All you had to do was stumble once, and you wouldn't stop sliding and tumbling and bouncing till you hit the bottom. Up ahead the track was moon-silvered, to the place where the cliff over-hung, where the shadows were black and blacker than night. And behind . . . behind us came Dimitrios, his presence made clear by the sound his boots made shoving rocks and pebbles out of his way.

'Come on,' I said, starting on up again.

'But where to?' Hysteria was in her whisper.

'That clump of rocks there.' Ahead, on the right, weathered out of the scree, a row of long boulders like leaning graveyard slabs tilted at the moon. I got between two of them, pulled Julie off the track, and jammed her behind me. It was last-ditch stuff; there was no way out other than the way we'd come in. I loaded my gun, hauling on the propulsive rubbers until the spear was engaged. And then there was nothing else to do but wait.

'Now be quiet,' I hissed, crouching down. 'He may not see us, go straight on by.'

Across the little valley, headlights blazed. Then came the echoing roar of revving engines. A moment more, and I could identify humped silhouettes making their way like beetles down the ridge of the far spur toward the indigo sea, then slicing the gloom with scythes of light as they turned onto the dirt ramp. Two cars and a motorcycle. Down on the valley's floor, they raced for the taverna.

Dimitrios came struggling out of the dusk, up out of

the darkness, his breathing loud, laboured, gasping as he climbed in our tracks. His silhouette where he paused for breath was scarecrow-lean, and he'd lost his floppy, wide-brimmed hat. But I suspected a strength in him that wasn't entirely his own. From where she peered over my shoulder Julie had spotted him too. I heard her sharp intake of breath, breathed '*Shh!*' so faintly I wasn't even sure she'd hear me.

He came on, the thin moonlight turning his eyes yellow, and turning his machete silver. Level with the boulders he drew, and almost level with our hiding place, and paused again. He looked this way and that, cocked his head, and listened. Behind me, Julie was trembling. She trembled so hard I was sure it was coming right through me, through the rocks, too, and the earth, and right through the soles of his boots to Dimitrios.

He took another two paces up the track, came level with us. Now he stood out against the sea and the sky, where the first pale stars were beginning to switch themselves on. He stood there, looking up the slope toward the cave under the cliff, and small, dark silhouettes were falling from the large blot of his head. Not droplets of sweat, no, for they were far too big, and too brittle-sounding when they landed on the loose scree.

Again Julie snatched a breath, and Dimitrios's head slowly came round until he seemed to be staring right at us.

Down in the valley the cars and the motorcycle were on the move again, engines revving, headlight beams slashing here and there. There was some shouting. Lights began to blaze in the taverna, the chalets. Flashlights cut narrow searchlight swaths in the darkness.

Dimitrios seemed oblivious to all this; still looking in our direction, he scratched at himself under his right arm-pit. His actions rapidly became frantic, until with a soft, gurgling cry, he tore open his shirt. He let his machete fall clatteringly to the track and clawed wildly at himself with both hands! He was shedding tick-things as a dog sheds fleas. He tore open his trousers, dropped them, staggered as he stepped out of them. Agonized sulphur eyes burned yellow in his blot of a face as he tore at his thighs.

I saw all of this, every slightest action. And so did Julie. I felt her swell up behind me, scooping in air until she must surely burst – and then she let it out again. But silently, screaming like a maniac in the night – and nothing but air escaping her!

A rock slid away from under my foot, its scrape a deafening clatter to my petrified mind. The sound froze Dimitrios, too – but only for a moment. Then he stooped, regained his machete. He took a pace toward us, inclined his head. He couldn't see us yet, but he knew we were there. Then – *God*, I shall dream of this for the rest of my life!—

He reached down a hand and stripped a handful of living, crawling filth from his loins, and lobbed it in our direction as casually as tossing crumbs to starveling birds!

The next five seconds were madness.

I stumbled out from cover, lifted my gun, and triggered it. The spear struck him just below the rib cage, went deep into him. He cried out, reeled back, and yanked the gun from my hand. I'd forgotten to unfasten the nylon cord from the spear. Behind me, Julie was crumpling to the ground; I was aware of the latter, turned to grab her before she could sprawl. There were tick-things crawling about, and I mustn't let her fall on them.

I got her over my shoulder in a fireman's lift, went charging out onto the track, skipping and stamping my feet, roaring like a maddened bull. And I was mad: mad with shock, terror, loathing. I stamped and kicked and danced, never letting my feet stay in one place for more than a fraction of a second, afraid something would climb up onto me. And the wonder is I didn't carry both of us flying down the steep scree slope to the valley's floor.

Dimitrios was halfway down the track when I finally got myself under a semblance of control. Bouncing toward our end of the valley, a car came crunching and lurching across the scrub. I fancied it was Nichos's taxi. And sure enough, when the car stopped and its headlight beams were still, Nichos's voice came echoing up, full of concerned enquiry:

'Mister, lady – you OK?'

'Look out!' I shouted at the top of my voice, but only at the second attempt. 'He's coming down! Dimitrios is coming down!'

And now I went more carefully, as in my mind the danger receded, and in my veins the adrenalin raced less rapidly. Julie moaned where she flopped loosely across my shoulder, and I knew she'd be all right.

The valley seemed alight with torches now, and not only the electric sort. Considering these people were Greeks, they seemed remarkably well organized. That was a thought I'd keep in mind, something else I would have to ask about. There was some shouting down there, too, and flaring torches began to converge on the area at the foot of the goat track.

Then there echoed up to me a weird, gurgled cry: a cry of fear, protestation – relief? A haunting, sobbing shriek – cut off at highest pitch by the dull boom of a shot fired, and a moment later by a blast that was the twin of the first. From twin barrels, no doubt.

When I got down, Julie was still out of it, for which I was glad. They'd poured gasoline over Dimitrios's body and set fire to it. Fires were burning everywhere: the chalets, taverna, gardens. Cleansing flames leaping. Figures moved in the smoke and against a yellow roaring background, searching, burning. And I sat in the back of Nichos's taxi, cradling Julie's head. Mercifully, she remained unconscious right through it.

Even with the windows rolled up, I could smell something of the smoke, and something that wasn't smoke . . .

In Makelos town, Julie began to stir. I asked for her to be sedated, kept down for the night. Then, when she was sleeping soundly and safely in a room at the mayor's house, I began asking questions. I was furious at the beginning, growing more furious as I started to get the answers.

I couldn't be sorry for the people of Makelos, though I did feel something for Elli, Dimitrios's wife. She'd run to Nichos, told him what was happening. And he'd alerted the townspeople. Elli had been a sort of prisoner at the taverna for the past ten days or so, after her husband had 'gone funny'. Then, when she'd started to notice things, he'd told her to keep quiet and carry on as normal, or she'd be the loser. And he meant she'd lose all the way. She reckoned he'd got the parasites off the goats, accidentally, and she was probably right, for the goats had been the first to die. Her explanation was likely because the goats used to go up there sometimes, to the cave under the mountain. And that was where the things bred, in that cave and in the well it contained, which now and then overflowed, and found its way to the sea.

But Elli, poor peasant that she was: on her way to alert Nichos, she'd seen her husband kill George's wife and push her over the cliffs into the sea. Then she'd hid herself off the road until he'd turned his three-wheeler round and started back toward the taverna.

As for the corpse under the tarpaulin: that was Dimitrios's grandfather, who along with his grandson had been a survivor of the first outbreak. He'd been lucky that time, not so lucky this time.

And the tick things? They were . . . a *disease*, but they

could never be a plague. The men from Athens had taken some of them away with them that first time. But away from their well, away from the little shaded valley and from Makelos, they'd quickly died. This was their place, and they could exist nowhere else. Thank God!

Last time the chemicals hadn't killed them off, obviously, or maybe a handful of eggs had survived to hatch out when the poisons had dissolved away. For they *were* survivors, these creatures, the last of their species, and when they went, their secret would go with them. But a disease? I believe so, yes.

Like the common cold, or rabies, or any other disease, but far worse because they're visible, apparent. The common cold makes you sneeze, so that the disease is propagated, and hydrophobia makes its victims claw and bite, gets passed on in their saliva. The secret of the tick-things was much the same sort of thing: they made their hosts pass them on. It was the way their intelligent human hosts did it that made them so much more terrible.

In the last outbreak, only Greeks – Makelosians – had been involved; this time it was different. This time, too, the people would take care of the problem themselves: they'd pour hundreds of gallons of gasoline and fuel oil into the well, set the place on fire. And then they'd dynamite the cliff, bring it down to choke the well for ever, and they'd never, *ever*, let people go into that little valley again. That was their promise, but I'd made myself a couple of promises, too. I was angry and frightened, and I knew I was going to stay that way for a long time to come.

We were out of there first thing in the morning, on the first boat to the mainland. There were smart-looking men to meet us at the airport in Athens, Greek officials from some ministry or other. They had interpreters with them, and nothing was too much trouble. They, too, made promises, offers of compensation, anything our hearts desired.

We nodded and smiled wearily, said yes to this, that, and
the other, anything so that we could just get aboard that
plane. It had been our shortest holiday ever: we'd been in
Greece just forty-eight hours, and all we wanted now was
to be out of it as quickly as possible. But when we were
back home again – *that* was when we told our story!

It was played down, of course: the Common Market,
international tensions, a thousand other economic and
diplomatic reasons. Which is why I'm now telling it all
over again. I don't want anybody to suffer what we went
through, what we're still going through. And so if you
happen to be mad on the Mediterranean islands . . . well,
I'm sorry, but that's the way it was.

As for Julie and me: we've moved away from the sea, and
come summer, we won't be going out in the sun too much
or for too long. That helps a little. But every now and then,
I'll wake up in the night, in a cold sweat, and find Julie doing her horrible thing: nightmaring about Dimitrios, hiding
from him, holding her breath so that he won't hear her—

—And sometimes screaming her silent screams . . .

DE MARIGNY'S CLOCK

Not too many years before I was born, H.P. Lovecraft had written a story called The Terrible Old Man. *The basic similarity of themes between that tale and this present one didn't strike me until quite recently, but since I've always loved Lovecraft, I suppose it's possible I was subconsciously influenced sufficiently to write it 'after' HPL. Certainly the fate of the villains is . . . ah, but that would be telling.*

Something else in this story that you'll find in Lovecraft is the extraordinary timepiece of the title . . .

Any intrusions, other than those condoned or invited, upon the privacy of Titus Crow at his bungalow retreat, Blowne House, on the outskirts of London, were almost always automatically classified by that gentleman as open acts of warfare. In the first place for anyone to make it merely to the doors of Crow's abode without an invitation – often even *with* one – was a sure sign of the appearance on the scene of a forceful and dogmatic character; qualities which were almost guaranteed to clash with Crow's own odd nature. For Blowne House seemed to exude an atmosphere all its own, an exhalation of impending *something* which usually kept the place and its grounds free even from birds and mice; and it was quite unusual for Crow himself to invite visitors. He kept strange hours and busied himself with stranger matters and, frankly, was almost antisocial even in his most 'engaging' moments. Over the years the reasons for this apparent inhospitality had grown, or so it seemed to Crow, increasingly clear-cut. For one thing, his library contained quite a large number of rare and highly costly books, many of them long out of print and some of them never officially *in* print, and London apparently abounded with unscrupulous 'collectors' of such items. For another his studies, usually in occult matters and obscure archaeological, antiquarian or anthropological research, were such as required the most concentrated attention and personal involvement, completely precluding any disturbances from outside sources.

Not that the present infringement came while Crow was engaged with any of his many and varied activities – it did not; it came in the middle of the night, rousing him from deep and dreamless slumbers engendered by a long day of frustrated and unrewarding work on de Marigny's clock. And Titus Crow was not amused.

'What the hell's going on here? Who are you and what are you doing in my house?' He had sat bolt upright in bed almost as soon as the light went on. His forehead had come straight into contact with a wicked-looking automatic held in the fist of a most unbeautiful thug. The man was about five feet eight inches in height, thick-set, steady on legs which were short in comparison with the rest of his frame. He had a small scar over his left eye and a mouth that slanted downward – cynically, Crow supposed – from left to right. Most unbeautiful.

'Just take it easy, guv', and there'll be no bother,' the thug said, his voice soft but ugly. Crow's eyes flicked across the room to where a second hoodlum stood, just within the bedroom door, a nervous grin twisting his pallid features. 'Find anything, Pasty?' the man with the pistol questioned, his eyes never leaving Crow's face for a second.

'Nothing, Joe,' came the answer, ' a few old books and bit of silver, nothing worth our while – yet. He'll tell us where it is, though, won't you, chum?'

'Pasty!' Crow exclaimed, 'Powers of observation, indeed! I was just thinking, before hearing your name, what a thin, pasty creature you look – Pasty.' Crow grinned, got out of bed and put on his flame-red dressing-gown. Joe looked him up and down appraisingly. Crow was tall and broad-shouldered and it was plain to see that in his younger days he had been a handsome man. Even now there was a certain tawniness about him, and his eyes were still very bright and more than intelligent. Overall his aspect conveyed an impression of hidden power, which Joe did not particularly care much for. He decided it would be best to show his authority at the earliest opportunity. And Crow obligingly supplied him with that opportunity in the next few seconds.

The jibe the occultist had aimed at Pasty had meanwhile found its way home. Pasty's retaliation was a threat: 'Lovely colour, that dressing-gown,' he said, 'it'll match up nicely if you bleed when I rap you on your head.' He laughed harshly, slapping a metal cosh into his open palm. 'But before that, you will tell us where it is, won't you?'

'Surely,' Crow answered immediately, 'it's third on the left, down the passage . . . *ugh!*' Joe's pistol smacked into Crow's cheek, knocking him sprawling. He carefully got up, gingerly feeling the red welt on his face.

'Now that's just to show you that we don't want any more funnies, see?' Joe said.

'Yes, I see,' Crow's voice trembled with suppressed rage, 'just what do you want?'

'Now is that so difficult to figure out?' Pasty asked, crossing the room. 'Money . . . we want your money! A fine fellow like you, with a place like this—' the lean man glanced appraisingly about the room, noting the silk curtains, the boukhara rugs, the original erotic illustrations by Aubrey Beardsley in their rosewood frames – 'ought to have a good bit of ready cash lying about . . . we want it!'

'Then I'm sorry to have to disappoint you,' Crow told him happily, seating himself on his bed, 'I keep my money in a bank – what little I've got.'

'Up!' ordered Joe briefly. 'Off the bed.' He pulled Crow to one side, nodding to Pasty, indicating some sort of action involving the bed. Crow stepped forward as Pasty yanked back the covers from the mattress and took out a sharp knife.

'Now wait . . .' he began, thoroughly alarmed.

'Hold it, guv', or I might just let Pasty use his blade on you!' Joe waved his gun in Crow's face, ordering him back. 'You see, you'd be far better off to tell us where the money is without all this trouble. This way you're just going to see your little nest wrecked around you.' He waited, giving Crow the opportunity to speak up, then indicated to Pasty that he should go ahead.

Pasty went ahead!

He ripped open the mattress along both sides and one end, tearing back the soft outer covering to expose the stuffing and springs beneath, then pulling out the interior in great handfuls, flinging them down on the floor in total disregard of Crow's utter astonishment and concern.

'See, guv', you're a recluse – in our books, anyway – and retiring sorts like you hide their pennies in the funniest places. Like in mattresses . . . or behind wall-pictures!' Joe gave Pasty a nod, waving his pistol at the Beardsleys.

'Well for God's sake, just *look* behind them,' Crow snarled, again starting forward, 'there's no need to rip them off the walls.'

'Here!' Pasty exclaimed, turning an enquiring eye on the outraged householder, 'these pictures worth anything then?'

'Only to a collector – you'd never find a fence for stuff like that,' Crow replied.

'Hah! Not so stupid, our recluse!' Joe grinned, 'But being clever won't get you anywhere, guv', except hospital maybe . . . OK, Pasty, leave the man's dirty pictures alone. You—' He turned to Crow, ' – your study; we've been in there, but only passing through. Let's go, guv'; you can

give us a hand to, er, shift things about.' He pushed
Crow in the direction of the door.

Pasty was last to enter the study. He did so shivering,
an odd look crossing his face. Pasty did not know it
but he was a singularly rare person, one of the world's
few truly 'psychic' men. Crow was another – one who
had the *talent* to a high degree – and he sensed Pasty's
sudden feeling of apprehension.

'Snug little room, isn't it?' he asked, grinning cheerfully
at the uneasy thug.

'Never mind how pretty the place is – try the panelling,
Pasty,' Joe directed.

'Eh?' Pasty's mind obviously was not on the job. 'The
panelling?' His eyes shifted nervously round the room.

'Yes, the panelling!' Joe studied his partner curiously.
'What's wrong with you, then?' His look of puzzlement
turned to one of anger, 'Now come on, Pasty boy, get a
grip! At this rate we'll be here all bleeding night!'

Now it happened that Titus Crow's study was the pride
of his life, and the thought of the utter havoc his un-
welcome visitors could wreak in there was a terrifying
thing to him. He determined to help them in their abor-
tive search as much as he could; they would not find
anything – there was nothing to find! – but this way
he could at least ensure as little damage as possible before they realized there was no money in the house and
left. They were certainly unwilling to believe anything he
said about the absence of substantive funds! But then
again, to anyone not knowing him reasonably well – and
few did – Crow's home and certain of its appointments
might certainly point to a man of considerable means.
Yet he was merely comfortable, not wealthy, and, as he
had said, what money he did have was safe in a bank.
The more he helped them get through with their search
the quicker they would leave! He had just made up his

mind to this effect when Pasty found the hidden recess by the fireside.

'Here!' The nervous look left Pasty's face as he turned to Joe. 'Listen to this.' He rapped on a square panel. The sound was dull, hollow. Pasty swung his cosh back purposefully.

'No, wait – I'll open it for you.' Crow held up his hands in protest.

'Go on then, get it open,' Joe ordered. Crow moved over to the wall and expertly slid back the panel to reveal a dim shelf behind. On the shelf was a single book. Pasty pushed Crow aside, lifted out the book and read off its title:

'The ... what? ... *Cthaat Aquadingen*! Huh!' Then his expression quickly turned to one of pure disgust and loathing. '*Ughhh!*' He flung the book away from him across the room, hastily wiping his hands down his jacket. Titus Crow received a momentary but quite vivid mental message from the mind of the startled thug. It was a picture of things rotting in vaults of crawling darkness, and he could well understand why Pasty was suddenly trembling.

'That ... damn book's *wet*!' the shaken crook exclaimed nervously.

'No, just sweating!' Crow informed. 'The binding is, er, human skin, you see. Somehow it still retains the ability to sweat – a sure sign that it's going to rain.'

'Claptrap!' Joe snapped. 'And you get a grip of yourself,' he snarled at Pasty. 'There's something about this place I don't like either, but I'm not letting it get me down.' He turned to Crow, his mouth strained and twisting in anger: 'And from now on you speak when you're spoken to.' Then carefully, practicedly, he turned his head and slowly scanned the room, taking in the tall bookshelves with their many volumes, some ancient, others relatively modern, and he glanced at Pasty and grinned knowingly.

'Pasty,' Joe ordered, 'get them books off the shelves – I want to see what's behind them. How about it, recluse, you got anything behind there?'

'Nothing, nothing at all,' Crow quickly answered, 'for goodness sake don't go pulling them down; some of them are coming to pieces as it is. *No!*'

His last cry was one of pure protestation; horror at the defilement of his collection. The two thugs ignored him. Pasty, seemingly over his nervousness, happily went to work, scattering the books left, right and centre. Down came the collected works of Edgar Allan Poe, the first rare editions of Machen's and Lovecraft's fiction; then the more ancient works, of Josephus, Magnus, Levi, Borellus, Erdschluss and Wittingby; closely followed by a connected set on oceanic evil: Gaston Le Fe's *Dwellers in the Depths*, Oswald's *Legends of Liqualia*, Gantley's *Hydrophinnae*, the German *Unter-Zee Kulten* and Hartrack's *In Pressured Places* . . .

Crow could merely stand and watch it all, a black rage growing in his heart, and Joe, not entirely insensitive to the occultist's mood, gripped his pistol a little tighter and unsmilingly cautioned him: 'Just take it easy, hermit. There's still time to speak up – just tell us where you hide your money and it's all over. No? OK, what's next?' His eyes swept the now littered room again, coming to rest in a dimly lighted corner where stood a great clock.

In front of the clock – an instrument apparently of the 'grandfather' class; at least, from a distance of that appearance – stood a small occasional table bearing an adjustable reading-lamp, one or two books and a few scattered sheets of notepaper. Seeing the direction in which Joe's actions were leading him, Crow smiled inwardly and wished his criminal visitor all the best. If Joe could make anything of that timepiece, then he was a cleverer man than Titus Crow; and if he could actually *open* it, as is possible and perfectly normal with more orthodox clocks, then Crow would be eternally grateful to him. For the sarcophagus-like thing in the dim corner was that same instrument with which Crow had busied himself all the previous day and on many, many other days since first he purchased it more than ten years earlier. And none of his studies had done him a bit of good! He was still as unenlightened with regard to the clock's purpose as he had been a decade ago.

Allegedly the thing had belonged to one Etienne-Laurent de Marigny, once a distinguished student of occult and oriental mysteries and antiquities, but where de Marigny had come by the coffin-shaped clock was yet another mystery. Crow had purchased it on the assurance of its auctioneer that it was, indeed, that same timepiece mentioned in certain of de Marigny's papers as being 'a door on all space and time; one which only certain adepts – not all of this world – could use to its intended purpose!' There were, too, rumours that a certain Eastern mystic, the Swami Chandraputra, had vanished forever from the face of the Earth after squeezing himself into a cavity hidden beneath the panel of the lower part of the clock's coffin shape. Also, de Marigny had supposedly had the ability to open at will that door into which the Swami vanished – but that was a secret he had taken with him to the grave. Titus Crow had never been able to find even a keyhole; and while the clock weighed what it should for its size, yet when one rapped on the lower panel the sounds such rappings produced were not hollow as might be expected. A curious fact – a curious history altogether – but the clock itself was even more curious to gaze upon or listen to.

Even now Joe was doing just those things: looking at and listening to the clock. He had switched on and adjusted the reading-lamp so that its light fell upon the face of the peculiar mechanism. At first sight of that clock-face Pasty had gone an even paler shade of grey, with all his nervousness of a few minutes earlier instantly returned. Crow sensed his perturbation; he had had similar feelings while working on the great clock, but he had also had the advantage of understanding where such fears originated. Pasty was experiencing the same sensations he himself had known when first he saw the clock in the auction rooms. Again he gazed at it as he had then; his eyes following the flow of the weird hieroglyphs carved about the dial and the odd movements of the four hands, movements coinciding with no chronological system of earthly origin; and for a moment there reigned an awful silence in the study of Titus Crow. Only the strange clock's enigmatic and oddly paced ticking disturbed a quiet which otherwise might have been that of the tomb.

'That's no clock like any I've ever seen before!' exclaimed an awed Joe. 'What do you make of *that*, Pasty?'

Pasty gulped, his Adam's apple visibly bobbing. 'I . . . I don't like it! It . . . it's shaped like a damned *coffin*! And why has it four hands, and how come they *move* like that?' He stopped to compose himself a little, and with the cessation of his voice came a soft whispering from beyond the curtained windows. Pasty's eyes widened and his face went white as death. '*What's that?*' His whisper was as soft as the sounds prompting it.

'For God's sake get a grip, will you?' Joe roared, shattering the quiet. He was completely oblivious to Pasty's psychic abilities. 'It's *rain*, that's what it is – what did you bleeding think it was, spooks? I don't know what's come over you, Pasty, damned if I do. You act as if the place was haunted or something.'

'Oh, but it is!' Crow spoke up. 'At least the garden is. A very unusual story, if you'd care to hear it.'

'We don't care to hear it,' Joe snarled. 'And I warned you before – speak when you're spoken to. Now, this . . . *clock*! Get it open, quick.'

Crow had to hold himself to stop the ironic laughter he felt welling inside. 'I can't,' he answered, barely concealing a chuckle. 'I don't know how!'

'You what?' Joe shouted incredulously. 'You don't know how? What the hell d'you mean?'

'I mean what I say,' Crow answered. 'So far as I know that clock's not been opened for well over thirty years!'

'Yes? S . . . so where does it p . . . plug in?' Pasty enquired, stuttering over the words.

'Should it plug in?' Crow answered with his own question. Joe, however, saw just what Pasty was getting at; as, of course, had the 'innocent' Titus Crow.

'Should it plug in, he asks!' Joe mimed sarcastically. He turned to Pasty. 'Good point, Pasty boy – now,' he turned back to Crow, menacingly, 'tell us something, recluse. If your little toy here isn't electric, and if you can't get it open – *then just how do you wind it up?*'

'I don't wind it up – I know nothing whatsoever of the mechanical principles governing it,' Crow answered. 'You see that book there on the occasional table? Well, that's Walmsley's *Notes on Deciphering Codes, Cryptograms and Ancient Inscriptions*; I've been trying for years merely to understand the hieroglyphs on the dial, let alone *open* the thing. And several notable gentlemen students of matters concerning things not usually apparent or open to the man in the street have opinionated to the effect that yonder *device* is not a clock at all! I refer to Etienne-Laurent de Marigny, the occultist Ward Phillips of Rhode Island in America, and Professor Gordon Walmsley of Goole in Yorkshire; all of them believe it to be a space-time machine – *believed* in the case of the first two mentioned, both of those gentlemen now being dead – and I don't

know enough about it yet to decide whether or not I agree
with them! There's no money in it, if that's what you're
thinking.'

'Well, I warned you, guv',' Joe snarled, 'space-time
machine! – My God! – H. G. bloody Wells, he thinks he
is! Pasty, tie him up and gag him. I'm sick of his bleeding
claptrap. He's got us nervous as a couple of cats, he has!'

'I'll say no more,' Crow quickly promised, 'you carry
on. If you can get it open I'll be obliged to you; I'd like
to know what's inside myself.'

'Come off it, guv',' Joe grated, then: 'OK, but one
more word – you end up immobile, right?' Crow nodded
his acquiescence and sat on the edge of his great desk to
watch the performance. He really did not expect the thugs
to do much more than make fools of themselves. He had
not taken into account the possibility – the probability –
of violence in the solution of the problem. Joe, as a child,
had never had much time for the two-penny wire puzzles
sold in the novelty shops. He tried them once or twice, to
be sure, but if they would not go first time – well, you could
usually *make* them go – with a hammer! As it happened
such violence was not necessary.

Pasty had backed up to the door. He was still slapping his
cosh into his palm, but it was purely a reflex action now; a
nervous reflex action. Crow got the impression that if Pasty
dropped his cosh he would probably faint.

'The panels, Pasty,' Joe ordered. 'The panels in the
clock.'

'You do it,' Pasty answered rebelliously, 'that's no
clock and I'm not touching it. There's something wrong
here.'

Joe turned to him in exasperation. 'Are you crazy or
something? It's a clock and nothing more! And this joker
just doesn't want us to see inside. Now what does that
suggest to you?'

'OK, OK – but you do it this time. I'll stay out of the way and watch funnyman here. I've got a feeling about that thing, that's all.' He moved over to stand near Crow who had not moved from his desk. Joe took his gun by the barrel and rapped gently on the panel below the dial of the clock at about waist height. The sound was sharp, solid. Joe turned and grinned at Titus Crow. There certainly seemed to be *something* in there. His grin rapidly faded when he saw Crow grinning back. He turned again to the object of his scrutiny and examined its sides, looking for hinges or other signs pointing to the thing being a hollow container of sorts. Crow could see from the crook's puzzled expression that he was immediately at a loss. He could have told Joe before he began that there was not even evidence of jointing; it was as if the body of the instrument was carved from a solid block of timber – timber as hard as iron.

But Crow had underestimated the determined thug. Whatever Joe's shortcomings as a human being, as a safe-cracker he knew no peer. Not that de Marigny's clock was in any way a safe, but apparently the same principles applied! For as Joe's hands moved expertly up the sides of the panelling there came a loud click and the mad ticking of the instrument's mechanism went totally out of kilter. The four hands on the carven dial stood still for an instant of time before commencing fresh movements in alien and completely inexplicable sequences. Joe stood nimbly back as the large panel swung silently open. He stepped just a few inches too far back, jolting the occasional table. The reading-lamp went over with a crash, momentarily breaking the spell of the wildly oscillating hands and crazy ticking of de Marigny's clock. The corner was once more thrown in shadow and for a moment Joe stood there un-decided, put off stroke by his early success. Then he gave a grunt of triumph, stepped forward and thrust his empty left hand into the darkness behind the open panel.

Pasty sensed the *outsideness* at the same time as Crow. He leapt across the room shouting: 'Joe, Joe – for God's sake, leave it alone ... *leave it alone!*' Crow, on the other hand, spurred by no such sense of comradeship, quickly stood up and backed away. It was not that he was in any way a coward, but he knew something of Earth's darker mysteries – and of the mysteries of other spheres – and besides, he sensed the danger of interfering with an action having origin far from the known side of nature.

Suddenly the corner was dimly illumined by an eerie, dappled light from the open panel; and Joe, his arm still groping beyond that door, gave a yell of utter terror and tried to pull back. The ticking was now insanely aberrant, and the wild sweeps of the four hands about the dial were completely confused and orderless. Joe had braced himself against the frame of the opening, fighting some unseen menace within the strangely lit compartment, trying desperately to withdraw his arm. Against all his effort his left shoulder abruptly jammed forward, into the swirling light, and at the same moment he stuck the barrel of his gun into the opening and fired six shots in rapid succession.

By this time Pasty had an arm round Joe's waist, one foot braced against the base of the clock, putting all his strength into an attempt to haul his companion away from whatever threatened in the swirling light of the now fearsome opening. He was fighting a losing battle. Joe was speechless with terror, all his energies concentrated on escape from the clock; great veins stuck out from his neck and his eyes seemed likely at any moment to pop from his head. He gave one bubbling scream as his head and neck jerked suddenly forward into the maw of the mechanical horror ... and then his body went limp.

Pasty, still wildly struggling with Joe's lower body, gave a last titanic heave at that now motionless torso and actually managed to retrieve for a moment Joe's head from the weirdly lit door.

Simultaneously Pasty and Titus Crow saw something – something that turned Pasty's muscles to water, causing him to relax his struggle so that Joe's entire body bar the legs vanished with a horrible *hisss* into the clock – something that caused Crow to throw up his hands before his eyes in the utmost horror!

In the brief second or so that Pasty's efforts had partly freed the sagging form of his companion in crime, the fruits of Joe's impulsiveness had made themselves hideously apparent. The cloth of his jacket near the left shoulder and that same area of the shirt immediately beneath had been *removed*, seemingly *dissolved* or burnt away by some unknown agent; and in place of the flesh which should by all rights have been laid bare by this mysterious vanishment, *there had been a great blistered, bubbling blotch of crimson and brown – and the neck and head had been in the same sickening state!*

Surprisingly, Pasty recovered first from the shock. He made one last desperate, fatal, grab at Joe's disappearing legs – and the fingers of his right hand crossed the threshold of the opening into the throbbing light beyond. Being in a crouching position and considerably thinner than his now completely vanished friend, Pasty did not stand a chance. Simultaneous with Crow's cry of horror and warning combined, he gave a sobbing shriek and seemed simply to dive headlong into the leering entrance.

Had there been an observer what happened next might have seemed something of an anticlimax. Titus Crow, as if in response to some agony beyond enduring, clapped his hands to his head and fell writhing to the floor. There he stayed, legs threshing wildly for some three seconds, before his body relaxed as the terror of his experience drove his mind to seek refuge in oblivion.

Shortly thereafter, of its own accord, the panel in the clock swung smoothly back into place and clicked shut; the four hands steadied to their previous, not quite so deranged motions, and the ticking of the hidden mechanism slowed and altered its rhythm from the monstrous to the merely abnormal . . .

Titus Crow's first reaction on waking was to believe himself the victim of a particularly horrible nightmare; but then he felt the carpet against his cheek and, opening his eyes, saw the scattered books littering the floor. Shakily he made himself a large jug of coffee and poured himself a huge brandy, then sat, alternately sipping at both until there was none of either left. And when both the jug and the glass were empty he started all over again.

It goes without saying that Crow went nowhere near de Marigny's clock! For the moment, at least, his thirst for knowledge in *that* direction was slaked.

As far as possible he also kept from thinking back on the horrors of the previous night; particularly he wished to forget the hellish, psychic impression received as Pasty went into the clock. For it appeared that de Marigny, Phillips and Walmsley had been right! The clock was, in fact, a space-time machine of sorts. Crow did not know *exactly* what had caused the hideous shock to his highly developed psychic sense; but in fact, even as he had felt that shock and clapped his hands to his head, somewhere out in the worlds of Aldebaran, at a junction of forces neither spatial, temporal, nor of any intermediate dimension recognized by man except in the wildest theories, the Lake of Hali sent up a few streamers of froth and fell quickly back into silence.

And Titus Crow was left with only the memory of the feel of unknown acids burning, of the wash of strange tides outside nature, and of the rushing and tearing of great beasts designed in a fashion beyond man's wildest conjecturing . . .

THE LUSTSTONE

The Luststone *is a meeting of ancient and modern horrors – or at least, that's the theme. The story was written in five weeks in 1981, and if you think that's a long time to write a short story, or even a long one, perhaps I had better explain that in its original form it was a novel of 60,000 words! And it was pornographic. I just wanted to see if I could do it – and did it so well that I submitted it only once and scrapped it! I didn't want my name associated with it. But I did keep parts of it, which I believed might be cannibalized later.*

Seven or eight years went by; Weird Tales magazine asked me if I had any new stories; it was my opportunity to do something with The Luststone. *By then enough time had passed that I could see a new direction for the story and was able to turn a minus into a plus.*

I find The Luststone *very visual. It's funny, but of all the stories and novels I've written, this one is probably the most filmable. And if they gave it an 'adults only' rating it wouldn't any longer be for the sex . . .*

One

The ice was only a memory now, a racial memory whose legends had come down the years, whose evidence was graven in the land in hollow glacial tracts. Of the latter: time would weather the valley eventually, soften its contours however slowly. But the memories would stay, and each winter the snows would replenish them.

That was why the men of the tribes would paint themselves yellow in imitation of the sun-god, and stretch themselves in a line across the land east to west and facing north, and beat back the snow and ice with their clubs. And *frighten* it back with their screams and their leapings. With their magic they defeated winter and conjured spring, summer, and autumn, and thus were the seasons perpetuated.

The tribes, too, were perpetuated; each spring the tribal wizards – the witch-doctors – would perform those fertility rites deemed necessary to life, by means of which the grass was made to grow, the beasts to mate, and Man the weapon-maker to increase and prosper upon the face of the earth. It was the time of the sabretooth and the mammoth, and it was the springtime of Man, the thinking animal whose destiny is the stars. And even in those far dim primal times there were visionaries.

Chylos of the mighty Southern Tribe was one such: Chylos

the Chief, the great wizard and seer whose word was law in the mid-South. And in that spring some ten thousand years ago, Chylos lay on his bed in the grandest cave of all the caves of the Southern Tribe, and dreamed his dream.

He dreamed of invaders!

Of men not greatly unlike the men of the tribes, but fiercer far and with huge appetites for ale, war, and women. Aye, and there were gross-bearded ones, too, whose dragon-prowed ships were as snakes of the sea, whose horned helmets and savage cries gave them the appearance of demons! But Chylos knew that he dreamed only of the far future and so was not made greatly fearful.

And he dreamed that in that distant future there were others who came from the east with fire and thunder, and in his dreams Chylos heard the agonized screams of the descendants of his tribe, men, women, and children; and saw visions of black war, red rape, and rivers of crimson blood. A complex dream it was, and alien these invaders: with long knives and axes which were not of stone, and again wearing horned helmets upon their heads to make them more fearsome yet. From the sea they came, building mounds and forts where they garrisoned their soldiers behind great earthworks.

And some of them carried strange banners, covered with unknown runes and wore kilts of leather and rode in horse-drawn chairs with flashing spokes in their wheels; and their armies were disciplined thousands, moving and fighting with one mind . . .

Such were Chylos's dreams, which brought him starting awake; and so often had he dreamed them that he knew they must be more than mere nightmares. Until one morning, rising from his bed of hides, he saw that it was spring again and knew what must be done. Such visions as he had dreamed must come to pass, he felt it in his old bones, but not for many years. Not for years

beyond his numbering. Very well: the gods themselves had
sent Chylos their warning, and now he must act. For he
was old and the earth would claim him long before the
first invaders came, and so he must unite the tribes now
and bring them together. And they must grow strong and
their men become great warriors.

And there must be that which would remain long after
Chylos himself was gone: a reminder, a monument, a *Power*
to fuel the loins of the men and make the tribes strong.
A driving force to make his people lusty, to ensure their
survival. There must be children – many children! And
their children in their turn must number thousands,
and theirs must number ... such a number as Chylos
could not envisage. Then when the invaders came the
tribes would be ready, unconquerable, indestructible.

So Chylos took up his staff and went out into the central
plain of the valley, where he found a great stone worn
round by the coming and going of the ice; a stone half
as tall again as a man above the earth, and as much or
more of its mass still buried in the ground. And upon
this mighty stone he carved his runes of fertility, powerful
symbols that spelled LUST. And he carved designs which
were the parts of men and women: the rampant pods and
rods of seed, and the ripe breasts and bellies of dawning
life. There was nothing of love in what he drew, only of
lust and the need to procreate; for man was much more
the animal in those dim forgotten days and love as such
one of his weaknesses. But when Chylos's work was done,
still he saw that it was not enough.

For what was the stone but a stone? Only a stone carved
with cryptic runes and symbols of sexuality, and nothing
more. It had no power. Who would remember it in a
hundred seasons, let alone years? Who would know what
it meant?

He called all the leaders of the tribes together, and

because there was a recent peace in the land they came. And Chylos spoke to those headmen and wizards, telling them of his dreams and visions, which were seen as great omens. Together the leaders of the tribes decided what must be done; twenty days later they sent all of their young men and women to Chylos the Seer, and their own wizards went with them.

Meanwhile a pit had been dug away from the foot of the great stone, and wedged timbers held back that boulder from tumbling into the pit. And of all the young men and women of the tribes, Chylos and the Elders chose the lustiest lad and a broad-hipped lass with the breasts of a goddess; and they were proud to be chosen, though for what they knew not.

But when they saw each other, these two, they drew back snarling; for their markings were those of tribes previously opposed in war! And such had been their enmity that even now when all the people were joined, still they kept themselves apart each tribe from the other. Now that the pair had been chosen to be together – and because of their markings, origins, and tribal taboos, the greatest of which forbade intercourse between them – they spoke thus:

'What is the meaning of this?' cried the young man, his voice harsh, affronted. 'Why am I put with this woman? She is not of my tribe. She is of a tribe whose very name offends me! I am not at war with her, but neither may I know her.'

And she said: 'Do my own Elders make mock of me? Why am I insulted so? What have I done to deserve this? Take this thing which calls itself a man away from me!'

But Chylos and the Elders held up their hands, saying: 'Be at peace, be at ease with one another. All will be made plain in due time. We bestow upon you a great honour. Do not dishonour your tribes.' And the chosen ones were subdued, however grudgingly.

And the Elders whispered among each other and said: 'We chose them and the gods were our witnesses and unopposed. They are more than fit for the task. Joining them like this may also more nearly fuse their tribes, and bring about a lasting peace. It must be right.' And they were all agreed.

Then came the feasting, of meats dipped in certain spices and herbs known only to the wizards and flavoured with the crushed horn of mammoth; and the drinking of potent ales, all liberally sprinkled with the potions of the wizards. And when the celebrant horde was feasted and properly drunk, then came the oiled and perfumed and grotesquely-clad dancers, whose dance was the slow-twining dance of the grossly endowed gods of fertility. And as the dance progressed so drummers took up the beat, until the pulses of the milling thousands pounded and their bodies jerked with the jerking of the male and female dancers.

Finally the dance ended, but still the drummers kept to their madly throbbing beat; while in the crowd lesser dances had commenced, not so practised but no less intense and even more lusty. And as the celebrants paired off and fell upon each other, thick pelts were tossed into the pit where the great stone balanced, and petals of spring flowers gathered with the dew upon them, making a bower in the shadow of the boulder; and this was where the chosen couple were made to lie down, while all about the young people of the tribes spent themselves in the ritual spring orgy.

But the pair in the pit – though they had been stripped naked, and while they were drunk as the rest – nevertheless held back and drew apart, and scowled at each other through slitted eyes. Chylos stood at the rim and screamed at them: 'Make love! Let the earth soak up your juices!' He prodded the young man with a spear and commanded him: 'Take her! The gods demand it! What? And would you have the trees die, and all the animals, and the ice come down again to destroy us all? *Do you defy the gods?*'

At that the young man would obey, for he feared the gods, but she would not have him. 'Let him in!' Chylos screamed at her. 'Would you be barren and have your breasts wither, and grow old before your time?' And so she wrapped her legs about the young man. But he was uncertain, and she had not accepted him; still, it seemed to Chylos that they were joined. And as the orgy climbed to its climax he cried out his triumph and signalled to a pair of well-muscled youths where they stood back behind the boulder. And coming forward they took up hammers and with mighty blows knocked away the chocks holding back the great stone from the pit.

The boulder tilted – three hundred tons of rock keeling over – and in the same moment Chylos clutched his heart, cried out and stumbled forward, and toppled into the pit! – and the rune-inscribed boulder with all its designs and great weight slammed down into the hole with a shock that shook the earth. But such was the power of the orgy that held them all in sway, that only those who coupled in the immediate vicinity of the stone knew that it had moved at all!

Now, with the drumming at a standstill, the couples parted, fell back, lay mainly exhausted. A vast field, as of battle, with steam rising as a morning mist. And the two whose task it had been to topple the boulder going amongst them, seeking still-willing, however aching flesh in which to relieve their own pent passions.

Thus was the deed done, the rite performed, the magic worked, the luststone come into being. Or thus it was intended. And old Chylos never knowing that, alas, his work was for nothing, for his propitiates had failed to couple . . .

*   *   *

Three winters after that the snows were heavy, meat was scarce, and the tribes warred. Then for a decade the gods and their seasonal rites were put aside, following which that great ritual orgy soon became a legend and eventually a myth. Fifty years later the luststone and its carvings were moss-covered, forgotten; another fifty saw the stone a shrine. One hundred more years passed and the domed, mossy top of the boulder was hidden in a grove of oaks: a place of the gods, taboo.

The plain grew to a forest, and the stone was buried beneath a growing mound of fertile soil; the trees were felled to build mammoth-pens, and the grass grew deep, thick, and luxurious. More years saw the trees grow up again into a mighty oak forest; and these were the years of the hunter, the declining years of the mammoth. Now the people were farmers, of a sort, who protected limited crops and beasts against Nature's perils. There were years of the long-toothed cats and years of the wolf. And now and then there were wars between the tribes.

And time was the moon that waxed and waned, and the hills growing old and rounded, and forests spanning the entire land; and the tribes flourished and fought and did little else under the green canopy of these mighty forests . . .

Through all of this the stone slept, buried shallow in the earth, keeping its secret; but lovers in the forest knew where to lie when the moon was up. And men robbed by the years or by their own excesses could find a wonder there, when forgotten strength returned, however fleetingly, to fill them once more with fire.

As for old Chylos's dream: it came to pass, but his remedy was worthless. Buried beneath the sod for three thousand years the luststone lay, and felt the tramping feet of the nomad-warrior Celts on the march. Five thousand more years saw the Romans come to Britain, then the Anglo-Saxons, the Vikings, and still the luststone lay there.

There were greater wars than ever Chylos had dreamed, more of rape and murder than he ever could have imagined. War in the sea, on the land and in the air.

And at last there was peace again, of a sort. And finally—

Finally . . .

Two

Garry Clemens was a human calculator at a betting shop in North London; he could figure the numbers, combinations and value of a winning ticket to within a doesn't matter a damn faster than the girls could feed the figures into their machines. All the punters knew him; generally they'd accept without qualms his arbitration on vastly complicated accumulators and the like. With these sort of qualifications Garry could hold down a job any place they played the horses – which was handy because he liked to move around a lot and betting on the races was his hobby. One of his hobbies, anyway.

Another was rape.

Every time Garry took a heavy loss, then he raped. That way (according to his figuring) he won every time. If he couldn't take it out on the horse that let him down, then he'd take it out on some girl instead. But he'd suffered a spate of losses recently, and that had led to some trouble. He hated those nights when he'd go back to his flat and lie down on his bed and have nothing good to think about for that day. Only bad things, like the two hundred he'd lost on that nag that should have come in at fifteen to one, or the filly that got pipped at the post and cost him a cool grand. Which was why he'd finally figured out a way to ease his pain.

Starting now he'd take a girl for every day of the week,

and that way when he took a loss – no matter which day it fell on – he'd always have something good to think about that night when he went to bed. If it was a Wednesday, why, he'd simply think about the Wednesday girl, et cetera . . .

But he'd gone through a bad patch and so the rapes had had to come thick and fast, one and sometimes two a week. His Monday girl was a redhead he'd gagged and tied to a tree in the centre of a copse in a built-up area. He'd spent a lot of time with her, smoked cigarettes in between and talked dirty and nasty to her, raped her three times. Differently each time. Tuesday was a sixteen-year-old kid down at the bottom of the railway embankment. No gag or rope or anything; she'd been so shit-scared that after he was through she didn't even start yelling for an hour. Wednesday (Garry's favourite) it had been a heavily pregnant coloured woman he'd dragged into a burned-out shop right in town! He'd made that one do everything. In the papers the next day he'd read how she lost her baby. But that hadn't bothered him too much.

Thursday had been when it started to get sticky. Garry had dragged this hooker into a street of derelict houses but hadn't even got started when along came this copper! He'd put his knife in the tart's throat – so that she wouldn't yell – and then got to Hell out of there. And he'd reckoned himself lucky to get clean away. But on the other hand, it meant he had to go out the next night, too. He didn't like the tension to build up too much.

But Friday had been a near-disaster, too. There was a house-party not far from where he lived, and Garry had been invited. He'd declined, but he was there anyway – in the garden of the house opposite, whose people weren't at home. And when this really stacked piece had left the party on her own about midnight, Garry had jumped her. But just when he'd knocked her cold and was getting her out of her clothes, then the owners of the house turned up and saw him in the garden. He'd had to cut and run like the wind then, and even now it made his guts churn when he thought about it.

So he'd kept it quiet for a couple of weeks before starting again, and then he'd finally found his Thursday girl. A really shy thing getting off a late-night tube, who he'd carried into a parking lot and had for a couple of hours straight. And she hadn't said a word, just panted a lot and been sick. It turned out she was dumb – and Garry chuckled when he read that. No wonder she'd been so quiet. Maybe he should look for a blind one next time . . .

A week later, Friday, he'd gone out again, but it was a failure; he couldn't find anyone. And so the very next night he'd taken his Saturday girl – a middle-aged baglady! So what the Hell! – a rape is a rape is a rape, right? He gave her a bottle of some good stuff first, which put her away nicely, then gave her a Hell of a lot of bad stuff in as many ways as he knew how. She probably didn't even feel it, wouldn't even remember it, so afterwards he'd banged her face on the pavement a couple of times so that when she woke up at least she'd know *something* had happened! Except she hadn't woken up. Well, at least that way she wouldn't be talking about it. And by now he knew they'd have his semen type on record, and that they'd also have *him* if he just once slipped up. But he didn't intend to.

Sunday's girl was a lady taxi driver with a figure that was a real stopper! Garry hired her to take him out of town, directed her to a big house in the country and stopped her at the bottom of the drive. Then he hit her on the head, ripped her radio out, drove into a wood and had her in the back of the cab. He'd really made a meal of it, especially after she woke up; but as he was finishing she got a bit too active and raked his face – which was something he didn't much like. He had a nice face, Garry,

and was very fond of it. So almost before he'd known that
he was doing it, he'd gutted the whore!

But the next day in the papers the police were talking
about skin under her fingernails, and now he knew they
had his blood-group but definitely, too. *And* his face was
marked; not badly, but enough. So it had been time to take
a holiday.

Luckily he'd just had a big win on the gee-gees; he
phoned the bookie's and said he wasn't up to it – couldn't
see the numbers too clearly – he was taking time off. With
an eye-patch and a bandage to cover the damage, he'd
headed west and finally holed up in Chichester.

But all of that had been twelve days ago, and he was
fine now, and he still had to find his girl-Friday. And
today *was* Friday, so ... Garry reckoned he'd rested up
long enough.

This morning he'd read about a Friday night dance at a
place called Athelsford, a hick village just a bus-ride away.
Well, and he had nothing against country bumpkins, did
he? So Athelsford it would have to be ...

It was the middle of the long hot summer of '76. The
weather forecasters were all agreed for once that this one
would drag on and on, and reserves of water all over
the country were already beginning to suffer. This was
that summer when there would be shock reports of the
Thames flowing backwards, when rainmakers would be
called in from the USA to dance and caper, and when a
certain Government Ministry would beg householders to
put bricks in their WC cisterns and thus consume less of
precious water.

The southern beaches were choked morning to night
with kids on their school holidays, sun-blackened treasure
hunters with knotted hankies on their heads and metal
detectors in their hands, and frustrated fishermen with

their crates of beer, boxes of sandwiches, and plastic bags of smelly bait. The pubs were filled all through opening hours with customers trying to drown their thirsts or themselves, and the resorts had never had it so good. The nights were balmy for lovers from Land's End to John o' Groat's, and nowhere balmier than in the country lanes of the Southern Counties.

Athelsford Estate in Hampshire, one of the few suburban housing projects of the Sixties to realize a measure of success (in that its houses were good, its people relatively happy, and – after the last bulldozer had clanked away – its countryside comparatively unspoiled) suffered or enjoyed the heatwave no more or less than anywhere else. It was just another small centre of life and twentieth-century civilization, and apart from the fact that Athelsford was 'rather select' there was little as yet to distinguish it from a hundred other estates and small villages in the country triangle of Salisbury, Reading, and Brighton.

Tonight being Friday night, there was to be dancing at The Barn. As its name implied, the place had been a half-brick, half-timber barn; but the Athelsfordians being an enterprising lot, three of their more affluent members had bought the great vault of a place, done it up with internal balconies, tables, and chairs, built a modest car park to one side – an extension of the village pub's car park – and now it was a dance hall, occasionally used for weddings and other private functions. On Wednesday nights the younger folk had it for their discotheques (mainly teenage affairs, in return for which they kept it in good repair), but on Friday nights the Barn became the focal point of the entire estate. The Barn and The Old Stage.

The Old Stage was the village pub, its sign a coach with rearing horses confronted by a highwayman in tricorn hat. Joe McGovern, a widower, owned and ran the pub, and many of his customers jokingly associated him with the highwayman on his sign. But while Joe was and always would be a canny Scot, he was also a fair man and down to earth. So were his prices. Ten years ago when the estate was new, the steady custom of the people had saved The Old Stage and kept it a free house. Now Joe's trade was flourishing, and he had plenty to be thankful for.

So, too, Joe's somewhat surly son Gavin. Things to be thankful for, and others he could well do without. Gavin was, for example, extremely thankful for The Barn, whose bar he ran on Wednesday and Friday nights, using stock from The Old Stage. The profits very nicely supplemented the wage he earned as a county council labourer working on the new road. The wage he *had* earned, anyway, before he'd quit. That had only been this morning but already he sort of missed the work, and he was sure he was going to miss the money. But ... oh, he'd find other work. There was always work for good strong hands. He had that to be thankful for, too: his health and strength.

But he was *not* thankful for his kid sister, Eileen: her 'scrapes and narrow escapes' (as he saw her small handful of as yet entirely innocent friendships with the local lads), and her natural, almost astonishing beauty, which drew them like butterflies to bright flowers. It was that, in large part, which made him surly; for he knew that in fact she wasn't just a 'kid' sister any more, and that sooner or later she ...

Oh, Gavin loved his sister, all right – indeed he had transferred to her all of his affection and protection when their mother died three years ago – but having lost his mother he wasn't going to lose Eileen, too, not if he could help it.

Gavin was twenty-two, Eileen seventeen. He was over six feet tall, narrow-hipped, wide in the shoulders: a tapering wedge of muscle with a bullet-head to top it off. Most of the village lads looked at Eileen, then looked at Gavin, and didn't look at Eileen again. But those of them who looked at her twice reckoned she was worth it.

She was blonde as her brother was dark, as sweet and slim as he was huge and surly; five-seven, with long shapely legs and a waist like a wisp, and blue eyes with lights in them that danced when she smiled; the very image of her mother. And that was Gavin's problem – for he'd loved his mother a great deal, too.

It was 5.30 p.m. and brother and sister were busy in workclothes, loading stock from the back door of The Old Stage onto a trolley and carting it across the parking lot to The Barn. Joe McGovern ticked off the items on a stock list as they worked. But when Gavin and Eileen were alone in The Barn, stacking the last of the bottles onto the shelves behind the bar, suddenly he said to her: 'Will you be here tonight?'

She looked at her brother. There was nothing surly about Gavin now. There never was when he spoke to her; indeed his voice held a note of concern, of agitation, of some inner struggle which he himself couldn't quite put his finger on. And she knew what he was thinking and that it would be the same tonight as always. Someone would dance with her, and then dance with her again – and then no more. Because Gavin would have had 'a quiet word with him.'

'Of course I'll be here, Gavin,' she sighed. 'You know I will. I wouldn't miss it. I love to dance and chat with the girls – *and* with the boys – when I get the chance! Why does it bother you so?'

'I've told you often enough why it bothers me,' he answered gruffly, breathing heavily through his nose. 'It's all those blokes. They've only one thing on their minds. They're the same with all the girls. But you're not just any girl – you're my sister.'

'Yes,' she answered, a trifle bitterly, 'and don't they just know it! You're always there, in the background, watching, somehow threatening. It's like having two fathers – only one of them's a tyrant! Do you know, I can't remember the last time a boy wanted to walk me home?'

'But . . . you *are* home!' he answered, not wanting to fight, wishing now that he'd kept his peace. If only she was capable of understanding the ways of the world. 'You live right next door.'

'Then simply *walk* me!' she blurted it out. 'Oh, anywhere! Gavin, can't you understand? It's *nice* to be courted, to have someone who wants to hold your hand!'

'That's how it starts,' he grunted, turning away. 'They want to hold your hand. But who's to say how it finishes, eh?'

'Well not much fear of that!' she sighed again. 'Not that I'm that sort of girl anyway,' and she looked at him archly. 'But even if I was, with you around – straining at the leash like . . . like a great hulking watchdog – nothing's very much likely to even get started, now is it?' And before he could answer, but less harshly now: 'Now come on,' she said, 'tell me what's brought all this on? You've been really nice to me this last couple of weeks. The hot weather may have soured some people but you've been really sweet – like a Big Brother should be – until out of the blue, like this. I really don't understand what gets into you, Gavin.'

It was his turn to sigh. 'Aren't you forgetting something?' he said. 'The assault – probably with sexual motivation – just last week, Saturday night, in Lovers' Lane?'

Perhaps Eileen really ought not to pooh-pooh that, but she believed she understood it well enough. 'An assault,' she said. 'Motive: "probably" sexual – the most excitement Athelsford has known in . . . oh, as long as *I* can remember! And the "victim": Linda Anstey. Oh, my, *what* a surprise! *Hah!* Why, Linda's always been that way! Every kid in the school had fooled around

with her at one time or another. From playing kids'
games to ... well, everything. It's the way she is and
everyone knows it. All right, perhaps I'm being unfair
to her: she might have asked for trouble and she might
not, but it seems hardly surprising to me that if it was
going to happen to someone, Linda would be the one!'

'But it *did* happen,' Gavin insisted. 'That kind of bloke
does exist – plenty of them.' He stacked the last half-dozen
cans and made for the exit; and changing the subject (as
he was wont to do when an argument was going badly for
him, or when he believed he'd proved his point sufficiently)
said: 'Me, I'm for a pint before I get myself ready for
tonight. Fancy an iced lemonade, kid?' He paused, turned
back towards her, and grinned, but she suspected it was
forced. If only she could gauge what went on in his mind.

But: 'Oh, all right!' she finally matched his grin, 'if
you're buying.' She caught up with him and grabbed him,
standing on tip-toe to give him a kiss. 'But Gavin – promise
me that from now on you won't worry about me so much,
OK?'

He hugged her briefly, and reluctantly submitted: 'Yeah,
all right.'

But as she led the way out of The Barn and across the car
park, with the hot afternoon sun shining in her hair and her
sweet, innocent body moving like that inside her coveralls,
he looked after her and worried all the harder; worried the
way an older brother *should* worry, he thought, and yet
somehow far more intensely. And the worst of it was that
he *knew* he was being unreasonable and obsessive! But (and
Gavin at once felt his heart hardening) ... oh, he recognized well enough the way the village Jack-the-Lads looked
at Eileen, and knew how much they'd like to get their itchy
little paws on her – the grubby-minded, horny ...

... But there Gavin's ireful thoughts abruptly evaporated, the scowl left his face, and he frowned as a vivid

picture suddenly flashed onto the screen of his mind. It
was something he'd seen just this morning, across the
fields where they were laying the new road; something
quite obscene which hadn't made much of an impression
on him at the time, but which now . . . and astonished, he
paused again. For he couldn't for the life of him see how
he'd connected up a thing like that with Eileen! And it just
as suddenly dawned on him that the reason he knew how
the boys felt about his sister was because he sometimes felt
that way too. Oh, not about *her* – no, of course not – but
about . . . a boulder? Well, certainly it had been a boulder
that did it to him this morning, anyway.

And: *Gavin, son,* he told himself, *sometimes I think you're
maybe just a tiny wee bit sick!* And then he laughed, if only
to himself.

But somehow the pictures in his mind just wouldn't go
away, and as he went to his upstairs room in The Old Stage
and slowly changed into his evening gear, so he allowed
himself to go over again the peculiar occurrences of the
morning . . .

Three

That Friday morning, yes, and it had been hot as a furnace.
And every member of the road gang without exception
looking forward to the coming weekend, to cool beers in
cool houses with all the windows thrown open; so that as
the heat-shimmering day had drawn towards noon they'd
wearied of the job and put a lot less muscle into it.

Also, and to make things worse, this afternoon they'd be
a man short; for this was Gavin McGovern's last morning
and he hadn't been replaced yet. And even when he was
. . . well, it would take a long time to find someone else
who could throw a bulldozer around like he could. The

thing was like a toy in his hands. But . . . seeing as how he lived in Athelsford and had always considered himself something of a traitor anyway, working on the link road, he'd finally decided to seek employment elsewhere.

Foreman John Sykes wasn't an Athelsfordian, but he made it his business to know something about the people working under him – especially if they were local to the land where he was driving his road. He'd got to know Big Gavin pretty well, he reckoned, and in a way envied him. He certainly wouldn't mind it if *his* Old Man owned a country pub! But on the other hand he could sympathize with McGovern, too. He knew how torn he must feel.

This was the one part of his job that Sykes hated: when the people up top said the road goes here, and the people down here said oh no it doesn't, not in *our* back garden! Puffed up, awkward, defiant, little bastards! But at the same time Sykes could sympathize with them also, even though they were making his job as unpleasant as they possibly could. And that was yet another reason why the work hadn't gone too well this morning.

Today it had been a sit-in, when a good dozen of the locals had appeared from the wood at the end of Lovers' Lane, bringing lightweight fold-down garden chairs with them to erect across the road. And there they'd sat with their placards and sandwiches on the new stretch of tarmac, heckling the road gang as they toiled and sweated into their dark-stained vests and tried to build a bloody road which wasn't wanted. And which didn't seem to want to be built! They'd stayed from maybe quarter-past nine to a minute short of eleven, then got up and like a gaggle of lemmings waddled back to the village again. Their 'good deed' for the day – *Goddam!*

Christ, what a day! For right after that . . . *big* trouble, mechanical trouble! Or rather an obstruction which had caused mechanical trouble. Not the more or less passive, placard-waving obstruction of people – which was bad enough – but a rather more physical, much more tangible obstruction. Namely, a bloody great boulder!

The first they'd known of it was when the bulldozer hit it while lifting turf and muck in a wide swath two feet deep. Until then there had been only the usual stony debris – small, rounded pebbles and the occasional blunt slab of scarred rock, nothing out of the ordinary for these parts – and Sykes hadn't been expecting anything quite this big. The surveyors had been across here, hammering in their long iron spikes and testing the ground, but they'd somehow missed this thing. Black granite by its looks, it had stopped the dozer dead in its tracks and given Gavin McGovern a fair old shaking! But at least the blade had cleared the sod and clay off the top of the thing. Like the dome of a veined, bald, old head it had looked, sticking up there in the middle of the projected strip.

'See if you can dig the blade under it,' Sykes had bawled up at Gavin through clouds of blue exhaust fumes and the clatter of the engine. 'Try to lever the bastard up, or split it. We have to get down a good forty or fifty inches just here.'

Taking it personally – and with something less than an hour to go, eager to get finished now – Gavin had dragged his sleeve across his brown, perspiration-shiny brow and grimaced. Then, tilting his helmet back on his head, he'd slammed the blade of his machine deep into the earth half a dozen times until he could feel it biting against the unseen curve of the boulder. Then he'd gunned the motor, let out the clutch, shoved, and lifted all in one fluid movement. Or at least in a movement that should have been fluid. For instead of finding purchase the blade had ridden up, splitting turf and topsoil as it slid over the fairly smooth surface of the stone; the dozer had lurched forward, slewing round when the blade finally snagged on a rougher part of the surface; the offside caterpillar had parted in a shriek of hot, tortured metal.

Then Gavin had shut her off, jumped down, and stared disbelievingly at his grazed and bleeding forearm where it had scraped across the iron frame of the cab. 'Damn – *damn!*' he'd shouted then, hurling his safety helmet at the freshly turned earth and kicking the dozer's broken track.

'Easy, Gavin,' Sykes had gone up to him. 'It's not your fault, and it's not the machine's. It's mine, if anybody's. I had no idea there was anything this big here. And by the look of it this is only the tip of the iceberg.'

But Gavin wasn't listening; he'd gone down on one knee and was examining part of the boulder's surface where the blade had done a job of clearing it off. He was frowning, peering hard, breaking away small scabs of loose dirt and tracing lines or grooves with his strong, blunt fingers. The runic symbols were faint but the carved picture was more clearly visible. There were other pictures, too, with only their edges showing as yet, mainly hidden under the curve of the boulder. The ganger got down beside Gavin and assisted him, and slowly the carvings took on clearer definition.

Sykes was frowning, too, now. What the Hell? A floral design of some sort? Very old, no doubt about it. Archaic? Prehistoric?

Unable as yet to make anything decisive of the pictures on the stone, they cleared away more dirt. But then Sykes stared harder, slowly shook his head, and began to grin. The grin spread until it almost split his face ear to ear. Perhaps not prehistoric after all. More like the work of some dirty-minded local kid. And not a bad artist, at that!

The lines of the main picture were primitive but clinically correct, however exaggerated. And its subject was completely unmistakable. Gavin McGovern continued to stare at it, and his bottom jaw had fallen open. Finally, glancing at Sykes out of the corner of his eye, he grunted: 'Old, do you think?'

Sykes started to answer, then shut his mouth and stood up. He thought fast, scuffed some of the dirt back with his booted foot, bent to lean a large, flat flake of stone against the picture, mainly covering it from view. Sweat trickled down his back and made it itch under his wringing shirt. Made it itch like the devil, and the rest of his body with it. The boulder seemed hot as Hell, reflecting the blazing midday sunlight.

And 'Old?' the ganger finally answered. 'You mean, like ancient? Naw, I shouldn't think so ... Hey, and Gavin, son – if I were you, I wouldn't go mentioning this to anyone. You know what I mean?'

Gavin looked up, still frowning. 'No,' he shook his head, 'what do you mean?'

'What?' said Sykes. 'You mean to say you can't see it? Why, only let this get out and there'll be people coming from all over the place to see it! Another bloody Stonehenge, it'll be! And what price your Athelsford then, eh? Flooded, the place would be, with all sorts of human debris come to see the famous dirty caveman pictures! You want that, do you?'

No, that was the last thing Gavin wanted. 'I see what you mean,' he said, slowly. 'Also, it would slow you down, right? They'd stop you running your road through here.'

'That, too, possibly,' Sykes answered. 'For a time, anyway. But just think about it. What would you rather have: a new road pure and simple – or a thousand yobs a day tramping through Athelsford and up Lovers' Lane to ogle this little lot, eh?'

That was something Gavin didn't have to think about for very long. It would do business at The Old Stage a power of good, true, but then there was Eileen. Pretty soon they'd be coming to ogle her, too. 'So what's next?' he said.

'You leave that to me,' Sykes told him. 'And just take my word for it that this time tomorrow this little beauty will be so much rubble, OK?'

Gavin nodded; he knew that the ganger was hot stuff with a drill and a couple of pounds of explosive. 'If you say so,' he spat into the dust and dirt. 'Anyway, I don't much care for the looks of the damned thing!' He scratched furiously at his forearm where his graze was already starting to scab over. 'It's not right, this dirty old thing. Sort of makes me hot and . . . itchy!'

'Itchy, yeah,' Sykes agreed. And he wondered what sort of mood his wife, Jennie, would be in tonight. If this hot summer sun had worked on her the way it was beginning to work on him, well tonight could get to be pretty interesting. Which would make a welcome change!

Deep, dark, and much disturbed now, old Chylos had felt unaccustomed tremors vibrating through his fossilized bones. The stamping of a thousand warriors on the march, roaring their songs of red death? Aye, perhaps. And:

'Invaders!' Chylos breathed the word, without speaking, and indeed without breathing.

'No,' Hengit of the Far Forest tribe contradicted him. *'The mammoths are stampeding, the earth is sinking, trees are being felled. Any of these things, but no invaders. Is that all you dream about, old man? Why can't you simply lie still and sleep like the dead thing you are?'*

'And even if there were invaders,' the revenant of a female voice now joined in, Alaze of the Shrub Hill folk, *'would you really expect a man of the Far Forest tribe to come to arms? They are notorious cowards! Better you call on me, Chylos, a woman to rise up against these invaders — if there really were invaders, which there are not.'*

Chylos listened hard – to the earth, the sky, the distant sea – but no longer heard the thundering of booted feet, nor warcries going up into the air, nor ships with muffled oars creeping and creaking in the mist. And so he sighed and said: *'Perhaps you are right – but nevertheless we should be ready! I, at least, am ready!'*

And: *'Old fool!'* Hengit whispered of Chylos into the dirt and the dark.

And: *'Coward!'* Alaze was scathing of Hengit where all three lay broken, under the luststone . . .

7.15 p.m.

The road gang had knocked off more than two hours ago and the light was only just beginning to fade a little. An hour and a half to go yet to the summer's balmy darkness, when the young people would wander hand in hand, and occasionally pause mouth to mouth, in Lovers' Lane. Or perhaps not until later, for tonight there was to be dancing at The Barn. And for now . . . all should be peace and quiet out here in the fields, where the luststone raised its veined dome of a head through the broken soil. All *should* be quiet – but was not.

'Levver!' shouted King above the roar of the bikes, his voice full of scorn. 'What a bleedin' player you turned out to be! What the 'ell do yer call this, then?'

'The end o' the bleedin' road,' one of the other bikers shouted. 'That's where!'

'Is it ever!' cried someone else.

Leather grinned sheepishly and pushed his Nazi-style crash-helmet to the back of his head. 'So I come the wrong way, di'n I? 'Ell's teef, the sign said bleedin' Affelsford, dinnit?'

'Yers,' King shouted. 'Also NO ENTRY an' WORKS IN PRO-bleedin'-GRESS! 'Ere, switch off, you lot. I can't 'ear meself fink!'

As the engines of the six machines clattered to a halt, King got off his bike and stretched, stamping his feet. His real name was Kevin; but as leader of a chapter of Hell's Angels, who needed a name like that? A crude crown was traced in lead studs on the back of his leather jacket and a golden sovereign glittered where it dangled from his left earlobe. No more than twenty-five or -six years of age, King kept his head clean-shaven under a silver helmet painted with black eye-sockets and fretted nostrils to resemble a skull. He was hard as they come, was King, and the rest of them knew it.

'That's the place I cased over there,' said Leather, pointing. He had jumped up onto the dome of a huge boulder, the luststone, to spy out the land. 'See the steeple there? That's Affelsford – and Comrades, does it have *some* crumpet!'

'Well, jolly dee!' said King. 'Wot we supposed to do, then? Ride across the bleedin' fields? Come on, Levver my son – you was the one rode out here and onced it over. 'Ow do we bleedin' *get* there?' The rest of the Angels sniggered.

Leather grinned. 'We goes up the motorway a few 'undred yards an' spins off at the next turnin', that's all. I jus' made a simple mistake, di'n I.'

'Yers,' said King, relieving himself loudly against the luststone. 'Well, let's not make no more, eh? I gets choked off pissin' about an' wastin' valuable time.'

By now the others had dismounted and stood ringed around the dome of the boulder. They stretched their legs and lit 'funny' cigarettes. 'That's right,' said King, 'light up. Let's have a break before we go in.'

'Best not leave it too late,' said Leather. 'Once the mood is on me I likes to get it off . . .'

'One copper, you said,' King reminded him, drawing deeply on a poorly constructed smoke. 'Only one bluebottle in the whole place?'

'S'right,' said Leather. 'An' 'e's at the other end of town. We can wreck the place, 'ave our fun wiv the girlies, be out again before 'e knows we was ever in!'

' 'Ere,' said one of the others. 'These birds is the real fing, eh, Levver?'

Leather grinned crookedly and nodded. 'Built for it,' he answered. 'Gawd, it's ripe, is Affelsford.'

The gang guffawed, then quietened as a dumpy figure approached from the construction shack. It was one of Sykes's men, doing night-watchman to bolster his wages. 'What's all this?' he grunted, coming up to them.

'Unmarried muvvers' convention,' said King. 'Wot's it look like?' The others laughed, willing to make a joke of it and let it be; but Leather jumped down from the boulder and stepped forward. He was eager to get things started, tingling – even itchy – with his need for violence.

'Wot's it ter you, baldy?' he snarled, pushing the little man in the chest and sending him staggering.

Baldy Dawson was one of Sykes's drivers and didn't have a lot of muscle. He did have common sense, however, and could see that things might easily get out of hand. 'Before you start any rough stuff,' he answered, backing away, 'I better tell you I took your bike numbers and phoned 'em through to the office in Portsmouth.' He had done no such thing, but it was a good bluff. 'Any trouble – my boss'll know who did it.'

Leather grabbed him by the front of his sweat-damp shirt. 'You little—'

'Let it be,' said King. 'E's only doin' 'is job. Besides, 'e 'as an 'ead jus' like mine!' He laughed.

'Wot?' Leather was astonished.

'Why spoil fings?' King took the other's arm. 'Now listen, Levver me lad – all you've done so far is bog everyfing up, right? So let's bugger off into bleedin' Affelsford an' 'ave ourselves some fun! You want to see some blood –

OK, me too – but for Chrissakes, let's get somefing for our money, right?'

They got back on their bikes and roared off, leaving Baldy Dawson in a slowly settling cloud of dust and exhaust fumes. 'Young bastards!' He scratched his naked dome. 'Trouble for someone before the night's out, I'll wager.'

Then, crisis averted, he returned to the shack and his well-thumbed copy of *Playboy* . . .

Four

'*This time,*' said Chylos, with some urgency, '*I cannot be mistaken.*'

The two buried with him groaned – but before they could comment:

'*Are you deaf, blind – have you no feelings?*' he scorned. '*No, it's simply that you do not have my magic!*'

'*It's your "magic" that put us here!*' finally Hengit answered his charges. '*Chylos, we don't need your magic!*'

'*But the tribes do,*' said Chylos. '*Now more than ever!*'

'*Tribes?*' this time it was Alaze who spoke. '*The tribes were scattered, gone, blown to the four winds many lifetimes agone. What tribes do you speak of, old man?*'

'*The children of the tribes, then!*' he blustered. '*Their children's children! What does it matter? They are the same people! They are of our blood! And I have dreamed a dream . . .*'

'*That again?*' said Hengit. '*That dream of yours, all these thousands of years old?*'

'*Not the old dream,*' Chylos denied, '*but a new one! Just now, lying here, I dreamed it! Oh, it was not unlike the old one, but it was vivid, fresh, new! And I cannot be mistaken.*'

And now the two lying there with him were silent, for they too had felt, sensed, something. And finally: *'What did you see . . . in this dream?'* Alaze was at least curious.

'I saw them as before,' said Chylos, *'with flashing spokes in the wheels of their battle-chairs; except the wheels were not set side by side but fore and aft! And helmets upon their heads, some with horns! They wore shirts of leather picked out in fearsome designs, monstrous runes; sharp knives in their belts, aye, and flails – and blood in their eyes! Invaders – I cannot be mistaken!'*

And Hengit and Alaze shuddered a little in their stony bones, for Chylos had inspired them with the truth of his vision and chilled them with the knowledge of his prophecy finally come true. But . . . what could they do about it, lying here in the cold earth? It was as if the old wizard read their minds.

'You are not bound to lie here,' he told them. *'What are you now but will? And my will remains strong! So let's be up and about our work. I, Chylos, have willed it – so let it be!'*

'Our work? What work?' the two cried together. *We cannot fight!'*

'You could if you willed it,' said Chylos, *'and if you have not forgotten how. But I didn't mention fighting. No, we must warn them. The children of the children of the tribes. Warn them, inspire them, cause them to lust after the blood of these invaders!'* And before they could question him further:

'Up, up, we've work to do!' Chylos cried. *'Up with you and out into the night, to seek them out. The children of the children of the tribes . . . !'*

From the look of things, it was all set to be a full house at The Barn. Athelsfordians in their Friday-night best were gravitating first to The Old Stage for a warm-up drink or two, then crossing the parking lot to The Barn to secure good tables up on the balconies or around the dance floor. Another hour or two and the place would be in full swing. Normally Gavin McGovern would be pleased with the way things were shaping up, for what with tips and all it would mean a big bonus for him. And his father at the pub wouldn't complain, for what was lost on the swings would be regained on the roundabouts. And yet . . .

There seemed a funny mood on the people tonight, a sort of scratchiness about them, an abrasiveness quite out of keeping. When the disco numbers were playing the girls danced with a sexual aggressiveness Gavin hadn't noticed before, and the men of the village seemed almost to be eyeing each other up like tomcats spoiling for a fight. Pulling pints for all he was worth, Gavin hadn't so far had much of a chance to examine or analyse the thing; it was just that in the back of his mind some small dark niggling voice seemed to be urgently whispering: *'Look out! Be on your guard! Tonight's the night! And when it happens you won't believe it!* But . . . it could simply be his imagination, of course.

Or (and Gavin growled his frustration and self-annoyance as he felt that old obsession rising up again) it could simply be that Eileen had found herself a new dancing partner, and that since the newcomer had walked into the place they'd scarcely been off the floor. A fact which in itself was enough to set him imagining all sorts of things, and uppermost the sensuality of women and sexual competitiveness, readiness, and willingness of young men. And where Gavin's sister was concerned, much too willing!

But Eileen had seen Gavin watching her, and as the dance tune ended she came over to the bar with her young man in tow. This was a ploy she'd used before: a direct attack is often the best form of defence. Gavin remembered his promise, however, and in fact the man she was with seemed a very decent sort at first glance: clean and bright, smartly dressed, seriously intentioned. Now Gavin would see if his patter matched up to his looks.

'Gavin,' said Eileen, smiling warningly, 'I'd like you to meet Gordon Cleary – Gordon's a surveyor from Portsmouth.'

'How do you do, Gordon,' Gavin dried his hands, reached across the bar to shake with the other, discovered the handshake firm, dry, and no-nonsense. But before they could strike up any sort of conversation the dance floor had emptied and the bar began to crowd up. 'I'm sorry,' Gavin shrugged ruefully. 'Business. But at least you were here first and I can get you your drinks.' He looked at his sister.

'Mine's easy,' she said, smiling. 'A lemonade, please.' And Gavin was pleased to note that Cleary made no objection, didn't try to force strong drink on her.

'Oh, a shandy for me,' he said, 'and go light on the beer, please, Gavin, for I'll be driving later. And one for yourself, if you're ready.'

The drinks were served and Gavin turned to the next party of customers in line at the bar. There were four of them: Tod Baxter and Angela Meers, village sweethearts, and Allan Harper and his wife, Val. Harper was a PTI at the local school; he ordered a confusing mixture of drinks, no two alike; Gavin, caught on the hop, had a little trouble with his mental arithmetic. 'Er, that's two pounds – er—' He frowned in concentration.

'Three pounds and forty-seven pence, on the button!' said Gordon Cleary from the side. Gavin looked at him and saw his eyes flickering over the price list pinned up behind the bar.

'Pretty fast!' he commented, and carried on serving. But to himself he said: *except I hope it's only with numbers* . . .

Gavin wasn't on his own behind the bar; at the other end, working just as hard, Bill Salmons popped corks and pulled furious pints. Salmons was ex-Army, a parachutist who'd bust himself up jumping. You wouldn't know it, though, for he was strong as a horse. As the disc jockey got his strobes going again and the music started up, and as the couples gradually gravitated back towards the dance floor, Gavin crossed quickly to Salmons and said: 'I'm going to get some of this sweat off. Two minutes?'

Salmons nodded, said: 'Hell of a night, isn't it? Too damned *hot!*'

Gavin reached under the bar for a clean towel and headed for the gents' toilet. Out of the corner of his eye he saw that Eileen and Gordon Cleary were back on the floor again. Well, if all the bloke wanted was to dance . . . that was OK.

In the washroom Gavin took off his shirt, splashed himself with cold water, and towelled it off, dressed himself again. A pointless exercise: he was just as hot and damp as before! As he finished off Allan Harper came in, also complaining of the heat.

They passed a few words; Harper was straightening his tie in a mirror when there came the sound of shattering glass from the dance hall, causing Gavin to start. 'What—?' he said.

'Just some clown dropped his drink, I expect,' said Harper. 'Or fainted for lack of air! It's about time we got some decent air-conditioning in this—'

And he paused as there sounded a second crash – which this time was loud enough to suggest a table going over. The music stopped abruptly and some girl gave a high-pitched shriek.

We warned you! said several dark little voices in the back of Gavin's mind. 'What the Hell—?' he started down the corridor from the toilets with Harper hot on his heels.

Entering the hall proper the two skidded to a halt. On the other side of the room a village youth lay sprawled among the debris of a wrecked table, blood spurting from his nose. Over him stood a Hell's Angel, swinging a bike chain threateningly. In the background a young girl sobbed, backing away, her dress torn down the front. Gavin would have started forward but Harper caught his arm. 'Look!' he said.

At a second glance the place seemed to be crawling with Angels. There was one at the entrance, blocking access; two more were on the floor, dragging Angela Meers and Tod Baxter apart. They had yanked the straps of Angela's dress down, exposing her breasts. A fifth Angel had clambered into the disco control box, was flinging records all over the place as he sought his favourites. And the sixth was at the bar.

Now it was Gavin's turn to gasp, 'Look!'

The one at the bar, King, had trapped Val Harper on her bar stool. He had his arms round her, his hands gripping the bar top. He rubbed himself grindingly against her with lewdly suggestive sensuality.

For a moment longer the two men stood frozen on the perimeter of this scene, nailed down by a numbness which, as it passed, brought rage in its wake. The Angel with the chain, Leather, had come across the floor and swaggered by them into the corridor, urinating in a semicircle as he went, saying: 'Evenin' gents. This the bog, then?'

What the Hell's happening? thought Harper, lunging towards the bar. There must be something wrong with the strobe lights: they blinded him as he ran, flashing rainbow colours in a mad kaleidoscope that flooded the entire room. The Angel at the bar was trying to get his hand down the front of Val's dress, his rutting movements exaggerated by the crazy strobes. Struggling desperately, Val screamed.

Somewhere at the back of his shocked mind, Harper noted that the Angels still wore their helmets. He also noted, in the flutter of the crazy strobes, that the helmets seemed to have grown horns! *Jesus, it's like a bloody Viking invasion!* he thought, going to Val's rescue . . .

It had looked like a piece of cake to King and his Angels. A gift. The kid selling tickets hadn't even challenged them. Too busy wetting his pants, King supposed. And from what he had seen of The Barn's clientele: pushovers! As soon as he'd spotted Val Harper at the bar, he'd known what he wanted. A toffy-nosed bird like her in a crummy place like this? She could only be here for one thing. And not a man in the place to deny him whatever he wanted to do or take.

Which is why it came as a total surprise to King when Allan Harper spun him around and butted him square in the face. Blood flew as the astonished Angel slammed back against the bar; his spine cracked against the bar's rim, knocking all the wind out of him; in another moment Bill Salmons's arm went round his neck in a stranglehold. There was no time for chivalry: Harper the PTI finished it with a left to King's middle and a right to his already bloody face. The final blow landed on King's chin, knocking him cold. As Bill Salmons released him he flopped forward, his death's-head helmet flying free as he landed face-down on the floor.

Gavin McGovern had meanwhile reached into the disc-jockey's booth, grabbed his victim by the scruff of the neck, and hurled him out of the booth and across the dance floor. Couples hastily got out of the way as the Angel slid on his back across the polished floor. Skidding to a halt, he brought out a straight-edged razor in a silvery flash of steel. Gavin was on him in a moment; he lashed out with a foot that caught the Angel in the throat, knocking him flat on his back again. The razor spun harmlessly away across the floor as its owner writhed and clawed at his throat.

Seeing their Angel at Arms on the floor like that, the pair who tormented Angela Meers now turned their attention to Gavin McGovern. They had already knocked Tod Baxter down, kicking him where he huddled. But they hadn't got in a good shot and as Gavin loomed large so Tod got to his feet behind them. Also, Allan Harper was dodging his way through the now strangely silent crowd where he came from the bar.

The Angel at the door, having seen something of the melee and wanting to get his share while there was still some going, also came lunging in through the wild strobe patterns. But this one reckoned without the now fully roused passions of the young warriors of the Athelsford tribe. Three of the estate's larger youths jumped him, and he went down under a hail of blows. And by then Allan Harper, Gavin McGovern and Tod Baxter had fallen on the other two. For long moments there were only the crazily flashing strobes, the dull thudding of fists into flesh, and a series of fading grunts and groans.

Five Angels were down; and the sixth, coming out of the toilets, saw only a sea of angered faces all turned in his direction. Faces hard and full of fury – *and* bloodied, crumpled shapes here and there, cluttering the dance floor. Pale now and disbelieving, Leather ran towards the exit, found himself surrounded in a moment. And now in the absolute silence there was bloodlust written on those faces that ringed him in.

They rolled over him like a wave, and his Nazi helmet flew off and skidded to a rocking halt . . . at the feet of Police Constable Charlie Bennett, Athelsford's custodian of the law, where he stood framed in the door of the tiny foyer.

Then the normal lights came up and someone cut the strobes, and as the weirdly breathless place slowly came back to life, so PC Bennett was able to take charge. And for the moment no one, not even Gavin, noticed that Eileen McGovern and her new friend were nowhere to be seen . . .

Five

Chylos was jubilant. *'It's done!'* he cried in his grave. *'The invaders defeated, beaten back!'*

And: *'You were right, old man,'* finally Hengit grudgingly answered. *'They were invaders, and our warnings and urgings came just in time. But this tribe of yours – pah! Like flowers, they were, weak and waiting to be crushed – until we inspired them.'*

And now Chylos was very angry indeed. *'You two!'* he snapped like a bowstring. *'If you had heeded me at the rites, these many generations flown, then were there no requirement for our efforts this night! But . . . perhaps I may still undo your mischief, even now, and finally rest easy.'*

'That can't be, old man, and you know it,' this time Alaze spoke up. *'Would that we could put right that of which you accuse us; for if our blood still runs in these tribes, then it were only right and proper. But we cannot put it right. No, not even with all your magic. For what are we now but worm-fretted bones and dust? There's no magic can give us back our flesh . . .'*

'There is,' Chylos chuckled then. *'Oh, there is! The magic of this stone. No, not your flesh but your will. No, not your limbs but your lust. Neither your youth nor your beauty nor even your hot blood, but your spirit! Which is all you will need to do what must be done. For if the tribes may not be imbrued with your seed, strengthened by your blood – then it must be with your spirit. I may not do it for I was old even in those days, but it*

is still possible for you. If I will it – and if you will it.
   'Now listen, and I shall tell you what must be done . . .'

Eileen McGovern and 'Gordon Cleary' stood outside The
Barn in the deepening dusk and watched the Black Maria
come and take away the battered Angels. As the police
van made off down the estate's main street Eileen leaned
towards the entrance to the disco, but her companion
seemed concerned for her and caught her arm. 'Better
let it cool down in there,' he said. 'There's bound to be
a lot of hot blood still on the boil.'

'Maybe you're right,' Eileen looked up at him. 'Certainly you were right to bundle us out of there when it
started! So what do you suggest? We could go and cool
off in The Old Stage. My father owns it.'

He shrugged, smiled, seemed suddenly shy, a little awkward. 'I'd rather hoped we could walk together,' he said.
'The heat of the day is off now – it's cool enough out
here. Also, I'll have to be going in an hour or so. I'd
hoped to be able to, well, talk to you in private. Pubs
and dance halls are fine for meeting people, but they're
dreadfully noisy places, too.'

It was her turn to shrug. It would be worth it if only
to defy Gavin. And afterwards she'd make him see how
there was no harm in her friendships. 'All right,' she said,
taking Cleary's arm. 'Where shall we walk?'

He looked at her and sighed his defeat. 'Eileen, I don't
know this place at all. I wouldn't know one street or lane
from the next. So I suppose I'm at your mercy!'

'Well,' she laughed. 'I do know a pretty private place.'
And she led him away from The Barn and into an avenue
of trees. 'It's not far away, and it's *the* most private place of
all.' She smiled as once more she glanced up at him in
the flooding moonlight. 'That's why it's called Lovers'
Lane . . .'

* * *

Half an hour later in The Barn, it finally dawned on Gavin McGovern that his sister was absent. He'd last seen her with that Gordon Cleary bloke. And what had Cleary said: something about having to drive later? Maybe he'd taken Eileen with him. They must have left during the ruckus with the Angels. Well, at least Gavin could be thankful for that!

But at eleven o'clock when The Barn closed and he had the job of checking and then shifting the stock, still she wasn't back. Or if she was she'd gone straight home to The Old Stage and so to bed. Just before twelve midnight Gavin was finished with his work. He gratefully put out the lights and locked up The Barn, then crossed to The Old Stage where his father was still checking the night's take and balancing the stock ledger.

First things first, Gavin quietly climbed the stairs and peeped into Eileen's room; the bed was still made up, undisturbed from this morning; she wasn't back. Feeling his heart speeding up a little, Gavin went back downstairs and reported her absence to his father.

Burly Joe McGovern seemed scarcely concerned. 'What?' he said, squinting up from his books. 'Eileen? Out with a young man? For a drive? So what's your concern? Come on now, Gavin! I mean, she's hardly a child!'

Gavin clenched his jaws stubbornly as his father returned to his work, went through into the large private kitchen and dining room and flopped into a chair. Very well, then he would wait up for her himself. And if he heard that bloke's car bringing her back home, well he'd have a few words to say to him, too.

It was a quarter after twelve when Gavin settled himself down to wait upon Eileen's return; but his day had been long and hard, and something in the hot summer air had sapped his usually abundant energy. The evening's excitement, maybe. By the time his father went up to bed Gavin was fast asleep and locked in troubled dreams . . .

* * *

Quite some time earlier:

. . . In the warm summer nights, Lovers' Lane wasn't
meant for fast-walking. It was only a mile and a half
long, but almost three-quarters of an hour had gone by
since Eileen and her new young man had left The Barn
and started along its winding ways. Lovers' Lane: no, it
wasn't the sort of walk you took at the trot. It was a
holding-hands, swinging-arms-together, soft-talking walk;
a kissing walk, in those places where the hedges were
silvered by moonlight and lips softened by it. And it seemed
strange to Eileen that her escort hadn't tried to kiss her, not
once along the way . . .

But he had been full of talk: not about himself but
mainly the night – how much he loved the darkness, its
soft velvet, which he claimed he could feel against his skin,
the *aliveness* of night – and about the moon: the secrets
it knew but couldn't tell. Not terribly scary stuff but . . .
strange stuff. Maybe too strange. And so, whenever she
had the chance, Eileen had tried to change the subject, to
talk about herself. But oddly, he hadn't seemed especially
interested in her.

'Oh, there'll be plenty of time to talk about personalities
later,' he'd told her, and she'd noticed how his voice was
no longer soft but . . . somehow coarse? And she'd shivered
and thought: *time later? Well of course there will be . . .
won't there?*

And suddenly she'd been aware of the empty fields and
copses opening on all sides, time fleeting by, the fact that
she was out here, in Lovers' Lane, with . . . a total stranger?
What was this urgency in him, she wondered? She could
feel it now in the way his hand held hers almost in a
vice, the coarse, jerky tension of his breathing, the way
his eyes scanned the moonlit darkness ahead and to left
and right, looking for . . . what?

'Well,' she finally said, trying to lighten her tone as much as she possibly could, digging her heels in a little and drawing him to a halt, 'that's it – all of it – Lovers' Lane. From here on it goes nowhere, just open fields all the way to where they're digging the new road. And anyway it's time we were getting back. You said you only had an hour.'

He held her hand more tightly yet, and his eyes were silver in the night. He took something out of his pocket and she heard a click, and the something gleamed a little in his dark hand. 'Ah, but that was then and this is now,' Garry Clemens told her, and she snatched her breath and her mouth fell open as she saw his awful smile. And then, while her mouth was still open, suddenly he *did* kiss her – and it was a brutal kiss and very terrible. And now Eileen knew.

As if reading her mind, he throatily said: 'But if you're good and do *exactly* as you're told – then you'll live through it.' And as she filled her lungs to scream, he quickly lifted his knife to her throat, and in his now choking voice whispered, 'But if you're *not* good then I'll hurt you very, very much and you won't live through it. And one way or the other it will make no difference: I shall have you anyway, for you're my girl-Friday!'

'Gordon, I—' she finally breathed, her eyes wide in the dark, heart hammering, breasts rising and falling unevenly beneath her thin summer dress. And trying again: 'Tell me this is just some sort of game, that you're only trying to frighten me and don't mean any . . . of . . . it.' But she knew only too well that he did.

Her voice had been gradually rising, growing shrill, so that now he warningly hissed: 'Be *quiet*!' And he backed her up to a stile in the fence, pressing with his knife until she was aware of it delving the soft skin of her throat. Then, very casually, he cut her thin summer dress down the front to her waist and flicked back the two halves with the point of his knife. Her free hand fluttered like a trapped bird, to match the palpitations of her heart, but she didn't dare do anything with it. And holding that sharp blade to her left breast, he said:

'Now we're going across this stile and behind the hedge, and then I'll tell you all you're to do and how best to please me. And that's important, for if you *don't* please me – well, then it will be good night, Eileen, Eileen!'

'Oh, God! *Oh, God!*' she whispered, as he forced her over the fence and behind the tall hedge. And:

'Here!' he said. 'Here!'

And from the darkness just to one side of him, another voice, not Eileen's, answered, *'Yes, here! Here!'* But it was *such* a voice . . .

'What . . . ?' Garry Clemens gulped, his hot blood suddenly ice. 'Who . . . ?' He released Eileen's hand and whirled, scything with his knife – scything nothing! – only the dark, which now seemed to close in on him. But:

'Here,' said that husky, hungry, lusting voice again, and now Clemens saw that indeed there was a figure in the dark. A naked female figure, voluptuous and inviting. And, *'Here!'* she murmured yet again, her voice a promise of pleasures undreamed, drawing him down with her to the soft grass.

Out of the corner of his eye, dimly in his confused mind, the rapist saw a figure – fleeting, tripping, and staggering upright, fleeing – which he knew was Eileen McGovern where she fled wildly across the field. But he let her go. For he'd found a new and more wonderful, more exciting girl-Friday now. 'Who . . . who *are* you?' he husked as he tore at his clothes – astonished that she tore at them, too.

And: *'Alaze,'* she told him, simply. *'Alaze . . .'*

Eileen – running, crashing through a low thicket, flying under the moon – wanted to scream but had no wind for it. And in the end was too frightened to scream anyway. For she knew that someone ran with her, alongside her;

a lithe, naked someone, who for the moment held off from whatever was his purpose.

But for how long?

The rattle of a crate deposited on the doorstep of The Old Stage woke Gavin McGovern up from unremembered dreams, but dreams which nevertheless left him red-eyed and rumbling inside like a volcano. Angry dreams! He woke to a new day, and in a way to a new world. He went to the door and it was dawn; the sun was balanced on the eastern horizon, reaching for the sky; Dave Gorman, the local milkman, was delivering.

'Wait,' Gavin told him, and ran upstairs. A moment later and he was down again. 'Eileen's not back,' he said. 'She was at the dance last night, went off with some bloke, an outsider. He hasn't brought her back. Tell them.'

Gorman looked at him, almost said: *tell who?* But not quite. He knew who to tell. The Athelsford tribe.

Gavin spied the postman, George Lee, coming along the road on his early morning rounds. He gave him the same message: his sister, Eileen, a girl of the tribe, had been abducted. She was out there somewhere now, stolen away, perhaps hurt. And by the time Gavin had thrown water in his face and roused his father, the message was already being spread abroad. People were coming out of their doors, moving into the countryside around, starting to search. The tribe looked after its own . . .

And beneath the luststone:

Alaze was back, but Hengit had not returned. It was past dawn and Chylos could feel the sun warming their mighty headstone, and he wondered what had passed in the night: was his work now done and could he rest?

'*How went it?*' the old wizard inquired immediately, as Alaze settled back into her bones.

'*It went . . . well. To a point,*' she eventually answered.

'*A point? What point?*' He was alarmed. '*What went wrong? Did you not follow my instructions?*'

'*Yes,*' she sighed, '*but—*'

'*But?*' And now it was Chylos's turn to sigh. '*Out with it.*'

'*I found one who was lusty. Indeed he was with a maid, which but for my intervention he would take against her will! Ah, but when he saw me he lusted after her no longer! And I heeded your instructions and put on my previous female form for him. According to those same instructions, I would teach him the true passions and furies and ecstasies of the flesh; so that afterwards and when he was with women of the tribe, he would be untiring, a satyr, and they would always bring forth from his potent seed. But because I was their inspiration, my spirit would be in all of them! This was why I put on flesh; and it was a great magic, a gigantic effort of will. Except . . . it had been a long, long time, Chylos. And in the heat of the moment I relaxed my will; no, he relaxed it for me, such was his passion. And . . . he saw me as I was, as I am . . .*'

'*Ah!*' said Chylos, understanding what she told him. '*And afterwards? Did you not try again? Were there no others?*'

'*There might have been others, aye – but as I journeyed out from this stone, the greater the distance the less obedient my will. Until I could no longer call flesh unto myself. And now, weary, I am returned.*'

Chylos sagged down into the alveolate, crumbling relics of himself. '*Then Hengit is my last hope,*' he said.

At which moment Hengit returned – but hangdog, as Chylos at once observed. And: '*Tell me the worst,*' the old man groaned.

But Hengit was unrepentant. '*I did as you instructed,*' he commenced his story, '*went forth, found a woman, put on flesh. And she was of the tribe, I'm sure. Alas, she was a child in the ways of men, a virgin, an innocent. You had said: let her be lusty, willing – but she was not. Indeed, she was afraid.'*

Chylos could scarce believe it. *'But – were there no others?'*

'Possibly,' Hengit answered. *'But this was a girl of the tribe, lost and afraid and vulnerable. I stood close by and watched over her, until the dawn . . .'*

'Then that is the very end of it,' Chylos sighed, beaten at last. And his words were truer than even he might suspect.

But still, for the moment, the luststone exerted its immemorial influence . . .

Of all the people of Athelsford who were out searching in the fields and woods that morning, it was Gavin McGovern who found the rapist Clemens huddled beneath the hedgerow. He heard his sobbing, climbed the stile, and found him there. And in the long grass close by, he also found his knife still damp with dew. And looking at Clemens the way he was, Gavin fully believed that he had lost Eileen forever.

He cried hot, unashamed tears then, looked up at the blue skies she would never see again, and blamed himself. *My fault – my fault! If I'd not been the way I was, she wouldn't have needed to defy me!*

But then he looked again at Clemens, and his surging blood surged more yet. And as Clemens had lusted after Eileen, so now Gavin lusted after him – after his life!

He dragged him out from hiding, bunched his white hair in a hamlike hand, and stretched his neck taut across his knee. Then – three things, occurring almost simultaneously.

One: a terrific explosion from across the fields, where John Sykes had kept his word and reduced the luststone to so much rubble. Two: the bloodlust went out of Gavin like a light switched off, so that he gasped, released his victim, and thrust him away. And three, he heard the voice of his father, echoing from the near-distance and carrying far and wide in the brightening air:

'Gavin, we've found her! She's unharmed! She's all right!'

PC Bennett, coming across the field, his uniformed legs damp from the dewy grass, saw the knife in Gavin's hand and said, 'I'll take that, son.' And having taken it he also went to take charge of the gibbering, worthless, soul-shrivelled maniac thing that was Garry Clemens.

And so in a way old Chylos was right, for in the end nothing had come of all his works. But in several other ways he was quite wrong . . .

MOTHER LOVE

In Dagon's Bell & Other Discords, *I did something that every horror, SF, and fantasy writer does (or used to do, but I've been around for some time now!) at least once in his writing career: an aftermath story. I've always thought this sort of story has to be short, sharp, punchy. And that's the way I've done them. The story in* Dagon's Bell *was called* In the Glow-Zone, *and this one is called* Mother Love. *But there are mothers and there are mothers. And as any American will tell you, sometimes there are* real *mothers!*

With a high-pitched whine the bullet took a long groove out of the rock wall to his right, showering him with sharp splinters. He flung himself awkwardly to the ground, feeling a splash of blood on his face where one of the hot, flying fragments had caught him. Simultaneous with the second crack of the rifle, another bullet kicked up dirt in his eyes with a buzz and a thud as it buried itself in the ground a few inches in front of his nose. He waited for a few seconds, blood pounding, before peering cautiously from his prone position along the narrow rock passage to where the girl stood – tattered denims moulding the fine shape of her wide-spread legs – squinting down the sights of her weapon . . . sights which were centered squarely on him!

'Lady, if you're planning to scare me, you've done it already. If you're trying to kill me, aim a little more carefully – I hate the thought of bleeding to death . . . ' His voice carried to her, a hoarse, panting shout as she began to squeeze the trigger for the third shot. She eased her finger slowly out of the triggerguard to leave it lying there, a thought's distance from sudden death.

'What are you after?' The way she said it – menacing, low so he could hardly hear – it was more than a question; it was a warning, and he knew he would have to answer carefully. Only sixty feet separated them and there was nowhere he could run. If she was any good at all with that rifle she could put a neat hole right through his head before he made five yards.

'Lady, I seen your fire-smoke earlier in the day, and I smelled your cooking a mile off. Smelled pretty good to a man who hasn't ate in three days – and when I did last eat it was a rat I was lucky enough to catch!' His panting came a little easier now. 'But lady, if you want me to move on . . . you just say the word and I'll be on my way. I'd be plenty obliged, though, if you'd allow me a bite to eat first.'

'Get up,' she ordered. As he climbed to his feet she stared at the stump where his right arm should have been. 'You can't be a mutant – you're too old for that.'

He walked slowly, carefully up the defile, dusting himself off as he went towards the girl who was outlined, now, against the evening greens and browns of the small valley behind her. She had a nice set-up here, and she was alone – otherwise she wouldn't be toting that rifle herself. As he drew closer to her he saw the cave on the other side of the valley. Could hardly be more than a hundred yards across, that valley; more a saddle between the hills. Corn patch growing nicely . . . mutant strawberries . . . rabbits. She had real good legs . . .

She saw where he was looking.

'Hold it right there.' He came to a halt not ten feet away from her. 'I asked you a question!' She swung the rifle to point it significantly at his middle.

'Mutant? No, industrial accident, that's all – long before the war,' he answered. 'But I've been given the mutant treatment ever since. So has every cripple! Been kicked out of every town I ever went near for almost four years. It's no fun, lady – 'specially now they're burnin' mutants! Look, if you've any decency at all, you'll give me just a bite of what you've got cooking over there, and then I'll be on my way.'

She thought about it, began to shake her head negatively,

then changed her mind: 'You're . . . welcome – but I'll warn you now, there's three unmarked graves in the corner of this valley. You try anything . . . I'll have no more corners left.' She waved him past with the gun, taking a good look at him as he went. He was about thirty-five, forty perhaps. He'd probably put on age fast after the war. Feeling her eyes on his stump, he glanced back over his shoulder.

'Armless, I be,' he said in wry humour, gratified to see her relax a little. Then: 'How come you're up here on your own? You've been here some years by the look of the place.'

'I lived in the town on the coast back there, where the walls shine at night,' she gestured vaguely behind her. 'That place at the foot of the hills, just a heap of rubble now, you must have come through it to get up here. I was only eighteen then . . . when the war came. One of the first bombs landed in the sea, threw radioactive water all over the town. When my baby was born he was – different. The radiation . . .' She faltered, lost for words. '. . . My husband died quickly. What few people lived through it wanted to have my baby put . . . they wanted to kill him. Said it would be better for him. Said it would be better for both of us. I ran off. I stole the rifle, shells, some seeds and one or two other odds and ends. Been here ever since. I get along fine . . .'

'You still got the mu—?' He knew it was a mistake before the words were out. The air seemed to go hard.

'Mister,' she poked the barrel of the gun viciously between his shoulder-blades, 'if you're a mutant-hunter you're as good as dead!' He staggered from the pressure of the rifle in his back, turning to face her, going suddenly white as he saw her finger tightening on the trigger.

'No . . . ! No, just curious. Christ, I've been hunted myself – and it's obvious I couldn't be a mutant! What, me? A mutant-hunter! Why? – some places there's a bounty,

sure – but out here in the middle of nowhere? I mean . . .
do I look like a bounty hunter . . . ?' He was pathetic.

She relaxed again. 'My baby . . . he . . . he died! No
more questions.' It was an order.

They had crossed the valley and the sun was starting
to sink behind the hills. He peered eagerly into the pot
hanging over the fire. The cave was a dark blot behind
the glowing embers, with a homemade candle flickering at
its back.

This was sure a good thing she'd got, he mused to
himself, licking his lips.

She motioned with the rifle, indicating he should help
himself from the pot. He took up a battered tin plate and
heaped it with the thick, bubbling stew before dropping
the heavy iron spoon back into the pot. Juicy rabbit bones
protruded from the meat in the mess of stew on his plate.
Without another word he started eating. It was good.

As he ate he looked the girl over. She had a good face
to match her figure. He could hardly keep from staring
at the way her shirt swelled outwards with the pressure
of the firm breasts beneath it. And it was that above all
else – the way her shirt strained from her body – which
finally decided his course of action.

He licked his lips and reached casually for the spoon
again, crouching with the plate on his knees . . .

In a second he had straightened and the hot stuff was on
her neck. Before she even had time to yelp from the shock
he had brought her a savage, whip-lash, back-hand blow
across the face with the swing of a powerfully muscled left
arm. As she spun sideways he nimbly grabbed the falling
rifle out of midair and turned it on her. She started to
scramble to her feet, a red welt already blossoming on her
face.

'Stay put!' He held the rifle loosely in his hand, confi-
dent finger on the trigger, daring her to make a false move.

'I'll shoot you in the legs,' he said, grinning wolfishly, 'so's not to spoil you completely. You wouldn't want to be spoiled completely, now would you?'

She cringed away from him on the ground. 'You wouldn't . . . you—'

'Get up!' he snarled, the grin sliding from his face.

As she made to get to her feet he tossed the rifle behind him and slammed another roundly swinging blow to her face. She lurched backwards, falling, and before she could recover he stepped over her, planting his feet firmly, tearing the shirt from her supple body. 'Thing was ready to bust anyway . . .'

He licked his lips again as she screamed and tried to cover herself. 'Shirt sure didn't tell no lie . . .'

He grabbed her left wrist, twisting her arm up behind her back, forcing her to her feet.

'Sweetheart, your feeding's good – now let's see what your loving's like; the Good Lord knows you've waited a long time!'

'Don't . . . ! Don't do it. I fed you, I . . .'

'More fool you, sweetheart,' he rasped, cutting her off, 'but you may's well get used to me; I'm going to be here quite some time. You need a man about the place.'

He pushed her into the cave, noting that the candle at the rear stood beside a heavy black blanket, stretched luxuriously in a hollow on the floor.

The shadows moved in the dimness of the cave as he shoved her towards the sputtering candle. A few feet from the rear wall of rock she twisted under her own arm and pulled away from him. He laughed at the way her body moved as she tried to free herself. 'No good getting all hot and bothered now, sweetheart – not with the bed all laid out for us . . .'

'It's not a bed!' she screamed, jerking her arm back in desperate resistance. The sweat of anticipation on his straining fingers let him down. Her hand suddenly slipped through his and he crashed backwards, off balance, onto the 'bed.'

There was instant, horrible movement beneath him.

'No . . . !' the girl screamed. 'No! That's not stew, Baby, it's a man!'

But Baby, who had no ears, took no notice.

The edges of the 'bed' rose up in thickly glistening, black doughy flaps – like an inky, folding pancake – and flopped purposefully over the struggling man upon it. Subtly altered digestive juices squirted into his face and muscular hardness gripped him. He gave a shriek – just one – as the living envelope around him started to squeeze.

Hours later, when dawn was spreading like a pale stain over the horizon between the hills, the girl was still crying. Baby had taken a long time over his meal. He burped, ejecting the last bone and a few odd buttons. There wasn't even a back she could pat him on.

That day there was a new grave in the little valley in the hills. A very small one . . .

WHAT DARK GOD?

If my memory serves me well, this next one was intended for August Derleth's Arkham Collector, *a sort of house journal in which he advertised forthcoming Arkham House books. But it was still unpublished when he died in 1971 and was eventually used by editor and writer Jerry Page in a grab-bag of a book called* Nameless Places. What Dark God? *was my twelfth short story in the first six months of my writing career. I used to write 'em fast in those days. Incidentally, the esoteric references and paraphernalia of Black Magic are all genuine. Only the timetables have been changed to protect British Rail!*

> '... *Summanus* – whatever power he may be ...'
>
> Ovid's *Fasti*

The Tuscan Rituals? Now where had I heard of such a book or books before? Certainly very rare ... Copy in the British Museum? Perhaps! Then what on earth were *these* fellows doing with a copy? And such a strange bunch of blokes at that.

Only a few minutes earlier I had boarded the train at Bengham. It was quite crowded for a night train and the boozy, garrulous, and vociferous 'Jock' who had boarded it directly in front of me had been much upset by the fact that all the compartments seemed to be fully occupied.

'Och, they bleddy British trains,' he had drunkenly grumbled, 'either a'wiz emp'y or a'wiz fool. No orgynization whatsayever – ye no agree, ye sassenach?' He had elbowed me in the ribs as we swayed together down the dim corridor.

'Er, yes,' I had answered. 'Quite so!'

Neither of us carried cases and as we stumbled along, searching for vacant seats in the gloomy compartments, Jock suddenly stopped short.

'Noo what in hell's this – will ye look here? A compartment wi' the bleddy blinds doon. Prob'ly a young laddie an' lassie in there wi' six emp'y seats. Privacy be damned. Ah'm no standin' oot here while there's a seat in there . . .'

The door had proved to be locked – on the inside – but that had not deterred the 'bonnie Scot' for a moment. He had banged insistently upon the wooden frame of the door until it was carefully, tentatively opened a few inches; then he had stuck his foot in the gap and put his shoulder to the frame, forcing the door fully open.

'No, no . . .' The scrawny, pale, pin-stripe jacketed man who stood blocking the entrance protested. 'You can't come in – this compartment is reserved . . .'

'Is that so, noo? Well, if ye'll kindly show me the reserved notice,' Jock had paused to tap significantly upon the naked glass of the door with a belligerent fingernail, 'Ah'll bother ye no more – meanwhile, though, if ye'll hold ye're blether, *Ah'd appreciate a bleddy seat . . .*'

'No, no . . .' The scrawny man had started to protest again, only to be quickly cut off by a terse command from behind him:

'Let them in . . .'

I shook my head and pinched my nose, blowing heavily and puffing out my cheeks to clear my ears. For the voice from within the dimly-lit compartment had sounded hollow, unnatural. Possibly the train had started to pass through a tunnel, an occurrence which never fails to give me trouble with my ears. I glanced out of the exterior corridor window and saw immediately that I was wrong; far off on the dark horizon I could see the red glare of coke-oven fires. Anyway, whatever the effect had been which had given that voice its momentarily peculiar – resonance? – it had obviously passed, for Jock's voice sounded perfectly normal as he said: 'Noo tha's *better*; excuse a body, will ye?' He shouldered the dubious looking man in the doorway to one side and slid clumsily into a seat alongside a second stranger. As I joined them in the compartment, sliding the door shut behind me, I saw that there were four strangers in all; six people including Jock and myself, we just made comfortable use of the eight seats which faced inwards in two sets of four.

I have always been a comparatively shy person so it was only the vaguest of perfunctory glances which I gave to each of the three new faces before I settled back and took out the pocket-book I had picked up earlier in the day in London. Those merest of glances, however, were quite sufficient to put me off my book and to tell me that the three friends of the pin-stripe jacketed man appeared the very strangest of travelling companions – especially the extremely tall and thin member of the three, sitting stiffly in his seat beside Jock. The other two answered to approximately the same description as Pin-Stripe – as I was beginning mentally to tag him – except that one of them wore a thin moustache; but that fourth one, the tall one, was something else again.

Within the brief duration of the glance I had given him I had seen that, remarkable though the rest of his features were, his mouth appeared decidedly odd – almost as if it had been painted onto his face – the merest thin red line, without a trace of puckering or any other depression to show that there was a hole there at all. His ears were thick and blunt and his eyebrows were bushy over the most penetrating eyes it has ever been my unhappy lot to find staring at me. Possibly that was the reason I had glanced so quickly away; the fact that when I had looked at him I had found *him* staring at *me* – and his face had been totally devoid of any expression whatsoever. *Fairies?* The nasty thought had flashed through my mind unbidden; none the less, that would explain why the door had been locked.

Suddenly Pin-Stripe – seated next to me and directly opposite Funny-Mouth – gave a start, and, as I glanced up from my book, I saw that the two of them were staring directly into each other's eyes.

'Tell them . . .' Funny-Mouth said, though I was sure his strange lips had not moved a fraction, and again his voice had seemed distorted, as though his words passed through weirdly angled corridors before reaching my ears.

'It's, er – almost midnight,' informed Pin-Stripe, grinning sickly first at Jock and then at me.

'Aye,' said Jock sarcastically, 'happens every nicht aboot this time . . . Ye're very observant . . .'

'Yes,' said Pin-Stripe, choosing to ignore the jibe, 'as you say – but the point I wish to make is that we three, er, that is, we *four*,' he corrected himself, indicating his companions with a nod of his head, 'are members of a little-known, er, religious sect. We have a ceremony to perform and would appreciate it if you two gentlemen would remain quiet during the proceedings . . .' I heard him out and nodded my head in understanding and agreement – I am a tolerant person – but Jock was of a different mind.

'Sect?' he said sharply. 'Ceremony?' He shook his head in disgust. 'Well; Ah'm a member o' the Church O' Scotland and Ah'll tell ye noo – Ah'll hae no truck wi' bleddy heathen *ceremonies* . . .'

Funny-Mouth had been sitting ram-rod straight, saying not a word, doing nothing, but now he turned to look at Jock, his eyes narrowing to mere slits; above them, his eyebrows meeting in a black frown of disapproval.

'Er, perhaps it would be better,' said Pin-Stripe hastily, leaning across the narrow aisle towards Funny-Mouth as he noticed the change in that person's attitude, 'if they, er, *went to sleep* . . . ?'

This preposterous statement or question, which caused Jock to peer at its author in blank amazement and me to wonder what on earth he was babbling about, was directed at Funny-Mouth who, without taking his eyes off Jock's outraged face, nodded in agreement.

I do not know what happened then – it was as if I had been suddenly *unplugged* – I was asleep, yet not asleep – in a trance-like condition full of strange impressions and mind-pictures – abounding in unpleasant and realistic sensations, with dimly-recollected snatches of previously absorbed information floating up to the surface of my conscious mind, correlating themselves with the strange people in the railway compartment with me ...

And in that dream-like state my brain was still very active; possibly *fully* active. All my senses were still working; I could hear the clatter of the wheels and smell the acrid tang of burnt tobacco from the compartment's ash-trays. I saw Moustache produce a folding table from the rack above his head – saw him open it and set it up in the aisle, between Funny-Mouth and himself on their side and Pin-Stripe and his companion on my side – saw the designs upon it, designs suggestive of the more exotic work of Chandler Davies, and wondered at their purpose. My head must have fallen back, until it rested in the corner of the gently rocking compartment, for I saw all these things without having to move my eyes; indeed, I doubt very much if I *could* have moved my eyes and do not remember making any attempt to do so.

I saw that book – a queerly bound volume bearing its title, *The Tuscan Rituals*, in archaic, burnt-in lettering on its thick spine – produced by Pin-Stripe and opened reverently to lie on that ritualistic table, displayed so that all but Funny-Mouth, Jock, and I could make out its characters. But Funny-Mouth did not seem in the least bit interested in the proceedings. He gave me the impression that he had seen it all before, many times ...

Knowing I was dreaming – or was I? – I pondered that title, *The Tuscan Rituals*. Now where had I heard of such a book or books before? The *feel* of it echoed back into my subconscious, telling me I recognized that title – but in what connection?

I could see Jock, too, on the fixed border of my sphere of vision, lying with his head lolling towards Funny-Mouth – in a trance similar to my own, I imagined – eyes staring at the drawn blinds on the compartment windows. I saw the lips of Pin-Stripe, out of the corner of my right eye, and those of Moustache, moving in almost perfect rhythm and imagined those of Other – as I had named the fourth who was completely out of my periphery of vision – doing the same, and heard the low and intricate liturgy which they were chanting in unison.

Liturgy? Tuscan Rituals? Now what dark 'God' was this they worshipped? . . . And what had made *that* thought spring to my dreaming or hypnotized mind? And what was Moustache doing now?

He had a bag and was taking things from it, laying them delicately on the ceremonial table. Three items in all; in one corner of the table, that nearest Funny-Mouth. Round cakes of wheat-bread in the shape of wheels with ribbed spokes. Now who had written about offerings of round cakes of— . . . ?

Festus? Yes, *Festus* – but, again, in what connection?

Then I heard it. A *name*: chanted by the three worshippers, but not by Funny-Mouth who still sat aloofly upright. 'Summanus, Summanus, Summanus . . .' They chanted; and suddenly, it all clicked into place.

Summanus! Of whom Martianus Capella had written as being The Lord of Hell . . . I remembered now. It was Pliny who, in his *Natural History*, mentioned the dreaded *Tuscan Rituals*, 'books containing the Liturgy of Summanus . . .' Of course; Summanus – Monarch of Night – The Terror that Walketh in Darkness; Summanus, whose worshippers were so few and whose cult was surrounded with such mystery, fear, and secrecy that according to St Augustine even the most curious enquirer could discover no particular of it.

So Funny-Mouth, who stood so aloof to the ceremony in which the others were participating, must be a priest of the cult.

Though my eyes were fixed – my centre of vision being a picture, one of three, on the compartment wall just above Moustache's head – I could still clearly see Funny-Mouth's face and, as a blur to the left of my periphery, that of Jock. The liturgy had come to an end with the calling of the 'God's' name and the offering of bread. For the first time Funny-Mouth seemed to be taking an interest. He turned his head to look at the table and just as I was certain that he was going to reach out and take the breadcakes the train lurched and Jock slid sideways in his seat, his face coming into clearer perspective as it came to rest about half-way down Funny-Mouth's upper right arm. Funny-Mouth's head snapped round in a blur of hate. *Hate*, livid and pure, shone from those cold eyes, was reflected by the bristling eyebrows and tightening features; only the strange, painted-on mouth remained sterile of emotion. But he made no effort to move Jock's head.

It was not until later that I found out what happened then. Mercifully my eyes could not take in the whole of the compartment – or what was happening in it. I only knew that Jock's face, little more than an outline with darker, shaded areas defining the eyes, nose, and mouth at the lower rim of my fixed 'picture,' became suddenly contorted; twisted somehow, as though by some great emotion or pain. He said nothing, unable to break out of that damnable trance, but his eyes bulged horribly and his features writhed. If only I could have taken my eyes off him, or closed them even, to shut out the picture of his face writhing and Funny-Mouth staring at him so terribly.

Then I noticed the change in Funny-Mouth. He had been a chalky-grey colour before; we all had, in the weak glow from the alternatively brightening and dimming compartment ceiling light. Now he seemed to be *flushed*; pinkish waves of unnatural colour were suffusing his outré features and his red-slit mouth was fading into the deepening blush of his face. It almost looked as though . . . *My God! He did not have a mouth.* With that unnatural reddening of his features the painted slit had vanished completely; his face was *blank* beneath the eyes and nose.

What a God-awful dream. I knew it must be a dream now – it *had* to be a dream – such things do not happen in real life. Dimly I was aware of Moustache putting the bread-cakes away and folding the queer table. I could feel the rhythm of the train slowing down. We must be coming into Grenloe. Jock's face was absolutely convulsed now. A white, twitching, jerking, bulge-eyed blur of hideous motion which grew paler as quickly as that of Funny-Mouth – if that name applied now – reddened. Suddenly Jock's face stopped its jerking. His mouth lolled open and his eyes slowly closed. He slid out of my circle of vision towards the floor.

The train was moving much slower and the wheels were clacking over those groups of criss-crossing rails which always warn one that a train is approaching a station or depot. Funny-Mouth had turned his monstrous, nightmare face towards me. He leaned across the aisle, closing the distance between us. I mentally screamed, physically incapable of the act, and strained with every fibre of my being to break from the trance which I suddenly knew beyond any doubting *was not a dream and never had been* . . .

The train ground to a shuddering halt with a wheeze of steam and a squeal of brakes. Outside in the night the station-master was yelling instructions to a porter on the unseen platform. As the train stopped Funny-Mouth was jerked momentarily back, away from me, and before he could bring his face close to mine again Moustache was speaking to him.

'There's no time, Master – this is our stop . . .' Funny-Mouth hovered over me a moment longer, seemingly undecided, then he pulled away. The others filed past him out into the corridor while he stood, tall and eerie, just within the doorway. Then he lifted his right hand and snapped his fingers.

I could move. I blinked my eyes rapidly and shook myself, sitting up straight, feeling the pain of the cramp between my shoulder-blades. 'I say . . .' I began.

'*Quiet!*' ordered that echoing voice from unknown spaces – and of course, his painted, false mouth never moved. I was right; I had been hypnotized, not dreaming at all. That false mouth – Walker in Darkness – Monarch of Night – Lord of Hell – the Liturgy to Summanus . . .

I opened my mouth in amazement and horror, but before I could utter more than one word – '*Summanus . . .*' – something happened.

His waist-coat slid to one side near the bottom and a long, white, tapering tentacle with a blood-red tip slid into view. That tip hovered, snake-like, for a moment over my petrified face – and then struck. As if someone had taken a razor to it my face opened up and the blood began to gush. I fell to my knees in shock, too terrified even to yell out, automatically reaching for my handkerchief; and when next I coweringly looked up Funny-Mouth had gone.

Instead of seeing him – *It* – I found myself staring, from where I kneeled dabbing uselessly at my face, into the slack features of the sleeping Jock.

Sleeping?

I began to scream. Even as the train started to pull out of the station I was screaming. When no one answered my cries I managed to pull the communication-cord. Then, until they came to find out what was wrong, I went right on screaming. Not because of my face – *because of Jock* . . .

A jagged, bloody, two-inch hole led clean through his jacket and shirt and into his left side – the side which had been closest to . . . to that *thing – and there was not a drop of blood in his whole, limp body.* He simply lay there – half on, half off the seat – victim of 'a bleddy heathen ceremony' – substituted for the bread-cakes simply because the train had chosen an inopportune moment to lurch – a sacrifice to Summanus . . .

THE THIEF IMMORTAL

This next is a story about the most virulent vampire of all time. A mere glance, and . . . but please read on, for I'd hate to spoil it for you. Oh, and just to be topical, it's also a human tragedy and an ecological disaster story – on a grand scale! So if you thought the Gulf War was something . . .

Klaus August Scharme was born in a tiny village called Paradise close to Koln in the middle of the year 1940. The name of his birthplace has nothing to do with Scharme's story; the village was anything but paradisiacal, being a collection or huddle of farm buildings, some middling private dwellings and a grubby gasthaus, all reached along unmetalled roads which for at least four months of the year were little more than ruts around the perimeters of boggy fields.

Therefore, neither the date nor location of his origin was especially auspicious. The best we can say of them is that they were uninspired ... drab beginnings for a man whose longevity would make him a legend of godlike proportions, not only in his own lifetime but also in every one of the countless *millions* of lives which would come and be lived and go – often in unseemly haste – before Scharme himself was yet fifty years old.

But here the paradox: he achieved that age not as might be expected in 1990, but in the summer of 2097. And the following story includes the facts of how that came about.

Aged sixteen years and three months, Scharme left Paradise and became an apprentice signwriter. He took up lodgings in Koln at the house of his master, where for the next five years he learned how to paint those intricate

Kreise signs which signify with heraldic sigils the boundaries of the many and various districts of Germany. At that time such signs could be found on all major roads where they approached any specific district, and where for many years they had been the prey of avid 'art collectors' from England, France, the USA – the troops of NATO in general – energetically manœuvring and war-gaming across the long-since conquered German countryside. But this too is a mere detail and should not be allowed to detract . . . except that it also served as Scharme's launching point on his trajectory of four hundred years' duration.

It started as a dream: Scharme dreamed that he was growing old at an unprecedented rate. He aged a day for every hour, then a week for every minute, finally a year for every second, at which point he collapsed in upon himself, died, crumbled into dust and blew away.

He woke up screaming, and it was the morning of his twenty-first birthday. Perhaps the dream had come about through a subconscious awareness of his proximity to the age of manhood; perhaps it had dawned on him that the first part of his life was done, ended like a chapter closed. But that same day, as Scharme replaced a purloined sign upon its post, he saw speeding by him a military Land Rover . . . and reclining in the open back of the vehicle a good half-dozen of these very signs over which he laboured so long and hard! The driver of this vehicle, a young Corporal in British uniform, laughed and waved as he sped into the distance; Scharme, wide-eyed in anger where he gazed after him, thought: '*Damn you . . . you should age a year for every sign you've stolen!*'

At which he was horrified to see the Land Rover swerve violently from the road to strike a tree!

Leaping onto his bicycle, Scharme raced to the scene of the accident. The Corporal, alas, was dead; also, he was old; moreover (and as Scharme would later work it out), it was probably the instantaneous aging which had caused him to swerve – making Klaus August Scharme a murderer! And he knew it was so, for at the moment of his wish – that the Corporal should age commensurate with his thieving – he had felt *himself* the beneficiary of those years, some thirty-five in number. The Corporal had been twenty-five years of age; he was now sixty. Scharme had been twenty-one and still looked it, but some strange temporal instinct within told him that he would be fifty-six before he began to age again. Somehow – in some monstrous and inexplicable fashion – he had stolen all the young soldier's years!

And so for the next thirty-five years Scharme aged not at all but remained twenty-one; *but* – and most monstrously – in the twelve-month after that he aged altogether too many years, so that while by rights (?) he should only be twenty-two, his internal hourglass told him that in fact he had spilled the sands of ten whole years! It was the summer of 1997; K. A. Scharme had lived for fifty-seven years, should have aged by only twenty-two of them, and yet knew that physically he had aged *thirty*-two of them. In short, he knew that he was now getting old at ten times the normal rate, and that therefore he had started to pay the world back for the time he owed it. In just two and a half more years he'd be pushing sixty, and all the pleasures of an apparently eternal youth would be behind him and senility just around the corner. It was all grossly unfair and Scharme was very bitter about it.

So bitter, indeed, that the guilt he had felt over the past thirty-five years quite melted away. He determined to do something about his predicament, and of course it must be done quickly; when one is aging an entire year for every five weeks, time grows very short. But still Scharme was not a cruel man, and so chose his next victim (the very word left an unpleasant echo in his mind) with a deal of care and attention.

He chose, in fact, a crippled greypate who suffered incessant arthritic pains, stealing his last four years with the merest glance. The old man never knew what hit him but simply crumpled up in the street on his way to collect his pension. And Scharme was pleased that (a) the old boy would know no more pain, and (b) that the state was plainly a benefactor, likewise every taxpayer, and (c) that he himself, K. A. Scharme, would now live for a further four years at the constant age of only thirty-two and some few months. Which would surely be sufficient time to work out some sort of humane strategy.

Except ... no sooner had his mental meter clocked up the defunct dodderer's four years, than it inexplicably halved them, alloting Scharme only two! Alarmed, he returned home and collapsed before his TV, where at that very moment they were showing an interview with a prisoner on Death Row. It was reckoned that this one could stave off his execution by a maximum of only two years, and that only at great expense. Scharme decided to save him and the state both money and trouble, and snatched his two remaining years right through the screen! The prisoner died right there in full view of many millions (good riddance, the majority said) but Scharme only gasped as the stolen time registered within him at a mere fraction of the time perceived: namely, six months!

It didn't take much of a mathematician to work out the implications. Complete this sequence: If thirty-five equals thirty-five, and four equals two, and two equals one-half ...

Patently Scharme was only going to get one-eighth of his next victim's span of years; and after that one-sixteenth; then only one small thirty-second part, *und so weiter*. Which was precisely the way it was to work out.

But ... let's not leap ahead. Scharme now had two and a half years of other people's time in which to think about it and plan for his vastly extended future. Which, diligently, he now set about to do. Nor did it take him thirty months by any means but only one day. You'll see why if you apply yourself to his problem:

His seventh victim would yield only one sixty-fourth of his remaining span, his eighth perhaps four or five months ... *good God!* ... By the time the vampire Scharme had taken his tenth victim – and even were that tenth a newborn infant – he would only be gaining a matter of weeks! Twenty victims later and he'd be down to seconds! Then half-seconds, microseconds, nanoseconds! By which time, quite obviously, he'd have arrived at the point where he was taking multiples of lives, perhaps even entire races at a gulp. Was that his destiny, then: to be a mass murderer? To be guilty of invisible genocide? To be the man who murdered an entire planet just to save his own miserable life?

Well, miserable it might be, but it was the only one he had. And life was cheap, as he above all other men was only too well aware. And so now he must use his two and a half year advantage to its fullest, and work out the *real* way it was going to be.

Scharme's grandfather had once told him: 'It takes hard work to earn a sum of money, but after that all it takes is time. Money in the bank doubles every ten years or so. That's something you should remember, Klaus August Scharme . . .' And Scharme had remembered.

And so for now he lived as frugally as possible, saved every pfennig he could get his hands on, banked his wages and watched the interest grow month by month, year by year. And while his money was growing, so he experimented.

For instance: he knew he could steal the lives of men, but what about animals? Scharme had read somewhere that no man knows the true age of sharks; so little is known about them that their span of years is beyond our scope. And he'd also read that barring accidents or the intervention of man, a shark *might* live for as long as two or three hundred years! Likewise certain species of tortoise, lizard, crocodile. Testing out the sharks, crocs and such, Scharme gained himself a good many years. But at the same time he lost some, too. The problem was that he couldn't know in advance how long these creatures were destined to live! A hammerhead off the Great Barrier Reef earned him three whole years (miraculous!), but another, taken the same day, was worth only an hour or two. Obviously that one had been set to meet its fate anyway. As for crocodiles: he ensured that several of those would never make it to the handbag stage!

And so eventually, without for the moment doing any further damage (to the *human* race, anyway) Scharme clocked up one hundred years on his mental chronometer and was able to give it a rest. He was more or less happy now that he could take it easy for a full century and still come out the other end only thirty-two years and some few months old. But rich? Oh, be certain he'd come out rich!

Except . . . what then, he wondered? What if – in the summer of 2097 when he'd used up all his stolen time – what if he then began to age too fast again? And just how fast *would* he age? Would it be ten years for every ordinary year, as before – or a hundred – or . . . a thousand? Or would he simply wither and die before he even knew it, before he had time to steal any more life? Obviously he should not allow that to happen. But at least with an entire century to give it a deal of considered thought, he wasn't going to let the knowledge of it spoil what he already had. Or what he was going to have . . .

The spring of 2097 eventually came around, and Scharme was a multi-millionaire. Back in the Year 2000 he had had only 23,300 Deutsch Marks in his Koln bank; in 2010 it had been 75,000; in 2050 the sum was 3,000,100; and now he was worth close to one hundred millions. (Not in any bank in Koln, no, but in several numbered accounts in Switzerland.) And Scharme was still only thirty-two years old.

But as the spring of that year turned to summer the thief immortal was prepared and waiting, and he sat in his Hamburg mansion and listened to the clocks in his head and in his very atoms ticking off the seconds to his fate. And he knew he was taking a great chance but took it anyway, simply because *he had to know!*

And so the time narrowed down to zero and Scharme's internal time clock – the register of his years – recommenced the sweep which he had temporarily stilled back in 1997. And so horrified was Scharme, so petrified at what transpired, that he let the thing run for a full three seconds before he was able to do anything about it. And then, on the count of three and when he was capable again, he pointed a trembling but deadly finger at a picture of Japan in his Atlas and absorbed the lives of all its millions – yes, every one of them – at a stroke! *And saw that he had only clocked up five extra years!*

He killed off Indonesia for another ten before his panic subsided – and then took half the fish in the Mediterranean just to be absolutely sure. Then, when he saw that he'd clocked up thirty-eight and a half years, he was satisfied – for a brief moment. Until as an afterthought (perhaps on a point of simple economy or ecology), he also took half of the *fishermen* in the Med and so evened up the balance.

And he knew that he must *never* let time creep up on him again, because if he did then it were certainly the end. For during the span of those three monstrous, uncontrolled seconds Klaus August Scharme had aged almost a *half-billion* such units and was now fifty years old!

Ah, but he would never get any older . . . not until the very last second, anyway . . .

*   *   *

There had been no one left to bury the dead in the Japanese and Indonesian Islands; for fifty years they were pestholes; mercifully, being islands, their plagues were contained. That lesser ravage (men called it The Ravage) which had slain so many in and around the Mediterranean was guessed to have had the same origin as the Japan/Indonesian Plagues, but science had never tracked it to its source. It was generally assumed that Mother Nature had simply bridled at one of Man's nuclear, ecological or chemical indiscretions. No one ever had cause to relate the horror to the being of Klaus August Scharme. No, not even when his strange longevity finally became known.

That was the fault of his doctor; rather, it came about through that doctor's diligence. Scharme had gone through a phase of worrying about diseases. He had reasoned that if, in a normal lifetime, a man will suffer several afflictions of mind and body, how then a man with many lifetimes? What fatal cancers were blossoming in him even now? What tumours? What micro-biological mutations, even as he was a mutation, were killing him? And when he had submitted himself for the most minute examination, he'd also submitted his medical records . . .

The news broke: the world had taken unto its bosom, or created, what appeared to be an immortal! The Second Coming? It could be! A miracle to bring lasting peace and tranquillity? Possibly. And Klaus August Scharme became the most feted man in the history of the world. Churchmen, at first sceptical, eventually applauded; world leaders looked to him for his friendship and favours; wealth as great and even greater than his own billions was heaped at his feet.

And when the Maltese Plague struck in the Year 2163, Klaus August Scharme bought that island and sent in a million men to burn the bodies, cleanse the streets and build him his palace there. And still no one suspected that the Great Benefactor Scharme was in fact the Great Monster Scharme, a vampire thief drinking up the lives of men. But why should they?

Scharme gave work to the millions; he lavished billions of dollars, pounds, yen, lire, on charities across the face of the world; countless fortunes were spent in the search for the ultimate secret – that of eternal youth – which Scharme declared was fitting for all mankind and not just himself. He built hospitals, laboratories, schools, houses. He opened up the potential of the poorer countries; dug wells in the Sahara, repopulated ravaged islands (such as Japan, Indonesia), built dams and barriers to stem the floods in the Nile and Ganges; wiped out the locust (at a stroke, and without ever hinting at the miracle he employed); deliberately and systematically did all he could to provide the monies and the science requisite to prolonging the lives of men. Ah, of course he did! The longer men lived, the longer he would live. It was a question of careful culling, that was all . . .

In 2247 the whales died . . . but of no discernible disorder. Those largest of all Earth's creatures – protected, revered and preserved by man since the turn of the 21st Century – switched off like a light, wasted, erased to provide Scharme with life. And the thief immortal gaining only a moment or two from each huge, placid creature. Not all of them died; perhaps a dozen of each species were left to repopulate the oceans – naturally. Scharme was not an unreasonable man, and he was learning.

In the North Sea and the waters around England, across the Atlantic to the American coastline, there came the sudden and inexplicable decline of the cod; that was in 2287. But in the ensuing four years the rest of the food fishes surged and man did not go short. At the end of that period, in the spring of 2292, all the world's longest lived trees became firewood overnight. It was Nature, the Top Men said; it was Evolution, an ecological balancing act; it was the Survival of the Fittest. And in that last, at least, they were right; the survival of Klaus August Scharme.

But there were no more wars. World President Scharme in his impregnable Malta fortress, rearing two miles high from the sea, would not allow wars; they were destructive and cost him too many lives. Nor would he allow pollution or disease, and wherever possible he took all steps to avoid natural disasters. The world had become a very wonderful place in which to live – if one could live long enough and avoid those unpredictable places wherein an apparently outraged Nature was wont to strike so pitilessly and without warning.

Scharme had long ago discovered that it was not the number of lives he took which determined the ever-shortening half-life of his obscene talent but the number of times he used that talent. Whether he took the life of a single man or an entire species of toad made no difference: always the sum of the span of stolen time was halved. And by the year 2309 he was already well down into the micro-seconds. Patently it was wasteful – what? It was sheer madness! – to take single lives and he would never do that again; indeed he had not done so since the late 20th Century.

Towards the end of 2309 he took seven-eighths of all the world's corals and earned himself only nine weeks! And that same night, after worriedly pacing the floors of his incredible palace fortress Scharme eventually retired to dream his second inspirational dream. An inspiration, and a warning:

He saw a word: NECROMETER.

That single word above an instrument with one hundred little glass windows all in a row. Behind each window, on a black background, the same white digital number (or negative) gleamed like a long line of open mouths: one hundred '0's, a century of zeroes.

Scharme was in a dark room, seated at some sort of console. He was strapped into a sturdy metal chair-like frame, held upright and immobile as a man in an electric chair. Behind the NECROMETER a massive wall reached away out of sight both vertically and horizontally. The wall was made up of trillions of tiny lights no bigger than pinheads, each one like a minuscule firefly, lending the wall a soft haze of light.

Scharme looked at the word again: NECROMETER. And at the digital counter beneath it. Even as he watched, the number 1 clicked into place in the window on the far right, in the next moment became a 2, a 3, 4, 5 · · ·

The numbers began to flutter, reaching 1,000 in a moment, 10,000 in seconds. On the wall the tiny lights, singly, in small clusters, in masses, were blinking out, whole sections snuffing themselves before his eyes. On the NECROMETER the figure was into millions, tens of millions, billions; and a hideous fear, a soul-shrinking terror descended upon Scharme as he watched, strapped in his sturdy metal chair. If only he could break these straps he knew he could smash the counter, stop the lights from winking out, put an end to the wanton destruction of life, the death.

The death, yes. NECROMETER.

An instrument for measuring death!

But whose instrument? Obviously it belonged to Death himself. The entire – control room? – *was* Death!

Now the number on the counter was into the trillions, tens of trillions, hundreds of trillions, and entire sections of the wall were darkening like lights switched off in a skyscraper. In as little time as it takes to tell the quintillions were breached, the counter whirring and blurring and humming now in a mechanical frenzy of death-dealing activity. The wall was going out, Life itself was being extinguished.

Scharme struggled frantically, uselessly with his straps, straining against them, clawing at them with trapped, spastic hands. The counters were slowing down, the wall dimming, the NECROMETER had almost completed its task. The world – perhaps even the Universe – was almost empty of life.

Only two tiny lights remained on the dark wall: two faintly glowing pinheads. Close together, almost touching, they seemed to swell enormous in the eye of Scharme's mind, blooming into beacons that riveted his attention.

Two lights. He – his life – must be one of them. And the other?

The Conqueror Worm!

The Old Man!

The Grim Reaper!

The Nine of Spades!

The black lumpish machine bank atop the console above the NECROMETER split open like a hatching egg, its metal casing cracking and flaking away in chunks.

An eye, crimson with blood, stared out; a mouth, dripping the blood of nameless, numberless lives, smiled a monstrous smile, opening up into an awesome, gaping maw.

Scharme's straps snapped open. His chair tilted forward and flexed itself, ejecting him screaming down Death's endlessly echoing throat . . .

In the Year 2310 Scharme built the NECROMETER into a new wing of his massive Malta stronghold, and not a man of the thousands of technicians and scientists and builders who constructed it could ever have guessed at its purpose. Nor would they have thought of trying to do so. It was sufficient that the Immortal Man-god Master and Benefactor of the World Klaus August Scharme desired it, and so it was done. And Scharme's Computer of Life

– and more surely of Death – was fashioned almost exactly as his dream had prescribed.

Within its electrical memory were housed details of every known species of animal, insect and vegetable, the approximate spans of life of each, their locations upon a vast world globe which turned endlessly above the console. This last was lit from within, taking the place of the wall of lights; and this was Scharme's single improvement over his dream.

The computer contained details of every species that flew in the sky, walked or grew upon the ground, crawled beneath it or swam in the deeps of the seas. It kept as accurate as possible a record of births (and deaths, of course) and updated Scharme's precious seconds of vampiric life in a never-ending cycle of self-appointed self-serving sacrifice. It specified the region of the planet to be exploited, told Scharme whom or what to kill and when to do it, programmed his culling of life until it was the finest (and foulest) of fine arts.

And suddenly, with all the weight and worry of calculation and of decision-making taken from his shoulders, and with all of his long years of existence stretching out behind him and apparently before him, Scharme began to feel the inevitable *ennui* of his immortality. And until now, he had not once thought of taking a wife.

There were three main reasons for this.

First, despite all the years he had stolen, there had never seemed to be enough time for it. Second, he had feared to father children who might carry forward and spread his own mutation throughout the world, so robbing him of his future. Last, he knew how great was his power and mighty his position, and so would never be certain that a woman – any woman – would love him for himself and not for the glory of knowing him. All of which seemed valid arguments indeed . . . until the day he met Oryss.

Oryss was young, innocent and very beautiful: long-legged, firm-bodied, green-eyed and lightly tanned. And courting her, Scharme also discovered her to be without greed. Indeed, he was astonished that she turned him down on those very grounds: she could not marry him because people would say it was only his power and position which she loved. But while she visited him in his Maltese redoubt there occurred one of those unimaginable disasters with which, paradoxically, the world was now all too well acquainted. Her island, the island of Crete, was stricken with plague!

There were no survivors save Oryss; she could not go home to what was now a rotting pesthole; she became Scharme's wife and thus Queen of the World . . .

The years passed. She wanted children and he refused. Soon she was thirty-five and he was still fifty. But in three more years, when he saw how time was creeping up on her, Scharme began to despair. So that one day he called her to his most private place, the hall of the NECROMETER, and explained to her that machine's purpose. Except it had no purpose unless he also explained his talent, which he did. At first she was astonished, awed, frightened. And then she was quiet. Very quiet.

'What are you thinking?' he eventually asked her.

'Only of Crete,' she told him.

'The great whales have proliferated during the last hundred years,' he told her then. 'I would like to experiment, see if I can give you some of their time. I can't bear to see another wrinkle come into your face.'

'They were only laughter lines,' she said, sadly, as if she thought she might never laugh again.

'Here, hold my hands,' said Scharme. And there in the hall of the NECROMETER he willed half the whales dead and their time transferred to Oryss. And here the most astonishing thing of all: he discovered that his internal chronometer worked not only for him but also for his wife – *and that she had gained several millions of years!*

And he saw that because she was new to his art, it was for her as it had been at first for him: just as he had gained all of that almost forgotten Corporal's years, so had Oryss gained all of the years of the many whales. 'It could have been me!' he told himself then. 'If I had known at the beginning . . . it could have been me . . .' And while he clapped a hand to his forehead and reeled, and thought these things – things which he had always known, but which never before had been brought home so forcefully – so Oryss fainted at his feet.

He at once carried her to her bed, called his physicians, sat stroking her hand until the medical men were finished with their examination. And: 'What is it?' he whispered to them then, afraid that they would tell him the worst.

'Nothing, merely a faint,' they shrugged. But Scharme suspected it was much more than that. He felt it in his bones, a cold such as he had never known before, not even as a barefoot boy in Paradise in the winter. And mazed and mortally afraid he once more turned his eyes inwards and gazed upon the life-clock ticking in his being. Ah, and he saw how quickly the pendulum swung, how fast his time was running down! Too fast; the weight of Oryss's myriad years had tipped the scales; he had a month and then must take life again. Oh, a great many lives . . .

It was too much for him. Even for the Great Vampire Klaus August Scharme. To extend his life a single hour beyond the twenty-eight days remaining to him he must devour a hundred lifetimes, and for the next hour ten thousand, and for the next one hundred million! The figure would simply multiply itself each time he used his talent. Quickly he returned to the hall of the NECROMETER, fed the computer with these new figures, impatiently waited out the few seconds the machine stole from him to perform its task. And while he stood there trembling and waiting, so the NECROMETER balanced all the planet's teeming life against the single life of Klaus August Scharme, and finally delivered its verdict. He had only twenty-eight days, six hours, three minutes and forty-three seconds left – and not a second longer. Neither Scharme, nor any other living thing upon the face of the planet!

Gasping his horror, he fed new figures into the computer. What if he took *all* the Earth's life at a single stroke – with the exception, of course, of life in the air and on the land and in the waters around Malta? And the computer gave him back exactly the same result, for it had assumed that this was his question in the first instance!

At which, Scharme too fainted away . . .

But before he woke up he dreamed his third inspirational dream, whose essence was simplicity itself. He saw gigantic scales weighted on the one side with Oryss, and on the other with the planet Earth and all it contained. But for all that she was a single creature, still those cosmic scales were tilted in her favour. And between the pans of the scales, holding them aloft on arms which formed the pivot, stood Klaus August Scharme himself.

He awoke, and Oryss stood there close by, looking at the NECROMETER. Upon its screen were those terrible calculations which had caused her husband's faint. And from the look on her face Scharme supposed she understood them. And from the look on *his* face, she also understood that he had reached a decision.

'So,' she said then, 'it is ended.'

He climbed tiredly to his feet, burst into tears. 'It is the only way,' he said, folding her to his heart. 'But not yet, my love, not yet. I can wait . . . a day? Perhaps even a day and a night. But you must understand that what was mine to give is also mine to take away.'

'Not so,' she clasped him coldly. 'For when you gave me my millions of years, you also gave me your talent. I feel it within me, ticking like a clock.'

He gasped and thrust her away, but she was pointing at him and had already commenced to say: 'You should age one second for every man, woman and child, every beast, fish, fowl and creeping thing which you destroyed in the island of Crete!' Which was the end of him, for he had something a deal less than two and a half millions of seconds left, and of creeping things alone, that would have sufficed to kill him. But Oryss had loved her island dearly.

Long ago, Scharme had conceived of a time when someone might see his NECROMETER, understand its purpose and meaning and attempt to kill him. And he had determined that if that time should ever come, then that his executioner must die with him. Now, even as he crumbled to dust, he fell upon a certain lever.

The console of the NECROMETER cracked open into a gaping mouth and the floor of the hall lashed like a crippled snake. A convulsion which hurled the beautiful Oryss and the vile vampiric debris of Klaus August Scharme into eternity within the clashing cogs and wheels and electrical daggers of the great machine. Scharme's fortress blew apart from its roots upwards, and the island of Malta collapsed inwards, and great tidal waves washed outwards to the furthest corners of the world.

And Time Itself felt a wrenching and a reckoning, and Inviolable Life – so long held upon Scharme's monstrous leash – rebelled and added to the space-time confusion. So that for a split second all was chaos until the vast Engine which is the Universe backfired . . . !

Laughing and waving, the Corporal sped away in his Land Rover. Scharme's short ladder shuddered for a moment beneath the post to which he'd nailed his *Kreise* sign, then stood still and empty. The *Kreise* sign swung all askew upon a single nail, the job unfinished. And at the foot of the ladder lay a small pile of rags and a handful of grey dust, which the winds of time quickly blew away . . .

THE HOUSE OF THE TEMPLE

This one, with its Mythos background, is a favourite of mine. Note I don't say that it's a Cthulhu Mythos story. It is, but as Steve Jones pointed out in his introduction in the Mammoth Book of Terror, *'despite that it uses the trappings of HPL's Mythos, the terror induced by this gripping novella is purely Lumley's own.' Nice one, Steve – thanks!*

The House of the Temple is a tale of strange inheritance, which in a horror story usually means to inherit something you really don't want. The sins of the fathers, and all that . . .

1. The Summons

I suppose under the circumstances it is only natural that the police should require this belated written statement from me; and I further suppose it to be in recognition of my present highly nervous condition and my totally unwarranted confinement in this *place* that they are allowing me to draw the thing up without supervision. But while every kindness has been shown me, still I most strongly protest my continued detainment here. Knowing what I now know, I would voice the same protest in respect of detention in *any* prison or institute anywhere in Scotland ... anywhere in the entire British Isles.

Before I begin, let me clearly make the point that, since no charges have been levelled against me, I make this statement of my own free will, fully knowing that in so doing I may well extend my stay in this detestable place. I can only hope that upon its reading, it will be seen that I had no alternative but to follow the action I describe.

You the reader must therefore judge. My actual sanity – if indeed I am still sane – my very *being*, may well depend upon your findings ...

I was in New York when the letter from my uncle's solicitors reached me. Sent from an address in the Royal

Mile, that great road which reaches steep and cobbled to the esplanade of Edinburgh Castle itself, the large, sealed manila envelope had all the hallmarks of officialdom, so that even before I opened it I feared the worst.

Not that I had been close to my uncle in recent years (my mother had brought me out of Scotland as a small child, on the death of my father, and I had never been back) but certainly I remembered Uncle Gavin. If anything I remembered him better than I did my father; for where Andrew McGilchrist had always been dry and introverted, Uncle Gavin had been just the opposite. Warm, outgoing and generous to a fault, he had spoilt me mercilessly.

Now, according to the letter, he was dead and I was named his sole heir and beneficiary; and the envelope contained a voucher which guaranteed me a flight to Edinburgh from anywhere in the world. And then of course there was the letter itself, the contents of which further guaranteed my use of that voucher; for only a fool could possibly refuse my uncle's bequest, or fail to be interested in its attendant though at present unspecified conditions.

Quite simply, by presenting myself at the offices of Macdonald, Asquith and Lee in Edinburgh, I would already have fulfilled the first condition toward inheriting my uncle's considerable fortune, his estate of over three hundred acres and his great house where it stood in wild and splendid solitude at the foot of the Pentlands in Lothian. All of which seemed a very far cry from New York . . .

As to what I was doing in New York in the first place: Three months earlier, in mid-March of 1976 – when I was living alone in Philadelphia in the home where my mother had raised me – my fiancée of two years had given me back my ring, run off and married a banker from Baltimore. The novel I was writing had immediately metamorphosed from a light-hearted love story into a doom-laden tragedy, became meaningless somewhere in the transformation, and ended up in my waste-paper basket. That was that. I sold up and moved to New York, where an artist friend had been willing to share his apartment until I could find a decent place of my own.

I had left no forwarding address, however, which explained the delayed delivery of the letter from my uncle's solicitors; the letter itself was post-marked March 26th, and from the various marks, labels and redirections on the envelope, the US Mail had obviously gone to considerable trouble to find me. And they found me at a time when the lives of both myself and my artist friend, Carl Earlman, were at a very low ebb. I was not writing and Carl was not drawing, and despite the arrival of summer our spirits were on a rapid decline.

Which is probably why I jumped at the opportunity the letter presented, though, as I have said, certainly I would have been a fool to ignore or refuse the thing . . . Or so I thought at the time.

I invited Carl along if he so desired, and he too grasped at the chance with both hands. His funds were low and getting lower; he would soon be obliged to quit his apartment for something less ostentatious; and since he, too, had decided that he needed a change of locale – to put some life back into his artwork – the matter was soon decided and we packed our bags and headed for Edinburgh.

It was not until our journey was over, however – when we were settled in our hotel room in Princes Street – that I remembered my mother's warning, delivered to me deliriously but persistently from her deathbed, that I should never return to Scotland, certainly not to the old house. And as I vainly attempted to adjust to the jet-lag and the fact that it was late evening while all my instincts told me it should now be day, so my mind went back over what little I knew of my family roots, of the McGilchrist line itself, of that old and rambling house in the Pentlands where I had been born, and especially of the peculiar reticence of Messrs Macdonald, Asquith and Lee, the Scottish solicitors.

Reticence, yes, because I could almost feel the hesitancy in their letter. It seemed to me that they would have preferred *not* to find me; and yet, if I were asked what it was that gave me this impression, then I would be at a loss for an answer. Something in the way it was phrased, perhaps – in the dry, professional idiom of solicitors – which too often seems to me to put aside all matters of emotion or sensibility; so that I felt like a small boy offered a candy . . . and warned simultaneously that it would ruin my teeth. Yes, it seemed to me that Messrs Macdonald, Asquith and Lee might actually be *apprehensive* about my acceptance of their conditions – or rather, of my uncle's conditions – as if they were offering a cigar to an addict suffering from cancer of the lungs.

I fastened on that line of reasoning, seeing the conditions of the will as the root of the vague uneasiness which niggled at the back of my mind. The worst of it was that these conditions were not specified; other than to say that if I could not or would not meet them, still I would receive fifteen thousand pounds and my return ticket home, and that the residue of my uncle's fortune would then be used to carry out his will in respect of 'the property known as Temple House.'

Temple House, that rambling old seat of the McGilchrists where it stood locked in a steep re-entry; and the Pentland Hills a grey and green backdrop to its frowning, steep-gabled aspect; with something of the Gothic in its structure, something more of Renaissance Scotland, and an aura of antiquity all its own which, as a child, I could still remember loving dearly. But that had been almost twenty years ago and the place had been my home. A happy home, I had thought; at least until the death of my father, of which I could remember nothing at all.

But I did remember the pool – the deep, grey pool where it lapped at the raised, reinforced, east-facing garden wall – the pool and its ring of broken quartz pillars, the remains of the temple for which the house was named. Thinking back over the years to my infancy, I wondered if perhaps the pool had been the reason my mother had always hated the place. None of the McGilchrists had ever been swimmers, and yet water had always seemed to fascinate them. I would not have been the first of the line to be found floating face-down in that strange, pillar-encircled pool of deep and weedy water; and I had used to spend hours just sitting on the wall and staring across the breeze-rippled surface . . .

So my thoughts went as, tossing in my hotel bed late into the night, I turned matters over in my mind . . . And having retired late, so we rose late, Carl and I; and it was not until 2 p.m. that I presented myself at the office of Macdonald, Asquith and Lee on the Royal Mile.

2. The Will

Since Carl had climbed up to the esplanade to take in the view, I was alone when I reached my destination and entered MA and L's offices through a door of yellow-tinted bull's-eye panes, passing into the cool welcome of a dim and very *Olde Worlde* anteroom; and for all that this was the source of my enigmatic summons, still I found a reassuring air of charm and quiet sincerity about the place. A clerk led me into an inner chamber as much removed from my idea of a solicitor's office as is Edinburgh from New York, and having been introduced to the firm's Mr Asquith I was offered a seat.

Asquith was tall, slender, high-browed and balding, with a mass of freckles which seemed oddly in contrast with his late middle years, and his handshake was firm and dry. While he busied himself getting various documents, I was given a minute or two to look about this large and bewilderingly cluttered room of shelves, filing cabinets, cupboards and three small desks. But for all that the place seemed grossly disordered, still Mr Asquith quickly found what he was looking for and seated himself opposite me behind his desk. He was the only partner present and I the only client.

'Now, Mr McGilchrist,' he began. 'And so we managed to find you, did we? And doubtless you're wondering what it's all about, and you probably think there's something of a mystery here? Well, so there is, and for me and my partners no less than for yourself.'

'I don't quite follow,' I answered, searching his face for a clue.

'No, no of course you don't. Well now, perhaps this will explain it better. It's a copy of your uncle's will. As you'll see, he was rather short on words; hence the mystery. A more succinct document – which nevertheless hints at so much more – I've yet to see!'

'I Gavin McGilchrist,' (the will began) 'of Temple House in Lothian, hereby revoke all Wills, Codicils or Testamentary Dispositions heretofore made by me, and I appoint my Nephew, John Hamish McGilchrist of Philadelphia in the United States of America, to be the Executor of this my Last Will and direct that all my Debts, Testamentary and Funeral Expenses shall be paid as soon as conveniently may be after my death.

'I give and bequeath unto the aforementioned John Hamish McGilchrist everything I possess, my Land and the Property standing thereon, with the following Condition: namely that he alone shall open and read the Deposition which shall accompany this Will into the hands of the

Solicitors; and that furthermore he, being the Owner, shall destroy Temple House to its last stone within a Threemonth of accepting this Condition. In the event that he shall refuse this undertaking, then shall my Solicitors, Macdonald, Asquith and Lee of Edinburgh, become sole Executors of my Estate, who shall follow to the letter the Instructions simultaneously deposited with them.'

The will was dated and signed in my uncle's scratchy scrawl.

I read it through a second time and looked up to find Mr Asquith's gaze fixed intently upon me. 'Well,' he said, 'and didn't I say it was a mystery? Almost as strange as his death . . .' He saw the immediate change in my expression, the frown and the question my lips were beginning to frame, and held up his hands in apology. 'I'm sorry,' he said, 'so very sorry – for of course you know nothing of the circumstances of his death, do you? I had better explain:

'A year ago,' Asquith continued, 'your uncle was one of the most hale and hearty men you could wish to meet. He was a man of independent means, as you know, and for a good many years he had been collecting data for a book. Ah! I see you're surprised. Well, you shouldn't be. Your great-grandfather wrote *Notes of Nessie: the Secrets of Loch Ness*; and your grandmother, under a pseudonym, was a fairly successful romanticist around the turn of the century. You, too, I believe, have published several romances? Indeed,' and he smiled and nodded, 'it appears to be in the blood, you see?

'Like your great-grandfather, however, your Uncle Gavin McGilchrist had no romantic aspirations. He was a researcher, you see, and couldn't abide a mystery to remain unsolved. And there he was at Temple House, a bachelor and time on his hands, and a marvellous family tree to explore and a great mystery to unravel.'

'Family tree?' I said. 'He was researching the biography of a family? But which fam—' And I paused.

Asquith smiled. 'You've guessed it, of course,' he said. 'Yes, he was planning a book on the McGilchrists, with special reference to the curse . . .' And his smile quickly vanished.

It was as if a cold draught, coming from nowhere, fanned my cheek. 'The curse? My family had . . . a curse?'

He nodded. 'Oh, yes. Not the classical sort of curse, by any means, but a curse nevertheless – or at least your uncle thought so. Perhaps he wasn't really serious about it at first, but towards the end—'

'I think I know what you mean,' I said. 'I remember now: the deaths by stroke, by drowning, by thrombosis. My mother mentioned them on her own deathbed. A curse on the McGilchrists, she said, on the old house.'

Again Asquith nodded, and finally he continued. 'Well, your uncle had been collecting material for many years, I suspect since the death of your father; from local archives, historical annals, various chronicles, church records, military museums, and so on. He had even enlisted our aid, on occasion, in finding this or that old document. Our firm was founded one hundred and sixty years ago, you see, and we've had many McGilchrists as clients.

'As I've said, up to a time roughly a year ago, he was as hale and hearty a man as you could wish to meet. Then he travelled abroad; Hungary, Romania, all the old countries of antique myth and legend. He brought back many books with him, and on his return he was a changed man. He had become, in a matter of weeks, the merest shadow of his former self. Finally, nine weeks ago on March 22nd, he left his will in our hands, an additional set of instructions for us to follow in the event you couldn't be found, and the sealed envelope which he mentions in his will. I shall give that to you in a moment. Two days later, when his gillie returned to Temple House from a short holiday—'

'He found my uncle dead,' I finished it for him. 'I see . . . And the strange circumstances?'

'For a man of his years to die of a heart attack . . .' Asquith shook his head. 'He wasn't old. What? – an out-doors man, like him? And what of the shotgun, with both barrels discharged, and the spent cartridges lying at his feet just outside the porch? What had he fired at, eh, in the dead of night? And the look on his face – monstrous!'

'You saw him?'

'Oh, yes. That was part of our instructions; I was to see him. And not just myself but Mr Lee also. And the doctor, of course, who declared it could only have been a heart attack. But then there was the post-mortem. That was also part of your uncle's instructions . . .'

'And its findings?' I quietly asked.

'Why, that was the reason he wanted the autopsy, do you see? So that we should know he was in good health.'

'No heart attack?'

'No,' he shook his head, 'not him. But dead, certainly. And that look on his face, Mr McGilchrist – that terrible, pleading look in his wide, wide eyes . . .'

3. The House

Half an hour later I left Mr Asquith in his office and saw myself out through the anteroom and into the hot, cobbled road that climbed to the great grey castle. In the interim I had opened the envelope left for me by my uncle and had given its contents a cursory scrutiny, but I intended to study them minutely at my earliest convenience.

I had also offered to let Asquith see the contents, only to have him wave my offer aside. It was a private thing, he said, for my eyes only. Then he had asked me what I intended to do now, and I had answered that I would go to Temple House and take up temporary residence there. He then produced the keys, assured me of the firm's interest in my business – its complete confidentiality and its readiness to provide assistance should I need it – and bade me good day.

I found Carl Earlman leaning on the esplanade wall and gazing out over the city. Directly below his position the castle rock fell away for hundreds of feet to a busy road that wound round and down and into the maze of streets and junctions forming the city centre. He started when I took hold of his arm.

'What—? Oh, it's you, John! I was lost in thought. This fantastic view; I've already stored away a dozen sketches in my head. Great!' Then he saw my face and frowned. 'Is anything wrong? You don't quite look yourself.'

As we made our way down from that high place I told him of my meeting with Asquith and all that had passed between us, so that by the time we found a cab (a 'taxi') and had ourselves driven to an automobile rental depot, I had managed to bring him fully up to date. Then it was simply a matter of hiring a car and driving out to Temple House . . .

We headed south-west out of Edinburgh with Carl driving our Range Rover at a leisurely pace, and within three-quarters of an hour turned right off the main road onto a narrow strip whose half-metalled surface climbed straight as an arrow toward the looming Pentlands. Bald and majestic, those grey domes rose from a scree of gorse-grown shale to cast their sooty, mid-afternoon shadows over lesser mounds, fields and streamlets alike. Over our vehicle, too, as it grew tiny in the frowning presence of the hills.

I was following a small-scale map of the area purchased from a filling station (a 'garage'), for of course the district was completely strange to me. A lad of five on leaving Scotland – and protected by my mother's exaggerated fears at that, which hardly ever let me out of her sight – I had never been allowed to stray very far from Temple House.

Temple House . . . and again the name conjured strange phantoms, stirred vague memories I had thought long dead.

Now the road narrowed more yet, swinging sharply to the right before passing round a rocky spur. The ground rose up beyond the spur and formed a shallow ridge, and my map told me that the gully or re-entry which guarded Temple House lay on the far side of this final rise. I knew that when we reached the crest the house would come into view, and I found myself holding my breath as the Range Rover's wheels bit into the cinder surface of the track.

'There she is!' cried Carl as first the eaves of the place became visible, then its oak-beamed gables and greystone walls, and finally the entire frontage where it projected from behind the sheer rise of the gully's wall. And now, as we accelerated down the slight decline and turned right to follow a course running parallel to the stream, the whole house came into view where it stood half in shadow. That strange old house in the silent gully, where no birds ever flew and not even a rabbit had been seen to sport in the long wild grass.

'Hey!' Carl cried, his voice full of enthusiasm. 'And your uncle wanted this place pulled down? What in hell for? It's beautiful – and it must be worth a fortune!'

'I shouldn't think so,' I answered. 'It might look all right from here, but wait till you get inside. Its foundations were waterlogged twenty years ago. There were always six inches of water in the cellar, and the panels of the lower rooms were mouldy even then. God only knows what it must be like now!'

'Does it look the way you remember it?' he asked.

'Not quite,' I frowned. 'Seen through the eyes of an adult, there are differences.'

For one thing, the pool was different. The level of the water was lower, so that the wide, grass-grown wall of the dam seemed somehow taller. In fact, I had completely forgotten about the dam, without which the pool could not exist, or at best would be the merest pebble-bottomed pool and not the small lake which it now was. For the first time it dawned on me that the pool was artificial, not natural as I had always thought of it, and that Temple House had been built on top of the dam's curving mound where it extended to the steep shale cliff of the defile itself.

With a skidding of loose chippings, Carl took the Range Rover up the ramp that formed the drive to the house, and a moment later we drew to a halt before the high-arched porch. We dismounted and entered, and now Carl went clattering away – almost irreverently, I thought – into cool rooms, dark stairwells and huge cupboards, his voice echoing back to me where I stood with mixed emotions, savouring the atmosphere of the old place, just inside the doorway to the house proper.

'But this is *it*!' he cried from somewhere. 'This is for me! My studio, and no question. Come and look, John – look at the windows letting in all this good light. You're right about the damp, I can feel it – but that aside, it's perfect.'

I found him in what had once been the main living-room, standing in golden clouds of dust he had stirred up, motes illumined by the sun's rays where they struck into the room through huge, leaded windows. 'You'll need to give the place a good dusting and sweeping out,' I told him.

'Oh, sure,' he answered, 'but there's a lot wants doing before that. Do you know where the master switch is?'

'Umm? Switch?'

'For the electric light,' he frowned impatiently at me. 'And surely there's an icebox in the kitchen.'

'A refrigerator?' I answered. 'Oh, yes, I'm sure there is . . . Look, you run around and explore the place and do whatever makes you happy. Me, I'm just going to potter about and try to waken a few old dreams.'

During the next hour or two – while I quite literally 'pottered about' and familiarized myself once again with this old house so full of memories – Carl fixed himself up with a bed in his 'studio,' found the main switch and got the electricity flowing, examined the refrigerator and satisfied himself that it was in working order, then searched me out where I sat in the mahogany-panelled study upstairs to tell me that he was driving into Penicuik to stock up with food.

From my window I watched him go, until the cloud of dust thrown up by his wheels disappeared over the rise to the south, then stirred myself into positive action. There were things to be done – things I must do for myself, others for my uncle – and the sooner I started the better. Not that there was any lack of time; I had three whole months to carry out Gavin McGilchrist's instructions, or to fail to carry them out. And yet somehow . . . yes, there was this feeling of *urgency* in me.

And so I switched on the light against gathering shadows, took out the envelope left for me by my uncle – that envelope whose contents, a letter and a notebook, were for my eyes only – sat down at the great desk used by so many generations of McGilchrists, and began to read . . .

4. The Curse

'My dear, dear nephew,' the letter in my uncle's uneven script began, '—so much I would like to say to you, and so little time in which to say it. And all these years grown in between since last I saw you.

'When first you left Scotland with your mother I would have written to you through her, but she forbade it. In early 1970 I learned of her death, so that even my condolences would have been six months too late; well, you have them now. She was a wonderful woman, and of course she was quite right to take you away out of it all. If I'm right in what I now suspect, her woman's intuition will yet prove to have been nearer the mark than anyone ever could have guessed, and—

'But there I go, miles off the point and rambling as usual; and such a lot to say. Except – I'm damned if I know where to begin! I suppose the plain fact of the matter is quite simply stated – namely, that for you to be reading this is for me to be gone forever from the world of men. But gone . . . *where?* And how to explain?

'The fact is, I cannot tell it all, not and make it believable. Not the way I have come to believe it. Instead you will have to be satisfied with the barest essentials. The rest you can discover for yourself. There are books in the old library that tell it all – if a man has the patience to look. And if he's capable of putting aside all matters of common knowledge, all laws of science and logic; capable of unlearning all that life has ever taught him of truth and beauty.

'Four hundred years ago we weren't such a race of damned sceptics. They were burning witches in these parts then, and if they had suspected of anyone what I have come to suspect of Temple House and its grounds . . .

'Your mother may not have mentioned the curse – the curse of the McGilchrists. Oh, she believed in it, certainly, but it's possible she thought that to tell of it might be to invoke the thing. That is to say, by telling you she might bring the curse down on your head. Perhaps she was right, for unless my death is seen to be *entirely natural*, then certainly I shall have brought it down upon myself.

'And what of you, Nephew?

'You have three months. Longer than that I do not deem safe, and nothing is guaranteed. Even three months might be dangerously overlong, but I pray not. Of course you are at liberty, if you so desire, simply to get the thing over and done with. In my study, in the bottom right-hand drawer of my desk, you will find sufficient fuses and explosive materials to bring down the wall of the defile onto the house, and the house itself into the pool, which should satisfactorily put an end to the thing.

'But . . . you had an enquiring mind as a child. If you look where I have looked and read what I have read, then you shall learn what I've learned and know that it is neither advanced senility nor madness but my own intelligence which leads me to the one, inescapable conclusion – that this House of the Temple, this Temple House of the McGilchrists, is accursed. Most terribly . . .

'I could flee this place, of course, but I doubt if that would save me. And if it did save me, still it would leave the final questions unanswered and the riddle unsolved. Also, I loved my brother, your father, and I saw his face when he was dead. If for nothing else, that look on your father's dead face has been sufficient reason for me to pursue the thing thus far. I thought to seek it out, to know it, destroy it – but now . . .

'I have never been much of a religious man, Nephew, and so it comes doubly hard for me to say what I now say: that while your father is dead these twenty years and more, I now find myself wondering if he is truly at rest! And what will be the look on *my* face when the thing is over, one way or the other? Ask about that, Nephew, ask how *I* looked when they found me.

'Finally, as to your course of action from this point onward: do what you will, but in the last event be sure you bring about the utter dissolution of the seat of ancient evil known as Temple House. There are things hidden in the great deserts and mountains of the world, and others sunken under the deepest oceans, which never were meant to exist in any sane or ordered universe. Yes, and certain revenants of immemorial horror have even come among men. One such has anchored itself here in the Pentlands, and in a little while I may meet it face to face. If all goes well . . . But then you should not be reading this.

'And so the rest is up to you, John Hamish; and if indeed man has an immortal soul, I now place mine in your hands. Do what must be done and if you are a believer, then say a prayer for me . . .

Yr. Loving Uncle –
Gavin McGilchrist.'

I read the letter through a second time, then a third, and the shadows lengthened beyond the reach of the study's electric lights. Finally, I turned to the notebook – a slim, ruled, board-covered book whose like might be purchased at any stationery store – and opened it to page upon page of scrawled and at first glance seemingly unconnected jottings, references, abbreviated notes and memoranda concerning . . . Concerning what? Black magic? Witchcraft? The 'supernatural'? But what else would you call a curse if not supernatural?

Well, my uncle had mentioned a puzzle, a mystery, the McGilchrist curse, the thing he had tracked down almost to the finish. And here were all the pointers, the clues, the keys to his years of research. I stared at the great bookcases lining the walls, the leather spines of their contents dully agleam in the glow of the lights. Asquith had told me that my uncle brought many old books back with him from his wanderings abroad.

I stood up and felt momentarily dizzy, and was obliged to lean on the desk until the feeling passed. The mustiness of the deserted house, I supposed, the closeness of the room and the odour of old books. Books . . . yes, and I moved shakily across to the nearest bookcase and ran my fingers over titles rubbed and faded with age and wear. There were works here which seemed to stir faint memories – perhaps I had been allowed to play with those books as a child? – but others were almost tangibly strange to the place, whose titles alone would make aliens of them without ever a page being turned. These must be those volumes my uncle had discovered abroad. I frowned as I tried to make something of their less than commonplace names.

Here were such works as the German *Unter-Zee Kulten* and Feery's *Notes on the Necronomicon* in a French edition; and here Gaston le Fe's *Dwellers in the Depths* and a black-bound, iron-hasped copy of the *Cthäat Aquadingen*, its harsh title suggestive of both German and Latin roots. Here was Gantley's *Hydrophinnae*, and here the *Liber Miraculorem* of the Monk and Chaplain Herbert of Clairvaux. Gothic letters proclaimed of one volume that it was Prinn's *De Vermis Mysteriis*, while another purported to be the suppressed and hideously disquieting *Unaussprechlichen Kulten* of Von Junzt – titles which seemed to leap at me as my eyes moved from shelf to shelf in a sort of disbelieving stupefaction.

What possible connection could there be between these ancient, foreign volumes of elder madness and delirium and the solid, down-to-earth McGilchrist line of gentlemen, officers and scholars? There seemed only one way to find out. Choosing a book at random. I found it to be the *Cthäat Aquadingen* and returned with it to the desk. The light outside was failing now and the shadows of the hills were long and sooty. In less than an hour it would be dusk, and half an hour after that dark.

Then there would only be Carl and I and the night. And the old house. As if in answer to unspoken thoughts, settling timbers groaned somewhere overhead. Through the window, down below in the sharp shadows of the house, the dull green glint of water caught my eye.

Carl and I, the night and the old house—
And the deep, dark pool.

5. The Music

It was almost completely dark by the time Carl returned, but in between I had at least been able to discover my uncle's system of reference. It was quite elementary, really. In his notebook, references such as 'CA 121/7' simply indicated an item of interest in the *Cthäat Aquadingen*, page 121, the seventh paragraph. And in the work itself he had carefully underscored all such paragraphs or items of interest. At least a dozen such references concerning the *Cthäat Aquadingen* occurred in his notebook, and as night had drawn on I had examined each in turn.

Most of them were meaningless to me and several were in a tongue or glyph completely beyond my comprehension, but others were in a form of old English which I could transcribe with comparative ease. One such, which seemed a chant of sorts, had a brief annotation scrawled in the margin in my uncle's hand. The passage I refer to, as nearly as I can remember, went like this:

'Rise, O Nameless Ones;
It is Thy Season
When Thine Own of Thy Choosing,
Through Thy Spells & Thy Magic,
Through Dreams & Enchantry,
May know Thou art come.
They rush to Thy Pleasure,
For the Love of Thy Masters —
— the Spawn of Cthulhu.'

And the accompanying annotation queried: 'Would they have used such as this to call the Thing forth, I wonder, or was it simply a blood lure? What causes it to come forth now? When will it next come?'

It was while I was comparing references and text in this fashion that I began to get a glimmer as to just what the book was, and on further considering its title I saw that I had probably guessed correctly. 'Cthäat' frankly baffled me, unless it had some connection with the language or being of the pre-Nacaal Kthatans; but 'Aquadingen' was far less alien in its sound and formation. It meant (I believed), 'water-things', or 'things of the waters'; and the – *Cthäat Aquadingen* was quite simply a compendium of myths and legends concerning water sprites, nymphs, demons, naiads and other supernatural creatures of lakes and oceans, and the spells or conjurations by which they might be evoked or called out of their watery haunts.

I had just arrived at this conclusion when Carl returned, the lights of his vehicle cutting a bright swath over the dark surface of the pool as he parked in front of the porch. Laden down, he entered the house and I went down to the spacious if somewhat old fashioned kitchen to find him filling shelves and cupboards and stocking the refrigerator with perishables. This done, bright and breezy in his enthusiasm, he enquired about the radio.

'Radio?' I answered. 'I thought your prime concern was for peace and quiet? Why, you've made enough noise for ten since we got here!'

'No, no,' he said. 'It's not *my* noise I'm concerned about but yours. Or rather, the radio's. I mean, you've obviously found one for I heard the music.'

Carl was big, blond and blue-eyed; a Viking if ever I saw one, and quite capable of displaying a Viking's temper. He had been laughing when he asked me where the radio was, but now he was frowning. 'Are you playing games with me, John?'

'No, of course I'm not,' I answered him. 'Now what's all this about? What music have you been hearing?'

His face suddenly brightened and he snapped his fingers. 'There's a radio in the Range Rover,' he said. 'There has to be. It must have gotten switched on, very low, and I've been getting Bucharest or something.' He made as if to go back outside.

'Bucharest?' I repeated him.

'Hmm?' he paused in the kitchen doorway. 'Oh, yes – gypsyish stuff. Tambourines and chanting – and fiddles. Dancing around campfires. Look, I'd better switch it off or the battery will run down.'

'I didn't see a radio,' I told him, following him out through the porch and onto the drive.

He leaned inside the front of the vehicle, switched on the interior light and searched methodically. Finally he put the light out with an emphatic click. He turned to me and his jaw had a stubborn set to it. I looked back at him and raised my eyebrows. 'No radio?'

He shook his head. 'But I heard the music.'

'Lovers,' I said.

'Eh?'

'Lovers, out walking. A transistor radio. Perhaps they were sitting in the grass. After all, it is a beautiful summer night.'

Again he shook his head. 'No, it was right there in the air. Sweet and clear. I heard it as I approached the house. It came from the house, I thought. And you heard nothing?'

'Nothing,' I answered, shaking my head.

'Well then – damn it to hell!' he suddenly grinned. 'I've started hearing things, that's all! Skip it . . . Come on, let's have supper . . .'

*   *   *

Carl stuck to his 'studio' bedroom but I slept upstairs in a room adjacent to the study. Even with the windows thrown wide open, the night was very warm and the atmosphere sticky, so that sleep did not come easily. Carl must have found a similar problem for on two or three occasions I awakened from a restless half-sleep to sounds of his moving about downstairs. In the morning over breakfast both of us were a little bleary-eyed, but then he led me through into his room to display the reason for his nocturnal activity.

There on the makeshift easel, on one of a dozen old canvasses he had brought with him, Carl had started work on a picture . . . of sorts.

For the present he had done little more than lightly brush in the background, which was clearly the valley of the house, but the house itself was missing from the picture and I could see that the artist did not intend to include it. The pool was there, however, with its encircling ring of quartz columns complete and finished with lintels of a like material. The columns and lintels glowed luminously.

In between and around the columns vague figures writhed, at present insubstantial as smoke, and in the foreground the flames of a small fire were driven on a wind that blew from across the pool. Taken as a whole and for all its sketchiness, the scene gave a vivid impression of savagery and pagan excitement – strange indeed considering that as yet there seemed to be so little in it to excite any sort of emotion whatever.

'Well,' said Carl, his voice a trifle edgy, 'what do you think?'

'I'm no artist, Carl,' I answered, which I suppose in the circumstances was saying too much.

'You don't like it?' he sounded disappointed.

'I didn't say that,' I countered. 'Will it be a night scene?'

He nodded.

'And the dancers there, those wraiths . . . I suppose they *are* dancers?'

'Yes,' he answered, 'and musicians. Tambourines, fiddles . . .'

'Ah!' I nodded. 'Last night's music.'

He looked at me curiously. 'Probably . . . Anyway, I'm happy with it. At least I've started to work. What about you?'

'You do your thing,' I told him, 'and I'll do mine.'

'But what are you going to do?'

I shrugged. 'Before I do anything I'm going to soak up a lot of atmosphere. But I don't intend staying here very long. A month or so, and then—'

'And then you'll burn this beautiful old place to the ground.' He had difficulty keeping the sour note out of his voice.

'It's what my uncle wanted,' I said. 'I'm not here to write a story. A story may come of it eventually, even a book, but that can wait. Anyway, I won't burn the house.' I made a mushroom cloud with my hands. 'She goes – up!'

Carl snorted. 'You McGilchrists,' he said. 'You're all nuts!' But there was no malice in his statement.

There was a little in mine, however, when I answered: 'Maybe – but I don't hear music when there isn't any!'

But that was before I knew everything . . .

6. The Familiar

During the course of the next week Scotland began to feel the first effects of what is now being termed 'a scourge on the British Isles,' the beginning of an intense, ferocious and prolonged period of drought. Sheltered by the Pentlands, a veritable suntrap for a full eight to ten hours a day, Temple House was no exception. Carl and I took to lounging around in shorts and T-shirts, and with his blond hair and fair skin he was particularly vulnerable. If we had been swimmers, then certainly we should have used the pool; as it was we had to content ourselves by sitting at its edge with our feet in the cool mountain water.

By the end of that first week, however, the drought's effect upon the small stream which fed the pool could clearly be seen. Where before the water had rushed down from the heights of the defile, now it seeped, and the natural overflow from the sides of the dam was so reduced that the old course of the stream was now completely dry. As for our own needs: the large water tanks in the attic of the house were full and their source of supply seemed independent, possibly some reservoir higher in the hills.

In the cool of the late afternoon, when the house stood in its own and the Pentlands' shade, then we worked; Carl at his drawing or painting, I with my uncle's notebook and veritable library of esoteric books. We also did a little walking in the hills, but in the heat of this incredible summer that was far too exhausting and only served to accentuate a peculiar mood of depression which had taken both of us in its grip. We blamed the weather, of course, when at any other time we would have considered so much sunshine and fresh air a positive blessing.

By the middle of the second week I was beginning to make real sense of my uncle's fragmentary record of his research. That is to say, his trail was becoming easier to follow as I grew used to his system and started to detect a pattern.

There were in fact two trails, both historic, one dealing with the McGilchrist line itself, the other more concerned with the family seat, with the House of the Temple. Because I seemed close to a definite discovery, I worked harder and became more absorbed with the work. And as if my own industry was contagious, Carl too began to put in longer hours at his easel or drawing board.

It was a Wednesday evening, I remember, the shadows lengthening and the atmosphere heavy when I began to see just how my uncle's mind had been working. He had apparently decided that if there really was a curse on the McGilchrists, then that it had come about during the construction of Temple House. To discover why this was so, he had delved back into the years prior to its construction in this cleft in the hills, and his findings had been strange indeed.

It had seemed to start in England in 1594 with the advent of foreign refugees. These had been the members of a monkish order originating in the mountains of Romania, whose ranks had nevertheless been filled with many diverse creeds, colours and races. There were Chinamen amongst them, Hungarians, Arabs and Africans, but their leader had been a Romanian priest named Chorazos. As to why they had been hounded out of their own countries, that remained a mystery.

Chorazos and certain of his followers became regular visitors at the Court of Queen Elizabeth I – who had ever held an interest in astrology, alchemy and all similar magics and mysteries – and with her help they founded a temple 'somewhere near Finchley.' Soon, however, couriers from foreign parts began to bring in accounts of the previous doings of this darkling sect, and so the Queen took advice.

Of all persons, she consulted with Dr John Dee, that more than dubious character whose own dabbling with the occult had brought him so close to disaster in 1555 during the reign of Queen Mary. Dee, at first enamoured of Chorazos and his followers, now turned against them. They were pagans, he said; their women were whores and their ceremonies orgiastic. They had brought with them a 'familiar,' which would have 'needs' of its own, and eventually the public would rise up against them and the 'outrage' they must soon bring about in the country. The Queen should therefore sever all connections with the sect – and immediately!

Acting under Dee's guidance, she at once issued orders for the arrest, detention and investigation of Chorazos and his members ... but too late, for they had already flown. Their 'temple' in Finchley – a 'columned pavilion about a central lake' – was destroyed and the pool filled in. That was in late 1595.

In 1596 they turned up in Scotland, this time under the guise of travelling faith-healers and herbalists working out of Edinburgh. As a reward for their work among the poorer folk in the district, they were given a land grant and took up an austere residence in the Pentlands. There, following a pattern established abroad and carried on in England, Chorazos and his followers built their temple; except that this time they had to dam a stream in order to create a pool. The work took them several years; their ground was private property; they kept for the main well out of the limelight, and all was well ... for a while.

Then came rumours of orgiastic rites in the hills, of children wandering away from home under the influence of strange, hypnotic music, of a monstrous being conjured up from hell to preside over ceremonial murder and receive its grisly tribute, and at last the truth was out. However covertly Chorazos had organized his perversions, there now existed the gravest suspicions as to what he and the others of his sect were about. And this in the Scotland of James IV, who five years earlier had charged an Edinburgh jury with 'an Assize of Error' when they dismissed an action for witchcraft against one of the 'notorious' North Berwick Witches.

In this present matter, however, any decision of the authorities was pre-empted by persons unknown – possibly the inhabitants of nearby Penicuik, from which town several children had disappeared – and Chorazos's order had been wiped out *en masse* one night and the temple reduced to ruins and shattered quartz stumps.

Quite obviously, the site of the temple had been here, and the place had been remembered by locals down the centuries, so that when the McGilchrist house was built in the mid-18th Century it automatically acquired the name of Temple House. The name had been retained . . . but what else had lingered over from those earlier times, and what *exactly* was the nature of the McGilchrist Curse?

I yawned and stretched. It was after eight and the sinking sun had turned the crests of the hills to bronze. A movement, seen in the corner of my eye through the window, attracted my attention. Carl was making his way to the rim of the pool. He paused with his hands on his hips to stand between two of the broken columns, staring out over the silent water. Then he laid back his head and breathed deeply. There was a tired but self-satisfied air about him that set me wondering.

I threw the window wide and leaned out, calling down through air which was still warm and cloying: 'Hey, Carl – you look like the cat who got the cream!'

He turned and waved. 'Maybe I am. It's that painting of mine. I think I've got it beat. Not finished yet . . . but coming along.'

'Is it good?' I asked.

He shrugged, but it was a shrug of affirmation, not indifference. 'Are you busy? Come down and see for yourself. I only came out to clear my head, so that I can view it in fresh perspective. Yours will be a second opinion.'

I went downstairs to find him back in his studio. Since the light was poor now, he switched on all of the electric lights and led the way to his easel. I had last looked at the painting some three or four days previously, at a time when it had still been very insubstantial. Now—

Nothing insubstantial about it now. The grass was green, long and wild, rising to nighted hills of grey and purple, silvered a little by a gibbous moon. The temple was almost luminous, its columns shining with an eerie light. Gone the wraithlike dancers; they capered in cassocks now, solid, wild and weird with leering faces. I started as I stared at those faces – yellow, black and white faces, a half-dozen different races – but I started worse at the sight of the *thing* rising over the pool within the circle of glowing columns. Still vague, that horror – that leprous grey, tentacled, mushroom-domed monstrosity – and as yet mainly amorphous; but formed enough to show that it was nothing of this good, sane Earth.

'What the hell is it?' I half-gasped, half-whispered.

'Hmm?' Carl turned to me and smiled with pleased surprise at the look of shock on my blanched face. 'I'm damned if I know – but I think it's pretty good! It will be when it's finished. I'm going to call it *The Familiar* . . .'

7. The Face

For a long while I simply stood there taking in the contents of that hideous canvas and feeling the heat of the near-tropical night beating in through the open windows. It was all there: the foreign monks making their weird music, the temple glowing in the darkness, the dam, the pool and the hills as I had always known them, the *Thing* rising up in bloated loathsomeness from dark water, and a sense of realness I had never seen before and probably never again will see in any artist's work.

My first impulse when the shock wore off a little was to turn on Carl in anger. This was too monstrous a joke. But no, his face bore only a look of astonishment now – astonishment at my reaction, which must be quite obvious to him. 'Christ!' he said, 'is it that good?'

'That – *thing* – has nothing to do with Christ!' I finally managed to force the words out of a dry throat. And again I felt myself on the verge of demanding an explanation. Had he been reading my uncle's notes? Had he been secretly following my own line of research? But how could he, secretly or otherwise? The idea was preposterous.

'You really do *feel* it, don't you?' he said, excitedly taking my arm. 'I can see it in your face.'

'I . . . I feel it, yes,' I answered. 'It's a very . . . powerful piece of work.' Then, to fill the gap, I added: 'Where did you dream it up?'

'Right first time,' he answered. 'A dream – I think. Something left over from a nightmare. I haven't been sleeping too well. The heat, I guess.'

'You're right,' I agreed. 'It's too damned hot. Will you be doing any more tonight?'

He shook his head, his eyes still on the painting. 'Not in this light. I don't want to foul it up. No, I'm for bed. Besides, I have a headache.'

'What?' I said, glad now that I had made no wild accusation. 'You? – a strapping great Viking like you, with a headache?'

'Viking?' he frowned. 'You've called me that before. My looks must be deceptive. No, my ancestors came out of Hungary – a place called Stregoicavar. And I can tell you they burned more witches there than you ever did in Scotland!'

*   *   *

There was little sleep for me that night, though toward morning I did finally drop off, slumped across the great desk, drowsing fitfully in the soft glow of my desk light. Prior to that, however, in the silence of the night – driven on by a feeling of impending . . . something – I had delved deeper into the old books and documents amassed by my uncle, slowly but surely fitting together that great jigsaw whose pieces he had spent so many years collecting.

The work was more difficult now, his notes less coherent, his writing barely legible; but at least the material was or should be more familiar to me. Namely, I was studying the long line of McGilchrists gone before me, whose seat had been Temple House since its construction two hundred and forty years ago. And as I worked so my eyes would return again and again, almost involuntarily, to the dark pool with its ring of broken columns. Those stumps were white in the silver moonlight – as white as the columns in Carl's picture – and so my thoughts returned to Carl.

By now he must be well asleep, but this new mystery filled my mind through the small hours. Carl Earlman . . . It certainly sounded Hungarian, German at any rate, and I wondered what the old family name had been. Ehrlichman, perhaps? Arlmann? And not Carl but Karl.

And his family hailed from Stregoicavar. That was a name I remembered from a glance into Von Junzt's *Unspeakable Cults*, I was sure. Stregoicavar: it had stayed in my mind because of its meaning, which is 'witch-town.' Certain of Chorazos's order of pagan priests had been Hungarian. Was it possible that some dim ancestral memory lingered over in Carl's mind, and that the pool with its quartz stumps had awakened that in his blood which harkened back to older times? And what of the gypsy music he had sworn to hearing on our first night in this old house? Young and strong he was certainly, but beneath an often brash exterior he had all the sensitivity of an artist born.

According to my uncle's research my own great-grandfather, Robert Allan McGilchrist, had been just such a man. Sensitive, a dreamer, prone to hearing things in the dead of night which no one else could hear. Indeed, his wife had left him for his peculiar ways. She had taken her two sons with her; and so for many years the old man had lived here alone, writing and studying. He had been well known for his paper on the Lambton Worm legend of Northumberland: of a great worm or dragon that lived in a well and emerged at night to devour 'bairns and beasties and foolhardy wanderers in the dark.' He had also published a pamphlet on the naiads of the lochs of Inverness; and his limited edition book, *Notes on Nessie – the Secrets of Loch Ness* had caused a minor sensation when first it saw print.

It was Robert Allan McGilchrist, too, who restored the old floodgate in the dam, so that the water level in the pool could be controlled; but that had been his last work. A shepherd had found him one morning slumped across the gate, one hand still grasping the wheel which controlled its elevation, his upper body floating face-down in the water. He must have slipped and fallen, and his heart had given out. But the look on his face had been a fearful thing; and since the embalmers had been unable to do anything with him, they had buried him immediately.

And as I studied this or that old record or consulted this or that musty book, so my eyes would return to the dam, the pool with its fanged columns, the old floodgate – rusted now and fixed firmly in place – and the growing sensation of an onrushing doom gnawed inside me until it became a knot of fear in my chest. If only the heat would let up, just for one day, and if only I could finish my research and solve the riddle once and for all.

It was then, as the first flush of dawn showed above the eastern hills, that I determined what I must do. The fact of the matter was that Temple House frightened me, as I suspected it had frightened many people before me. Well, I had neither the stamina nor the dedication of my uncle. He had resolved to track the thing down to the end, and something – sheer hard work, the 'curse,' failing health, *something* – had killed him.

But his legacy to me had been a choice: continue his work or put an end to the puzzle for all time and blow Temple House to hell. So be it, that was what I would do. A day or two more – only a day or two, to let Carl finish his damnable painting – and then I would do what Gavin McGilchrist had ordered done. And with that resolution uppermost in my mind, relieved that at last I had made the decision, so I fell asleep where I sprawled at the desk.

The sound of splashing aroused me; that and my name called from below. The sun was just up and I felt dreadful, as if suffering from a hangover. For a long time I simply lay sprawled out. Then I stood up and eased my cramped limbs, and finally I turned to the open window. There was Carl, dressed only in his shorts, stretched out flat on a wide, thick plank, paddling out toward the middle of the pool!

'Carl!' I called down, my voice harsh with my own instinctive fear of the water. 'Man, that's dangerous – you can't swim!'

He turned his head, craned his neck and grinned up at me. 'Safe as houses,' he called, 'so long as I hang on to the plank. And it's cool, John, so wonderfully cool. This feels like the first time I've been cool in weeks!'

By now he had reached roughly the pool's centre and there he stopped paddling and simply let his hands trail in green depths. The level of the water had gone down appreciably during the night and the streamlet which fed the pool was now quite dry. The plentiful weed of the pool, becoming concentrated as the water evaporated, seemed thicker than ever I remembered it. So void of life, that water, with never a fish or frog to cause a ripple on the morass-green of its surface.

And suddenly that tight knot of fear was back in my chest, making my voice a croak as I tried to call out: 'Carl, get out of there!'

'What?' he faintly called back, but he didn't turn his head. He was staring down into the water, staring intently at something he saw there. His hand brushed aside weed—

'Carl!' I found my voice. 'For God's sake get out of it!'

He started then, his head and limbs jerking as if scalded, setting the plank to rocking so that he half slid off it. Then – a scrambling back to safety and a frantic splashing and paddling; and galvanized into activity I sprang from the window and raced breakneck downstairs. And Carl laughing shakily as I stumbled knee-deep in hated water to drag him physically from the plank, both of us trembling despite the burning rays of the new-risen sun and the furnace heat of the air.

'What happened?' I finally asked.

'I thought I saw something,' he answered. 'In the pool. A reflection, that's all, but it startled me.'

'What did you see?' I demanded, my back damp with cold sweat.

'Why, what would I see?' he answered, but his voice trembled for all that he tried to grin. 'A face, of course – my own face framed by the weeds. But it didn't look like me, that's all . . .'

8. The Dweller

Looking back now in the light of what I already knew – certainly of what I should have guessed at that time

– it must seem that I was guilty of an almost suicidal negligence in spending the rest of that day upstairs on my bed, tossing in nightmares brought on by the nervous exhaustion which beset me immediately after the incident at the pool. On the other hand, I had had no sleep the night before and Carl's adventure had given me a terrific jolt; and so my failure to recognize the danger – how close it had drawn – may perhaps be forgiven.

In any event, I forced myself to wakefulness in the early evening, went downstairs and had coffee and a frugal meal of biscuits, and briefly visited Carl in his studio. He was busy – frantically busy, dripping with sweat and brushing away at his canvas – working on his loathsome painting, which he did not want me to see. That suited me perfectly for I had already seen more than enough of the thing. I did take time enough to tell him, though, that he should finish his work in the next two days; for on Friday or at the very latest Saturday morning I intended to blow the place sky high.

Then I went back upstairs, washed and shaved, and as the light began to fail so I returned to my uncle's notebook. There were only three or four pages left unread, the first dated only days before his demise, but they were such a hodge-podge of scrambled and near-illegible miscellanea that I had the greatest difficulty making anything of them. Only that feeling of a burgeoning terror drove me on, though by now I had almost completely lost faith in making anything whatever of the puzzle.

As for my uncle's notes: a basically orderly nature had kept me from leafing at random through his book, or perhaps I should have understood earlier. As it is, the notebook is lost forever, but as best I can I shall copy down what I remember of those last few pages. After that – and after I relate the remaining facts of the occurrences of that fateful hideous night – the reader must rely upon his own judgement. The notes then, or what little I remember of them:

'Levi's or Mirandola's invocation: *"Dasmass Jeschet Boene Doess Efar Duvema Enit Marous."* If I could get the pronunciation right, perhaps . . . But what will the Thing be? And will it succumb to a double-barrelled blast? That remains to be seen. But if what I suspect is firmly founded . . . Is it a tick-thing, such as Von Junzt states inhabits the globular mantle of Yogg-Sothoth? (*Unaussprechlichen Kulten*, 78/16) – fearful hints – monstrous pantheon . . . And this merely a parasite to one of *Them*!

'The Cult of Cthulhu . . . immemorial horror spanning all the ages. The *Johansen Narrative* and the *Pnakotic Manuscript*. And the Innsmouth Raid of 1928; much was made of that, and yet nothing known for sure. Deep Ones, but . . . different again from this Thing.

'Entire myth-cycle . . . So many sources. Pure myth and legend? I think not. Too deep, interconnected, even plausible. According to Carter in SR, (AH '59) p. 250-51, *They* were driven into this part of the universe (or into this time-dimension) by "Elder Gods" as punishment for a rebellion. Hastur the Unspeakable prisoned in Lake of Hali (again the lake or pool motif) in Carcosa; Great Cthulhu in R'lyeh, where he slumbers still in his death-sleep; Ithaqua sealed away behind icy Arctic barriers, and so on. But Yogg-Sothoth was sent *outside*, into a parallel place, conterminous with all space and time. Since YS is everywhere and when, if a man knew the gate he could call Him out . . .

'Did Chorazos and his acolytes, for some dark reason of their own, attempt thus to call Him out?

And did they get this dweller in Him instead? And I believe I understand the reason for the pool. Grandfather knew. His interest in Nessie, the Lambton Worm, the Kraken of olden legend, naiads, Cthulhu ... Wendy Smith's burrowers feared water; and the sheer *weight* of the mighty Pacific helps keep C. prisoned in his place in R'lyeh – thank God! Water subdues these things ...

'But if water confines It, why does It *return* to the water? And how may It leave the pool if not deliberately called out? No McGilchrist ever called It out, I'm sure, not willingly; though some may have suspected that something was there. No swimmers in the family – not a one – and I think I know why. It is an instinctive, an ancestral fear of the pool! No, of the unknown *Thing* which lurks beneath the pool's surface ...'

The thing which lurks beneath the pool's surface ...

Clammy with the heat, and with a debilitating terror springing from these words on the written page – these scribbled thought-fragments which, I was now sure, were anything but demented ravings – I sat at the old desk and read on. And as the house grew dark and quiet, as on the previous night, again I found my eyes drawn to gaze down through the open window to the surface of the still pool.

Except that the surface was no longer still!

Ripples were spreading in concentric rings from the pool's dark centre, tiny mobile wavelets caused by – by what? Some disturbance beneath the surface? The water level was well down now and tendrils of mist drifted from the pool to lie soft, luminous and undulating in the moonlight, curling like the tentacles of some great plastic beast over the dam, across the drive to the foot of the house.

A sort of paralysis settled over me then, a dreadful lassitude, a mental and physical malaise brought on by excessive morbid study, culminating in this latest phenomenon of the old house and the aura of evil which now seemed to saturate its very stones. I should have done something – something to break the spell, anything rather than sit there and merely wait for what was happening to happen – and yet I was incapable of positive action.

Slowly I returned my eyes to the written page; and there I sat shivering and sweating, my skin crawling as I read on by the light of my desk lamp. But so deep my trancelike state that it was as much as I could do to force my eyes from one word to the next. I had no volition, no will of my own with which to fight that fatalistic spell; and the physical heat of the night was that of a furnace as sweat dripped from my forehead onto the pages of the notebook.

'. . . I have checked my findings and can't believe my previous blindness! It should have been obvious. It happens when the water level falls below a certain point. It *has* happened every time there has been extremely hot weather – when the pool has started to *dry up*! The Thing needn't be called out at all! As to why it returns to the pool after taking a victim: it must return before daylight. It is a fly-the-light. A haunter of the dark. A wampyre! . . . but not blood. Nowhere can I find mention of blood sacrifices. And no punctures or mutilations. What, then are Its "needs?" Did Dee know? Kelly knew, I'm sure, but his writings are lost . . .

'Eager now to try the invocation, but I wish that first I might know the true nature of the Thing. It takes the life of Its victim – but what else?'

'I have it! – God, I know – and I wish I did not know! But that *look* on my poor brother's face . . . Andrew, Andrew . . . I know now why you looked that way. But if I can free you, you shall be freed. If I wondered at the nature of the Thing, then I wonder no longer. The answers are all there, in the *Cthaat A.* and *Hydrophinnae*, if only I had known exactly where to look. Yibb-Tstll is one such; Bugg-Shash, too. Yes, and the pool-thing is another . . .

'There have been a number down the centuries – the horror that dwelled in the mirror of Nitocris; the sucking, hunting thing that Count Magnus kept; the red, hairy slime used by Julian Scortz – familiars of the Great Old Ones, parasites that lived on *Them* as lice live on men. Or rather, on their life-force! This one has survived the ages, at least until now. It does not take the blood but the very essence of Its victim. *It is a soul-eater!*

'I can wait no longer. Tonight, when the sun goes down and the hills are in darkness . . . But if I succeed, and if the Thing comes for me . . . We'll see how It faces up to my shotgun!'

My eyes were half-closed by the time I had finally scanned all that was written, of which the above is only a small part; and even having read it I had not fully taken it in. Rather, I had absorbed it automatically, without reading any immediate meaning into it. But as I re-read those last few lines, so I heard something which roused me up from my lassitude and snapped me alertly awake in an instant.

It was music: the faint but unmistakable strains of a whirling pagan tune that seemed to reach out to me from a time beyond time, from a hell beyond all known hells . . .

9. The Horror

Shocked back to mental alertness, still my limbs were stiff as a result of several hours crouched over the desk. Thus, as I sprang or attempted to spring to my feet, a cramp attacked both of my calves and threw me down by the window. I grabbed at the sill . . . and whatever I had been about to do was at once forgotten.

I gazed out the open window on a scene straight out of madness or nightmare. The broken columns where they now stood up from bases draped with weed seemed to glow with an inner light; and to my straining eyes it appeared that this haze of light extended uniformly upwards, so that I saw a revenant of the temple as it had once been. Through the light-haze I could also see the centre of the pool, from which the ripples spread outward with a rapidly increasing agitation.

There was a shape there now, a dark oblong illuminated both by the clean moonlight and by that supernatural glow; and even as I gazed, so the water slopping above the oblong seemed pushed aside and the slab showed its stained marble surface to the air. The music grew louder then, soaring wildly, and it seemed to me in my shocked and frightened condition that dim figures reeled and writhed around the perimeter of the pool.

Then – horror of horrors! – in one mad moment the slab tilted to reveal a black hole going down under the pool, like the entrance to some sunken tomb. There came an outpouring of miasmal gases, visible in the eerie glow, and then—

Even before the thing emerged I knew what it would be; how it would look. It was that horror on Carl's canvas, the soft-tentacled, mushroom-domed terror he had painted under the ancient, evil influence of this damned, doomed place. It was the dweller, the familiar, the tick-thing, the star-born wampyre . . . it was the curse of the McGilchrists.

Except I understood now that this was not merely a curse on the McGilchrists but on the entire world. Of course it had seemed to plague the McGilchrists as a personal curse – but only because they had chosen to build Temple House here on the edge of its pool. They had been victims by virtue of their *availability*, for I was sure that the pool-thing was not naturally discriminative.

Then, with an additional thrill of horror, I saw that the thing was on the move, drifting across the surface of the pool, its flaccid tentacles reaching avidly in the direction of the house. The lights downstairs were out, which meant that Carl must be asleep . . .

Carl!

The thing was across the drive now, entering the porch, the house itself. I forced cramped limbs to agonized activity, lurched across the room, out onto the dark landing and stumbled blindly down the stairs. I slipped, fell, found my feet again – and my voice, too.

'Carl!' I cried, arriving at the door of his studio. 'Carl, *for God's sake!*'

The thing straddled him where he lay upon his bed. It glowed with an unearthly, a rotten luminescence which outlined his pale body in a sort of foxfire. Its tentacles writhed over his naked form and his limbs were filled with fitful motion. Then the dweller's mushroom head settled over his face, which disappeared in folds of the thing's gilled mantle.

'Carl!' I screamed yet again, and as I lurched forward in numb horror so my hand found the light switch on the wall. In another moment the room was bathed in sane and wholesome electric light. The thing bulged upward from Carl – rising like some monstrous amoeba, some sentient, poisonous jellyfish from an alien ocean – and turned toward me.

I saw a face, a face I knew across twenty years of time fled, *my uncle's face!* Carved in horror, those well remembered features besought, pleaded with me, that an end be put to this horror and peace restored to this lonely valley; that the souls of countless victims be freed to pass on from this world to their rightful destinations.

The thing left Carl's suddenly still form and moved forward, flowed toward me; and as it came so the face it wore melted and changed. Other faces were there, hidden in the thing, many with McGilchrist features and many without, dozens of them that came and went ceaselessly. There were children there, too, mere babies; but the last face of all, the one I shall remember above all others – *that was the face of Carl Earlman himself!* And it, too, wore that pleading, that imploring look – the look of a soul in hell, which prays only for its release.

Then the light won its unseen, unsung battle. Almost upon me, suddenly the dweller seemed to wilt. It shrank from the light, turned and flowed out of the room, through the porch, back toward the pool. Weak with reaction I watched it go, saw it move out across the now still water, saw the slab tilt down upon its descending shape and heard the music fade into silence. Then I turned to Carl . . .

I do not think I need mention the look on Carl's lifeless face, or indeed say anything more about him. Except perhaps that it is my fervent prayer that he now rests in peace with the rest of the dweller's many victims, taken down the centuries. That is my prayer, but . . .

As for the rest of it:

I dragged Carl from the house to the Range Rover, drove him to the crest of the rise, left him there and returned to the house. I took my uncle's prepared charges from his study and set them in the base of the shale cliff where the house backed onto it. Then I lit the fuses, scrambled back into the Range Rover and drove to where Carl's body lay in the cool of night. I tried not to look at his face.

In a little while the fuses were detonated, going off almost simultaneously, and the night was shot with fire and smoke and a rising cloud of dust. When the air cleared the whole scene was changed forever. The cliff had come down on the house, sending it crashing into the pool. The pool itself had disappeared, swallowed up in shale and debris; and it was as if the House of the Temple, the temple itself and the demon-cursed pool had never existed.

All was silence and desolation, where only the moonlight played on jagged stumps of centuried columns, projecting still from the scree- and rubble-filled depression which had been the pool. And now the moon silvered the bed of the old stream, running with water from the ruined pool—

And at last I was able to drive on.

10. The Unending Nightmare

That should have been the end of it, but such has not been the case. Perhaps I alone am to blame. The police in Penicuik listened to my story, locked me in a cell overnight and finally conveyed me to this place, where I have been now for more than a week. In a way I supposed that the actions of the police were understandable; for my wild appearance that night – not to mention the ghastly, naked corpse in the Range Rover and the incredible story I incoherently told – could hardly be expected to solicit their faith or understanding. But I do *not* understand the position of the alienists here at Oakdeene.

Surely they, too, can hear the damnable music? – that music which grows louder hour by hour, more definite and decisive every night – the music which in olden days summoned the pool-thing to its ritual sacrifice. Or is it simply that they disagree with my theory? I have mentioned it to them time and time again and repeat it now: that there are *other* pools in the Pentlands, watery havens to which the thing might have fled from the destruction of its weedy retreat beside the now fallen seat of the McGilchrists. Oh, yes, and I firmly believe that it did so flee. And the days are long and hot and a great drought is on the land . . .

And perhaps, too, over the years, a very real curse has loomed up large and monstrous over the McGilchrists. Do souls have a flavour, I wonder, a distinctive texture of their own? Is it possible that the pool-thing has developed an appetite, a *taste* for the souls of McGilchrists? If so, then it will surely seek me out; and yet here I am detained in this institute for the insane.

Or could it be that I am now in all truth mad? Perhaps the things I have experienced and know to be true have driven me mad, and the music I hear exists only in my mind. That is what the nurses tell me and dear God, I pray that it is so! But if not – if not . . .

For there is that other thing, which I have not mentioned until now. When I carried Carl from his studio after the pool-thing left him, I saw his finished painting. Not the whole painting but merely a part of it, for when it met my eyes they saw only one thing: the finished face which Carl had painted on the dweller.

This is the nightmare which haunts me worse than any other, the question I ask myself over and over in the dead of night, when the moonlight falls upon my high, barred window and the music floods into my padded cell:

If they should bring me my breakfast one morning and find me dead – *will my face really look like that?*

BACK ROW

I did my share of back-row necking way back when in my teens. And sometimes I got lucky and didn't stop at the neck! More I daren't say because I don't want to spoil my clean-cut image. Oh, and a PS: this is the closest I get to breaking the promise I made in my introduction. So, just in case, have a bucket handy . . .

I'll tell it exactly the way it happened.

They were showing a love story at the Odeon, a classic from years dead and all but forgotten. The first time I'd seen this picture had been with my wife – would you believe, thirty years ago? The picture had outlasted her, if not our love. Maybe that's why I wanted to see it again.

I picked a rainy Wednesday afternoon. No kids hooting and gibbering in the back rows, maybe a pair or two of lovers in the double seats back there, snuggling up to each other and blissfully, deliciously secure and secretive in the dark. I'd been young myself, once. But what with this ancient film and the middle of the week, and the miserable weather, the old Odeon should be just about empty; maybe a few dodderers like myself, down at the front where their eyes wouldn't feel the strain.

But not me, I'd be up in the gods, in the next but back row. Along with my memories, my eyes seemed to be the only things that hadn't faded away on me.

I was there waiting for the doors to open, my collar turned up, a fifty-pence piece ready in my hand. That's one mercy: we oldies can get in cheap. Cheap? *Hah!* I remember when it was thruppence! And these two kids in front of me, why, they'd be paying maybe two pounds *each*! For a bit of privacy, if you can call it that, in a mouldy old flea-trap like the Odeon.

Behind me a handful of people had gathered, Darby and Joans, some of them, but mainly singles. Most of them were pensioners like myself, out chasing memories of their own, I supposed. And we all stood there waiting for the doors to open.

I had to look somewhere, and so I looked ahead of me, at these two kids. Well, I didn't actually look *at* them – I mean you don't, do you? I looked around them, over them, through them, the way you do. But something of them stuck to my mind – not very much, I'm afraid.

The lad would be eighteen, maybe nineteen, and the girl a couple of years younger. I didn't fix her face clearly, mind you, but she was what they call a looker: all pink and glowing, and a bit giggly, with a mass of shiny black hair under the hood of her bright red plastic rain mac. White teeth and a stub of a nose, and eyes that sparkled when she smiled. A right Little Red Riding-Hood! And all of it in little more than sixty-two or -three inches; but then again they say nice things come in small packages. Damned if I could see what she saw in *him*! But she clung to him so close it was like he'd hypnotized her. And you know, I had to have a little smile to myself? Jealousy, at my age!

About the lad: he was pale, gangly – or 'gawky' as we'd say in my neck of the woods – hollow-cheeked; he looked like someone had been neglecting him. A good feed would fix him up no end. But it probably wouldn't fix the fishy, unblinking stare that came through those thick-lensed spectacles of his. He wore a black mac a bit small for him, which made his wrists stick out like pipe-stems. A matched couple? Hardly, but they do say that opposites attract . . .

Anyway, before I could look at them more closely, if I'd wanted to, we went in.

The Odeon's a dowdy place. It always has been. Twenty years ago it was dowdy, since when it's well past the point of no return. The glitter's gone, I'm afraid, and no putting it back. But I'll say one thing for it: they've never called bingo there. When telly came in and the cinemas slumped, the old Odeon continued to show films; somehow it came through it, but not without its share of scars.

These days . . . well, you could plaster and paint all you liked, and you still wouldn't cover up all the wrinkles. It would be like an old woman putting on her warpaint: she'd still come out mutton dressed as lamb. But that's the old Odeon: even with the lights up full, still the place seems so dim as to be almost misty. Misty, yes, with that clinging miasma of old places. Not haunted, no, but old and creaking and about ready to be pulled down. Or maybe my eyes weren't so good after all, or perhaps there's a layer of dust on the light-bulbs in the high ceiling . . .

I went upstairs (taking it easy, you know, and leaning on my stick a bit) and headed for my usual seat near the back. And sure enough the young 'uns were right there ahead of me, not in my row but the one behind, at the very back; all very quiet and coy, they were, where they'd chosen one of the double seats. But I hadn't noticed them buying sweets or popcorn at the kiosk in the shabby foyer, so maybe they'd stay that way right through the show: nice and quiet.

Other patrons came upstairs, all heading for the front where there was a little more leg-room and they could lean on the mahogany balcony and look down on the screen. When the lights started to go down in that slow way of theirs, there couldn't have been more than two dozen people in all up there, and most of them in the front two rows. Me and the kids, we had the back entirely to ourselves. It was a poor showing even for a Wednesday; maybe there'd be more people in the cheap seats downstairs.

In the old days this was the part I'd liked the best: the lights dimming, organ music (but only recorded, even in my time), and the curtains on stage slowly swishing open to reveal a dull, pearly, vacant screen. Then there'd be The Queen and the curtains would close again while the lights died completely. Followed by a supporting film, a cartoon, the trailers, and finally the feature film. Oh, yes – and between the cartoon and the main show there'd be an intermission, when the ice cream ladies would come down the aisles with their trays. And at the end, The Queen again. Funny thing, but I can't go back as far as The King. I mean, I can, but my memory can't or won't! And even remembering what I can, I'm not sure I have it exactly right. That's what getting old does to you. Anyway, the whole thing from going in to coming out would last two and a half to maybe three whole hours! *That* was value.

Nowadays . . . you get the trailer, local advertisements, the Feature Film – and that's it. Or if you're lucky there *might* be a short supporting picture. And here's me saying I was surprised at the poor turnout.

Well, the trailers weren't much, and the local ads were totally colourless and not even up to date – Paul's Unisex Hairdressing Salon had shut down months ago! Then the briefest of brief intervals when the lights came half-way up; and suddenly it dawned on me that I hadn't heard a peep out of the young couple behind me in the back row. Well, maybe the very faintest whisper or giggle or two. Certainly nothing to complain about.

The seats were stepped down in tiers from the back to the balcony, so that my row of seats was maybe six inches lower than theirs. I sneaked a backward glance and my eyes trapped just a snapshot of the two sitting there very close, wasting half their seat, the girl crammed in one corner with the pale lad's black-clad arm thrown lightly round her red-clad shoulders. And his fish-eyes behind their thick lenses, swivelling to meet mine, expressionless but probably wishing I'd go away. Then it was dark again and the titles rolling, and me settling down to enjoy this old picture, along with one or two old-fashioned memories.

That was when it started; the carrying-on in the back row. Of course I had seen it coming: when I'd glanced back at them, those kids had still been wearing their rain macs. You don't have to be a dirty old man to see through that old ploy. It's amazing what can go on – or come off – under a rain mac.

Very soon buttons would slowly be giving way, one by one, to trembly, groping fingers under the shiny plastic; garments would be loosened, warm, naked flesh cautiously exposed – but not to view. No usherette's torch beam would find them out, and certainly not the prying eyes of some old duffer in the row in front. Indeed, the fact that I was there probably added to their excitement. It amused me to think of myself as a prop in their loveplay, a spanner in their wet works, whom they must somehow deceive even knowing that I wasn't deceived.

And all the time this sick-looking excuse for a youth pretending the exploratory hand had nothing to do with him, and the girl pretending to be completely unaware of its creeping advance toward her nipples. And they'd only be its first objective. All of this assuming, of course, that they were just beginners. Oh, yes – it's a funny business, love in the back row of a cinema.

First there was the heavy breathing. Ah, but there's heavy breathing and there's heavy breathing! And the moaning, very low at first but gradually becoming more than audible. I quickly changed my mind, restructured the scenario I'd devised for them. They weren't new to it, these two; by now *all* the buttons would be loose, and just about everything else for that matter! No exploratory work here. This was old ground, gone over many, many times before, together or with others; no prelude but a full-blown orchestration, which would gradually build to a crescendo.

Would they actually do it, I wondered? Right there in the back row? Fifteen minutes ago I'd seen myself as some sort of obstacle they'd have to overcome; now I was thinking they didn't give a damn about me, didn't care that I was there at all. I might as well not exist for these two, not here, not tonight. They had the darkness and each other – what the hell was the presence of one old man, who was probably deaf anyway?

A knee had found its way up onto the curved collar of my seat back; I felt its gentle pressure, then its vibration starting up like a mild electric current, building to a throb that came right through the wood and the padding to my shoulders. A knee-trembler, we'd called it in my day, when the body's passion is too great to be contained. And all the time the moaning increasing in pitch, until it rose just a little above the whirring of the projector where it aimed its white, flickering curtain of beams at the screen to form the moving pictures.

It dawned on me that I was a voyeur. Without even looking at them I was party to their every action. But an unwilling party . . . wasn't I? I had come here to watch a film, not to be caught up in the animal excitement of lusting lovers. And yet I was caught up in it!

They'd aroused me – *me*, an old man. With their panting and moaning and slobbering. I was sweating with their sweat and shaking with their vibrations; and all I could do was sit there, stricken and trembling like a man immobilized as by the touch of some strange female's hand in his most private place; yes, actually *feeling* as if some unknown woman had taken the seat next to mine and started to fondle me! That's how engrossed I had become with what was happening behind me, there in the back row.

Suddenly I was startled to realize that we were into the last reel. My God! – but what had happened here?

Where had my film and my memories gone? A little bit of nostalgia was all I had wanted. And I'd missed it all, everything, because of them.

Them . . .

Why, I could even smell them now! Musty, sweet, sweaty, sexual, biological! I could *smell* sex! And a mouth gobbling away at flesh only inches from my ears! And a frantic gasping coming faster and faster, bringing pictures of some half-exhausted dog steaming away on a bitch!

Lovers? Animal excitement? They *were* animals! Young animals – and right now they were feasting on each other like . . . like vampires! Oh, I *suppose* you could call it petting, kissing, 'canoodling' – but it wasn't the kind I'd used to do. Not the kind me and my lass had indulged in, all those years ago. Kissing? I could hear them *sucking* at each other, foaming away like hard acid eating into soft wood. And suddenly I was angry.

Angry with myself, with them, with everything. The film had only fifteen minutes to run and everything felt . . . ruined. Well, and now I'd ruin it for them. For him, any-way. *You won't come, you young bugger!* I thought. *You've denied me my pleasure, and now I'll deny you yours.*

Abruptly I turned the top half of my body, my head, and spat out: 'Now listen, you two—'

They were like one person, fused together, almost prone on their long seat. The hoods of their macs were up and crushed together, and I swear that I saw steam – the smoke of their sex – escaping from the darkness where their faces were locked like tightly clasped hands. The slobbering stopped on the instant, and a moment later . . . I heard a growl!

No, a snarl! A warning not to interfere.

Oh, pale and sickly he might have seemed, but he was young and I was old. His bones would bend where mine would break like twigs. I could feel his contempt like a physical thing; I *had been* feeling it for the last ninety minutes. Of course, for who else but a contemptuous lout would have dared all of this with me sitting there right in front of him? And the girl was just as bad if not worse!

'I . . . I . . . I'm disgusted!' I mumbled. And then I quickly turned my face back to the screen, and watched the rest of the film through a wash of hot, shameful tears . . .

Just before the lights went up I thought I heard them leave. At least I heard light footsteps treading the carpet along the back row, receding. Of course it could be the girl, on her own, going to 'tidy herself up' in the ladies. And because he might still be there behind me, sneering at me, I didn't look to see.

Then the film was over, and as the people down front began filing out, still I sat there. Because I could still feel someone behind me, hot and salty. Because it might be him and he'd look at me, fishy-eyed and threatening, through those steamed-up glasses of his.

Eventually I had to make a move. Maybe they'd both gone after all and I was just an old coward. I stood up, glanced into the back row, and saw—

God! What had he done to her?

The rain mac was open top to bottom. She – what was left of her – was slumped down inside it. There was very little flesh on her face, just raw red. Breasts had gone, right down to steaming ribs. The belly was open, eviscerated, a laid back gash that opened right down to the spread thighs. There were no innards, no sexual parts left at all down there. If I hadn't seen her before, I couldn't even have said it was a girl at all.

These were my thoughts before I noticed the true colour of the mac. I had only thought it was red at first glance, because my mind hadn't been able to accept so much red that wasn't plastic. And I saw his specs, crushed and broken on the blackened, blood-soaked baize of the double seat . . .

That's my statement, Sergeant, and there's nothing else I can tell you – except that there's something terrible loose in this town that eats living guts and looks like a pretty girl.

NAME AND NUMBER

*This one sprang from a personal interest in numerology, cryp-
tography, and biblical prophecy* not *bibliomancy! Believe me,
I'm not a Bible-puncher! But so many stories had been written
about the Antichrist, I just wanted to do it differently.*

After Francesco Cova had published Name and Number
in Kadath, *his superb but alas long-vanished magazine, he
wanted to know how I had worked it out. I could only tell
him I hadn't, that Titus Crow must take the credit himself.
Flippant? – you could say that, I suppose – but it really is
difficult to say how this one 'worked itself out.' It's one of
those peculiar stories that has to be written backwards.*

*Who was it said, 'You can prove anything with numbers?'
And who for that matter asked, 'What's in a name?' So
here's psychic detective Titus Crow posing a most peculiar
problem. Now put yourself in Henri de Marigny's shoes and
see how* you *make out. The clues are all there.*

Hey! – and no cheating!

I

Of course, nothing now remains of Blowne House, the sprawling bungalow retreat of my dear friend and mentor Titus Crow, destroyed by tempestuous winds in a 'freak storm' on the night of 4 October 1968, but . . .

Knowing all I know, or knew, of Titus Crow, perhaps it has been too easy for me to pass off the disastrous events of that night simply as a vindictive attack of dark forces; and while that is exactly what they were, I am now given to wonder if perhaps there was not a lot more to it than met the eye.

Provoked by Crow's and my own involvement with the Wilmarth Foundation (that vast, august and amazingly covert body, dedicated to the detection and the destruction of Earth's elder evil, within and outside of Man himself, and working in the sure knowledge that Man is but a small and comparatively recent phenomenon in a cosmos which has known sentience, good and evil, through vast and immeasurable cycles of time), dark forces did indeed destroy Blowne House. In so doing they effectively removed Titus Crow from the scene, and as for myself . . . I am but recently returned to it.

But since visiting the ruins of Crow's old place all these years later (perhaps because the time flown in between means so very little to me?), I have come to wonder more and more about the *nature* of that so well-remembered attack, the nature of the very winds themselves – those twisting, rending, tearing winds – which fell with such intent and purpose upon the house and bore it to the ground. In considering them I find myself casting my mind back to a time even more remote, when Crow first outlined for me the facts in the strange case of Mr Sturm Magruser V.

Crow's letter – a single handwritten sheet in a blank, sealed envelope, delivered by a taxi-driver and the ink not quite dry – was at once terse and cryptic, which was not unusual and did not at all surprise me. When Titus Crow was idling, then all who wished anything to do with him must also bide their time, but when he was in a hurry—

> Henri,
> (said the note)
>   *Come as soon as you can, midnight would be fine. I expect you will stay the night. If you have not eaten, don't – there is food here. I have something of a story to tell you, and in the morning we are to visit a cemetery!*
>
> > > > *Until I see you –*
> > > > (signed)
> > > > *Titus.*

The trouble with such invitations was this: I had never been able to refuse them. For Crow being what he was, one of London's foremost occultists, and my own interest in such matters amounting almost to obsession – why, for all its brevity, indeed by the very virtue of that brevity – Crow's summons was more a Royal Command!

And so I refrained from eating, wrote a number of letters which could not wait, enveloped and stamped them, and left a note for my housekeeper, Mrs Adams, telling her to post them. She was to expect me when she saw me, but in any matter of urgency I might be contacted at Blowne House. Doubtless the dear lady, when she read that address, would complain bitterly to herself about the influence of 'that dreadful Crow person,' for in her eyes Titus had always been to blame for my own deep interest in darkling matters. In all truth, however, my obsession was probably inherited, sealed into my personality as a permanent stamp of my father, the great New Orleans mystic Etienne-Laurent de Marigny.

Then, since the hour already approached twelve and I would be late for my 'appointment,' I 'phoned for a taxi and double-checked that my one or two antique treasures were safely locked away; and finally I donned my overcoat. Half an hour or so later, at perhaps a quarter to one, I stood on Crow's doorstep and banged upon his heavy oak door; and having heard the arrival of my taxi, he was there at once to greet me. This he did with his customary grin (or enigmatic smile?), his head cocked slightly to one side in an almost enquiring posture. And once again I was ushered into the marvellous Aladdin's Cave which was Blowne House.

Now Crow had been my friend ever since my father sent me out of America as a child in the late thirties, and no man knew him better than I; and yet his personality was such that whenever I met him – however short the intervening time – I would always be impressed anew by his stature, his leonine good looks, and the sheer weight of intellect which seemed invariably to shine out from behind those searching, dark eyes of his. In his flame-red, wide-sleeved dressing-gown, he might easily be some wizard from the pages of myth or fantasy.

In his study he took my overcoat, bade me sit in an easy chair beside a glowing fire, tossed a small log onto ruddy embers and poured me a customary brandy before seating himself close by. And while he was thus engaged I took my chance to gaze with fascination and unfeigned envy all about that marvellous room.

Crow himself had designed and furnished that large room to contain most of what he considered important to his world, and certainly I could have spent ten full years there in constant study of the contents without absorbing or even understanding a fifth part of what I read or examined. However, to give a brief and essentially fleshless account of what I could see from my chair:

His 'Library,' consisting of one entire wall of shelves, contained such works as the abhorrent *Cthaat Aquadingen* (in a binding of human skin!), Feery's *Original Notes on the Necronomicon* (the complete book, as opposed to my own abridged copy), Wendy-Smith's translation of the *G'harne Fragments*, a possibly faked but still priceless copy of the *Pnakotic Manuscripts,* Justin Geoffrey's *People of the Monolith,* a literally fabulous *Cultes des Goules* (which, on my next birthday, having derived all he could from it, he would present to me), the *Geph Transcriptions,* Wardle's *Notes on Nitocris,* Urbicus' *Frontier Garrison,* circa AD 183, Plato on *Atlantis,* a rare, illustrated, pirated and privately printed *Complete Works of Poe* in three sumptuous volumes, the far more ancient works of such as Josephus, Magnus, Levi and Erdschluss, and a connected set of volumes on oceanic lore and legend which included such works as Gantley's *Hydrophinnae* and Konrad von Gerner's *Fischbuch* of 1598. And I have merely skimmed the surface . . .

In one dim corner stood an object which had been a source of fascination for me, and no less for Crow himself: a great hieroglyphed, coffin-shaped monstrosity of a grandfather clock, whose *tick* was quite irregular and abnormal, and whose four hands moved independently and without recourse to any time-system with which I was remotely familiar. Crow had bought the thing in an auction some years previously, at which time he had mentioned his belief that it had once belonged to my father – of which I had known nothing, not at that time.

As for the general decor and feel of the place:

Silk curtains were drawn across wide windows; costly boukhara rugs were spread on a floor already covered in fine Axminster; a good many Aubrey Beardsley originals – some of them most erotic – hung on the walls in equally valuable antique rosewood frames; and all in all the room seemed to exude a curiously mixed atmosphere of rich, warm, Olde Worlde gentility on the one hand, a strange and alien chill of outer spheres on the other.

And thus I hope I have managed to convey something of the nature of Titus Crow and of his study – and of his *studies* – in that bungalow dwelling on Leonard's Heath known as Blowne House . . . As to why I was there—

'I suppose you're wondering,' Crow said after a while, 'just why I asked you to come? And at such an hour on such a chilly night, when doubtless you've a good many other things you should be doing? Well, I'll not keep you in suspense – but first of all I would greatly appreciate your opinion of something.' He got up, crossed to his desk and returned with a thick book of newspaper cuttings, opening it to a previously marked page. Most of the cuttings were browned and faded, but the one Crow pointed out to me was only a few weeks old. It was a photograph of the head and shoulders of a man, accompanied by the following legend:

Mr Sturm Magruser, head of 'Magruser Systems UK,' the weapons manufacturing company of world repute, is on the point of winning for his company a £2,000,000 order from the Ministry of Defence in respect of an at present 'secret' national defence system. Mr Magruser, who himself devised and is developing the new system, would not comment when he was snapped by our reporter leaving the country home of a senior Ministry of Defence official, but it has been rumoured for some time that his company is close to a breakthrough on a defence system which will effectively make the atom bomb obsolete. Tests are said to be scheduled for the near future, following which the Ministry of Defence is expected to make its final decision . . .

'Well?' Crow asked as I read the column again.

I shrugged. 'What are you getting at?'

'It makes no impression?'

'I've heard of him and his company, of course,' I answered, 'though I believe this is the first time I've actually seen a picture of him – but apart from—'

'Ah!' Crow cut in. 'Good! This is the first time you've seen his picture: and him a prominent figure and his firm constantly in the news and so on. Me too.'

'Oh?' I was still puzzled.

'Yes, it's important, Henri, what you just said. In fact, I would hazard a guess that Mr Magruser is one of the world's least photographed men.'

'So? Perhaps he's camera shy.'

'Oh, he is, he is – and for a very good reason. We'll get to it – eventually. Meanwhile, let's eat!'

Now this is a facet of Crow's personality which did annoy me: his penchant for leaping from one subject to another, willy-nilly, with never a word of explanation, leaving one constantly stumbling in the dark. He could only do it, of course, when he knew that his audience was properly hooked. But in my case I do not expect he intended any torment; he merely offered me the opportunity to use my mind. This I seized upon, while he busied himself bringing out cold cuts of fried chicken from his kitchen.

II

Sturm Magruser ... A strange name, really. Foreign, of course. Hungarian, perhaps? As the 'Mag' in 'Magyar'? I doubted it, even though his features were decidedly eastern or middle-eastern; for they were rather pale, too. And what of his first name, Sturm? If only I were a little more proficient in tongues, I might make something of it. And what of the man's reticence, and of Crow's comment that he stood amongst the least photographed of men?

We finished eating. 'What do you make of the "V" after his name?' Crow asked.

'Hmm? Oh, it's a common enough vogue nowadays,' I answered, 'particularly in America. It denotes that he's the fifth of his line, the fifth Sturm Magruser.'

Crow nodded and frowned. 'You'd think so, wouldn't you? But in this case it can't possibly be. No, for he changed his name by deed-poll after his parents died.' He had grown suddenly intense, but before I could ask him why, he was off again. 'And what would you give him for nationality, or rather origin?'

I took a stab at it. 'Romanian?'

He shook his head. 'Persian.'

I smiled. 'I was way out, wasn't I?'

'What about his face?' Crow pressed.

I picked up the book of cuttings and looked at the photograph again. 'It's a strange face, really. Pale somehow . . .'

'He's an albino.'

'Ah!' I said. 'Yes, pale and startled – at least in this picture – displeased at being snapped, I suppose.'

Again he nodded. 'You suppose correctly . . . All right, Henri, enough of that for the moment. Now I'll tell you what I made of this cutting – Magruser's picture and the story – when first I saw it. Now as you know I collect all sorts of cuttings from one source or another, tidbits of fact and fragments of information which interest me or strike me as unusual. Most occultists, I'm told, are extensive collectors of all sorts of things. You yourself are fond of antiques, old books and *outré* bric-a-brac; much as I am, but as yet without my dedication. And yet if you examine all of my scrapbooks you'll probably discover that this would appear to be the most mundane cutting of them all. At least on the surface. For myself, I found it the most frightening and disturbing.'

He paused to pour more brandy and I leaned closer to him, fascinated to find out exactly what he was getting at. 'Now,' he finally continued, 'I'm an odd sort of chap, as you'll appreciate, but I'm not eccentric – not in the popular sense of the word. Or if I am,' he hurried on, 'it's of my choosing. That is to say, I believe I'm mentally stable.'

'You are the sanest man I ever met,' I told him.

'I wouldn't go that far,' he answered, 'and you may soon have reason for re-evaluation, but for the moment I *am* sane. How then might I explain the loathing, the morbid repulsion, the absolute shock of horror which struck me almost physically upon opening the pages of my morning newspaper and coming upon that picture of Magruser? I could not explain it – not immediately . . .' He paused again.

'Presentiment?' I asked. 'A forewarning?'

'Certainly!' he answered. 'But of what, and from where? And the more I looked at that damned picture, the more sure I became that I was seeing something monstrous! Seeing him – that face, startled, angered, trapped by the camera – and despite the fact that I could not possibly know him, I *recognized* him.'

'Ah,' I said. 'You mean that you've known him before, under his former name?'

Crow smiled, a trifle wearily I thought. 'The world has known him before under several names,' he answered. Then the smile slipped from his face. 'Talking of names, what do you make of his forename?'

'Sturm? I've already considered it. German, perhaps?'

'Good! Yes, German. His mother was German, his father Persian, both nationalized Americans in the early 1900s. They left America to come here during McCarthy's UnAmerican Activities witch-hunts. Sturm Magruser, incidentally, was born on 1 April 1921. An important date, Henri, and not just because it was April Fool's Day.'

'A fairly young man,' I answered, 'to have reached so powerful a position.'

'Indeed,' Crow nodded. 'He would have been forty-three in a month's time.'

'Would have been?' I was surprised by Crow's tone of finality. 'Is he dead then?'

'Mercifully, yes,' he answered, 'Magruser and his project with him! He died the day before yesterday, on 4 March 1964, also an important date. It was in yesterday's news, but I'm not surprised you missed it. He wasn't given a lot of space, and he leaves no mourners that I know of. As to his "secret weapon,"' (and here Crow gave an involuntary little shudder), 'the secret has gone with him. For that, too, we may be thankful.'

'Then the cemetery you mentioned in your note is where he's to be interred?' I guessed.

'Where he's to be cremated,' he corrected me. 'Where his ashes are to be scattered to the winds.'

'Winds!' I snapped my fingers. 'Now I have it! "Sturm" means "storm" – it's the German word for storm!'

Crow nodded. 'Again correct,' he said. 'But let's not start to add things up too quickly.'

'Add things up?' I snorted. 'My friend, I'm completely lost!'

'Not completely,' he denied. 'What you have is a jig-saw puzzle without a picture to work from. Difficult, but once you have completed the frame the rest will slowly piece itself together. Now then, I was telling you about the time three weeks ago when I saw Magruser's picture.

'I remember I was just up, still in my dressing-gown, and I had just brought the paper in here to read. The curtains were open and I could see out into the garden. It was quite cold but relatively mild for the time of the year. The morning was dry and the heath seemed to beckon me, so that I made up my mind to take a walk. After reading the day's news and after breakfast, I would dress and take a stroll outdoors. Then I opened my newspaper – and Sturm Magruser's face greeted me!

'Henri, I dropped the paper as if it were a hot iron! So shaken was I that I had to sit down or risk falling. Now I'm a fairly sturdy chap, and you can well imagine the sort of shock my system would require to disturb it. Then as I sat down in my chair and stooped to recover the newspaper – the other thing.

'Out in the garden, a sudden stirring of wind. The hedgerow trembling and last year's leaves blowing across my drive. And birds startled to flight, as by the sudden presence of someone or thing I could not see. And the sudden gathering and rushing of spiralling winds, dust-devils that sucked up leaves and grit and other bits of debris and shot them aloft. Dust-devils, Henri, in March – in England – half-a-dozen of them that paraded all about Blowne House for the best part of thirty minutes! In any other circumstance, a marvellous, fascinating phenomenon.'

'But not for you?'

'No.' He shook his head. 'Not then. I'll tell you what they signified for me, Henri. They told me that just as I had recognized *something*, so I had been recognized! Do you understand?'

'Frankly, no,' and it was my turn to shake my head.

'Let it pass,' he said after a moment. 'Suffice it to say that there were these strange spiralling winds, and that I took them as a sign that indeed my psychic sense had detected something unutterably dangerous and obscene in this man Sturm Magruser. And I was so frightened by my discovery that I at once set about to discover all I could of him, so that I should know what the threat was and how best to deal with it.'

'Can I stop you for a moment?' I requested.

'Eh? Oh, certainly.'

'Those dates you mentioned as being important, Magruser's birth and death dates. In what way important?'

'Ah! We shall get to that, Henri,' he smiled. 'You may or may not know it, but I'm also something of a numerologist.'

Now it was my turn to smile. 'You mean like those fellows who measure the great pyramid and read in their findings the secrets of the universe?'

'Do not be flippant, de Marigny!' he answered at once, his smile disappearing in an instant. 'I meant no such thing. And in any case, don't be in too great a hurry to discredit the pyramidologists. Who are you to say what may or may not be? Until you have studied a thing for yourself, treat it with respect.'

'Oh!' was all I could say.

'As for birth and death dates, try these: 1889, 1945.'

I frowned, shrugged, said: 'They mean nothing to me. Are they, too, important?'

'They belong to Adolf Hitler,' he told me, 'and if you add the individual numbers together you'll discover that they make five sets of nine. Nine is an important number in occultism, signifying death. Hitler's number, 99999, shows him to have been a veritable Angel of Death, and no one could deny that! Incidentally, if you multiply five and nine you get forty-five, which are the last numbers in 1945 – the year he died. This is merely one example of an ancient science. Now please, Henri, no more scoffing at numerology . . .'

Deflated, still I was beginning to see a glimmer of light in Crow's reasoning. 'Ah!' I said again. 'And Sturm Magruser, like Hitler, has dates which add up to forty-five? Am I right? Let me see: the 1st of the 4th 1921 – that's eighteen – and the 4th of the 3rd 1964. That's forty-five!'

Crow nodded, smiling again. 'You're a clever man, Henri, yes – but you've missed the most important aspect of the thing. But never mind that for now, let me get back to my story . . .

'I have said that I set about to discover all I could of this fellow with the strange name, the camera-shy manner, the weight of a vast international concern behind him – and the power to frighten the living daylights out of me, which no other man ever had before. And don't ask me how, but I knew I had to work fast. There wasn't a great deal of time left before . . . before whatever was coming came.

'First, however, I contacted a friend of mine at the British Museum, the Curator of the Special Books Department, and asked him to search something out for me in the *Necronomicon*. I must introduce you one day, Henri. He's a marvellous chap. Not quite all there, I fancy – he can't be to work in that place – but so free of vice and sin, so blindly naïve and innocent, that the greatest possible evils would bounce right off him, I'm sure. Which is just as well, I suppose. Certainly I would never ask an enquiring or susceptible mind that it lay itself open to the perils of Alhazred's book.

'And at last I was able to concentrate on Magruser. This was about midday and my mind had been working frantically for several hours, so that already I was beginning to feel tired – mentally if not physically. I was also experiencing a singular emotion, a sort of morbid suspicion that I was being watched, and that the observer lurked somewhere in my garden!

'Putting this to the back of my mind, I began to make discreet telephone enquiries about Magruser – but no sooner had I voiced his name than the feeling came over me again, more strongly than before. It was as if a cloud of unutterable malignity, heavy with evil, had settled suddenly over the entire house. And starting back from the telephone, I saw once again the shadow of a nodding dust-devil where it played with leaves and twigs in the centre of my drive.'

III

'Now my fear turned to anger. Very well, if it was war . . . then I must now employ weapons of my own. Or if not weapons, defences, certainly.

'I won't go into details, Henri, but you know the sort of thing I mean. I have long possessed the necessary knowledge to create barriers of a sort against evil influences; no occultist or student of such things worth his salt would ever be without them. But it had recently been my good fortune to obtain a certain – shall we call it "charm"? – allegedly efficacious above all others.

'As to how this "charm" happened my way:

'In December Thelred Gustau had arrived in London from Iceland, where he had been studying Surtsey's volcanic eruption. During that eruption, Gustau had fished from the sea an item of extreme antiquity – indeed, a veritable time-capsule from an age undreamed of. When he contacted me in mid-December, he was still in a high fever of excitement. He needed my skills, he said, to help him unravel a mystery "predating the very dinosaurs." His words.

'I worked with him until mid-January, when he suddenly received an offer from America in respect of a lecture tour there. It was an offer he could not refuse – one which would finance his researches for several years to come – and so, off he went. By that time I had become so engrossed with the work I almost went with him. Fortunately I did not.' And here he paused to refill our glasses.

'Of course,' I took the opportunity to say, 'I knew you were extremely busy with something. You were so hard to contact, and then always at Gustau's Woolwich address. But what exactly were you working on?'

'Ah!' he answered. 'That is something which Thelred Gustau himself will have to reveal – which I expect he'll do shortly. Though who'll take him seriously, heaven only knows. As to what I may tell you of it – I'll have to have your word that it will be kept in the utmost secrecy.'

'You know you have it,' I answered.

'Very well . . . During the course of the eruption, Surtsey ejected a . . . a *container*, Henri, the "time-capsule" I have mentioned. Inside – fantastic!

'It was a record from a prehistoric world, Theem'hdra, a continent at the dawn of time, and it had been sent to us down all the ages by one of that continent's greatest magicians, the wizard Teh Atht, descendant of the mighty Mylakhrion. Alas, it was in the unknown language of that primal land, in Teh Atht's own hand, and Gustau had accidentally lost the means of its translation. But he did have a key, and he had his own great genius, and—'

'And he had you,' I smiled. 'One of the country's greatest paleographers.'

'Yes,' said Crow, matter-of-factly and without pride, 'second only to Professor Gordon Walmsley of Goole.

Anyway, I helped Gustau where I could, and during the work I came across a powerful spell against injurious magic and other supernatural menaces. Gustau allowed me to make a copy for myself, which is how I came to be in possession of a fragment of elder magic from an age undreamed of. From what I could make of it, Theem'hdra had existed in an age of wizards, and Teh Atht himself had used this very charm or spell to ward off evil.

'Well, I had the thing, and now I decided to employ it. I set up the necessary paraphernalia and induced within myself the required mental state. This took until well into the afternoon, and with each passing minute the sensation of impending doom deepened about the house, until I was almost prepared to flee the place and let well alone. And, if I had not by now been certain that such flight would be a colossal desertion of duty, I admit I would have done so.

'As it was, when I had willed myself to the correct mental condition, and upon the utterance of certain words – the effect was instantaneous!

'Daylight seemed to flood the whole house; the gloom fled in a moment; my spirits soared, and outside in the garden a certain ethereal watchdog collapsed in a tiny heap of rubbish and dusty leaves. Teh Atht's rune had proved itself effective indeed . . .'

'And then you turned your attention to Sturm Magruser?' I prompted him after a moment or two.

'Not that night, no. I was exhausted, Henri. The day had taken so much out of me. No, I could do no more that night. Instead I slept, deeply and dreamlessly, right through the evening and night until the jangling of my telephone awakened me at 9 o'clock on the following morning.'

'Your friend at the Rare Books Department?' I guessed.

'Yes, enlisting my aid in narrowing down his field of research. As you'll appreciate, the *Necronomicon* is a large volume – compared to which Feery's *Notes* is a pamphlet

– and many of its sections appear to be almost repetitious in their content. The trouble was, I wasn't even certain that it contained what I sought; only that I believed I had read it there. If not–' and he waved an expansive hand in the direction of his own more than appreciable occult library, 'then the answer must be here somewhere – whose searching out would form an equally frustrating if not utterly impossible task. At least in the time allowed.'

'You keep hinting at this urgency,' I frowned. 'What do you mean, "the time allowed"?'

'Why,' he answered, 'the time in which Magruser must be disposed of, of course!'

'Disposed of?' I could hardly believe my ears.

Crow sighed and brought it right out in the open: 'The time in which I must kill him!' he said.

I tried to remain calm, tried not to seem too flippant when I said, 'So, you had resolved to do away with him. This was necessary?'

'Very. And once my enquiries began to produce results, why, then his death became more urgent by the minute! For over the next few days I turned up some very interesting and very frightening facts about our Mr Magruser, not the least of them concerning his phenomenal rise from obscurity and the amount of power he controlled here and abroad. His company extended to no less than seven different countries, with a total of ten plants or factories engaged in the manufacture of weapons of war. Most of them conventional weapons – for the moment. Ah, yes! And those numbers too, Henri, are important.

'As for his current project – the completion of this "secret" weapon or "defence system," in this I was to discover the very root and nature of the evil, after which I was convinced in my decision that indeed Magruser must go!'

The time was now just after three in the morning and the fire had burned very low. While Crow took a break from talking and went to the kitchen to prepare a light snack, I threw logs on the fire and shivered, not merely because of the chill the night had brought. Such was Crow's story and his method of delivery that I myself was now caught up in its cryptic strangeness, the slowly strangling threads of its skein. Thus I paced the floor and pondered all he had told me, not least his stated intention to – murder? – Sturm Magruser, who now apparently was dead.

Passing Crow's desk I noticed an antique Family Bible in two great volumes, the New Testament lying open, but I did not check book or chapter. Also littering his desk were several books on cryptology, numerology, even one on astrology, in which 'science' Crow had never to my knowledge displayed a great deal of faith or interest. Much in evidence was a well-thumbed copy of Walmsley's *Notes on Deciphering Codes, Cryptograms and Ancient Inscriptions,* also an open notebook of obscure jottings and diagrams. My friend had indeed been busy.

Over cheese and crackers we carried on, and Crow took up his tale once more by hinting of the awesome power of Magruser's 'secret' weapon.

'Henri,' he began, 'there is a tiny island off the Orkneys which, until mid-1961, was green, lovely, and a sanctuary for sea birds. Too small and isolated to settle, and far too cold and open to the elements in winter, the place was never inhabited and only rarely visited. Magruser bought it, worked there, and by February '62—'

'Yes?'

'A dustbowl!'

'A dustbowl?' I repeated him. 'Chemicals, you mean?'

Crow shrugged. 'I don't know how his weapon works exactly, only what it produces. Also that it needs vast amounts of energy to trigger it. From what I've been able to discover, he used the forces of nature to fuel his experiment in the Orkneys, the enormous energies of an electrical storm. Oh, yes, and one other thing: the weapon was *not* a defence system!'

'And of course you also know,' I took a stab at it, 'what he intended to do with this weapon?'

'That too, yes,' he nodded. 'He intended to destroy the world, reduce us to savagery, return us to the Dark Ages. In short, to deliver a blow from which the human race would never recover.'

'But—'

'No, let me go on. Magruser intended to turn the world into a desert, start a chain reaction that couldn't be stopped. It may even have been worse than I suspected. He may have aimed at total destruction – no survivors at all!'

'You had proof?'

'I had evidence. As for proof: he's dead, isn't he?'

'You did kill him, then?'

'Yes.'

After a little while I asked, 'What evidence did you have?'

'Three types of evidence, really,' he answered, relaxing again in his chair. 'One: the evidence of my own five senses – and possibly that sixth sense by which I had known him from the start. Two: the fact that he had carried out his experiments in other places, several of them, always with the same result. And three—'

'Yes?'

'That too was information I received through government channels. I worked for MOD as a very young man, Henri. Did you know that? It was the War Department in those days. During the war I cracked codes for them, and I advised them on Hitler's occult interests.'

'No,' I said, 'I never knew that.'

'Of course not,' he replied. 'No man has *my* number, Henri,' and he smiled. 'Did you know that there's supposed to be a copy of the *Necronomicon* buried in a filled-in bunker just across the East German border in Berlin? And did you know that in his last hour Hitler was approached in his own bunker by a Jew – can you imagine that? – a Jew who whispered something to him before he took his life? I believe I know what that man whispered, Henri. I think he said these words: "I know you, Adolf Hitler!"'

'Titus,' I said, "there are so many loose ends here that I'm trying to tie together. You've given me so many clues, and yet—"

'It will all fit, Henri,' he calmed me. 'It will fit. Let me go on . . .

'When I discovered that Magruser's £2,000,000 "order" from the MOD was not an order at all but merely the use of two million pounds' worth of equipment – and as soon as I knew what that equipment was – then I guessed what he was up to. To clinch matters there finally came that call from the British Museum, and at last I had all the information I needed. But that was not until after I had actually met the man face to face.

'First the government "equipment" Magruser had managed to lay his hands on: two million pounds' worth of atomic bombs!'

IV

'*What?*' I was utterly astonished. 'You're joking!'

'No,' he answered, 'I am not joking. They were to provide the power he needed to trigger his doomsday weapon, to start the chain reaction. A persuasive man,

Magruser, Henri, and you may believe that there's hell to pay right now in certain government circles. I have let it be known – anonymously, of course – just exactly what he was about and the holocaust the world so narrowly escaped. Seven countries, Henri, and seven atomic bombs. Seven simultaneous detonations powering his own far more dreadful weapon, forging the links in a chain reaction which would spread right across the world!'

'But . . . how . . . when was this to happen?' I stammered.

'Today,' he answered, 'at ten o'clock in the morning, a little more than five hours from now. The bombs were already in position in his plants, waiting for the appointed time. By now of course they have been removed and the plants destroyed. And now Britain too will have to answer to the heads of six foreign powers; and certain lesser heads will roll, you may be sure. But very quietly, and the world as a whole shall never know.'

'But what was his purpose?' I asked. 'Was he a madman?'

He shook his head. 'A madman? No. Though he was born of human flesh, he was not even a man, not completely. Or perhaps he was more than a man. A force? A power . . .

'A week ago I attended a party at the home of my friend in the MOD. Magruser was to be there, which was why I *had* to be there – and I may tell you that took a bit of arranging. And all very discreetly, mind you, for I could not let any other person know of my suspicions. Who would have believed me anyway?

'At the party, eventually I cornered Magruser – as strange a specimen as ever you saw – and to come face to face with him was to confirm my quarry's identity. I now knew beyond any question of doubt that indeed he was the greatest peril the world has ever faced! If I sound melodramatic, Henri, it can't be helped.

'And yet to look at him . . . any other man might have felt pity. As I have said, he was an albino, with hair white as snow and flesh to match, so that his only high points seemed to lie in pallid pulses beating in his throat and forehead. He was tall and spindly, and his head was large but not overly so; though his cranium did display a height and width which at one and the same time hinted of imbecility and genius. His eyes were large, close together, pink, and their pupils were scarlet. I have known women – a perverse group at best – who would call him attractive, and certain men who might envy him his money, power and position. As for myself, I found him repulsive! But of course my prejudice was born of knowing the truth.

'He did not wish to be there, that much was plain, for he had that same trapped look about him which came through so strongly in his photograph. He was afraid, Henri, afraid of being stopped. For of course he knew that someone, somewhere, had recognized him. What he did not yet know was that I was that someone.

'Oh, he was nervous, this Magruser. Only the fact that he was to receive his answer that night, the go-ahead from the ministry, had brought him out of hiding. And he did receive that go-ahead, following which I cornered him, as I have said.'

'Wait,' I begged him. 'You said he knew that someone had recognized him. How did he know?'

'He knew at the same moment I knew, Henri, at the very instant when those spinning winds of his sprang up in my garden! But I had destroyed them, and fortunately before he could discover my identity. Oh, you may be sure he had tried to trace me, but I had been protected by the barriers I had placed about Blowne House. Now, however, I too was out in the open . . .'

'But I still can't see how the British government could be tricked into giving him a handful of atomic bombs!' I pressed. 'Are we all in the hands of lunatics?'

Crow shook his head. 'You should know by now,' he said, 'that the British give nothing for nothing. What the government stood to gain was far greater than a measly £2,000,000. Magruser had promised to deliver a power-screen, Henri, a dome of force covering the entire land, to be switched on and off at will, making the British Isles totally invulnerable!'

'And we believed him?'

'Oh, there had been demonstrations, all faked, and it had been known for a long time that he was experimenting with a "national defence system." And remember, my friend, that Magruser had never once stepped out of line. He was the very model of a citizen, a man totally above suspicion who supported every welfare and charity you could name. Why, I believe that on occasion he had even funded the government itself; but for all this he had not the means of powering his damnable weapons. And now you begin to see something of the brilliance of the man, something of his fiendishness.

'But to get back to what I was saying: I finally cornered him, we were about to be introduced, I even stuck out my hand for him to shake, and—

'At that very moment a window blew in and the storm which had been blowing up for over an hour rushed into the room. Rushing winds, Henri, and fifty ladies and gentlemen spilling their drinks and hanging onto their hats – and a whirling dervish of a thing that sucked up invitation cards and flowers from vases and paper napkins and flew *between* Magruser and myself like . . . like one of hell's own devils!

'How his pink eyes narrowed and glared at me then, and in another moment he had stepped quickly out of my reach. By the time order was restored Magruser was gone. He had rushed out of the house to be driven away, probably back to his plant outside Oxford.

'Well, I too left in something of a hurry, but not before my friend had promised not to tell Magruser who I was. Later, Magruser did indeed call him, only to be fobbed off with the answer that I must have been a gatecrasher. And so I was safe from him – for the moment.

'When I arrived home my telephone was ringing, and at first I was of a mind not to pick it up – but ... it was the information I had been waiting for, a quotation from the Mad Arab himself, Abdul Alhazred.' Here Crow paused to get up, go to his desk, rummage about for a second or two and return with a scrap of paper. He seated himself once more and said: 'Listen to this, Henri:

'Many and multiform are ye dim horrors of Earth, infesting her ways from ye very prime. They sleep beneath ye unturned stone; they rise with ye tree from its root; they move beneath ye sea, and in subterranean places they dwell in ye inmost adyta. Some there are long known to man, and others as yet unknown, abiding ye terrible latter days of their revealing. One such is an evil born of a curse, for ye Greatest Old One, before He sent Him down into His place to be sealed therein and sunken under ye sea, uttered a cry which rang out to ye very corners of ye All; and He cursed this world then and forever. And His curse was this: that whoso-ever inhabit this world which was become his prison, there should breed amongst them and of their flesh great traitors who would ever seek to destroy them and so leave ye world cleared off for ye day of His return. And when they heard this great curse, them that held Him thrust Him down where He could do no more harm. And because they were good, they sought to eradicate ye harm He had willed, but could not do so. Thus they worked a counter-spell, which was this: that there would always be ones to know the evil ones when they arose and waxed strong, thus protecting ye innocents from His great curse. And this also did they arrange: that in their fashion ye evil ones would reveal themselves, and that any man with understanding might readily dispose of such a one by seizing him and saying unto him, "I know you," and by revealing his number . . .'

'And in the end it was as simple as that, Henri . . .

'Late as the evening had grown, still I set about to strengthen those psychic or magical protections I had built about Blowne House. Also, I placed about my own person certain charms for self-protection when I was abroad and outside the safety of these stout walls; all of which took me until the early hours of the morning. That day – that very day – Sturm Magruser would be collecting his deadly detonators, the triggers for his devilish device; and in my mind's eye I pictured a vehicle pulling up at some innocuous-seeming but well-guarded and lethally supplied establishment, and the driver showing a pass, and documents being signed in triple-triplicate and the subsequent very careful loading of seven heavy crates.

'There would be a pair of executive jets waiting on the private runway inside Magruser's Oxford plant, and these would take six of the atomic bombs off to their various destinations around the globe. And so it can be seen that my time was running down. Tired as I was, worn down by worry and work, still I must press on and find the solution to the threat.'

'But surely you had the solution?' I cut in. 'It was right there in that passage from Alhazred.'

'I had the means to destroy him, Henri, yes – but I did not have the means of delivery! The only thing I could be sure of was that he was still in this country, at his centre of operations. But how to get near him, now that he knew me?'

'He knew you?'

Crow sighed. 'My face, certainly, for we had now met. Or almost. And if I knew my quarry, by now he might also have discovered my name and particulars. Oh, yes, Henri. For just as I have my means, be sure Magruser had his. Well, obviously I could not stay at Blowne House, not after I realized how desperate the man must be to find me. I must go elsewhere, and quickly.

'And I did go, that very night. I drove up to Oxford.'

'To Oxford?'

'Yes, into the very lion's den, as it were. In the morning I found a suitable hotel and garaged my car, and a little later I telephoned Magruser.'

'Just like that?' Again I was astonished. 'You telephoned him?'

'No, not just like that at all,' he answered. 'First I ordered and waited for the arrival of a taxi. I dared not use my Mercedes for fear that by now he knew both the car and its number.' He smiled tiredly at me. 'You are beginning to see just how important numbers really are, eh, Henri?'

I nodded. 'But please go on. You said you phoned him?'

'I tried the plant first and got the switchboard, and was told that Mr Magruser was at home and could not be disturbed. I said that it was important, that I had tried his home number and was unable to obtain him, and that I must be put through to him at once.'

'And they fell for that? Had you really tried his home number?'

'No, it's not listed. And to physically go near his estate would be sheer lunacy, for surely the place would be heavily guarded.'

'But then they *must* have seen through your ruse,' I argued. 'If his number was ex-directory, how could you possibly tell them that you knew it?'

Again Crow smiled. 'If I was the fellow I pretended to be, I would know it,' he answered.

I gasped. 'Your friend from the ministry? You used his name.'

'Of course,' said Crow. 'And now we see again the importance of names, eh, my friend? Well, I was put through and eventually Magruser spoke to me, but I knew that it was him before ever he said a word. The very sound of his breathing came to me like an exhalation from a tomb! "This is Magruser," he said, his voice full of suspicion. "Who is speaking?"

'"Oh, I think you know me, Sturm Magruser," I answered. "Even as I know you!"

V

'There was a sharp intake of breath. Then: "Mr Titus Crow," he said. "You are a most resourceful man. Where are you?"

'"On my way to see you, Magruser," I answered.

'"And when may I expect you?"

'"Sooner than you think. I have your number!"

'At that he gasped again and slammed the 'phone down; and now I would discover whether or not my preliminary investigation stood me in good stead. Now, too, I faced the most danger-fraught moments of the entire business.

'Henri, if you had been Magruser, what would you do?'

'Me? Why I'd stay put, surrounded by guards – and they'd have orders to shoot you on sight as a dangerous intruder.'

'And what if I should come with more armed men than you? And would your guards, if they were ordinary chaps, obey that sort of order in the first place? How could you be *sure* to avoid any encounter with me?'

I frowned and considered it. 'I'd put distance between us, get out of the country, and—'

'Exactly!' Crow said. 'Get out of the country.'

I saw his meaning. 'The private airstrip inside his plant?'

'Of course,' Crow nodded. 'Except I had ensured that I was closer to the plant than he was. It would take me fifteen to twenty minutes to get there by taxi. Magruser would need between five and ten minutes more than that . . .

'As for the plant itself – proudly displaying its sign, *Magruser Systems, UK* – it was large, set in expensive grounds and surrounded by a high, patrolled wire fence. The only entrance was from the main road and boasted an electrically operated barrier and a small guard-room sort of building to house the security man. All this I saw as I paid my taxi fare and approached the barrier.

'As I suspected, the guard came out to meet me, demanding to know my name and business. He was not armed that I could see, but he was big and heavy. I told him I was MOD and that I had to see Mr Magruser.

'"Sorry, sir," he answered. "There must be a bit of a flap on. I've just had orders to let no one in, not even pass-holders. Anyway, Mr Magruser's at home."

'"No, he's not," I told him, "he's on his way here right now, and I'm to meet him at the gate."

'"I suppose that'll be all right then, sir," he answered, "just as long as you don't want to go in."

'I walked over to the guard-room with him. While we were talking, I kept covert watch on the open doors of a hangar spied between buildings and installations. Even as I watched, a light aircraft taxied into the open and mechanics began running to and fro, readying it for flight. I was also watching the road, plainly visible from the guard-room window, and at last was rewarded by the sight of Magruser's car speeding into view a quarter-mile away.

'Then I produced my handgun.'

'What?' I cried. 'If all else failed you planned to shoot him?'

'Not at all. Oh, I might have tried it, I suppose, but I doubt if a bullet could have killed him. No, the gun had another purpose to serve, namely the control of any merely human adversary.'

'Such as the security man?'

'Correct. I quickly relieved him of his uniform jacket and hat, gagged him and locked him in a small back room. Then, to make absolutely certain, I drove the butt of my weapon through the barrier's control panel, effectively ruining it. By this time Magruser's car was turning off the road into the entrance, and of course it stopped at the lowered barrier. There was Magruser, sitting on my side and in the front passenger seat, and in the back a pair of large young men who were plainly bodyguards.

'I pulled my hat down over my eyes, went out of the guard-room and up to the car, and as I had prayed Magruser himself wound down his window. He stuck out his hand, made imperative, flapping motions, said, "Fool! I wish to be in. Get the barrier—"

'But at that moment I grabbed and held onto his arm, lowered my face to his and said, "Sturm Magruser, I know you – and I know your number!"

'"What? What?" he whispered – and his eyes went wide in terror as he recognized me.

'Then I told him his number, and as his bodyguards leapt from the car and dragged me away from him, he waved them back. "Leave him be," he said, "for it is too late now." And he favoured me with such a look as I shall never forget. Slowly he got out of the car, leaning heavily upon the door, facing me. "That is only half my number," he said, "but sufficient to destroy me. Do you know the rest of it?"

'And I told him the rest of it.

'What little colour he had drained completely from him and it was as if a light had gone out behind his eyes. He would have collapsed if his men hadn't caught and supported him, seating him back in the car. And all the time his eyes were on my face, his pink and scarlet eyes which had started to bleed.

'"A very resourceful man," he croaked then, and, "So little time." To his driver he said, "Take me home . . ."'

'Even as they drove away I saw him slump down in his seat, saw his head fall on one side. He did not recover.'

After a long moment I asked, 'And you got away from that place?' I could think of nothing else to say, and my mouth had gone very dry.

'Who was to stop me?' Crow replied. 'Yes, I got away, and returned here. Now you know it all.'

'I know it,' I answered, wetting my lips, 'but I still don't understand it. Not yet. You must tell me how you—'

'No, Henri.' He stretched and yawned mightily. 'The rest is for you to find out. You know his name and you have the means to discover his number. The rest should be fairly simple. As for me: I shall sleep for two hours, then we shall take a drive in my car for one hour; following which we shall pay, as it were, our last respects to Sturm Magruser V.'

Crow was good as his word. He slept, awakened, breakfasted and drove – while I did nothing but rack my brains and pore over the problem he had set me. And by the time we approached our destination I believed I had most of the answers.

Standing on the pavement outside the gardens of a quiet country crematorium between London and Oxford, we gazed in through spiked iron railings across plots and head-stones at the pleasant-seeming, tall-chimneyed building which was the House of Repose, and I for one wondered what words had been spoken over Magruser. As we had arrived, Magruser's cortege, a single hearse, had left. So far as we were aware, none had remained to join us in paying 'our last respects.'

Now, while we waited, I told Crow, 'I think I have the answers.'

Tilting his head on one side in that old-fashioned way of his, he said, 'Go on.'

'First his name,' I began. 'Sturm Magruser V. The name Sturm reveals something of the nature of his familiar winds, the dust-devils you've mentioned as watching over his interests. Am I right?'

Crow nodded. 'I have already allowed you that, yes,' he said.

'His full name stumped me for a little while, however,' I admitted, 'for it has only thirteen letters. Then I remembered the "V," symbolic for the figure five. That makes eighteen, a double nine. Now, you said Hitler had been a veritable Angel of Death with his 99999 . . . which would seem to make Magruser the very Essence of Death itself!'

'Oh? How so?'

'His birth and death dates,' I reminded. 'The 1st of April 1921, and the 4th of March 1964. They, too, add up to forty-five, which, if you include the number of his name, gives Magruser 9999999. Seven nines!' And I gave myself a mental pat on the back.

After a little while Crow said, 'Are you finished?' And from the tone of his voice I knew there was a great deal I had overlooked.

VI

I sighed and admitted: 'I can't see what else there could be.'

'Look!' Crow said, causing me to start.

I followed his pointing finger to where a black-robed figure had stepped out onto the patio of the House of Repose. The bright wintry sun caught his white collar and made it a burning band about his neck. At chest height he carried a bowl, and began to march out through the garden with measured tread. I fancied I could hear the quiet murmur of his voice carrying on the still air, his words a chant or prayer.

'Magruser's mortal remains,' said Crow, and he automatically doffed his hat. Bre-headed, I simply stood and watched.

'Well,' I said after a moment or two, 'where did my calculations go astray?'

Crow shrugged. 'You missed several important points, that's all. Magruser was a "black magician" of sorts, wouldn't you say? With his demonic purpose on Earth and his "familiar winds," as you call them? We may rightly suppose so; indeed the Persian word "magu" or "magus" means magician. Now then, if you remove Magus from his name, what are you left with?'

'Why,' I quickly worked it out, "with R, E, R. Oh, yes – and with V."

'Let us rearrange them and say we are left with R, E, V and R,' said Crow. And he repeated, "R, E, V and R.

Now then, as you yourself pointed out, there are thirteen letters in the man's name. Very well, let's look at—"

'Rev. 13!' I cut him off. 'And the family Bible you had on your desk. But wait! You've ignored the other R.'

Crow stared at me in silence for a moment. 'Not at all,' he finally said, 'for R is the *eighteenth* letter of the alphabet. And thus Magruser, when he changed his name by deed-poll, revealed himself!'

Now I understood, and now I gasped in awe at this man I presumed to call friend, the vast intellect which was Titus Crow. For clear in my mind I could read it all in the eighteenth verse of the thirteenth chapter of the Book of Revelation.

Crow saw knowledge written in my dumbfounded face and nodded. 'His birthdate, Henri, adds up to eighteen – 666, the Number of the Beast!'

'And his ten factories in seven countries,' I gasped. 'The ten horns upon his seven heads! And the Beast in Revelations rose up *out of the sea!*'

'Those things, too,' Crow grimly nodded.

'And his death date, 999!'

Again, his nod and, when he saw that I was finished: 'But most monstrous and frightening of all, my friend, his very name – which, if you read it in reverse order—'

'Wh-what?' I stammered. But in another moment my mind reeled and my mouth fell open.

'*Resurgam!*'

'Indeed,' and he gave his curt nod. 'I shall rise again!'

Beyond the spiked iron railings the priest gave a sharp little cry and dropped the bowl, which shattered and spilled its contents. Spiralling winds, coming from nowhere, took up the ashes and bore them away . . .

SNARKER'S SON

In Fruiting Bodies *I included a story called* No Way Home: *a parallel universe story. And in* Dagon's Bell *I likewise included* The Whisperer, *which might well have been an intrusion from a parallel universe. So to complete the trilogy of collected stories, the inclusion of* Snarker's Son *in the current volume seemed a must. Before I give the story away entirely, I suppose I'd better stop right here . . .*

'All right, all right!' Sergeant Scott noisily submitted. 'So you're lost. You're staying with your dad here in the city at a hotel – you went sightseeing and you got separated – I accept all that. But look, son, we've had lost kids in here before, often, and they didn't try on all this silly stuff about names and spellings and all!'

Sergeant Scott had known – had been instinctively 'aware' all day – that this was going to be one of *those* shifts. Right up until ten minutes ago his intuition had seemed for once to have let him down. But now . . .

'It's true,' the pallid, red-eyed nine-year-old insisted, hysteria in his voice. 'It's all true, everything I've said. This town *looks* like Mondon – but it's not! And . . . and before I came in here I passed a store called Woolworths – but it should have been "Wolwords!"'

'All right, let's not start that again,' the policeman put up quieting hands. 'Now: you say you came down with your father from . . . from Sunderpool? That's in England?'

'No, I've *told* you,' the kid started to cry again. 'It's "Eenland!" We came down on holiday from Sunderpool by longcar, and—'

'Longcar?' Sergeant Scott cut in, frowning. 'Is that some place on the north-east coast?'

'No, it's not a place! A longcar is . . . well, a *longcar*!

Like a buzz but longer, and it goes on the longcar lanes. You know . . . ?' The boy looked as puzzled as Sergeant Scott, to say nothing of accusing.

'No, I don't know!' the policeman shook his head, trying to control his frown. 'A "buzz?"' Scott could feel the first twinges of one of his bilious headaches coming on, and so decided to change the subject.

'What does your father do, son? He's a science-fiction writer, eh? – And you're next in a long line?'

'Dad's a snarker,' the answer came quite spontaneously, without any visible attempt at deceit or even flippancy. In any case, the boy was obviously far too worried to be flippant. A 'nut', Scott decided – but nevertheless a nut in trouble.

Now the kid had an inquisitive look on his face. 'What's science fiction?' he asked.

'Science fiction,' the big sergeant answered with feeling, 'is that part of a policeman's lot called "desk-duty" – when crazy lost kids walk into the station in tears to mess up said policeman's life!'

His answer set the youngster off worse than before.

Sighing, Scott passed his handkerchief across the desk and stood up. He called out to a constable in an adjacent room:

'Hey, Bob, come and look after the desk until Sergeant Healey gets in, will you? He's due on duty in the next ten minutes or so. I'll take the kid and see if I can find his father. If I can't – well, I'll bring the boy back here and the job can go through the usual channels.'

'All right, Sergeant, I'll watch the shop,' the constable agreed as he came into the duty-room and took his place at the desk. 'I've been listening to your conversation! Right rum 'un that,' he grinned, nodding towards the tearful boy. 'What an imagination!'

Imagination, yes. And yet Scott was not quite sure.

There was 'something in the air', a feeling of impending – *strangeness* – hard to define.

'Come on, son,' he said, shaking off his mood. 'Let's go.'

He took the boy's hand. 'Let's see if we can find your dad. He's probably rushing about right now wondering what's become of you.' He shook his head in feigned defeat and said: 'I don't know – ten o'clock at night, just going off duty – and *you* have to walk in on me!'

'Ten o'clock – *already*?' The boy looked up into Scott's face with eyes wider and more frightened than ever. 'Then we only have half an hour!'

'Eh?' the policeman frowned again as they passed out into the London street (or was it 'Mondon', Scott wondered with a mental grin). 'Half an hour? What happens at half past ten, son? Do you turn into a pumpkin or something?' His humour was lost on his small charge.

'I mean the *lights*!' the boy answered, in what Scott took to be exasperation. 'That's when the lights go out. At half past ten they put the lights out.'

'They do?' the sergeant had given up trying to penetrate the boy's fertile but decidedly warped imagination. 'Why's that, I wonder?' (Let the kid ramble on; it was better than tears at any rate.)

'Don't you know *anything*?' the youngster seemed half-astonished, half-unbelieving, almost as if he thought Scott was pulling his leg.

'No,' the sergeant returned, 'I'm just a stupid copper! But come on – where did you give your father the slip? You said you passed Woolworths getting to the police station. Well, Woolworths is down this way, near the tube.' He looked at the boy sharply in mistaken understanding. 'You didn't get lost on the tube, did you? Lots of kids do when it's busy.'

'The Tube?' Scott sensed that the youngster spoke the

words in capitals – and yet it was only a whisper. He had to hold on tight as the boy strained away from him in something akin to horror. 'No one goes down in The Tube any more, except—' He shuddered.

'Yes?' Scott pressed, interested in this particular part of the boy's fantasy despite himself and the need, now, to have done with what would normally be a routine job. 'Except who?'

'Not *who*,' the boy told him, clutching his hand tighter. 'Not who, but—'

'But?' again, patiently, Scott prompted him.

'Not who but *what*!'

'Well, go on,' said the sergeant, sighing, leading the way down the quiet, half-deserted street towards Woolworths. '*What*, er, goes down in the tube?'

'Why, Tubers, of course!' Again there was astonishment in the youngster's voice, amazement at Scott's obvious deficiency in general knowledge. 'Aren't you Mondoners thick!' It was a statement of fact, not a question.

'Right,' said Scott, not bothering to pursue the matter further, seeing the pointlessness of questioning an idiot. 'We've passed Woolworths – now where?'

'Over there, I think, down that street. Yes! – that's where I lost my father – down there!'

'Come on,' Scott said, leading the boy across the road, empty now of all but the occasional car, down into the entrance of the indicated street. In fact it was little more than an alley, dirty and unlighted. 'What on earth were you doing down here in the first place?'

'We weren't down here,' the youngster answered with a logic that made the sergeant's head spin. 'We were in a bright street, with lots of lights. Then I felt a funny buzzing feeling, and . . . and then I was here! I got frightened and ran.'

At that moment, their footsteps echoing hollowly on the

cobbles of the alley, the sergeant felt a weird vibration that began in his feet and travelled up his body to his head, causing a burst of bright, painfully bilious stars to flash across his vision – and simultaneous with this peculiar sensation the two turned a corner to emerge with startling abruptness into a much brighter side street.

'That was the buzzing I told you about,' the boy stated unnecessarily.

Scott was not listening. He was looking behind him for the broken electric cable he felt sure must be lying there just inside the alley (the sensation must surely have been caused by a mild electric shock), but he couldn't see one. Nor could he see anything else that might have explained that tingling, nerve-rasping sensation he had known. For that matter, where was the entrance (or exit) from which he and the boy had just this second emerged?

Where was the alley?

'Dad!' the kid yelled, suddenly tugging himself free to go racing off down the street.

Scott stood and watched, his head starting to throb and the street lights flaring garishly before his eyes. At the boy's cry a lone man had turned, started to run, and now Scott saw him sweep the lad up in his arms and wildly hug him, intense and obvious relief showing in his face.

The policeman forgot the problem of the vanishing alley and walked up to them, hands behind his back in the approved fashion, smiling benignly. 'Cute lad you've got there, sir – but I should curb his imagination if I were you. Why, he's been telling me a story fit to—'

Then the benign smile slid from his face. '*Here!*' he cried, his jaw dropping in astonishment.

But despite his exclamation, Scott was nevertheless left standing on his own. For without a word of thanks both man and boy had made off down the street, hands linked, running as if the devil himself was after them!

'Here!' the policeman called again, louder. 'Hold on a bit—'

For a moment the pair stopped and turned, then the man glanced at his watch (reminding Scott curiously of the White Rabbit in *Alice in Wonderland*) before picking up the boy again and holding him close. 'Get off the street!' he yelled back at Scott as he once more started to run. 'Get off the streets, man.' His white face glanced back and up at the street lights as he ran, and Scott saw absolute fear shining in his eyes. 'It'll soon be half past ten!'

The policeman was still in the same position, his jaw hanging slack, some seconds later when the figure of the unknown man, again hugging the boy to him, vanished round a distant corner. Then he shrugged his shoulders and tried to pull himself together, setting his helmet more firmly on his aching head.

'Well I'll be—' he grinned nervously through the throb of his headache. 'Snarker's son, indeed!'

Alone, now, Scott's feeling of impending – *something* – returned, and he noticed suddenly just how deserted the street was. He had never known London so quiet before. Why, there wasn't a single soul in sight!

And a funny thing, but here he was, only a stone's throw from his station, where he'd worked for the last fifteen years of his life, and yet – damned if he could recognise the street! Well, he knew he'd brought the boy down a dark, cobbled alley from the right, and so . . .

He took the first street on the right, walking quickly down it until he hit another street he knew somewhat better—

—Or did he?

Yes, yes, of course he did. The street was deserted now, quite empty, but just over there was good old . . .

Good old Wolwords!

Lights blazed and burst into multicoloured sparks before

Scott's bilious eyes. His mind spun wildly. He grabbed hold of a lamp-post to steady himself and tried to think the thing out properly.

It must be a new building, that place – yes, that had to be the answer. He'd been doing a lot of desk-duties lately, after all. It was quite possible, what with new techniques and the speed of modern building, that the store had been put up in just a few weeks.

The place didn't *look* any too new, though . . .

Scott's condition rapidly grew worse – understandably in the circumstances, he believed – but there was a tube station, nearby. He decided to take a train home. He usually walked the mile or so to his flat, the exercise did him good; but tonight he would take a train, give himself a rest.

He went dizzily down one flight of steps, barely noticing the absence of posters and the unkempt, dirty condition of the underground. Then, as he turned a corner, he came face to face with a strange legend, dripping in red paint on the tiled wall:

ROT THE TUBERS!

Deep creases furrowed the sergeant's forehead as he walked on, his footsteps ringing hollowly in the grimy, empty corridors, but his headache just wouldn't let him think clearly.

Tubers, indeed! What the hell – Tubers . . . ?

Down another flight of steps he went, to the deserted ticket booths, where he paused to stare in disbelief at the naked walls of the place and the dirt- and refuse-littered floor. For the first time he really saw the *condition* of the place. What had happened here? Where was everyone?

From beyond the turnstiles he heard the rumble of a distant train and the spell lifted a little. He hurried forward then, past the empty booths and through the unguarded turnstiles, dizzily down one more flight of concrete steps, under an arch and out on to an empty platform. Not even a drunk or a tramp shared the place with him. The neons flared hideously, and he put out a hand against the naked wall for support.

Again, through the blinding flashes of light in his head, he noticed the absence of posters: the employment agencies, the pretty girls in lingerie, the film and play adverts, spectacular films and *avant-garde* productions – where in hell were they all?

Then, as for the first time he truly felt upon his spine the chill fingers of a slithering horror, there came the rumble and blast of air that announced the imminent arrival of a train – and he smelled the rushing reek of that which most certainly was *not* a train!

Even as he staggered to and fro on the unkempt platform, reeling under the fetid blast that engulfed him, the Tuber rushed from out its black hole – a *Thing* of crimson viscosity and rhythmically flickering cilia.

Sergeant Scott gave a wild shriek as a rushing feeler swept him from the platform and into the soft, hurtling plasticity of the thing – another shriek as he was whisked away into the deep tunnel and down into the bowels of the earth. And seconds later the minute hand of the clock above the empty, shuddering platform clicked down into the vertical position.

Ten-thirty – and all over Mondon, indeed throughout the length and breadth of Eenland, the lights went out.

RISING WITH SURTSEY

This one goes a long way back. It was written in December '67, revised in '68, and got a further (slight) revision when editor James Turner wanted to use it in an updated, excellent Tales of the Cthulhu Mythos, *1990. Lovecraft's influence is very strong here, but since this was only my tenth story ever, from my very first year of writing, that's hardly surprising. I think it was also my most ambitious story to date: a homage, most certainly, to Lovecraft, but also to August Derleth of Arkham House, without whose dedication HPL might have languished in the crumbling pages of ancient copies of* Weird Tales *forever. Wherefore, what would the story be without its purple prose?*

One last thing:

Unlike Gustaf Johansen's narrative concerning R'lyeh's upheaval from the sea floor, the details of Surtsey's rising are very well documented . . .

It appears that with the discovery of a live coelacanth – a fish thought to have been extinct for over seventy millions of years – we may have to revise our established ideas of the geological life spans of certain aquatic animals . . .

– LINKAGE'S
WONDERS OF THE DEEP

Surname	– Haughtree
Christian Names	– Phillip
Date of Birth	– 2 Dec 1927
Age (years)	– 35
Place of Birth	– Old Beldry, Yorks.
Address	– Not applicable
Occupation	– Author

WHO STATES: (Let here follow the body of the statement)

I have asked to be cautioned in the usual manner but have been told that in view of my alleged *condition* it is not necessary . . . The implication is obvious, and because of it I find myself obliged to begin my story in the following way:

I must clearly impart to the reader – before advising any unacquainted perusal of this statement – that I was never a fanatical believer in the supernatural. Nor was I ever given to hallucinations or visions, and I have never suffered from my nerves or been persecuted by any of the mental illnesses. There is no record to support any evidence of madness in any of my ancestors – and Dr Stewart was quite wrong to declare me insane.

It is necessary that I make these points before permitting the reading of this, for a merely casual perusal would soon bring any conventionally minded reader to the incorrect conclusion that I am either an abominable liar or completely out of my mind, and I have little wish to reinforce Dr Stewart's opinions . . .

Yet I admit that shortly after midnight on the 15th November 1963 the body of my brother did die by my hand; but at the same time I must clearly state that I am *not* a murderer. It is my intention in the body of this statement – which will of necessity be long, for I insist I must tell the whole story – to prove conclusively my innocence. For, indeed, I am guilty of no heinous crime, and that act of mine which terminated life in the body of my brother was nothing but the reflex action of a man who had recognized a hideous threat to the sanity of the whole world. Wherefore, and in the light of the allegation of madness levelled against me, I must now attempt to tell this tale in the most detailed fashion; I must avoid any sort of garbled sequence and form my sentences and paragraphs with meticulous care, refraining from even *thinking* on the end of it until that horror is reached . . .

Where best to start?

If I may quote Sir Amery Wendy-Smith:

There are fabulous legends of Star-Born creatures who inhabited this Earth many millions of years before Man appeared and who were still here, in certain black places, when he eventually evolved. They are, I am sure, to an extent here even now.

It may be remembered that those words were spoken by the eminent antiquary and archeologist before he set out upon his last, ill-fated trip into the interior of Africa. Sir Amery was hinting, I know, at the same breed of hell-spawned horror which first began to make itself apparent to me at that ghastly time eighteen months ago; and I take this into account when I remember the way in which he returned, alone and raving, from that dark continent to civilization.

At that time my brother Julian was just the opposite of myself, insofar as he was a firm believer in dark mysteries. He read omnivorously of fearsome books uncaring whether they were factual – as Frazer's *Golden Bough* and Miss Murray's *Witch-Cult* – or fanciful – like his collection of old, nigh-priceless volumes of *Weird Tales* and similar popular magazines. Many friends, I imagine, will conclude that his original derangement was due to this unhealthy appetite for the monstrous and the abnormal. I am not of such an opinion, of course, though I admit that at one time I was.

Of Julian: he had always been a strong person physically, but had never shown much strength of character. As a boy he had had the size to easily take on any bully – but never the determination. This was also where he failed as a writer, for while his plots were good he was unable to make his characters live. Being without personality himself, it was as though he was only able to reflect his own weaknesses into his work. I worked in partnership with him, filling in plots and building life around his more or less clay figures. Up until the time of which I write, we had made a good living and had saved a reasonable sum. This was just as well, for during the period of Julian's illness, when I hardly wrote a word, I might well have found myself hard put to support both my brother and myself. Fortunately, though sadly, he was later taken completely off my hands; but that was after the onset of his trouble . . .

It was in May 1962 that Julian suffered his actual breakdown, but the start of it all can be traced back to the 2nd of February of that year – Candlemas – a date which I know will have special meaning to anyone with even the slightest schooling in the occult. It was on that night that he dreamed his dream of titanic basalt towers – dripping with slime and ocean ooze and fringed with great sea-mats – their weirdly proportioned bases buried in grey-green muck and their non-Euclidean-angled parapets fading into the watery distances of that unquiet submarine realm.

At the time we were engaged upon a novel of eighteenth-century romance, and I remember we had retired late. Still later I was awakened by Julian's screams, and he roused me fully to listen to an hysterical tale of nightmare. He babbled of what he had seen lurking *behind* those monolithic, slimy ramparts, and I remember remarking – after he had calmed himself somewhat – what a strange fellow he was, to be a writer of romances and at the same time a reader and dreamer of horrors. But Julian was not so easily chided, and such was his fear and loathing of the dream that he refused to lie down again that night but spent the remaining hours of darkness sitting at his typewriter in the study with every light in the house ablaze.

One would think that a nightmare of such horrible intensity might have persuaded Julian to stop gorging himself with his nightly feasts of at least two hours of gruesome reading. Yet, if anything, it had the opposite effect – but now his studies were all channelled in one certain direction. He began to take a morbid interest in anything to do with oceanic horror, collecting and avidly reading such works as the German *Unter-Zee Kulten*, Gaston le Fe's *Dwellers in the Depths*, Gantley's *Hydrophinnae*, and the evil *Cthaat Aquadingen* by an unknown author. But it was his collection of fictional books which in the main claimed his interest. From these he culled most of his knowledge of the Cthulhu Mythos – which he fervently declared was not myth at all – and often expressed a desire to see an original copy of the *Necronomicon* of the mad Arab Abdul Alhazred, as his own copy of Feery's *Notes* was practically useless, merely hinting at what Julian alleged Alhazred had explained in detail.

In the following three months our work went badly. We failed to make a deadline on a certain story and, but for the fact that our publisher was a personal friend, might have suffered a considerable loss financially. It was all due to the fact that Julian no longer had the urge to write. He was too taken up with his reading to work and could no longer even be approached to talk over story plots. Not only this, but that fiendish dream of his kept returning with ever increasing frequency and vividness. Every night he suffered those same silt-submerged visions of obscene terrors the like of which could only be glimpsed in such dark tomes as were his chosen reading. But did he really suffer? I found myself unable to make up my mind. For as the weeks passed, my brother seemed to become all the more uneasy and restless by day, whilst eagerly embracing the darkening skies of evening and the bed in which he sweated out the horrors of hideous dream and nightmare . . .

We were leasing, for a reasonable monthly sum, a moderate house in Glasgow where we had separate bedrooms and a single study which we shared. Although he now looked forward to them, Julian's dreams had grown even worse and they had been particularly bad for two or three nights when, in the middle of May, it happened. He had been showing an increasing interest in certain passages in the

Cthaat Aquadingen and had heavily underscored a section in that book which ran thus:

> *Rise!*
> *O Nameless Ones:*
> *That in Thy Season*
> *Thine Own of Thy choosing.*
> *Through Thy Spells and Thy Magic,*
> *Through Dreams and Enchantry,*
> *May know of Thy Coming;*
> *And rush to Thy Pleasure,*
> *For the Love of Our Master,*
> *Knight of Cthulhu,*
> *Deep Slumberer in Green,*
> *Othuum . . .*

This and other bits and pieces culled from various sources, particularly certain partly suppressed writings by a handful of authors, all allegedly 'missing persons' or persons who had died in strange circumstances – namely: Andrew Phelan, Abel Keane, Claiborne Boyd, Nayland Colum, and Horvath Blayne – had had a most unsettling effect upon my brother, so that he was close to exhaustion when he eventually retired late on the night that the horror really started. His condition was due to the fact that he had been studying his morbid books almost continually for a period of three days, and during that time had taken only brief snatches of sleep – and then only during the daylight hours, never at night. He would answer, if ever I attempted to remonstrate with him, that he did not *want* to sleep at night 'when the time is so near' and that 'there was so much that would be strange to him in the Deeps.' Whatever *that* was supposed to mean . . .

After he had retired that night I worked on for an hour or so before going to bed myself. But before leaving our study I glanced at that with which Julian had last been so taken up, and I saw – as well as the above nonsense, as I then considered it – some jottings copied from the *Life of St Brendan* by the sixth-century Abbot of Clonfert in Galway:

> All that day the brethren, even when they were no longer in view of the island, heard a loud wailing from the inhabitants thereof, and a noisome stench was perceptible at a great distance. Then St Brendan sought to animate the courage of the brethren, saying: 'Soldiers of Christ, be strong in faith unfeigned and in the armour of the spirit, for we are now on the confines of hell!'

I have since studied the *Life of St Brendan*, and have found that which made me shudder in awful recognition – though at the reading I could not correlate the written word and my hideous disquiet; there was just something in the book which was horribly disturbing – and, moreover, I have found other references to historic oceanic eruptions; namely, those which sank Atlantis and Mu, those recorded in the *Liber Miraculorem* of the monk and chaplain Herbert of Clairvaux in France in the years 1178–80, and that which was closer to the present and which is known only through the medium of the suppressed *Johansen Narrative*. But at the time of which I write, such things only puzzled me and I could never, not even in my wildest dreams, have guessed what was to come.

I am not sure how long I slept that night before I was eventually roused by Julian and half awoke to find him crouching by my bed, whispering in the darkness. I could feel his hand gripping my shoulder, and though I was only half-awake I recall the pressure of that strong hand and something of what he said. His voice had the trance-like quality of someone under deep hypnosis, and his hand jerked each time he put emphasis on a word.

'They are *preparing* ... They will *rise* ... They have not mustered *The Greater Power*, nor have they the blessing of *Cthulhu*, and the rising will not be *permanent* nor go recorded ... But the effort will suffice for the *Mind-Transfer* ... For the *Glory* of Othuum ...

'Using those *Others* in Africa, those who took Sir Amery Wendy-Smith, *Shudde-M'ell* and his hordes, to relay their messages and dream-pictures, they have finally defeated the magic *spell* of deep water and can now *control* dreams as of old – despite the oceans which cover them! Once more they have *mastery* of dreams, but to perform the Transfer they need not even break the surface of the water – a *lessening* of the pressure will suffice.

'Ce'haie, ce'haie!!!

'*They rise even now;* and He knows me, searching me out ... And my mind, which they have prepared in dreams, will be here to meet Him, for I am *ready* and they need wait no longer. My ignorance is nothing – I do not *need* to know or understand! They will *show* me; as, in dreams, they have showed me the *Deep Places*. But they are unable to draw from my weak mind, or from *any* mortal brain, *knowledge of the surface* ... The mental images of men are not *strongly* enough transmitted ... And the deep water – even though, through the work of *Shudde-M'ell*, they have mostly conquered its ill effects – *still* interferes with those blurred images which they *have* managed to obtain ...

'*I am the chosen one* ... Through *His* eyes in my *body* will they again acquaint themselves *entirely* with the surface; that in time, when the stars are *right*, they may perform the *Great Rising* ... Ah! The Great Rising! The *damnation* of *Hastur*! The dream of *Cthulhu* for countless ages ... When *all* the deep dwellers, the dark denizens, the *sleepers* in silted cities, will *again* confound the world with their powers ...

'For that is not dead which can lie *forever*, and when mysterious times have passed, *it shall be again as it once was* . . . Soon, when the Transfer is done, He shall walk the Earth *in my guise,* and I the great deeps *in His!* So that where they ruled *before* they may one day rule *again* – aye – even the brethren of *Yibb-Tstll* and the sons of dreaming *Cthulhu* and their servants – *for the Glory of R'lyeh . . .*'

That is as much of it as I can remember, and even then not at all clearly, and as I have said, it was nothing to me at that time but gibberish. It is only since then that I have acquainted myself with certain old legends and writings; and in particular, in connection with the latter part of my brother's fevered mouthings, the inexplicable couplet of the mad Arab Abdul Alhazred:

'That is not dead which can eternal lie,
And with strange aeons even death may die.'

But I digress.

It took me some time, after the drone of Julian's outré monologue had died away, to realize that he was no longer in the room with me and that there was a chill morning breeze blowing through the house. In his own room his clothes still hung neatly where he had left them the night before – but Julian had gone, leaving the door to the house swinging open.

I dressed quickly and went out to search the immediate neighbourhood – with negative results. Then, as dawn was breaking, I went into a police-station to discover – to my horror – that my brother was in 'protective custody.' He had been found wandering aimlessly through the northern streets of the city mumbling about 'giant Gods' waiting for something in the ocean deeps. He did not seem to realize that his sole attire was his dressing-gown, nor did he appear to recognize me when I was called to identify him. Indeed, he seemed to be suffering from the after-effects of some terrible shock which had left him in a trauma-like state, totally incapable of rational thought. He would only mumble unguessable things and stare blankly towards the northern wall of his cell; an awful, mad light glowing in the back of his eyes . . .

My tasks were sufficient that morning to keep me amply occupied, and horribly so; for Julian's condition was such that on the orders of a police psychiatrist he was transferred from his police-station cell to Oakdeene Sanatorium for 'observation.' Nor was it easy to get him attended to at the sanatorium. Apparently the supervisors of that institute had had their own share of trouble the previous night. When I did eventually get home, around noon, my first thought was to check the daily newspapers for any reference to my brother's behaviour. I was glad, or as glad as I could be in the circumstances, to find that Julian's activities had been swamped from a more prominent place of curious interest – which they might well have otherwise claimed – by a host of far more serious events.

Strangely, those other events were similar to my brother's trouble in that they all seemed concerned with mental aberrations in previously normal people or, as at Oakdeene, increases in the activities of the more dangerous inmates of lunatic asylums all over the country. In London a businessman of some standing had hurled himself bodily from a high roof declaring that he must 'fly to Yuggoth on the rim.' Chandler Davies, who later died raving mad at Woodholme, painted 'in a trance of sheer inspiration' an evil black and grey *G'harne Landscape* which his outraged and frightened mistress set on fire upon its completion. Stranger still, a Cotswold rector had knifed to death two members of his congregation who, he later protested to the police, 'had no right to exist,' and from the coast, near

Harden in Durham, strange midnight swimmers had been seen to make off with a fisherman who screamed of 'giant frogs' before disappearing beneath the still sea . . . It was as if, on that queer night, some madness had descended – or, as I now believe, had risen – to blanket the more susceptible minds of certain people with utter horror.

But all these things, awful as they were, were not that which I found most disturbing. Looking back on what Julian had murmured in my bedroom while I lay in half-slumber, I felt a weird and inexplicable chill sweep over me as I read, in those same newspapers, of an amateur seismologist who believed he had traced *a submarine disturbance in the ocean between Greenland and the northern tip of Scotland* . . .

What was it Julian had whispered about a *rising* which would not go recorded? Certainly something had been recorded happening in the depths of the sea! . . . But, of course, that was ridiculous, and I shook off the feeling of dread which had gripped me on reading the item. Whatever that deep oceanic disturbance had been, its cause could only be coincidental to my brother's behaviour.

So it was that rather than ponder the reason for so many outré happenings that ill-omened night I thanked our lucky stars that Julian had got away with so light a mention in the press; for what had occurred could have been damaging to both of us had it been given greater publicity.

Not that any of this bothered Julian! Nothing bothered him, for he stayed in that semi-conscious state in which the police had found him for well over a year. During that year his weird delusions were of such a fantastic nature that he became, as it were, the psychological pet and project of a well-known Harley Street alienist. Indeed, after the first month or so, so strong did the good doctor's interest in my brother's case become, he would accept no fee for Julian's keep or treatment; and, though I visited Julian frequently, whenever I was in London, Dr Stewart would never listen to my protests or hear of me paying for his services. Such was his patient's weird case that the doctor declared himself extremely fortunate to be in a position where he had the opportunity to study such a fantastic mind. It amazes me now that the same man who proved so understanding in his dealings with my brother should be so totally devoid of understanding with me; yet that is the pass to which the turn of events has brought me. Still, it was plain my brother was in good hands, and in any case I could hardly afford to press the matter of payment; Dr Stewart's fees were usually astronomical.

It was shortly after Dr Stewart 'took Julian in' that I began to study my brother's star-charts, both astronomical and astrological, and delved deep into his books on the supernatural arts and sciences. I read many peculiar volumes during that period and became reasonably familiar with the works of Fermold, Lévi, Prinn, and Gezrael, and – in certain darker reaches of the British Museum – I shuddered to the literacy lunacy of Magnus, Glynnd, and Alhazred. I read the *R'lyeh Text* and the *Johansen Narrative* and studied the fables of lost Atlantis and Mu. I crouched over flaking tomes in private collections and tracked down all sources of oceanic legend and myth with which I came into contact. I read the manuscript of Andrew Phelan, the deposition of Abel Keane, the testament of Claiborne Boyd, the statement of Nayland Colum, and the narrative of Horvath Blayne. The papers of Jefferson Bates fell to my unbelieving scrutiny, and I lay awake at nights thinking of the hinted fate of Enoch Conger.

And I need never have bothered.

All the above delvings took the better part of a year to complete, by which time I was no nearer a solution to my brother's madness than when I began. No, perhaps that is not quite true. On reflection I think it quite possible that a man might go mad after exploring such dark avenues as these I have mentioned – and especially a man such as Julian, who was more than normally sensitive to begin with. But I was by no means satisfied that this was the whole answer. After all, his interest in such things had been lifelong; I could still see no reason why such an interest should suddenly accumulate so terribly. No, I was sure that the start of it all had been that Candlemas dream.

But at any rate, the year had not been totally lost. I still did not believe in such things – dark survivals of elder times; great ancient gods waiting in the ocean depths; impending doom for the human race in the form of nightmare ocean-dwellers from the beginning of time – how could I and retain my own sanity? But I had become fairly erudite as regards these darker mysteries of elder Earth. And certain facets of my strange research had been of particular interest to me. I refer to what I had read of the oddly similar cases of Joe Slater, the Catskill Mountains vagabond in 1900–01, Nathaniel Wingate Peaslee of Miskatonic University in 1908–13, and Randolph Carter of Boston, whose disappearance in 1928 was so closely linked with the inexplicable case of the Swami Chandraputra in 1930. True, I had looked into other cases of alleged demonic possession – all equally well authenticated – but those I have mentioned seemed to have a special significance, as they paralleled more than roughly that case which I was researching and which involved so terribly my brother.

But time had passed quickly and it was a totally unexpected shock to me, though one of immeasurable relief and pleasure, to find in my letter-box one July morning in 1963 a letter from Dr Stewart which told of Julian's rapid improvement. My joy and amazement can be well imagined when, on journeying down to London the very next day, to the practice of Dr Stewart, I found my brother returned – so far as could be ascertained in such a short time – to literally complete mental recovery. Indeed, it was the doctor himself who, on my arrival, informed me that Julian's recovery was now complete, that my brother had *fully* recovered almost overnight: but I was not so sure – there appeared to be one or two anomalies.

These apart, though, the degree of recovery which had been accomplished was tremendous. When I had last seen my brother, only a month earlier, I had felt physically sickened by the unplumbed depths of his delusions. I had, on that occasion, gone to stand beside him at the barred window from which I was told he always stared blindly northwards, and in answer to my careful greeting he had said: 'Cthulhu, Othuum, Dagon: the Deep Ones in Darkness; all deeply dreaming, awaiting awakening . . .' Nor had I been able to extract anything from him at all except such senseless mythological jargon.

What a transformation! Now he greeted me warmly – though I imagined his recognition of me to be a trifle slow – and after I had delightedly talked with him for a while I came to the conclusion that so far as I could discern, and apart from one new idiosyncrasy, he seemed to be the same man I had known before the onset of the trouble. This oddity I have mentioned was simply that he seemed to have developed a weird photophobia and now wore large, shielded, dark-lensed spectacles which denied one the slightest glimpse of his eyes even from the sides. But, as I later found out, there was an explanation even for these enigmatic-looking spectacles.

While Julian prepared himself for the journey back to Glasgow, Dr Stewart took me to his study where I could sign the necessary release documents and where he could tell me of my brother's fantastic recovery. It appeared that one morning only a week earlier, on going to his exceptional patient's room, the doctor had found Julian huddled beneath his blankets. Nor would my brother come out or allow himself to be brought out until the doctor had agreed to bring him that pair of very dark-lensed spectacles. Peculiar though this muffled request had been, it had delighted the astonished alienist, constituting as it did the first conscious recognition of existence that Julian had shown since the commencement of his treatment.

And the spectacles had proved to be worth their weight in gold, for since their advent Julian had rapidly progressed to his present state of normalcy. The only point over which the doctor seemed unhappy was that to date my brother had point-blank refused to relinquish the things; he declared simply that the light *hurt his eyes!* To some degree, however, the good doctor informed me, this was only to be expected. During his long illness Julian had departed so far from the normal world as it were, that his senses, unused, had partly atrophied – literally ceasing to function. His recovery had left him in the position of a man who, trapped in a dark cave for a long period of time, is suddenly released to face the bright outside world: which also explained in part the clumsiness which had attended Julian's every physical action during the first days of his recovery. One of the doctor's assistants has found occasion to remark upon the most odd way in which my brother had tended to wrap his arms around things which he wanted to lift or examine – even small things – as though he had forgotten what his fingers were for! Also, at first, the patient had tended to waddle rather than walk, almost in the manner of a penguin, and his recently reacquired powers of intelligent expression had lapsed at times in the queerest manner – when his speech had degenerated to nothing more than a guttural, hissing parody of the English language. But all these abnormalities had vanished in the first few days, leaving Julian's recovery as totally unexplained as had been his decline.

*   *   *

In the first-class compartment on the London–Glasgow train, on our way north, having exhausted the more obvious questions I had wanted to put to my restored brother – questions to which, incidentally, his answers had seemed guardedly noncommittal – I had taken out a pocketbook and started to read. After a few minutes, startled by a passing train, I had happened to glance up ... and was immediately glad that Julian and I were alone in the compartment. For my brother had obviously found something of interest in an old newspaper, and I do not know what others might have thought of the look upon his face ... As he read his face bore an unpleasant and, yes, almost *evil* expression. It was made to look worse by those strange spectacles; a mixture of cruel sarcasm, black triumph, and tremendous contempt. I was taken aback, but said nothing, and later – when Julian went into the corridor for a breath of fresh air – I picked up the newspaper and turned to the section he had been reading, which perhaps had caused the weird distortion of his features. I saw at once what had affected him, and a shadow of the old fear flickered briefly across my mind as I read the article. It was not strange that what I read was new to me – I had hardly seen a newspaper since the horror began a year previously – but it was as though this was the same report I had read at that time. It was all there, almost a duplicate of the occurrences of that night of evil omen: the increased activities of lunatics all over the country, the sudden mad and monstrous actions of previously normal people, the cult activity and devil-worship in The Midlands, the sea-things sighted off Harden on the coast, and more inexplicable occurrences in the Cotswolds.

A chill as of strange ocean-floors touched my heart, and I quickly thumbed through the remaining pages of the paper – and almost dropped the thing when I came across that which I had more than half expected. For submarine disturbances had been recorded in the ocean between Greenland and the northern tip of Scotland. And more – I instinctively glanced at the date at the top-centre of the page, *and saw that the newspaper was exactly one week old* ... It had first appeared on the stands on the very morning when Dr Stewart had found my brother huddled beneath the blankets in the room with the barred windows.

Yet apparently my fears were groundless. On our return to the house in Glasgow the first thing my brother did, to my great delight and satisfaction, was destroy all his old books of ancient lore and sorcery; but he made no attempt to return to his writing. Rather he mooned about the house like some lost soul, in what I imagined to be a mood of frustration over those mazed months of which he said he could remember nothing. And not once, until the night of his death, did I see him without those spectacles. I believe he even wore the things to bed – but the significance of this, and something he had mumbled that night in my room, did not dawn on me until much later.

But of those spectacles: I had been assured that this photophobia would wear off, yet as the days went by it became increasingly apparent that Dr Stewart's assurances had gone for nothing. And what was I to make of that *other* change I had noticed? Whereas before Julian had been almost shy and retiring, with a weak chin and a personality to match, he now seemed to be totally out of character, in that he asserted himself over the most trivial things whenever the opportunity arose, and his face – his lips and chin in particular – had taken on a firmness completely alien to his previous physiognomy.

It was all most puzzling, and as the weeks passed I became ever more aware that far from all being well with that altered brother of mine something was seriously wrong.

Apart from his brooding, a darker horror festered within him. Why would he not admit the monstrous dreams which constantly invaded his sleep? Heaven knows he slept little enough as it was; and when he did he often roused me from my own slumbers by mumbling in the night of those same horrors which had featured so strongly in his long illness.

But then, in the middle of October, Julian underwent what I took to be a real change for the better. He became a little more cheerful and even dabbled with some old manuscripts long since left abandoned – though I do not think he did any actual work on them – and towards the end of the month he sprang a surprise. For quite some time, he told me, he had had a wonderful story in mind, but for the life of him he could not settle to it. It was a tale he would have to work on himself; and it would be necessary for him to do much research, as his material would have to be very carefully prepared. He asked that I bear with him during the period of his task and allow him as much privacy as our modest house could afford. I agreed to everything he suggested, though I could not see why he found it so necessary to have a lock put on his door; or, for that matter, why he cleared out the spacious cellar beneath the house 'for future use.' Not that I questioned his actions. He had asked for privacy, and as far as I could assist him he would have it. But I admit to having been more than somewhat curious.

From then on I saw my brother only when we ate – which for him was not any too often – and when he left his room to go to the library for books, a thing he did with clockwork regularity every day. With the first few of these excursions I made a point of being near the door of the house when he returned, for I was puzzled as to what form his work was going to take and I thought I might perhaps gain some insight if I could see his books of reference.

If anything, the materials Julian borrowed from the library only served to add to my puzzlement. What on Earth could he want with Lauder's *Nuclear Weapons and Engines*, Schall's *X-Rays*, Couderc's *The Wider Universe*, Ubbelohde's *Man and Energy*, Keane's *Modern Marvels of Science*, Stafford Clarke's *Psychiatry Today*, Schubert's *Einstein*, Geber's *The Electrical World*, and all the many volumes of *The New Scientist* and *The Progress of Science* with which he returned each day heavily burdened? Still, nothing he was doing gave me any cause to worry as I had in the old days, when his reading had been anything but scientific and had involved those dreadful works which he had now destroyed. But my partial peace of mind was not destined to last for very long.

One day in mid-November – elated by a special success which I had achieved in the writing of a difficult chapter in my own slowly shaping book – I went to Julian's room to inform him of my triumph. I had not seen him at all that morning, but the fact that he was out did not become apparent until, after knocking and receiving no reply, I entered his room. It had been Julian's habit of late to lock his door when he went out, and I was surprised that on this occasion he had not done so. I saw then that he had left the door open purposely so that I might see the note he had left for me on his bedside table. It was scribbled on a large sheet of white typing paper in awkward, tottering letters, and the message was blunt and to the point:

> Phillip,
>   Gone to London for four or five days.
> Research. Brit. Museum ...
>   Julian

Somewhat disgruntled, I turned to leave the room and as I did so noticed my brother's diary lying open at the foot of his bed where he had thrown it. The book itself did not surprise me – before his trouble he had always kept such notes – and not being a snoop I would have left the room there and then had I not glimpsed a word – *or name* – which I recognized on the open, hand-written pages: '*Cthulhu.*'

Simply that . . . yet it set my mind awhirl with renewed doubts. Was Julian's trouble reasserting itself? Did he yet require pyschiatric treatment and were his original delusions returning? Remembering that Dr Stewart had warned me of the possibility of a relapse, I considered it my duty to read all that my brother had written – which was where I met with a seemingly insurmountable problem. The difficulty was simply this: I was *unable* to read the diary, for it was written in a completely alien, cryptically cuneiform script the like of which I had ever seen only in those books which Julian had burned. There was a distinct resemblance in those weird characters to the minuscules and dot-groups of the *G'harne Fragments* – I remembered being struck by an article on them in one of Julian's books, an archeological magazine – but only a resemblance; the diary contained nothing I could understand except that one word, *Cthulhu*, and even that had been scored through by Julian, as if on reflection, and a weird squiggle of ink had been crammed in above it as a replacement.

I was not slow to come to a decision as to what my proper course of action should be. That same day, taking the diary with me, I went down to Wharby on the noon train. That article on the *G'harne Fragments* which I had re-membered reading had been the work of the curator of the Wharby Museum, Professor Gordon Walmsley of Goole; who, incidentally, had claimed the first translation of the fragments over the claim of the eccentric and long-vanished antiquarian and archeologist Sir Amery Wendy-Smith. The professor was an authority on the Phitmar Stone – that contemporary of the famous Rosetta Stone with its key

inscriptions in two forms of Egyptian hieroglyphs – and
the Geph Columns Characters, and had several other trans-
lations or feats of antiquarian deciphering to his credit.
Indeed, I was extremely fortunate to find him in at the
museum, for he planned to fly within the week to Peru
where yet another task awaited his abecedarian talents.
None the less, busy with arrangements as he was, he was
profoundly interested in the diary; enquiring where the
hieroglyphics within had been copied, and by whom and
to what purpose? I lied, telling him my brother had copied
the inscriptions from a black stone monolith somewhere in
the mountains of Hungary; for I knew that just such a stone
exists, having once seen mention of it in one of my brother's
books. The professor squinted his eyes suspiciously at my
lie but was so interested in the diary's strange characters
that he quickly forgot whatever it was that had prompted
his suspicion. From then until I was about to leave his
study, located in one of the museum's rooms, we did
not speak. So absorbed did he become with the diary's
contents that I think he completely forgot my presence in
the room. Before I left, however, I managed to extract a
promise from him that the diary would be returned to my
Glasgow address within three days and that a copy of his
translation, if any, would accompany it. I was glad that he
did not ask me why I required such a translation.

My faith in the professor's abilities was eventually borne
out – but not until far too late. For Julian returned to
Glasgow on the morning of the third day – earlier by
twenty-four hours than I had been led to believe, and
his diary still had not been returned – nor was he slow
to discover its loss.

I was working half-heartedly at my book when my
brother made his appearance. He must have been to his
own room first. Suddenly I felt a presence in my room

with me. I was so lost in my half-formed imaginings and ideas that I had not heard my door open; none the less I knew something was in there with me. I say *something;* and that is the way it was! I was being observed – but not, I felt, by a human being! Carefully, with the short hair of my neck prickling with an uncanny life of its own, I turned about. Standing in the open doorway with a look on his face which I can only describe as being utterly hateful was Julian. But even as I saw him, his horribly writhing features composed themselves behind those enigmatic dark glasses and he forced an unnatural smile.

'I seem to have mislaid my diary, Phillip,' he said slowly. 'I'm just in from London and I can't seem to find the thing anywhere. I don't suppose you've seen it, have you?' There was the suggestion of a sneer in his voice, an unspoken accusation. 'I don't need the diary really, but there are one or two things in it which I wrote in code – ideas I want to use in my story. I'll let you in on a secret! It's a *fantasy* I'm writing! I mean – horror, science fiction, and fantasy – they're all the rage these days; it's about time we broke into the field. You shall see the rough work as soon as it's ready. But now, seeing as you obviously haven't seen my diary, if you'll excuse me, I want to get some of my notes together.'

He left the room quickly, before I could answer, and I would be lying if I said I was not glad to see him go. And I could not help but notice that with his departure the feeling of an alien presence also departed. My legs felt suddenly weak beneath me as a dreadful aura of foreboding settled like a dark cloud over my room. Nor did that feeling disperse – rather it tightened as night drew on.

Lying in my bed that night I found myself going again and again over Julian's strangeness, trying to make some sense of it all. A fantasy? Could it be? It was so unlike Julian; and why, if it was only a story, had his look been

so terrible when he was unable to find his diary? And why
write a story in a diary at all? Oh! He had liked reading
weird stuff – altogether too much, as I have explained – but
he had never before shown any urge to *write* it! And what
of the books he had borrowed from the library? They had
not seemed to be works he could possibly use in connection
with the construction of a fantasy! And there was something else, something which kept making brief appearances
in my mind's eye but which I could not quite bring into
focus. Then I had it – the thing which had been bothering
me ever since I first saw that diary: *where in the name of
all that's holy had Julian learned to write in hieroglyphics?*

That cinched it!

No, I did not believe that Julian was writing a story at
all. That was only an excuse he had created to put me off
the track. But what track? What did he think he was doing?
Oh! It was obvious; he was on the verge of another breakdown, and the sooner I got in touch with Dr Stewart the
better. All these tumultuous thoughts kept me awake until a
late hour, and if my brother was noisy again that night I did
not hear him. I was so mentally fatigued that when I
eventually nodded off I slept the sleep of the dead.

Is it not strange how the light of day has the power to
drive away the worst terrors of night? With the morning
my fears were much abated and I decided to wait a few
more days before contacting Dr Stewart. Julian spent all
morning and afternoon locked in the cellar, and finally –
again becoming alarmed as night drew near – I determined
to reason with him, if possible, over supper. During the
meal I spoke to him, pointing out how strangely he seemed
to be acting and lightly mentioning my fears of a relapse.
I was somewhat taken aback by his answers. He argued
it was my own fault he had had to resort to the cellar
in which to work, stating that the cellar appeared to be

the only place where he could be sure of any privacy. He laughed at my mention of a relapse, saying he had never felt better in his life! When he again mentioned 'privacy' I knew he must be referring to the unfortunate incident of the missing diary and was shamed into silence. I mentally cursed Professor Walmsley and his whole museum.

Yet, in direct opposition to all my brother's glib explanations, that night was the worst; for Julian gibbered and moaned in his sleep, making it impossible for me to get any rest at all; so that when I arose, haggard and withdrawn, late on the morning of the 13th, I knew I would soon have to take some definite action.

I saw Julian only fleetingly that morning, on his way from his room to the cellar, and his face seemed pale and cadaverous. I guessed that his dreams were having as bad an effect upon him as they were on me; yet rather than appearing tired or hag-ridden he seemed to be in the grip of some feverish excitement.

Now I became more worried than ever and even scribbled two letters to Dr Stewart, only later to ball them up and throw them away. If Julian was genuine in whatever he was doing, I did not want to spoil his faith in me – what little of it was left – and if he was not genuine? I was becoming morbidly curious to learn the outcome of his weird activities. None the less, twice that day, at noon and later in the evening, when as usual my fears got the better of me, I hammered at the cellar door demanding to know what was going on in there. My brother completely ignored these efforts of mine at communication, but I was determined to speak to him. When he finally came out of the cellar, much later that night, I was waiting for him at the door. He turned the key in the lock behind him, carefully shielding the cellar's contents from my view, and regarded me curiously from behind those horrid dark glasses before offering me the merest parody of a smile.

'Phillip, you've been very patient with me,' he said, taking my elbow and leading me up the cellar steps, 'and I know I must have seemed to be acting quite strangely and inexplicably. It's all very simple really, but for the moment I can't explain just what I'm about. You'll just have to keep faith with me and wait. If you're worried that I'm heading for another bout of, well, *trouble* – you can forget it. I'm perfectly all right. I just need a little more time to finish off what I'm doing – and then, the day after tomorrow, I'll take you in there' – he nodded over his shoulder – 'into the cellar, and show you what I've got. All I ask is that you're patient for just one more day. Believe me, Phillip, you've got a revelation coming which will shake you to your very roots; and afterwards – you'll understand everything. Don't ask me to explain it all now – you wouldn't believe it! But seeing *is* believing, and when I take you in there you'll be able to see for yourself.'

He seemed so reasonable, so sensible – if a trifle feverish – and so excited, almost like a child about to show off some new toy. Wanting to believe him, I allowed myself to be easily talked around and we went off together to eat a late meal.

Julian spent the morning of the 14th transferring all his notes – great sheaves of them which I had never suspected existed – together with odds and ends in small cardboard boxes, from his room to the cellar. After a meagre lunch he was off to the library to 'do some final checking' and to return a number of books lately borrowed. While he was out I went down to the cellar – only to discover that he had locked the door and taken the key with him. He returned and spent the entire afternoon locked in down there, to emerge later at night looking strangely elated. Still later, after I had retired to my room, he came and knocked on my door.

'The night is exceptionally clear, Phillip, and I thought I'd have a look at the sky ... the stars have always fascinated me, you know? But the window in my room doesn't really show them off too well; I'd appreciate it if you'd allow me to sit in here and look out for a while?'

'By all means do, old fellow, come on in,' I answered, agreeably surprised. I left my easy chair and went to stand beside him after he crossed the room to lean on the windowsill. He peered through those strange, dark lenses up and out into the night. He was, I could see, intently studying the constellations, and as I glanced from the sky to his face I mused aloud: 'Looking up there, one is almost given to believe that the stars have some purpose other than merely making the night look pretty.'

Abruptly my brother's manner changed. 'What d'you mean by that?' He snapped, staring at me in an obviously suspicious fashion. I was taken aback. My remark had been completely innocuous.

'I mean that perhaps those old astrologers had something after all,' I answered.

'Astrology is an ancient and exact science, Phillip – you shouldn't talk of it so lightly.' He spoke slowly, as though restraining himself from some outburst. Something warned me to keep quiet, so I said no more. Five minutes later he left. Pondering my brother's odd manner, I sat there a while longer; and, as I looked up at the stars winking through the window across the room, I could not help but recall a few of those words he had mumbled in the darkness of my bedroom so long ago at the onset of his breakdown. He had said:

'That in time, *when the stars are right,* they may perform the Great Rising ...'

There was no sleep at all for me that night; the noises and mutterings, the mouthings and gibberings which came, loud and clear, from Julian's room would not permit it.

In his sleep he talked of such eldritch and inexplicable things as the Deep Green Waste, the Scarlet Feaster, the Chained Shoggoth, the Lurker at the Threshold, Yibb-Tstll, Tsathoggua, the Cosmic Screams, the Lips of Bugg-Shash, and the Inhabitants of the Frozen Chasm. Towards morning, out of sheer exhaustion, I eventually nodded off into evil dreams which claimed my troubled subconscious until I awoke shortly before noon on the 15th.

Julian was already in the cellar, and as soon as I had washed and dressed, remembering his promise to 'show me' what he had got, I started off down there. But at the top of the cellar steps my feet were suddenly arrested by the metallic *clack* of the letter-box flap in the front door of the house.

The diary!

Unreasonably fearing that Julian might also have heard the noise, I raced back along the passage to the door, snatched up the small stamped and addressed brown-paper parcel which lay on the inside door-mat, and fled with the thing to my room. I locked myself in and ripped open the parcel. I had tried Julian's door earlier and knew it to be unlocked. Now I planned to go in and drop the diary down behind the headboard of his bed while he was still in the cellar. In this way he might be led to believe he had merely misplaced the book. But, after laying aside the diary to pick up and read the stapled sheets which had fallen loose and fluttered to the floor, I forgot all about my planned deception in the dawning knowledge of my brother's obvious impending insanity. Walmsley had done as he had promised. I cast his brief, eagerly enquiring letter aside and quickly, in growing horror, read his translation of Julian's cryptical notes. It was all there, all the proof I needed, in neat partially annotated paragraphs; but I did not need to read it all. Certain words and phrases, lines and sentences, seemed to leap upon the paper, attracting my frantically searching eyes:

'This shape/form? sickens me. Thanks be there is not long to wait. There is difficulty in the fact that this form/body/shape? would not obey me at first, and I fear it may have alerted – (?—?) to some degree. Also, I have to hide/protect/conceal? that of me which also came through with the transfer/journey/passage?

'I know the mind of (?—?) fares badly in the Deeps . . . and of course his eyes were ruined/destroyed? completely . . .

'Curse the water that quiets/subdues? Great (?)'s power. In these few times/periods? I have looked upon/seen/ observed? much and studied what I have seen and read – but I have had to gain such knowledge secretly. The mind-sendings/mental messages (telepathy?) from my kin/brothers? at (?—?) near that place which men call Devil–(?) were of little use to me, for the progress these beings/creatures? have made is fantastic in the deep times/moments/periods? since their (?) attack on those at Devil–(?).

'I have seen much and I know the time is not yet ripe for the great rising/coming? They have developed weapons of (?) power. We would risk/chance? defeat – and that must never be.

'But if (??????? they ???) turn their devices against themselves (??? bring ?) nation against nation (?? then ??) destructive/cataclysmic? war rivalling (name – possibly *Azathoth*, as in *Pnakotic Mss*).

'The mind of (?—?) has broken under the strain of the deeps . . . It will now be necessary to contact my rightful shape in order to rebecome one/re-enter? it.

'*Cthulhu?* (?) triumph (???) I am eager to return to my own shape/form/body? I do not like the way this brother – (the word brother implying falseness?) has looked at me . . . but he suspects nothing . . .'

There was more, much more, but I skipped over the vast majority of the translation's remaining contents and finished by reading the last paragraph which, presumably, had been written in the diary shortly before Julian took himself off to London:

'(Date?) . . . six more (short periods of time?) to wait . . . Then the stars should be right/in order/positioned? and if all goes well the transfer can be performed/accomplished?'

That was all; but it was more than enough! That reference about my not 'suspecting' anything, in connection with those same horrors which had been responsible for his first breakdown, was sufficient finally to convince me that my brother was seriously ill!

Taking the diary with me, I ran out of my room with one thought in my mind. Whatever Julian thought he was doing I had to stop him. Already his delvings constituted a terrible threat to his health, and who could say but that the next time a cure might not be possible? If he suffered a second attack, there was the monstrous possibility that he would remain permanently insane.

Immediately I started my frantic hammering, he opened the cellar door and I literally fell inside. I say I fell; indeed, I did – I fell from a sane world into a lunatic, alien, nightmare dimension totally outside any previous experience. As long as I live I shall never forget what I saw. The floor in the centre of the cellar had been cleared, and upon it, chalked in bold red strokes, was a huge and unmistakable evil symbol. I had seen it before in those books which were now destroyed . . . and now I recoiled at what I had later read of it! Beyond the sign, in one corner, a pile of ashes was all that remained of Julian's many notes. An old iron grating had been fixed horizontally over bricks, and the makings of a fire were already upon it. A cryptographic script, which

I recognized as being the blasphemous *Nyhargo Code,* was scrawled in green and blue chalk across the walls, and the smell of incense hung heavily in the air. The whole scene was ghastly, unreal, a living picture from Eliphas Lévi – nothing less than the lair of a sorcerer! Horrified, I turned to Julian – in time to see him lift a heavy iron poker and start the stunning swing downwards towards my head. Nor did I lift a finger to stop him. I could not – *for he had taken off those spectacles, and the sight of his terrible face had frozen me rigid as polar ice* . . .

Regaining consciousness was like swimming up out of a dead, dark sea. I surfaced through shoals of night-black swimmers to an outer world where the ripples of the ocean were dimly lit by the glow from a dying orange sun. As the throbbing in my head subsided, those ripples resolved themselves into the pattern of my pin-stripe jacket – but the orange glow remained! My immediate hopes that it had all been a nightmare were shattered at once; for as I carefully raised my head from its position on my chest the whole room slowly came under my unbelieving scrutiny. Thank God Julian had his back to me and I could not see his face. Had I but *glimpsed* again, in those first moments of recovery, those hellish eyes I am certain the sight would have returned me to instant oblivion.

I could see now that the orange glow was reflected from the now blazing fire on the horizontal grill, and I saw that the poker which had been used to strike me down was buried in the heart of the flames with red-heat creeping visibly up the metal towards the wooden handle. Glancing at my watch, I saw that I had been unconscious for many hours – it was fast approaching the midnight hour. That one glance was also sufficient to tell me that I was tied to the old wicker-chair in which I had been seated, for I saw the ropes. I flexed my muscles against my bonds and noticed, not without a measure of satisfaction, that there was a certain degree of slackness in them. I had managed to keep my mind from dwelling on Julian's facial differences, but, as he turned towards me, I steeled myself to the coming shock.

His face was an impassive white mask in which shone, cold and malevolent and indescribably alien, *those eyes!* As I live and breathe, I swear they were twice the size they ought to have been – and they bulged, uniformly scarlet, outwards from their sockets in chill, yet aloof hostility.

'Ah! You've returned to us, dear brother. But why d'you stare so? Is it that you find this face so awful? Let me assure you, you don't find it half so hideous as I!'

Monstrous truth, or what I thought was the truth, began to dawn in my mazed and bewildered brain. 'The dark spectacles!' I gasped. 'No wonder you had to wear them, even at night. You couldn't bear the thought of people seeing those diseased eyes!'

'Diseased? No, your reasoning is only partly correct. I had to wear the glasses, yes; it was that or give myself away – which wouldn't have pleased those who sent me in the slightest, believe me. For Cthulhu, beneath the waves on the far side of the world, has already made it known to Othuum, my master, of his displeasure. They have spoken in dreams, and Cthulhu is *angry!*' He shrugged, 'Also, I needed the spectacles; these eyes of mine are accustomed to piercing the deepest depths of the ocean! Your surface world was an agony to me at first – but now I am used to it. In any case, I don't plan to stay here long, and when I go I will take this body with me,' he plucked at himself in contempt, 'for my pleasure.'

I knew that what he was saying was not, could not, be possible, and I cried out to him, begging him to recognize his own madness. I babbled that modern medical science could probably correct whatever was wrong with his eyes. My words were drowned out by his cold laughter. 'Julian!' I cried.

'Julian?' he answered. 'Julian Haughtree?' He lowered his awful face until it was only inches from mine. 'Are you blind, man? *I am Pesh-Tlen, Wizard of deep Gell-Ho to the North!*' He turned away from me, leaving my tottering mind to total up a nerve-blasting sum of horrific integers. The Cthulhu Mythos – those passages from the *Cthaat Aquadingen* and the *Life of St Brendan* – Julian's dreams; 'They can now control dreams as of old.' The Mind Transfer – 'They will rise' – 'through his eyes in my body' – giant gods waiting in the ocean deeps – 'He shall walk the Earth in my guise' – a submarine disturbance off the coast of Greenland! *Deep Gell-Ho to the North . . .*

God in heaven! Could such things be? Was this all, in the end, not just some fantastic delusion of Julian's but an incredible fact? This thing before me! Did he – *it* – really see through the eyes of a monster from the bottom of the sea? And if so – *was it governed by that monster's mind?*

After that, it was not madness which gripped me – not then – rather was it the refusal of my whole being to accept that which was unacceptable. I do not know how long I remained in that state, but the spell was abruptly broken by the first, distant chime of the midnight hour.

At that distant clamour my mind became crystal clear and the eyes of the being called Pesh-Tlen blazed even more unnaturally as he smiled – if that word describes what he *did* with his face – in final triumph. Seeing that smile, I knew that something hideous was soon to come and I struggled against my bonds. I was gratified to feel them slacken a little more about my body. The – creature – had meanwhile turned away from me and had taken the poker from the fire. As the chimes of the hour continued to ring out faintly from afar it raised its arms, weaving strange designs in the air with the tip of the redly glowing poker, and commenced a chant or invocation of such a loathsome association of discordant tones and pipings that my soul seemed to shrink inside me at the hearing. It was fantastic that what was grunted, snarled, whistled, and hissed with such incredible fluency could ever have issued from the throat of something I had called brother, regardless what force motivated his vocal cords; but, fantastic or not, I heard it. Heard it? Indeed, as that mad cacophony died away, tapering off to a high-pitched, screeching end – *I saw its result!*

Writhing tendrils of green smoke began to whirl together in one corner of the cellar. I did not see the smoke arrive, nor could I say whence it came – it was just suddenly there! The tendrils quickly became a column, rapidly thickening, spinning faster and faster, forming – *a shape!*

Outside in the night freak lightning flashed and thunder rumbled over the city in what I have since been told was the worst storm in years – but I barely heard the thunder or the heavy downpour of rain. All my senses were concentrated on the silently spinning, rapidly coalescing thing in the corner. The cellar had a high ceiling, almost eleven feet, but what was forming seemed to fill that space easily.

I screamed then, and mercifully fainted. For once again my mind had been busy totalling the facts as I knew them, and I had mentally questioned Pesh-Tlen's reason for calling up this horror from the depths – or from wherever else it came. Upstairs in my room, unless Julian had been up there and removed it, the answer lay where I had thrown it – Walmsley's translation! Had not Julian, or Pesh-Tlen, or whatever the thing was, written in that diary: *'It will now be necessary to contact my natural form in order to re-enter it'*?

My black-out could only have been momentary, for as I regained consciousness for the second time I saw that the thing in the corner had still not completely formed. It had stopped spinning and was now centrally opaque, but its outline was infirm and wavering, like a scene viewed through smoke. The creature that had been Julian was standing to one side of the cellar, arms raised towards the semi-coherent object in the corner, features strained and twitching with hideous expectancy.

'Look,' it spoke coldly, half turning towards me. 'See what I and the Deep Ones have done! Behold, mortal, your brother – *Julian Haughtree!*'

For the rest of my days, which I believe will not number many, I will never be able to rid my memory of that sight! While others lie drowning in sleep I will claw desperately at the barrier of consciousness, not daring to close my eyes for fear of that which lingers yet beyond my eyelids. As Pesh-Tlen spoke those words – the thing in the corner finally materialized!

Imagine a black, glistening, ten-foot heap of twisting, ropey tentacles and gaping mouths ... Imagine the outlines of a slimy, alien face in which, sunk deep in gaping sockets, are the remains of ruptured *human* eyes ... Imagine shrieking in absolute clutching, leaping fear and horror – and imagine the thing which I have here described answering your screams in a madly familiar voice; *a voice which you instantly recognize!*

'Phillip! Phillip, where are you? What's happened? I can't see ... We came up out of the sea, and then I was whirled away somewhere and I heard your voice.' The horror rocked back and forth. 'Don't let them take me back, Phillip!'

The voice was that of my brother, all right – but not the old *sane* Julian I had known! That was when I, too, went mad; but it was a madness with a purpose, if nothing else. When I had previously fainted, the sudden loosening of my body must have completed the work which I had started on the ropes. As I lurched to my feet they fell

from me to the floor. The huge, blind monstrosity in the
corner had started to lumber in my direction, vaguely
twisting its tentacles before it as it came. At the same time
the red-eyed demon in Julian's form was edging carefully
towards it, arms eagerly outstretched.

'Julian,' I screamed, 'look out – only by contact can
he re-enter – and then he intends to kill you, to take you
back with him to the deeps.'

'Back to the deeps? No! No, he can't! I won't go!'
The lumbering horror with my brother's mad voice spun
blindly around, its flailing tentacles knocking the hybrid
sorcerer flying across the floor. I snatched the poker from
the fire where it had been replaced and turned threateningly
upon the sprawling half-human.

'Stand still, Julian!' I gibbered over my shoulder at the
horror from the sea as the wizard before me leapt to his
feet. The lumberer behind me halted. 'You, Pesh-Tlen,
get back.' There was no plan in my bubbling mind; I
only knew I had to keep the two – *things* – apart. I danced
like a boxer, using the glowing poker to ward off the
suddenly frantic Pesh-Tlen.

'But it's time – it's time! The contact must be now!'
The red-eyed thing screeched. 'Get out of my way ...'
Its tones were barely human now. 'You can't stop me
... I must ... must ... must make strong ... strong
contact! I must ... *bhfg – ngyy fhtlhlh hegm – yeh'hhg
narcchhh'yy!* You won't cheat me!'

A pool of slime, like the trail of a great snail, had quickly
spread from the giant shape behind me; and, even as he
screamed, Pesh-Tlen suddenly leapt forward straight onto
it, his feet skidding on the evil-smelling mess. He completely
lost his balance. Arms flailing he fell, face down, sicken-
ingly, onto the rigid red-hot poker in my hand. Four inches
of the glowing metal slid, like a warm knife through butter,
into one of those awful eyes. There was a hissing sound,

almost drowned out by the creature's single shrill scream of agony, and a small cloud of steam rose mephitically from the thing's face as it pitched to the floor.

Instantly the glistening black giant behind me let out a shriek of terror. I spun round, letting the steaming poker fall, to witness that monstrosity from the ocean floor rocking to and fro, tentacles wrapped protectively round its head. After a few seconds it became still, and the rubbery arms fell listlessly away to reveal the multi-mouthed face with its ruined, rotting eyes.

'You've killed him, I know it,' Julian's voice said, calmer now. 'He is finished and I am finished – already I can feel them recalling me.' Then, voice rising hysterically: *'They won't take me alive!'*

The monstrous form trembled and its outline began to blur. My legs crumpled beneath me in sudden reaction, and I pitched to the floor. Perhaps I passed out again – I don't know for sure – but when I next looked in its direction the horror had gone. All that remained was the slime and the grotesque corpse.

I do not know where my muscles found the strength to carry my tottering and mazed body out of that house. Sanity did not drive me, I admit that, for I was quite insane. I wanted to stand beneath the stabbing lightning and scream at those awful, rain-blurred stars. I wanted to bound, to float in my madness through eldritch depths of unhallowed black blood. I wanted to cling to the writhing breasts of Yibb-Tstll. Insane – insane, I tell you, I gibbered and moaned, staggering through the thunder-crazed streets until, with a roar and a crash, sanity-invoking lightning smashed me down . . .

You know the rest. I awoke to this world of white sheets; to you, the police psychiatrist, with your soft voice . . . Why must you insist that I keep telling my story? Do you honestly think to make me change it? It's *true*, I tell you! I admit to killing my brother's body – but it wasn't *his mind* that I burned out! You stand there babbling of awful eye diseases. *Julian had no eye disease!* D'you really imagine that the other eye, the unburnt one which you found in that body – in my brother's face – was his? And what of the pool of slime in the cellar and the stink? Are you stupid or something? You've asked for a statement, and here it is! Watch, damn you, watch while I scribble it down . . . you damn great crimson eye . . . always watching me . . . who would have thought that the lips of Bugg-Shash could *suck* like that? Watch, you redness you . . . and look out for the Scarlet Feaster! *No, don't take the paper away* . . .

NOTE:
Sir,

Dr Stewart was contacted as you suggested, and after seeing Haughtree he gave his expert opinion that the man was madder than his brother ever had been. He also pointed out the possibility that the disease of Julian Haughtree's eyes had started soon after his partial mental recovery – probably brought on by constantly wearing dark spectacles. After Dr Stewart left the police ward, Haughtree became very indignant and wrote the above statement.

Davies, our specialist, examined the body in the cellar himself and is convinced that the younger brother must, indeed, have been suffering from a particularly horrible and unknown ocular disease.

It is appreciated that there are one or two remarkable coincidences in the wild fancies of both brothers in relation to certain recent factual events – but these are, surely, only coincidences. One such event is the rise of the volcanic island of Surtsey. Haughtree must somehow have heard of Surtsey after being taken under observation. He asked to be allowed to read the following newspaper account, afterwards yelling very loudly and repeatedly: 'By God! They've named it after the wrong mythos!' Thereafter he was put into a straitjacket of the arm-restricting type:

—— BIRTH OF AN ISLAND ——

Yesterday morning, the 16th November, the sun rose on a long, narrow island of tephra, lying in the sea to the north of Scotland at latitude 63°18′ North and longitude 20°36½′ West. Surtsey, which was born on the 15th November, was then 130 feet high and growing all the time. The fantastic 'birth' of the island was witnessed by the crew of the fishing vessel *Isleifer II*, which was lying west of Geirfuglasker, southernmost of the Vestmann Islands. Considerable disturbance of the sea – which hindered clear observation – was noticed, and the phenomena, the result of submarine volcanic activity, involved such awe-inspiring sights as columns of smoke reaching to two and a half miles high, fantastic lightning storms, and the hurling of lava-bombs over a wide area of the ocean. Surtsey has been named after the giant Surter, who – in Norse Mythology – 'Came from the South with Fire to fight the God Freyr at Ragnarok,' which battle preceded the end of the world and the Twilight of the Gods. More details and pictures inside.

Still in the 'jacket,' Haughtree finally calmed himself and begged that further interesting items in the paper be read to him. Dr Davies did the reading, and when he reached the following report Haughtree grew very excited:

—— BEACHES FOULED ——

Garvin Bay, on the extreme North coast, was found this morning to be horribly fouled. For a quarter of a mile deposits of some slimy, black grease were left by the tide along the sands. The stench was so great from these unrecognizable deposits that fishermen were unable to put to sea. Scientific analysis has already shown the stuff to be of an organic base, and it is thought to be some type of oil. Local shipping experts are bewildered, as no known tankers have been in the area for over three months. The tremendous variety of dead and rotting fish also washed up has caused the people of nearby Belloch to take strong sanitary precautions. It is hoped that tonight's tide will clear the affected area . . .

At the end of the reading Haughtree said: 'Julian said they wouldn't take him alive.' Then, still encased in the jacket, he somehow got off the bed and flung himself through the third-story window, of his room in the police ward. His rush at the window was of such tremendous ferocity and strength that he took the bars and frame with him. It all happened so quickly there was nothing anyone could do to stop him.

Submitted as an appendix to my original report.

Sgt. J.T. Muir

23 November 1963. Glasgow City Police

DAVID'S WORM

The last of my witch's dozen, David's Worm *was written in 1969. At first I couldn't find a buyer. Then it went into* Year's Best Horror Stories No. 2, *and from there must have gone into translation for eventually it was adapted for both German and Italian radio. Anyway, it's had a long outing, and it's only right that the trail of the slimy beast ends here!*

Professor Lees – chief radio-biologist at the Kendall nuclear research and power station – was showing his son some slides he had prepared weeks earlier from pond and sea water in irradiated test tubes. David was only seven, but already he could understand much of what his famous father said.

'Look,' the professor explained as the boy peered eagerly into the microscope. 'That's an *amoeba*, quite dead, killed off by radiation. Just like a little jelly-fish, isn't it? And this . . .' he swapped slides, '. . . is a tiny-wee plant called a *diatom*. It's dead too – they all are – that's what hard radiation does to living things . . .'

'What's this one?' David asked, changing the slides himself.

'That's a young flatworm, David. It's a tiny fresh-water animal. Lives in pools and streams. Funny little thing. That one's a type with very strange abilities. D'you know, when one *planarian* (that's what they're called) eats another—' David looked up sharply at his father, who smiled at the boy's expression. 'Oh, no! They're not cannibals – at least I don't think so – but if a dead worm is chopped up and fed to another, why! The live worm "inherits" the knowledge of the one it's eaten!'

'Knowledge?' David looked puzzled. 'Are they clever, then?'

'Noooo – not strictly *clever*, but they can be taught simple things: like how a drop in temperature means it's feeding time; stuff like that. And, as I've said, when one of them is dead and chopped up, whatever he knew before he died is passed on to the planarian who eats him.'

'And they're not cannibals?' David still looked puzzled.

'Why, no,' the professor patiently explained. 'I don't suppose for one minute they'd eat each other if they *knew* what they were eating – we do chop them up first!' He frowned. 'I'm not absolutely sure though . . . you could, I suppose, call them *unwilling* cannibals if you wished. Is it important?'

But David was not listening. Suddenly his attention seemed riveted on the tiny creature beneath the microscope.

'He moved—!'

'No he didn't, David – that's just your imagination. He *couldn't* move, he's dead.' None the less the scientist pulled his son gently to one side to have a look himself. It wasn't possible – no, of course not. He had been studying the specimens for three weeks, since the experiment, watching them all die off; and since then there had not been a sign of returning life in any of them. Certainly there could be none now. Even if the sustained blast of hard radiation had not killed them off proper (which of course it had), then colouring them and fixing them to the slides certainly must have. No, they were dead, all of them, merely tiny lumps of useless gelatin . . .

The next day was Saturday and David was not at school. He quit the house early saying he was going fishing at the pool. Shortly after he left, his father cleaned off his many slides, hardly missing the one with the tiny planarium worm – the one in David's pocket!

David *knew* he had seen the worm move under the microscope; a stiff, jerky movement, rather like the slug he had pinned to the garden with a twig through its middle one evening a few weeks earlier . . .

David's pool was his own. It lay in the grounds of the house, set far back from the road, in the copse that marked the boundary of his father's land. In fact it was a run-off from the river, filled nine months of the year by high waters flooding the creek running to it. There were fish, but David had never caught any of the big ones; not with his bent pin. He had seen them often enough in the reeds – even a great pike – but his catches were never any bigger than the occasional newt or minnow. That Saturday it was not even his intention to fish; that had only been an excuse to his mother to allow him to get down to the pool.

The truth was that David was a very humane boy really and the idea that the flatworm had been *alive* on that slide, no matter how, was abhorrent to him. His father had said that the creature was a fresh-water dweller; well, if it *was* alive, David believed it should be given another chance. Immersion in water, its natural habitat, might just do the trick!

He put the slide down on a stone in a part of the pool not quite so shaded by the surrounding trees, so that the creature upon it might benefit from what was left of the late summer sun. There he could see it just beneath the surface of the water. He kept up a watch on the tiny speck on the slide for almost an hour before growing tired of the game. Then he went home to spend the rest of the day in the library – boning up on planarian worms . . .

In defiance of everything the books said, 'Planny' (as David christened the creature the day after he saw it detach itself from the slide and swim almost aimlessly away) grew up very strangely indeed. Instead of adopting a worm-shape as it developed, with a lobey, spade-shaped head, it took on one more like an amoeba. It was simply a shapeless blob – or, at best, a roundish blob.

Now one might ask: 'Just how did David manage, in such a large pool, to follow the comings and goings of such a small animal?' And the answer would be that Planny did not stay small for very long. Indeed no, for even on that morning when he got loose from the slide he trebled his size: that is, he *converted* many times his own weight in less wily, even smaller denizens of David's pool. In just a day or two he was as big as a Ping-Pong ball; and David had taken to getting up very early, before school, so that he could go down to the copse to check the creature's rate of growth.

Two weeks later there was not a single minnow left in the pool, nor a stickleback, and even the numbers of the youngest of the larger fish were on a rapid decline.

David never discovered just how Planny swam. He could see that there were no fins or anything, no legs, yet somehow the animal managed quite nimbly in the water without such extensions – and especially after dining on the first of the larger fish. It had been noticeable, certainly, how much the freakish flatworm 'learned' from the minnows: how to hunt and hide in the reeds, how to sink slowly to the bottom if ever anything big came near, things like that. Not that Planny really *needed* to hide, but he was not aware of that yet; he only had the experience ('inherited' of course) of the minnows and other fish he had eaten. Minnows, being small, have got to be careful . . . so David's worm was careful too! Nor did he get much from the bigger fish; though they did help his self-assurance somewhat and his speed in the water; for naturally, they had the bustling attitude of most aquatic adults.

Then, when Planny was quite a bit bigger, something truly memorable happened!

He was all of five weeks reborn when he took the pike. David was lucky enough to see the whole bit. That old pike had been stalking Planny for a week, but the radiation-transformed worm had successfully managed to avoid him right until the best possible moment: that is, until their sizes were more or less equal . . . in mass if not in shape.

David was standing at the pool-side, admiring Planny as he gently undulated through the water, when the ugly fish came sliding out of the reed-patch; its wicked eyes fixed firmly on the vaguely globular, greyish-white thing in the water. David's worm had eyes too, two of them, and they were fixed equally firmly on the pike.

The boy gawked at the way it happened. The fish circled once, making a tight turn about his revolving 'prey,' then flashed in to the attack at a speed which left David breathless. The boy knew all about this vicious species of fish, especially about the powerful jaws and great teeth; but the pike in question might never have had any teeth at all – might well have been a caviar sandwich – for all Planny worried! He simply *opened up*, seeming to split down the middle and around his circumference until David, still watching from the poolside, thought he must tear himself in two. But he did not. David saw a flash of rapidly sawing rows of rasp-like teeth marching in columns along Planny's insides – and then the creature's two almost-halves ground shut on the amazed pike.

Planny seemed to go mad then, almost lifting himself (or being lifted) out of the water as the fish inside him thrashed about. But not for long. In a few seconds his now somewhat *elongated* shape became very still, then wobbled tiredly out of sight into deeper water to sleep it off . . .

For a full four days after this awesome display David's worm was absent from its rebirth-place. There had been some rain and the creek was again swollen; which was as well for the oddly mutated flatworm, for there were no fish left in the pool. In fact, there was not much of *anything* left in the pool – at least, not until the afternoon of the pike's vanquishment, when heavy rain brought the river waters to restock the Planny-depleted place. For that ugly, sadly vulnerable fish had been the pool's last natural inhabitant, and until the rain came it would have been perfectly true to say of David's pool that it was the most sterile stretch of open water in the whole world!

Now it is probably just as well that the majority of tales told by fishermen are usually recognized for what they usually are, for certainly a few strange stories wafted up from the riverside during that four-day period, and not *all* of them from rod-and-liners. Who can say what the result might have been had anyone really tried to check these stories out?

For Planny was coming along nicely, thank you, and in no time at all he had accumulated all the nastiness of quite a large number of easily devoured pike of all sizes. He had developed a taste for them. Also, he had picked up something of the unreasonable antagonism of a particularly unfriendly, yappy little dog whose master called for him in vain from the river bank until late into the fourth night.

On the fifth morning, having almost given up hope of ever seeing the curious creature again, David went down to the pool as usual. Planny was back, and much bigger! Not only had he put on a lot of weight but his capacity for learning had picked up too. The little dog had gone down (or rather *in*!) almost without a burp, and Planny's very efficient digestive system had proved only slightly superior to his 'natural' talent for, well, *picking* brains . . .

But while the animal's hidden abilities were not so obvious, his growth assuredly was!

David gaped at the creature's size – almost two feet in diameter now – as it came sliding out of the reed-patch with the top three inches of its spongy, greyish-white bulk sticking up out of the water. The eyes were just below the surface, peering out liquidly at the boy on the bank. It is not difficult to guess what was going on in Planny's composite knowledge-cells ... or brain ... or ganglia ... or whatever! The way he had been hiding in the reeds and the way he carefully came out of them undoubtedly highlighted a left-over characteristic from his earlier, minnow period; the gleam in his peculiar eyes (of which David was innocently unaware) was suspiciously like that glassiness, intense and snide, seen in the eyes of doggies as they creep up on the backsides of postmen; and there was also something of a very real and greedy *intent* in there somewhere. Need we mention the pike?

Up into the shallows Planny came, flattening a little as his body edged up out of the water, losing something of its buoyancy; and David – innocent David – mistakenly saw the creature's approach as nothing if not natural. After all, had he not saved the poor thing's life? – and might he not therefore expect Planny to display friendship and even loyalty and gratitude? Instinctively he reached out his hand ...

Now dogs are usually loyal only to their rightful masters – and minnows are rarely loyal at all, except perhaps to other minnows. But pike? Why the pike is a notoriously unfriendly fish, showing never a trace of gratitude or loyalty to anyone ...

Approximately one hundred and thirty yards away and half an hour later, Professor Lees and his wife rose up from their bed and proceeded to the kitchen where they always had breakfast. A rather pungent, stale-water smell had seemingly invaded the house; so that the scientist's wife, preceding her husband, sniffed suspiciously at the air, dabbing at her nose with the hem of her dressing gown as she opened the kitchen door and went in.

Her throbbing scream of horror and disbelief brought

her husband in at the run through the open kitchen door a few seconds later. There was his wife, crouched defensively in a corner, fending off a hideously wobbly *something* with her bleeding, oddly dissolved and pulpy hands.

David's father did not stop to ponder what or why, fortunately he was a man of action. Having seen at a glance the destructive properties of Planny's weird acid make-up, he jumped forward, snatching the patterned cloth from the table as he went. Flinging the table-cloth over the bobbing, roughly globular thing on the floor, he hoisted it bodily into the air. Fortunately for the professor, Planny had lost much of his bulk in moisture-seepage during his journey from the pool, but even so the creature was heavy. Three quick steps took the scientist to the kitchen's great, old-fashioned all-night fire. Already feeling the acid's sting through the thin linen, he kicked open the heavy iron fire-door and bundled his wobbly, madly pulsating armful – table-cloth and all – straight in atop the glowing coals, slamming the door shut on it. Behind him his wife screamed out something ridiculous and fainted, and almost immediately – even though he had put his slippered foot against it – the door burst open and an awfully wounded Planny leapt forth in a hissing cloud of poisonous steam. Slimy and dripping, shrunken and mephitic, the creature wobbled drunkenly, dementedly about the floor; only to be bundled up again in the space of a few seconds, this time in the scientist's sacrificed dressing gown, and hurled once more to the fire. And this time, so as to be absolutely sure, David's father put his hands to the hot iron door, holding it firmly shut. He threw all his weight into the job, staying his ground until his fingers and palms, already blistered through contact with Planny's singular juices, blackened and cracked. Only then, and when the pressures from within ceased, did he snatch his steaming, monstrously damaged hands away . . .

It was only in some kind of blurred daze that Professor

Lees managed to set the wheels of action in motion from that time onwards. Once the immediate panic had subsided a sort of shocked lethargy crept over him; but in spite of this he cleaned up his unconscious wife's bubbly hands as best he could, and his own – though that proved so painful he almost fainted himself – and then, somehow, he phoned for the doctor and the police.

Then, after a further minute or so, still dazed but re-membering something of the strange things his wife had screamed before she fainted, David's father went upstairs to look for his son. When he found the boy's room empty he became once more galvanized into frantic activity. He began rushing about the house calling David's name before remembering his son's odd habit of the last month or so – how he would get up early in the morning and go off down to the pool before school.

As he left the house a police car was just pulling up on the drive outside. He shouted out to the two constables, telling them they would find his wife in the house . . . would they look after her? Then, despite the fact that they called out after him for an explanation, he hurried off towards the copse.

At first the policemen were appalled by the loathsome stench issuing undiluted from the house; then, fighting back their nausea, they went in and began doing what they could to improve Mrs Lees' lot. The doctor arrived only a moment later. He could see instantly what was wrong – there had been some sort of accident with acid. Relieved at the arrival of this sure-handed professional, the bewildered policemen followed the scientist's tracks to the pool.

There they found him sitting at the pool-side with his head in his tattily bandaged hands. He had seen the slide on the stone in the pool; and, in a dazed sort of fashion, he had noted the peculiar, flattened *track* in the grass between the house and the copse. And then, being clever, totalling up these fragile facts, he had finally arrived at the impossible solution . . .

It all hinged, of course, on those mad things his wife had screamed before fainting. Now, thinking back on those things, David's father could see the connections. He *remembered* now that there had been a slide missing from his set. He recalled the way in which David had declared the flatworm – the *planarian* worm – on a certain slide to be alive.

Quite suddenly he took one hand from his face and shoved it into his mouth right up to the bandaged knuckles. Just for a moment his eyes opened up very wide; and then he let both his hands fall and turned his face up to the patient policemen.

'God . . . God . . . *God-oh-God!*' he said then. 'My wife! She said . . . she said . . .'

'Yes, sir—' one of the officers prompted him, 'what did she say?'

Aimlessly the professor got to his feet. 'She said that – that it was sitting at the breakfast table – sitting there in David's chair – *and she said it called her Mummy!*'

ALSO AVAILABLE FROM
HODDER AND STOUGHTON PAPERBACKS

All these books are available at your local bookshop or newsagent, or can be ordered direct from the publisher. Just tick the titles you want and fill in the form below.

Prices and availability subject to change without notice.

HODDER AND STOUGHTON PAPERBACKS, P.O. Box 11, Falmouth, Cornwall.

Please send cheque or postal order for the value of the book, and add the following for postage and packing.

UK including BFPO – £1.00 for one book, plus 50p for the second book, and 30p for each additional book ordered up to a £3.00 maximum.

OVERSEAS INCLUDING EIRE – £2.00 for the first book, plus £1.00 for the second book, and 50p for each additional book ordered.
OR Please debit this amount from my Access/Visa Card (delete as appropriate).

Card Number   ☐☐☐☐☐☐☐☐☐☐☐☐☐☐☐☐

AMOUNT £ ....

EXPIRY DATE ....

SIGNED ....

NAME ....

ADDRESS ....